SUPER-DETECTIVE
JIM ANTHONY
THE COMPLETE SERIES

VOL. 6

WRITTEN BY

ROBERT LESLIE BELLEM & W.T. BALLARD

ILLUSTRATIONS BY

JOSEPH SZOKOLI

STEEGER BOOKS

2025

PUBLISHING HISTORY

"Murder's Migrants" originally appeared in the March 1943 issue of *Super-Detective* (Volume 4, Number 3). Copyright © 1943 by Trojan Publishing Corporation.

"Death for a Flying Dutchman" originally appeared in the April 1943 issue of *Super-Detective* (Volume 4, Number 4). Copyright © 1943 by Trojan Publishing Corporation.

"Homicide Heiress" originally appeared in the June 1943 issue of *Super-Detective* (Volume 4, Number 5). Copyright © 1943 by Trojan Publishing Corporation.

"Curse of the Masters" originally appeared in the August 1943 issue of *Super-Detective* (Volume 4, Number 6). Copyright © 1943 by Trojan Publishing Corporation.

"Pipeline to Murder" originally appeared in the October 1943 issue of *Super-Detective* (Volume 5, Number 1). Copyright © 1943 by Trojan Publishing Corporation.

Visit *steegerbooks.com* for more books like this.

TABLE OF

CONTENTS

all stories written by Robert Leslie Bellem & W.T. Ballard

MURDER'S
MIGRANTS

THEY WERE USING JIM ANTHONY'S NAME AND REPUTATION
IN ONE OF THE MOST GIGANTIC CRIMINAL PLOTS IN HISTORY.
BUT JUST HOW WAS EACH INVOLVED—THE FAT MAN, THE
COLLEGIATE REPORTER, THE RHYMING PHOTOGRAPHER, THE
SOCIETY GIRL, AND THE CLEVER, GOOD-LOOKING SECRETARY?

GRIMLY, DOGGEDLY, THE HUNTED man fled onward through a gathering fog which had subtly deepened into night without bringing him any actual awareness of the change. In the chaos of his tortured brain there was no place for thoughts of time or weather; there was only a constant, gnawing hunger for revenge that goaded him forward like a living automaton.

Long ago he had lost all count of the days, the hours, consumed by his harried journey. Sometimes it seemed as if he had been on this endless trail for years, centuries—ever conscious that he was being pursued; that somewhere on the wet road behind him lurked ruthless killers who had failed once, but who were closing in for a second chance to strike.

He held no hope of escape, for he realized the power of the person he had grown to hate during these past few hellish days with a hatred such as he had never before experienced. He knew that he was doomed to die very soon; but he prayed with all his waning strength that he would be spared just long enough to kill the one who was responsible.

It was a strange sensation to Nick Uvaldi, this burning urge to end another man's life. The feeling was foreign to him; as fantastic as the circumstances in which he now found himself. It marked the bitter finish of what, to him, had always seemed a career of incredibly good fortune.

Where else except here in America could he, the son of an immigrant Greek shoemaker, have been permitted to enter one of the country's leading technical schools? In what other land could he have graduated with honors despite his insignificant, unimportant family background?

This, he told himself, was democracy at work; the liberty and equality to be found only in the United States. And for the privilege of citizenship in such a country he owed a heartfelt debt—a debt he was willing to pay with his blood, his life. It was a payment he would make willingly; but he was fanatically determined that another man should die with him.

An enemy of America!

SLOGGING THROUGH THE darkness, Nick Uvaldi thought again of his academic life after graduation. Still in his middle twenties, he'd been retained by the school to do experimental work in its shining laboratories; and he might have been there yet if it hadn't been for the war.

The cowardly Jap assault on Pearl Harbor had changed everything. He'd tried to enlist, only to be rejected for an unsuspected physical defect. Then he had decided to fight on the industrial front if he couldn't wear a uniform; surely a man of his technical training could find a place in some war plant. He owed it to the land that had given him this training.

"Your death is to be an atonement
to the little men, Mr. Anthony,"
the man with the gun answered.

By sheer chance, then, he'd stumbled upon a certain employment office on lower Broadway in New York. They'd accepted his application; told him to report at six that same night, ready to travel. Vaguely he understood that he was headed for a California factory which was one of the far-flung enterprises set up by a famous young capitalist to assist a government engaged in titanic battle.

The bus rolled out on time, loaded with men who were being moved across the breadth of the nation to work in war production. Steadily for almost twenty-four hours the big vehicle lumbered westward; and the following evening it happened to halt in a little Pennsylvania mountain town so the passengers could eat in a dingy restaurant—at their own expense, of course, just as each of them had paid as much cash as he could afford toward the cost of the bus trip.

There were two drivers, and they went into the café kitchen, leaving their labor recruits out front. Once again it was sheer chance that drew Nick Uvaldi into the plot, allowing him to overhear a disturbing conversation.

"Where you takin' this load?" It was the cook who had asked the question.

One of the drivers chortled dourly. "New Mexico. We dump 'em a hundred miles from no place. It'll be days before any of them get to where they can squawk."

Nick hadn't understood. He pressed closer, listening; and he presently learned that he and his fellow passengers were the victims of an ugly, gigantic hoax. There weren't any jobs waiting for these men on the west coast. The bus load of workers—and hundreds more just like it—would be abandoned in the far desert, to make their way back to civilization as best they could!

He lost his head, then. He should have slipped away, returned to New York and reported his findings to the proper authorities. Instead he burst into the kitchen and confronted the two drivers; threatened them with exposure.

It was a foolish move. The cook was behind him—and a blackjack slugged home to Nick Uvaldi's skull. Stunned, he swayed on his feet. Another vicious, smashing blow felled him; and then the bus drivers began using their boots on his unprotected body.

Eventually he lost consciousness.

DARKNESS HAD FALLEN when his senses returned, and the bus had long since resumed its westward journey. But Nick wasn't on it. He was tightly trussed in the café kitchen, and preparations were already under way to murder him as soon as a grave had been dug in the cellar to receive his battered corpse.

He still couldn't quite remember how he'd managed to escape. There were gaps in his memory now; blank spots induced by that terrific beating he had taken. Somehow he must have inched himself to a table where butcher knives were kept; must have contrived to cut away his fetters. In his mind, the whole scene was jumbled and disconnected.

He got away, though. That much he knew. And he knew he'd stolen some of those sharp, expensive knives—which he later traded in a pawnshop for the gun that now made a comforting bulge in his pocket; the gun he planned to use on the man responsible for what had happened.

As his bruised, weary legs carried him along New York's riverfront he tried to rehearse what he meant to say when he faced the millionaire he was going to kill. But the words refused to form in his tired mind. They weren't important, anyhow. One bullet was worth a hundred speeches, he told himself. One deadly, well-aimed bullet would do his talking for him.

It was funny to think about murdering a millionaire. Especially this millionaire—a man who owned a vast newspaper empire of which the New York *Star* was the cornerstone; who owned the biggest hotel in Manhattan; who owned and directed a tremendous scope of business properties, all of which had supposedly been turned into non-profit organizations for the benefit of governmental war effort.

Non-profit, hell! If the real truth were known, the man was probably fattening his pockets in secret; milking additional millions from his industries at the expense of hard-working, hard-fighting Americans. At least that was what Nick Uvaldi concluded, knowing what he knew.

He thought of the hundreds, perhaps thousands like himself who'd been clipped for bus fare on the fake promise of jobs that didn't exist. Men who were even now being dumped and left to shift for themselves in the western desert. Lured away from their homes to be ditched, maybe even to starve to death! Was that a millionaire patriot's idea of benevolence, of serving his country? Faugh!

And they talked of the man's amazing abilities in other lines of endeavor: his scientific discoveries, his mechanical inventions, his charities—and his astounding feats of detection in the field of amateur criminology. Why, unquestionably, the fellow himself was either a criminal or a sadistic madman! How else could you explain his recruiting of labor for imaginary war work? Labor that was being chiseled for paltry dollars and then shipped to nowhere?

PAIN-WRACKED AND NOT quite sane, thanks to the punishment he had undergone, Nick Uvaldi had made up his mind to put an end to such things. Long ago he'd dismissed all thought of asking the law for help. The brutal beating inflicted on him had distorted his sense of proportion, destroyed his confidence in orderly police procedure. You couldn't depend on the cops, he told himself. They were crooked, corrupt—all of them. If you wanted justice done, you had to arrange it yourself. Well, he was ready for the grim task.

Provided he lived long enough, of course. His escape from that café in western Pennsylvania had resulted in relentless pursuit; more than once he had barely eluded the murderers who were trailing him to shut him up. His flight had been reported, he knew; because a dozen traps had been set and waiting for him on his long trip homeward.

Luck and a certain crazed cunning had enabled him to avoid those pitfalls, however. Thus far he had fooled his enemies. And now he was back in New York, prepared to serve the country he loved by executing a man whom he considered to be nothing better than a monster.

After that they could lynch him or electrocute him or do as they pleased. But first he must accomplish his purpose; and it would require careful strategy, for his proposed victim would be well guarded. He already had a scheme to get past those guards, though.

As he trudged onward he patted the gun in his pocket; *the gun with which he intended to kill Jim Anthony!*

CHAPTER II

DEATH'S DINNER-GUEST

THE SUPPER ROOM OF the Waldorf-Anthony Hotel was ablaze with lights, filled with the hum of conversation and the melodic under-current of music from a big name orchestra. And at a gleaming table in the very center of this tastefully furnished hotel restaurant sat the man who owned it; the man whose very name spelled the magic of accomplishment.

Jim Anthony.

Impeccably attired in white tie and tails, Jim made a striking figure against his opulent background. He would have been equally notable against any background. Tall, lean, muscular, his broad-shouldered body a dynamic reservoir of strength, he sat with the lithe ease of a finely trained athlete. From his swashbuckling Irish captain-of-industry father he had inherited this superlative physique along with one of America's greatest fortunes; and he had developed his physical perfection to the topmost limits, thanks to constant exercise—just as he had likewise developed and expanded his financial empire far beyond its original scope, thanks to his brilliant mind.

But it was his face that attracted and held your attention. Sunbronzed under sleek black hair, the nose jutting, the cheek bones high, the dark eyes hawk-like and penetrating, it was a face that reminded you of some American Indian chieftain—which was natural enough, for Jim's mother had been a full princess of the Comanche tribe.

From her, perhaps, had come his instinct for the hunt; an instinct which had turned his many-sided abilities toward the biggest game of all—the tracking down of wrongdoers. As a manhunter Jim Anthony had no equals; his fame as an amateur scientific criminologist was world-wide. Detection was his hobby, his avocation; countless were the mysteries he had solved, the murderers he had brought to justice after the police themselves had failed. In consequence, the mere mention of his name was enough to strike terror into the heart of any transgressor.

Tonight the millionaire criminologist had two dinner guests. The first was his lifelong friend and boon companion, the freckled, happy-go-lucky aviator, Tom Gentry. Earlier in the day, Jim had gone into conference with the skylarking flyer.

"I'll leave the ordering of the dinner to you, Tom," he had said. "Eating is one of your delights, so I'm depending on you to arrange an impressive spread."

"With girls, pappy? I've got three pips in my address book. Knockouts, no less. The kind you dream about on rainy Sunday afternoons. If you want to impress this frog—"

"Frog isn't a very polite term for a man as important as the one we're entertaining," Anthony grinned. "It would probably be a shock to him if he heard you call him that."

Gentry shrugged. "Okay. Frenchman, then."

"Free French. Remember, Dr. Montclair barely got out of Paris ahead of the Nazi occupation. If they'd caught him, he'd have been stood against a wall and shot."

TOM SIGHED WITH mock resignation. "So all right. Dr. Montclair, Free Frenchman. Former industrialist and efficiency expert in French war-material production. Now a refugee, staying here in the hotel. Joining up with you in an advisory capacity to help increase the output of your plants. Have I got all of it so I can show the right amount of awe?"

"I think so," the wealthy detective had to laugh in spite of himself. "You make it sound spectacular."

"Yeah. So the guy's a big shot. So he's still human, ain't he?"

"Quite."

"Then why don't we invite these three cuties I mentioned? I mean Montclair would have to be deaf, dumb, and blind not to get a kick out of them. We could make a night of it."

"Sorry, Tom. You're thinking more of yourself than of Montclair, I'm afraid. And he has more important things on his mind than girls."

The aviator bridled. "What's more important than girls? Name two!— Okay, okay, don't hit me! I give up. We'll dine stag if you say so." Then, ducking his millionaire pal's playful punch, Gentry went searching for the chef.

NOW THE THREE men were quietly enjoying a meal on which that chef had outdone himself. There was Jim Anthony, there was Tom Gentry, and there was Dr. Francois Montclair—a dapper little man whose prematurely grey hair and deeply wrinkled features betrayed more than a hint of the perils he had undergone in those dark days when his native land had fallen into the hands of invading enemy hordes.

At this particular moment the wealthy criminologist and his guests were between courses. Anthony was deep in conversation with Montclair and they were speaking French—which could have been Sanskrit as far as Gentry was concerned, for he couldn't understand a word of it. Bored, toying with his silver, the genial aviator was secretly wishing he'd disobeyed orders and invited at least one girl to the feast. Then he would have had somebody to talk to, anyhow.

His roving gaze strayed over the big room, pausing now and then to admire some particularly lovely and beautifully-gowned woman. Then, suddenly, he tensed.

A strange figure had appeared through the service doorway and was making its way toward the Anthony table; a youthful but battered-looking fellow whose hair was disheveled, whose face bore the marks of savage bruises, and whose eyes held a curious glitter. He carried a tray and wore a bus-boy's uniform jacket; but it didn't fit very well—which struck Tom Gentry as odd, because any employee of the Waldorf-Anthony Hotel whose duties required the wearing of livery always had that livery tailored to his exact measure.

Moreover, this oncoming chap's appearance had other peculiarities. Beneath the ill-fitting coat his trousers were dirty and torn, the cuffs

"Ugly word, blackmail. Don't like it." The fat man punctuated his words with the gun.

frayed and mud-spattered. His shoes, too, were muddy and shapeless, as if he had just come from a long hike through rough terrain. He walked with an unsteady gait; the unmistakable evidence of complete fatigue—or complete drunkenness. Yet he didn't seem drunk, aside from this. There was something cold and sober and purposeful about him.

Gentry let out an astonished exclamation. "Gosh, pappy, I wish you'd look at the new style in busboys!"

AT THE WORDS, Jim Anthony abruptly broke off what he'd been saying to his French guest; stared in the direction of the genial aviator's gesture. And as he narrowed his hawk-like eyes, he felt a subconscious premonition of danger inching through him; a warming sensation such as he always experienced at the approach of peril. This weird sixth sense was another of his heritages from his Indian mother; it had never failed him in the past and he could not ignore it now.

The short hair stirred at the nape of his neck when he saw that ragged figure in the uniform jacket, making for his table. Simultaneously he observed that the captain of waiters and the maitre de hotel had also spotted the strange intruder and were angling toward him, trying to intercept him. Shocked stupefaction was scrawled on their faces, for nothing like this had ever before occurred within the four walls of the famed Waldorf-Anthony Hotel.

They were too far away to do anything about it, though. By now the newcomer had almost reached the millionaire criminologist's table. Nick Uvaldi had timed his arrival with cunning cleverness; there was nobody between him and his intended victim. His lips began to move soundlessly. Then he swung aside the empty tray he was carrying—and revealed the pawn-shop revolver clenched in his fist.

"Look out!" Tom Gentry squalled as he caught sight of the ugly snub-nosed weapon. "Duck, Jim! It's a hold-up!"

"No. You will not move," the battered man's voice was as implacable as the mask of hate that twisted his features. "Be still, or I'll kill you right now. And I don't want to do that. Not until you know why you're to die."

Tom froze and so did the Frenchman, Francois Montclair. But Anthony had an appearance of complete relaxation; of utter indifference to jeopardy. Beneath this counterfeit calmness, however, his splendid muscles were invisibly taut and ready to erupt into surging motion at the first opportunity.

"All right, my friend," he said easily. "Tell me why I'm to die."

Throughout the great dining room a hush had fallen; a frightened, shivery silence as hundreds of eyes watched the unbelievable drama unfolding before them. In this silence, Nick Uvaldi's answer rang with the clarity of a bell.

"Your death is atonement to the little men, Mr. Anthony. The workers who are your dupes, your victims. The poor deluded fools you shipped to nowhere after stealing what money they had. I am their hand, striking out to punish a rat who thought himself too big to be touched."

The speech was meaningless to Anthony. All this talk of shipping workmen to nowhere after stealing their money—it sounded like the ravings of a demented person. Just the same, a crazy man could shoot you as quickly as a sane one; and for less cause. It wasn't a pleasant prospect.

Mentally Jim judged the distance between himself and the gun that was aimed at him; weighed his chances of lunging sidewise out of his chair and going for the flat automatic which he himself carried under his left armpit.

AND THEN, BEFORE he came to a decision, there came the thunderous crash of a pistol's report. And at the same precise second, every light in the room was switched off.

The windows were shielded by heavy drapes to prevent any inner glow from seeping to the dimmed-out street; and now the drapes performed a reverse service by cutting off any possible light that might have sifted into the room from outside. In the solid darkness that ensued, Jim Anthony hurled himself to the floor and whipped out his automatic.

"Tom!" he called. "Dr. Montclair! Are you both okay?"

"*Oui, Monsieur,*" came the Frenchman's answer. And then Tom's gasping blurt of relief: "Jeepers cripes, pappy, did he manage to plug you?"

"No. Be quiet." This time Jim's voice sounded from another direction, for he had crawled Indian fashion on his belly away from the position he occupied when he first spoke. Thus his assailant couldn't draw a bead on him by listening for the source of his words.

As it turned out, the trick proved unnecessary; there was no more gunfire. Rustles of whispering began to sweep across the restaurant like sibilant surf as dinner patrons stirred and gave voice to their excitement. A scowl darkened Anthony's unseen countenance at this; for the whispers drowned out what he was straining his hypersensitive ears to hear—the possible slither of movement marking his attacker's location.

He resorted to a Hindu trick he had learned years ago from a yogi in Calcutta; dilated the pupils of his eyes to abnormal size by sheer muscular control. By means of this trick he was enabled to see clearly in darkness where ordinary vision was useless. Crawling forward again, he peered ahead.

"By God!" he whispered.

A man's form lay sprawled before him, gun in hand. But the stiffening fingers would never pull the weapon's trigger. There was a bullet hole through the back of the man's skull. He'd been shot from behind, the slug traveling from some spot on the far side of the room.

The millionaire criminologist stood up. "Lights!" he called grimly. "Somebody get to the master switch."

In an instant his command was obeyed and brilliance once more filled the fashionable eating place. Nearby, a woman moaned; another screamed hysterically. Tom Gentry leaped to his feet, registering amazement as he saw Anthony standing over the limp body of the fake busboy.

"Guard the doors," Jim said tersely. "See that nobody leaves. Send the house detective to me and telephone police headquarters. This man has been murdered."

CHAPTER III

SHAKEDOWN SET-UP

THE EDITORIAL OFFICES OF *Focus Magazine* occupied a musty set of rooms in an old building in the Forties. In the largest of these offices a fat man sat at a battered desk; but instead of the galley proofs and photograph prints you might have expected to find on an editor's worktable, the green blotter was covered by a tray on which reposed one of the biggest porterhouse steaks ever seen in Manhattan.

Nobody could say this steak was actually raw; there were a few slight evidences that it had come into contact with a broiler—but briefly. Crimson juices ran from its seared edges, and a delicious aroma arose from the heaps of French-fried potatoes which flanked it. There was another plate nearby containing two whole heads of lettuce liberally doused with mayonnaise; steaming coffee rich with cream filled a cup to the brim, and a dozen rolls were stacked alongside, dripping melted butter.

The desk's owner had a napkin tucked under his multiple chins, and he was attacking the steak with all the vigor of a man who'd been starving on a desert island for the past six weeks. Aside from his appetite, though, he showed no signs of starvation. He wasn't just fat; he was almost obscenely gross.

His three hundred pounds literally overflowed his creaking office chair in all directions; his face was moonlike and puffy; and his eyes, although large enough by ordinary standards, were almost lost in the purses of flesh that pocketed them. Just now they glittered with childish pleasure as he popped the first tremendous morsel of meat into his mouth.

The mouth was like a slit; a trap that snapped shut so that no trace of the food's flavor could escape. And somehow, despite the man's well-tailored clothes and infantile gurglings of pleasure, you got the impression that he himself was a trap—a deadly snare awaiting any unwary prey that came too close.

FEASTING, HE PAID absolutely no attention to the girl who stood across the office and watched him. To an outsider, this might have been somewhat puzzling; for Lana McBride was eminently worth looking at from the crown of her beautifully coiffed yellow hair to the soles of her small, opened-toed pumps. As a private secretary and editorial assistant she was not only decorative, but efficient as well.

She proved this by remarking with disapproval: "You'll eat yourself into the grave one of these days, Gabe. That wouldn't be very good for business."

He twinkled at her fondly, but he did not stop chewing until he had swallowed the mouthful and washed it down with a gulp of fragrant coffee. Then, when he finally did condescend to answer, he had a curious manner of talking that omitted all unnecessary words—as if each syllable were a silver dollar he hated to part with.

"Glorious death," he grinned. Then he went back to his meal without offering to share it.

Lana McBride viewed her employer with a cross between amusement and disgust. For three years she'd been a slave to the various magazines published by L. Gabriel Stope, none of which had lived very long; and sometimes she wondered why she remained with him.

For all his other faults, though, he had imagination coupled with a complete absence of ethics; and there was always the chance of making a financial killing by staying in his service.

Take his current publishing venture, for instance: this *Focus Magazine*. He was launching it as a nickel pictorial weekly in competition with the established ten-cent picture publications; with any sort of financial backing it might be a huge success. But lack of money had delayed the initial issue week after week, and Lana McBride wasn't feeling too hopeful.

"If Higgie Smith doesn't bring home the bacon, I'm not even sure you can afford enough steaks to kill yourself," she retorted tartly.

"Bacon. Steaks. Got *you* talking food now." He waved a piece of lettuce at her. "Stop worrying. You saw Higgie's wire. Got the goods. Flying home. Should be here now."

AS IF ON cue, the office door opened and two men crowded into Stope's musty sanctum. The first was round, chubby, but not fat; he wore Kollege-Kut Klothes at least six years out of fashion, a pork-pie hat with the brim turned up front and back, and he carried a portable typewriter whose scarred case slapped him on the knees when he walked. This seemed to cause him perpetual surprise; but beneath the naive exterior of Higgins Smith, sole and only reporter on the staff of *Focus Magazine*, lurked shrewdness as sharp as a scalpel.

"Hi, Toots," he said to Lana. "You look gorgeous tonight." Then he turned to the fat man, who had not paused in his eating. "We're in, boss. But definitely! I don't know how you got your tip-off, maybe you had a crystal ball! All I can say is, you hit it smack on the nose."

"Of course. But did you?"

Higgie Smith was not disturbed by the fat man's cold voice. "Sure. Wait until you get a load of the interviews I got from a dozen of those poor devils in the Arizona badlands. And the pix Rhymer snapped. Show him, Rhymer," he said to the cadaverous individual who had followed him into the room.

This tall, skeletal caricature of humanity was Rhymer Koenig, *Focus Magazine's* only photographer, and his loose suit hung on him like the threadbare garments of a scarecrow. As he unslung his battered camera case, his beady eyes wolfishly surveyed that steak on Stope's desk. Then he cleared his scrawny throat.

"A hunk of that I'd like to eat. And then I crave to take a seat. Because, you see, my dogs are tired. I'd ask for dough but I might get fired."

Higgie made disparaging sounds. "There you go spouting poetry again. Skip it, bub. Let's have those prints."

From an inside pocket, Rhymer produced an envelope and dumped a series of pictures on the desk. With the same movement he snagged two sections of fried potato and lifted them toward his mouth.

Stope hit him on the fingers with a spoon. "Lay off."

"For you I do not like to work. You've crippled me, you dirty jerk!" the scarecrow nursed his hurt hand. He dropped the potatoes, however.

"I'll break your arm if you touch my food again," the fat man growled. Then he looked at the snapshots. "Good."

"You like 'em, do you?" Higgie Smith asked.

"Yes."

Higgie gathered them up, stowed them in his pocket. "We're glad to know it, Rhymer and I. You can have them when you kick in with our back salaries."

"Hold-up, eh?"

"Sort of. Remember, when you had us sign up with that employment agency, you gave us only enough cash for plane fare home. I didn't see any eating money."

"Airline feeds you," Stope said.

"This one didn't. The stewardess had tough luck with her buffet; spoiled all the grub. The other passengers ate at various way stations when we came down for refueling. Rhymer and I were broke. We had a doughnut apiece for breakfast. For lunch and supper we played like we weren't hungry."

THE FAT MAN opened the top drawer of his desk and put both hands in it. His left hand came out with a dollar bill. "Here," he said. "Take this. Buy hot dogs. Give me pictures."

"Oh, no. Not for any lousy buck."

Stope's other hand appeared. It had an automatic in it "Not for a buck. For this."

"Gabe!" the startled protest came from Lana McBride.

He cast her a frigid glance. "Quiet." Then, to Smith and the startled photographer. "Fools. I don't plant to publish those pix and interviews."

"What?" Higgie stiffened. "After all the trouble we went to, getting them? Why, you said yourself they'd create a sensation. Our circulation would hit half a million with the first issue!"

"Take too much time. Printer would get most of the gravy. I have a quicker way. Hell with half million *circulation.* I'll get half million *dollars.* Cash. Maybe more."

Lana McBride lifted her eyebrows on an indrawn breath. "Explain that, Gabe. We're just ignorant dopes."

"Yes," Stope agreed. "Jim Anthony. Millionaire. Controls a hundred factories. Threaten him with exposure. Publish the evidence; labor recruited, then dumped. Unions would call strikes in every Anthony plant."

The girl's eyes sharpened. "Blackmail!"

"Ugly word. Don't like it. We sell him *Focus* for a million dollars. Lock, stock, barrel. He suppresses story and layout. We retire. Rich."

In that instant all hell broke loose in the street.

"It's still blackmail," Lana said. "But it's a knockout. Put away the gun. Give him those pictures, Higgie. Let's all go call on Mr. Anthony."

L. Gabriel Stope twinkled affably, but his mouth had as much mirth as a snake's. "Knew you'd see it my way," he said. "Scram while I finish my steak."

CHAPTER IV

PHONY FOUNDATION

JIM ANTHONY'S LIVING QUARTERS took in the entire penthouse on the roof of the Waldorf-Anthony Hotel. Here, in his luxurious living room, he now faced Lieutenant Trotter of the New York homicide department.

Nearly three hours had passed since the lights had been doused in the hotel restaurant and the misguided, unfortunate Nick Uvaldi had met death in the ensuing darkness. In those three hours many alleys of investigation had been opened—and found to be blind.

First Jim himself had been bluntly accused of the killing. "In self defense, of course," Trotter had reluctantly stipulated. "But you're the one guy with a logical motive."

"How so?"

"He pulled a gun on you. He claimed you were mixed up in some labor beef. He was going to plug you—so you beat him to the trigger.

Anthony had smiled faintly. "I'd have to be a contortionist. I was in front of him; the bullet entered the back of his skull. Don't be absurd."

"Okay, then. He was drilled by one of these two guys at your table. Gentry or Dr. Montclair."

"They were in front of him, too. Why not give us the paraffin test and see if any of us discharged a firearm?"

This was done; and the results had shown negative. Tests were then made on the hands of every other person in the supper room, employees as well as patrons—all of whom had been detained by Jim's orders pending an investigation.

And again the results were uniformly negative.

There was only one plausible answer. After firing the fatal shot, the murderer must have escaped in the darkness; his moves had been covered by that concert of excited whispering which had prevented

Anthony's abnormally acute ears from hearing any sound of receding footfalls. At this point the police had been temporarily stymied; forced to release all the witnesses after the formality of taking their names and addresses.

Now, three hours later, Lieutenant Trotter had returned to the hotel for another interview with the millionaire criminologist. And the homicide official looked definitely unhappy about the whole thing.

"I don't get any part of it," he rasped around the fragments of a frayed cigar. "Something tells me you're holding out on me. In fact, I feel sure of it."

Jim wasn't particularly startled by this remark. He and Trotter had locked horns on many a previous occasion, and there was little love lost between them. Or at least Trotter showed truculent traces of animosity whenever his duties brought him into professional contact with the wealthy amateur detective. Perhaps it was jealousy; time and again Anthony had solved cases through sheer scientific ability where the police department had failed. Trotter seemed to resent this, although he usually received a lion's share of the credit.

NOW THE CRUSTY homicide lieutenant was singing the same old tune, hinting that the sun-bronzed millionaire knew more than he was telling.

"Why should I hold out on you?" Jim asked calmly.

"That's what I'd like to know. For instance, what was your connection with this Nick Uvaldi?"

"Nick Uvaldi? Never heard of him."

"He's the guy that got bumped," Trotter made an impatient gesture. "We've been checking on him. He was a graduate of a big-time technical school; worked in their research lab afterward. He quit to enlist but was turned down."

"And—?"

"So then he applied for war industry work through your foundation office on lower Broadway."

Inwardly, Jim Anthony tensed with surprise; although none of it was revealed on his impassive countenance. "My foundation office? Afraid I don't follow you."

"Look, pal," Trotter lifted a lip. "Don't make with the mysterious stuff. It won't buy you anything. We did a routine check on that outfit when it first opened, two weeks ago."

"I still don't follow you."

Trotter aimed a menacing finger. "Are you trying to tell me you aren't connected with this so-called Foundation for the Redistribution of War Manpower?"

"It's all news to me," Anthony said.

The homicide official puffed his reddening cheeks. "Don't pull that stuff! You're *behind* the thing! You and a lot more rich guys. Listen. If you say you don't know Dorothy Dawson Carradyne, you and I are going to tangle."

"Yes, I know Miss Carradyne," Jim admitted. "I've met her a few times. Quite a striking woman."

From his seat across the room, Tom Gentry remarked: "That's an understatement if I ever heard one, pappy. Striking? She's a wow!"

Trotter ignored the interruption; kept right on talking to the millionaire criminologist. "Okay. So you know her. How much do you know about her?"

From the amazing catalogue of his mental index file, Jim Anthony produced an instantaneous *dossier*. "Dorothy Dawson Carradyne," he said. "Last surviving member of an old New York family. Well established in society. Parents were wealthy but died penniless; bad investments. Dorothy was educated in Europe; had post-graduate work in Berlin until her own funds ran out. Came back to America a few years ago; plunged into social service activities."

"Yeah. And that's why you hired her. On account of her experience finding jobs for down-and-outers."

Jim shook his head. "I never hired her."

"Don't give me that!" Trotter bellowed. "I just talked with her less than thirty minutes ago. I routed her out, made her go down to her office. She looked through her records and identified this Nick Uvaldi guy who got killed while threatening you. He signed up with the Redistribution Foundation last week and shipped out with a bus-load of other workers for one of your California plants."

ANTHONY'S HAWK-LIKE EYES glittered. "My California plants have all the men they need. We're not hiring extra help until our expansion plans are complete."

"Nuts! I asked this Carradyne jane who she was fronting for. At first she wouldn't talk except to say some of the biggest capitalists in the country were furnishing funds out of their own pockets to help relocate labor; guys who didn't want their names mentioned."

"Did you learn any of those names?"

"Finally, yeah. And yours is at the top of the list as chairman. She showed me your personal letter asking her as a favor to take the job of running the outfit."

"I wrote no such letter."

Trotter made a bitter mouth. "Naturally you'd say that, after what happened. You're trying to get out from under. Here's a man, Nick Uvaldi, that's hired through a labor exchange you organized. He ships out on a bus to work in one of your plants. A few nights later he shows up again, back in town, and for some unknown reason threatens to blast you. But he gets blasted first, before he's able to explain what's eating on him. If you were anybody else but Jim Anthony, you'd be in the clink this minute—and you might land there yet if you don't tell me the score."

"Give me the key," he insisted.

"Sorry. I don't know the score. I intend to find out, though." The millionaire criminologist's tone was bleak.

Lieutenant Trotter's heavy features grew apoplectic. "You refuse to talk, hunh? Okay. Maybe I'll come up with some way to make you whistle. Just wait. And look out! This is one time I won't be taking any of your shenanigans." Whereupon he strode stiff-legged to Jim's private automatic elevator, entered it, closed the door and viciously punched the *down* button.

IN THE PENTHOUSE living room, Tom Gentry built three generous drinks; one for himself, one for Francois Montclair, and a double jigger for his wealthy friend. "After that little session I have an idea we need these," he said.

The dapper but haggard-looking French refugee made a wry face as he sipped. *"Mais oui!"* he agreed. "But what does it all mean? It is of a strangeness I do not comprehend, this talk of labor relocation foundations and letters one did not write! At the first I thought the poor devil who was killed must have been insane, a victim of persecution complex. But now one wonders if there is a deeper significance!"

"I'm sure of it," Anthony frowned. "And I'm going to dig until I find the answer—"

He was interrupted by the melodious bell of his private telephone, and there was annoyance in his manner as he uncradled the instrument. "Anthony talking."

From the lobby came the voice of a desk clerk. "Sorry to intrude, sir, but there are four persons down here demanding to see you. Three men and a lady. They decline to give their names, but insist that you receive them at once."

"Give them my regrets. I'm very busy."

There was a pause; then the clerk came back on the line. "I am asked to tell you they're calling to confer with you on a matter of vital importance. The transportation of labor."

When he heard this, Jim Anthony stiffened; a cold gleam came into his slitted eyes. He had planned to leave the penthouse at once and go see that Dorothy Dawson Carradyne who was allegedly in charge of the mysterious Foundation for the Redistribution of War Manpower. But Miss Carradyne could wait a while, now; because apparently someone else had turned up who might be a source of unexpected information.

He spoke into the phone. "Four people, you said? Three men and one lady?"

"Yes, sir."

"All right. Send them along in my elevator."

Tom Gentry stared. "Now what pappy?

"I don't know," the wealthy investigator said as he rang off. "But we'll soon learn."

CHAPTER V

CLOSE CALL

MANY CURIOUS-LOOKING CHARACTERS HAD stepped out of Jim Anthony's elevator into the foyer of his fabulous penthouse; but never had there been an odder assortment than this present delegation representing *Focus Magazine*.

Of course, Anthony didn't know, at first, that they represented this publication. In fact, he was not even aware *Focus Magazine* existed—which, actually, it didn't, since its initial edition had not been issued.

Lana McBride emerged first; and Tom Gentry emitted a soundless whistle of admiring appreciation when he caught a glimpse of her blonde loveliness. He frowned, though, when he saw the fat man who followed her.

This individual was forced to squeeze his three hundred unattractive pounds of flesh through the doorway of the cage, and his ponderous gait resembled the waddling of a monstrous, overfed duck. He, in turn, was trailed by one of the tallest, thinnest men Gentry had ever seen; a scarecrow carrying a camera in a battered case slung to his shoulder. Last to appear was a chap with apple-dumpling cheeks and naive blue eyes; an individual whose pork-pie hat and Kollege-Kut Klothes made him look like a fugitive from some obscure campus.

"A circus side-show, no less!" Gentry whispered to Francois Montclair. "The living skeleton, the ton of blubber, the shimmy dancer and the press agent!"

Oblivious to any such whispers, the fat man made directly for Jim Anthony and shoved out a pudgy hand. "Pleasure, Mr. Anthony. Nice to meet a fellow publisher. Introduce myself. Owner of *Focus Magazine*, L. Gabriel Stope. These," he indicated his companions. "My staff."

Anthony's eyebrows lifted imperceptibly and he seemed not to see the fat man's extended hand. "You wanted to see me regarding labor transportation, I believe you said?"

"Ah. Get to the point. No lost time. Like to do business on that basis." Stope moved to a table and spread a layout of snapshots. "Look. Interesting."

JIM CAST A glance at Tom Gentry, which the aviator missed because he had drawn the blonde girl aside and opened a conversation with her. She seemed calmly pleased at having gained the attention of such a fast worker, particularly when he was the best friend of a famous millionaire.

Her companions, the tall photographer and apple-cheeked reporter, stood as silent as museum statues; while Francois Montclair sat in a corner wearing the expression of one who suddenly finds himself in a madhouse without understanding how he happened to get there. Anthony, too, experienced a momentary sensation of being in the presence of a group of escapees from a lunatic asylum; then his uncanny sixth sense began to function, warning him that although these people might appear crazy, they were in reality as dangerous as a time bomb.

Jim turned to study the pictures which L. Gabriel Stope had placed on the table-top. The first showed a doorway in front of which stood a cluster of men. The door itself bore the lettered legend:

FOUNDATION FOR THE REDISTRIBUTION
OF WAR MANPOWER

Anthony scowled. That blasted foundation again!

The next photograph was of a large bus crowded with passengers. Some of these men were recognizable as having appeared in the first snapshot; but the principal point of interest was the canvas sign on the side of the bus: *Anthony Enterprises.*

Once more he scowled, for he knew of no such vehicle in his industrial empire!

There were several other snaps, most of them not quite as sharp as the first pair. They revealed the same bus halted and silhouetted against a barren desert background. The passengers were huddled beyond, their faces angry, while the uniformed bus driver held them at bay with a threatening gun.

"Nice, hah?" Stope said. "Rhymer Koenig. Good photographer. Miniature camera inside his vest. Snapped pix through his buttonhole. Driver didn't suspect."

Jim faced the fat man. "What's the gag?"

"No gag. Don't pull innocent act. Evidence all against you. Obvious. Can't figure your purpose, but you've been recruiting workers on east coast, promising jobs, shipping them west, then stranding them."

The millionaire's nostrils quivered, flared. "So that's it! Now we're getting somewhere."

"Sure. Suppose I publish pictures and story in *Focus Magazine?* Big expose. Make you mighty unpopular with American labor. Unions may act. Call strikes in all your plants. Complete breakdown of war production. Government might step in. Anthony the hero becomes Anthony the heel."

"Do you intend to publish this expose?"

Stope smiled unpleasantly. "Depends on you."

"I see. Blackmail."

"Nasty word. Don't like it. You're a publisher. Own a chain of newspapers. Why not own a picture magazine too? Sell you *Focus* including title, good will, editorial material on hand. Including labor relocation pix and story. You can suppress the layout then if you like. Do as you please. Your own property."

"And the price?" Jim purred silkily.

THE ANSWER CAME, surprisingly enough, from the lips of that tall, skinny figure who carried a camera. "No matter how or where you look, you see we've got you on the hook. Your reputation's not worth shucks, unless we're paid a million bucks."

"Quiet, Rhymer!" the fat man snarled. Then he waddled close to the scarecrow photographer and deliberately hit him in the mouth. He was smiling again, though, when he turned back to Anthony. "Wrong. Not one million. *Two* million."

"That's pretty steep."

"No. Cheap. Just buttons to a man as rich as you."

The millionaire pretended to consider this. Presently he announced: "I'll let you know by noon tomorrow."

"Noon. Very good. One minute later, deal's off. We print a complete exposure. Understood?" He pivoted like a cumbersome pig, gestured to his staff. Silently they trailed him into the elevator and the cage wafted them downward.

THE INSTANT THEY had vanished, Francois Montclair leaped to his feet. "Criminals! *Cochons!* They will make you the most hated man in *les Etais Unis!*"

Anthony's stoic face was grimly expressionless. "I'm afraid I may be that in any event, if someone has been using my name in connection with the fake recruiting of labor. Provided those pictures were true, there's at least one bus load of workers already stranded somewhere in the west. Maybe scores more. Once those men manage to get back to civilization, hell's going to pop."

"Yeah," Tom Gentry said sourly. "Strikes, government investigations, maybe a Federal indictment—gosh, Jim, what do you plan to do?"

"Move," the wealthy criminologist answered. "Move fast, before the storm breaks. You get on the phone, Tom. Contact this Dorothy Dawson Carradyne woman either at her home or the Foundation office. Ask information for its number. Tell her we want to see her at that office within the next half hour."

Gentry leaped to obey.

Meantime, Jim drew his French associate aside. "Listen, Dr. Montclair. In France you were an industrial efficiency expert. That's why I invited you into my organization. Now I need your abilities."

"Oui, Monsieur Anthony. I am at your service."

"Good. I'm giving you carte-blanche authority; placing my entire resources at your disposal. I want you to start sending out telegrams to every city, village, and hamlet west of the Mississippi River. Notify all police stations, sheriffs' offices, state constabulary posts to be on the lookout for migrant workers who've been dumped from busses bearing my name."

"And—?"

"Spare no expense. Have searching parties sent out. Pick up every last man who may have been victimized. See that each one is given a hundred dollars cash. Plus a ticket to California on the first available Pullman. And the guarantee of a job in war industry, with salary commencing from the time each man left his home. Got that?"

"I comprehend."

"Okay. Then get busy!" And Anthony saw Montclair to the elevator; despatched him down to his own suite on the fifth floor of the hotel.

"Listen, Gabe," she said, "if
you think you can squeeze
us out of the gravy—"

By that time, Tom Gentry had finished phoning. "I talked to the Carradyne cookie, pappy. Boy, has she got a voice that makes your ears tingle!"

"Never mind her voice. Was she at the office?"

The freckled flyer nodded. "She said the cops had pulled her down there and hounded her with questions until she was worried sick. Claimed she was on the point of trying to reach you for instructions when I called. She's waiting for us."

"Fine. Let's go."

"Hey, wait. Don't you want me to phone the garage and have your car brought around?"

"We'll take a cab. It's quicker," Jim said.

In this, he was both right and wrong. He might save time in a taxi; that was true. But the decision came very close to costing him his freedom.

THE ATTACK CAME with vicious swiftness. It was a Yellow that Anthony and Gentry had chosen; and as it circled the block to get headed in the right direction for lower Broadway, another cab pulled abreast. Something small and white, like a pellet or thumb-sized capsule, was hurled from this second taxi into the tonneau of Jim's conveyance. The instant it landed, it burst with a tiny puff. Billowing fumes arose.

Simultaneously, a shot was fired and Anthony's cabby lurched forward over his wheel. He died instantly with a bullet through his brain—and the Yellow went out of control.

Tom Gentry yowled: "Damnation—!" and then as he sucked in his breath to yell again, the billowing fumes engulfed him. They entered his mouth, his nostrils; sifted stranglingly into his lungs. He choked, moaned; streams of unsolicited tears began to spurt from his eyes. "God—" he gasped.

"Don't breathe!" Anthony spoke just the two words; wasted no more of the precious air with which he had filled his own mighty chest a split second before the pellet had burst. Meanwhile his cab, which fortunately had been rolling along in slow second gear, was slanting over toward the far curb with the murdered driver's body slumped on the steering wheel, cramping it.

And that other taxi was crowding in.

The millionaire criminologist moved with the speed of lightning. His eyes were smarting now from the effects of the gas that drifted around him; his nostrils felt inflamed as if by a myriad stinging needles. But he controlled his lungs, held his breath; and with the butt of his automatic he smashed the glass partition between himself and the front compartment.

Then he reached through the jagged aperture, stretching until he found the ignition switch. He flipped it off. Braked by the compression of a dead motor, the cab slowly halted.

The second car also stopped. Its driver bounced to the street and two more men erupted from the tonneau, wearing masks and carrying guns. They deployed to Anthony's taxi, yanked its door open. "Come on, chumps. Out!"

Jim Anthony obeyed—but a lot faster than they anticipated. Like a surging streak of motion he flashed into view, using his automatic as a blackjack. A clubbing blow sent one of his assailants reeling backward, stunned. A second smashing impact dropped another masked thug to the street, unconscious.

"Boy!" came a whining bleat from the driver of the murder-cab. "The guy breathes tear gas an' *likes* it! I don't want no part of snatchin' anybody like that!" And he scuttled to his machine, slid under the wheel, clashed his gears.

AS THE VEHICLE roared forward, the first hood made a desperate grab for it; the thug Anthony had slugged groggy but hadn't quite felled. He caught a hand-hold, leaped to the running board and clung there as the taxi gathered speed.

Anthony could have drawn a bead on him, picked him off with one

It was obvious that she would never talk again.

shot. But it would have been the same as cold-blooded homicide and he couldn't bring himself to kill a defenseless man—not even an outlaw. Moreover, the police could be depended upon to capture the two fleeing gunsels sooner or later. Particularly since they'd left the third member of their trio stretched out senseless on the street.

Unfortunately, the thug clinging to the escaping cab must have thought of the same possibility; for as the machine rocketed around the next corner he snapped a bullet backward. It hit the prone gunman with deadly accuracy; tore a tunnel all the way through his heart.

Which made two murders in as many minutes: the innocent driver of Anthony's cab, and this masked thug who would never again regain consciousness to squeal on his companions.

CHAPTER VI

FORGERY'S FILES

ANTHONY CATAPULTED BACK TO his Yellow; wasted no time on vain regrets or useless oaths. He hauled Tom Gentry out into the open air.

"God, pappy… my eyes… my lungs… on fire…" the aviator sobbed without meaning to, any more than he meant the tears that streamed down his freckled cheeks.

"You'll be okay. It was just tear gas." From his pocket, the millionaire criminologist extracted a flat black kit which he always carried; a kit compactly packed with a varied and sometimes startling assortment of scientific equipment.

Opening the kit, he produced a vial of colorless liquid which he spilled on a clean handkerchief, soaking it. Then he used the handkerchief to sponge Tom's face and nostrils, carefully squeezing a few droplets of the fluid into each of the flyer's watery eyes. Then, finally, he wadded the cloth over Gentry's nose and mouth.

"Breathe in. Deep. Through the handkerchief's folds. Inhale as much of this volatile stuff as you can."

Tom obeyed; and in a moment he began sputtering in amazement. "I—I'm okay again!" he exclaimed. "I ain't weeping! And I can take a breath without it burning like hell!"

"Right," Anthony said. "I used a special neutralizing chemical of my own formula; works only on tear gas. Now let's get out of here. I think I hear a mounted cop coming and we haven't got time to answer questions."

The genial aviator looked around, shuddered, started loping with his wealthy friend. "Gosh—two stiffs! We might be just as dead if you hadn't—"

"I don't think so. Had they wanted to kill us, they could have shot us down the way they did our cabby. Instead, all they used on us was gas, hoping to put us out of action so they'd have no trouble kidnaping us."

"It was a snatch?"

"So one of them said, accidentally."

"But why, Jim?" Then Gentry snapped his fingers. "I've got it! That fat guy from *Focus Magazine!* He wanted to make sure you wouldn't run out before he could collect!"

"Possibly, although I doubt it. I'm beginning to see something deeper in all this mess. Maybe somebody doesn't want me to investigate this Manpower Relocation outfit."

Tom beckoned a cab and they piled in. "Say!" he whispered. "That's right! I *did* tell the Dorothy Dawson Carradyne quail we were coming to see her—!"

"And we still are. In fact, here's the address," Anthony remarked a few minutes later. "Let's go."

THE OFFICE OF the foundation was on the building's second floor. A sign on the wall by the staircase pointed upward; but the elevators didn't seem to be running, so Jim and Gentry took the stairs.

The door they wanted was directly opposite the stair-head, and they entered a big waiting room lined with bare wooden benches. Then an inner door opened and Dorothy Dawson Carradyne came forward to greet them.

She was tall, graceful, completely feminine in spite of her man-tailored suit. Her jet black hair was also cut man-fashion in a short bob that shaped to her head like a raven cap, accentuating the patrician quality of her chiseled features. She wore low heeled shoes; the sensible kind. But her stockings were of sheer nylon.

"Mr. Anthony!" she said, her voice rich and throaty. "Thank goodness you got here."

"Did you think maybe we wouldn't, babe?" Tom Gentry popped off, his light tone masking suspicion.

"Why—why, no, of course not. I knew you'd come, sooner or later. You phoned, you know." With this she dismissed the flyer and returned her attention to Jim. "I can't understand all the things that seem to have been happening tonight, Mr. Anthony. The murder of that Uvaldi man, and the—the police asking me so many questions—"

The wealthy criminologist made a wry grimace. "There are a lot of things I don't understand myself. For instance, Lieutenant Trotter tells me you're under the impression that I'm backing this labor relocation foundation."

"Under the impression?" she stared at him. "And why shouldn't I be? I have your letter asking me to undertake the work."

"May I see that letter?"

She nodded, conducted him to an inner office and produced a thin sheaf of correspondence from a file. "All your communications are here, together with those I've received from other members of the board. Naturally I've never spoken to any of you personally about the work; I was given to understand that you were all very busy, which was why you placed me in charge. I—I've tried to do a good job. I rented the most inexpensive offices I could find, kept my costs to a minimum—"

"Where did the money come from?" Jim interrupted her.

"Why, from the bank account you set up in my name."

"You used that money for buscharter as well as office rental?"

Her puzzled frown grew deeper. "But Mr. Anthony, you know I had nothing to do with the transportation end. I was merely notified by letter to have so many workers of certain types ready to leave at a certain date and hour. I had them here, the bus would arrive, and that was all there was to it."

"How many loads of men have you shipped?"

She looked at a paper on her desk. "Thirteen the second week. None at all the first week. And only one this week."

"You've been operating three weeks, then?"

"We've been open that long. But operating for only ten days, actually. It took time to get established." Then she added casually: "Of course I don't know how many bus loads have been shipped west from Philadelphia and Baltimore and—"

"Snow on a mountain, pappy!" Tom Gentry burst out. "They got *branches!*"

PRESENTLY THE MILLIONAIRE detective began inspecting the correspondence which he was supposed to have written. All the letters were on Foundation stationery, with a list of sponsors printed along one side: names that represented the ownership and management of some of the nation's greatest industries. Anthony's own name headed the list in larger type, just as his purported signature was boldly appended to many of the communications.

Beyond doubt, it was his genuine signature; no forger could possibly have made such a clever copy. As he leafed through the letters, though, a curious fact struck his eye. In each instance, his name had been signed in exactly the same way as the last; no slightest variation could be found.

He called this to the attention of Gentry and the Carradyne girl. "No matter how carefully a man writes his name, he never does it quite the same way twice," he remarked. "There are inevitable discrepancies. Ask any handwriting expert."

"Meaning what?" Tom asked.

For reply, Jim again had recourse to his flat, compact kit of scientific equipment. From a stoppered glass tube he spilled a few drops of chemical on one of his suppose signatures; then added a smear of jelly-like substance from a tiny plastic jar. The reaction was immediate and astonishing. As if the "James Anthony" had been scrawled with acid, it ate through the paper and vanished, leaving in its place the signature's silhouette sharply cut like a stencil.

Dorothy Dawson Carradyne muttered a guttural: *"Herr Lieber Gott!"* and then flushed with embarrassment. "Forgive me for lapsing into German. After all, I spent so many years as a student in Berlin… and your experiment was so startling—"

Jim's well-schooled features betrayed no expression as he politely accepted this glib explanation of her slip. In fact, he ignored it and pointed to the letter.

"One of the cleverest forgeries I ever encountered," he announced quietly. "Accomplished by a new method. This was not an ordinary ink."

"Then what was it?" Gentry demanded.

"Somebody procured a copy of my autograph and made a photoengraving of it. These letters were not signed by hand. An impression of my signature was struck in some sort of small printing press—exactly the way counterfeit money is engraved!"

The brunette woman's eyes widened. "But—but why?"

For a raging second Tom
considered hurling himself in
and snatching a drumstick.

"That's something. I'm not yet prepared to answer. However, I think you must realize by now the obvious fact that I had nothing whatever to do with this so-called Foundation."

"It—it w-would seem so," she admitted reluctantly. "Although I can't understand why anyone would go to all this trouble just to make a f-fool of me!"

Anthony faced her. "Disregard yourself for a moment. Consider the others who've been duped; the hundreds of men who were shipped out of town in my name and then left stranded."

"Stranded—?" she recoiled, as if this had been an angle unknown to her previously. "Then your California factories had no jobs waiting for those men?"

Jim nodded grimly. "That's the story. I'd like to see your records on Nick Uvaldi, the murdered man."

"Of course." She thumbed through an index box, withdrew a card and handed it over.

HE STUDIED IT, noting the date and hour of departure of the bus on which Uvaldi had been a passenger. Then he made a hasty mental calculation as to approximately how far west the vehicle might have traveled before the doomed man left it to come back to New York in time for his appointment with death.

After a moment Jim returned the card. "Thanks. And now, if you don't mind, I'd like those letters for police inspection. I want expert opinion on them."

Surprisingly enough, she refused. With a swift gesture she snatched up the sheaf of correspondence, thrust it in a drawer of the steel file by her desk, closed the drawer, locked it and then quickly unfastened her tailored jacket. Dropping the file key into a pocket of her blouse, she re-buttoned the coat.

"Sorry, Mr. Anthony," she said firmly. "This whole affair has placed me in an extremely awkward position. Those letters are all I have to indicate that I was acting under your authorization; or rather, that I thought I was. And while I have duplicate records and photostats of the letters in my bank safety deposit box, I prefer to keep the original correspondence in my possession until I've had time to consult an attorney."

If her action angered the wealthy detective, he revealed no hint of it; nor did he show the merest sign that her stubbornness had aroused his suspicions. Instead, he smiled. "Very well, Miss Carradyne. I can understand your feelings."

She seemed to lose some of her tension. "Thank you. If you have f-finished with me, I'd like to go home. I—I'm somewhat tired."

"That's understandable too. But I wish you'd stay here for just a little while longer. I have an errand to do, then I want to come back for one final look-around. It won't take long, I promise."

"We-e-ell, all right."

Jim moved toward the door and Gentry followed him. "What comes next, pappy?" the flyer asked in a low tone. "Could that fat Stope jerk and those other screwballs have schemed up this mess just to blackmail you?"

"Possibly. But it certainly cost them a terrific financial outlay to put their plans in operation."

"Not so terrific compared with the two million they're asking," Tom pointed out sagely. "If they stick you for that much dough, it's been a good gamble." Then he added: "Where we going now?"

"*You're* not going anywhere."

"Hunh?"

"You're to stay here, see that Miss Carradyne doesn't make a getaway with those letters. Keep your eye on her. I'll hunt up Lieutenant Trotter and bring him back with me. An official police request will make her part with that key."

Tom said: "Maybe I can get it without a police request." But his millionaire friend was already striding from the room and didn't hear the speculative remark.

As it turned out, Tom now found himself alone with the lovely Dorothy Dawson Carradyne; and he lost no time putting his strategy into motion. "Did anybody ever tell you how gorgeous you are, toots?"

She looked astounded. "Why—why, I—"

"You're wasting your life in this social service stuff, kitten. You ought to be behind footlights or something. Maybe the movies. You've got what it takes."

"Really?" she drawled, smiling a little. Her amusement didn't indicate displeasure, though. She was just the same as any other cutie, Tom told himself. None of them could resist flattery.

He moved closer to her. "Sure. Take me, for instance. I ain't very often impressed by beautiful women." He wondered if heaven would strike him dead for the outrageous lie.

"Aren't you?"

"No. But you do things to me."

"Such as… what?" she purred.

"Well, like making me want to kiss you." Audaciously he slipped an arm around her waist and pulled her to him; put his mouth on her lips.

At that moment the ceiling fell on him.

JIM ANTHONY HAILED a cruising cab and had himself driven to that side street where his first taxi had been attacked by those three thugs. Having left the corpses of two murdered men there—his original hacker and one of the masked gunsels—he had a hunch he would now find Lieutenant Trotter on the scene investigating the twin killings.

And he was right. The homicide official and a squad of his underlings had the street roped off to traffic while they bayed through the block like bloodhounds on a false scent. The bodies had been removed to the morgue by this time, although the wrecked Yellow still rested at the curb.

Trotter spotted the millionaire criminologist. "You!" he growled bitterly. "What are you doing here? Haven't I got enough grief on my hands without—?"

"I know, I know," Jim said in the tone of one who soothes a petulant child. "If you'll hold your temper, I'll try to give you a line on the two corpses you just found."

"What?" Trotter shouted. "You mean you know what happened to them? Why they were plugged?"

"I was here." And Anthony explained the attempted kidnaping, the manner in which he had frustrated it, and the subsequent escape of two of his thwarted abductors.

The headquarters man looked dazed. "I might have known you were mixed up in it somehow. Any time trouble begins cropping up in bunches I can figure you've got a finger in it." Then, a trifle more calmly, he asked: "Have you any idea why they tried to snatch you?"

"There are two possible theories."

"Well, spill them! Or is it a secret?"

Jim smiled bleakly. "First, someone may have wanted to put me out of action for a few days until a certain labor scandal breaks wide open. Second, it may be that somebody hoped to prevent my inspection of that relocation foundation's files."

"What about the files?"

"Those letters you saw were all forgeries. And now Miss Carradyne refuses to give them up. I'd like you to go back to her office with me and demand the forged correspondence."

Trotter announced that he would be glad to do this. "But as for a labor scandal, I don't get your drift."

BRIEFLY AND CONCISELY, Anthony furnished a resume of all he had learned, without revealing his sources of information. "You can see the possibilities," he concluded. "Hundreds of workers dumped on the desert in my name, left penniless and jobless after being promised employment—why, hell, it could cause strikes and walkouts in every plant I own. And a single day's stoppage of production would be a serious blow to American war effort at the rate we're turning out the goods."

"So that's why they tried to snatch you!" Trotter breathed. "To get you out of the way until it'd be too late to repair the damage!"

The millionaire criminologist inclined his head. "It's probable— although it wouldn't have done them as much good as they thought."

"Why not?"

"Because I already have my French associate at work. The man you met: Dr. Montclair. He's busy right now, setting the machinery in motion to rescue the stranded men and give them transportation, money, jobs."

"Smart enough," Trotter approved. "But who was behind this caper?"

Anthony's lips thinned. "Think it over a minute. Who'd gain by promoting disunity in this country? Who might have the biggest reason for fostering a rift between American capital and labor? Even though we mended that rift later by exposing the truth, we still would have lost thousands of man-hours that could never be made up."

"Good God; You mean—?"

"Yes. Axis agents. Saboteurs. A nation-wide plot to throw a temporary monkey wrench in our machinery," Jim said.

Trotter was appalled. "But who's responsible?" Then his big face darkened. "Say, that Carradyne woman was educated in Germany. And when I grilled her she accidentally used some German gab. Do you suppose—?"

"She spoke German to me, too. I've already thought of that. Which is why I'm asking you to go with me and have a showdown," Anthony reminded him.

"Yeah. What are we waiting for? Here's my car. Come on!" A vast impatience seemed to fill the homicide lieutenant as he realized they were wasting precious time.

But for all his sudden haste and the breakneck speed with which he presently sent his official sedan careening down Broadway, it developed that he might just as well have saved the effort. For when they finally burst into the offices of the fake Foundation for the Redistribution of War Manpower, he and Anthony discovered that Dorothy Dawson Carradyne was gone. Her files were looted and empty. And Tom Gentry lay sprawled on the carpetless floor of the inner office, as unconscious as a man who had been hit by a battering ram. In fact, from the appearance of the bruise on the back of his skull, it must have been a pile-driver that had bludgeoned him.

CHAPTER VII

REVELRY AT MIDNIGHT

"**I KISSED HER,**" **GENTRY** moaned when first aid measures eventually brought him back to his senses. "I kissed her just once. Pappy, did you ever kiss a girl and have it kick you into the middle of next week?"

Jim Anthony was in no mood for humor. "It was a blackjack, not the kiss, you idiot. I thought I left you here to guard her! Instead, you laid yourself wide open for an attack from behind. Won't you ever learn that crime and flirting don't mix?"

"Some day, maybe," the freckled aviator's tone was contrite. He rubbed the swelling on his scalp. "Anyhow, I'm certainly being educated the hard way."

Across the room, Trotter made irate noises. "Are you sure you didn't dish yourself that lump just to make the set-up look good?"

"Now, that's a lousy thing to say," Tom complained. "Why would I try to beat my own brains out?"

"It could be a cover-up," the homicide official peeled back his lips. Then he glared at Anthony. "I'm not forgetting that Uvaldi guy who got creamed in your hotel restaurant, my friend. He apparently had something on you—and he died. Whatever it was he knew or suspected, it was in connection with this Relocation Foundation."

The wealthy criminologist said: "Well?"

"Well, nuts! You've been feeding me a lot of baloney on forged letters and Axis saboteurs and melodramatic poppycock. How do I know any of it's true? Maybe you really are backing this relocation racket. Maybe it was some stinking scheme you hatched up to ship a lot of labor out west, strand them and then hire them at half pay—which they'd be forced to accept because they were stuck," Trotter theorized inelegantly.

Pretending to be drunk, he managed
to give her a lot of false information.

"And the disappearance of Miss Carradyne? The missing files of records?"

"Yeah. A neat gag when you saw you'd overstepped yourself. The dame drops out of sight and takes all the organization papers with her. So now nobody can prove or disprove your connection with the outfit. Gentry bumps himself on the conk to make it smell sweeter—but it's still got a stench as far as I'm concerned."

FROM PAST EXPERIENCE, Tom Gentry realized that the animosity existing between his millionaire friend and Lieutenant Trotter was one that could never be fully erased. It arose from deeply rooted differences in their natures, their habits of thinking, their training. Trotter had been schooled for direct action—the law of the nightstick, where every man is considered guilty until proven innocent. Anthony was the man of science, modern methods, rationalization. Between two such individuals friction was inevitable.

All the same, Tom couldn't restrain his temper as he heard the homicide official making his absurd insinuations. "Dizzy as I am, I've got a good notion to shove a few teeth down your throat!" he grunted at the headquarters man.

Anthony held up a warning hand. "Take it easy, Tom. If Trotter thinks I'm involved, that's his privilege. It's also his privilege to prove it—if he can."

"Is that a challenge?" the lieutenant asked.

"You may call it that."

"Okay. From now on, I'm breathing down your neck. Make one wrong move and I'll nail you, understand? And don't be coming to me with any more baloney about foreign spies. Don't look to me for help in chasing down blind alleys that you yourself arranged in advance. I'm after you and I'm going to get you, Mister Jim Anthony."

Then, snorting and muttering, Trotter tore out of the room in a towering rage.

"HEY, JIM," THE freckled flyer said plaintively. "What did drizzle-puss mean by foreign spies?" Anthony explained his saboteur theory. "The worst of it is," he ended, "I need those office records. First to prove my signature was forged; second, for the names and addresses of the men who were shipped west, so I can make amends."

Tom frowned. "But you've got Montclair working on that. The expert touch."

"He's shooting blind; putting out feelers in the dark. Chances are he'll miss connections with a lot of those fellows."

"What about Fatso from the picture magazine, Jim? Could he or one of his pals have bopped me, taken the files, and snatched Miss Carradyne? Or could she be in cahoots with the outfit?"

Anthony paced the floor. "Perhaps. Stope may think I'll pay off quicker if he offered me the foundation records along with his photos. If so, there's one flaw in his reasoning."

"What flaw?"

"The time element." Jim didn't elaborate on this. Instead, he said: "Let's take a look through his publishing office, Tom. We might find something." And they went down to hunt a cab.

Ten minutes later they stood before the musty suite in that dilapidated building in the Forties which comprised the headquarters of *Focus Magazine.* The corridors were dark, deserted; no lights could be discerned through the door's frosted glass panel, and the door itself was locked.

This didn't daunt Anthony, however. From a secret pocket in his coat he drew his prized steels, those famed implements with which he could work the cleverest lock ever invented. In a brief moment the door swung open. He and Tom entered.

But their visit proved fruitless; they found nothing remotely resembling the files of the labor relocation foundation. "If I only knew Stope's home address!" Jim whispered.

Astonishingly, Gentry came up with a possible solution. "We might get it from his blonde secretary. I can tell you where she lives. She gave me her address and phone number when I talked to her in your penthouse."

Anthony's lips pulled back in a quick, dark smile. "So that was why you fastened onto her. I believe if you were heading for the electric chair and passed a girl, you'd get her number."

"Why not? Maybe the current would fail, pappy."

LANA McBRIDE'S APARTMENT seemed to be the scene of unexpected revelry when the two friends arrived. At least you could hear conversation, merriment, the clink of glasses filtering through the door as the millionaire criminologist knocked.

It was the tall, skinny photographer who opened up. Like a slightly tipsy scarecrow he blinked at Anthony and Gentry, while in the room behind him a hush fell upon L. Gabriel Stope, Higgie Smith, and the McBride girl.

Then the cadaverous Koenig bowed drunkenly. "You find us in a celebration, drinking premature libation. Noon tomorrow is the deadline, or you'll be in every headline. Welcome to this little stash; I hope you brought two million cash."

CHAPTER VIII

BULLET TRAIL

OBLIVIOUS TO THE RHYMED greeting, Jim Anthony strode forward until he was face to face with the publisher of the picture weekly which didn't exist. "Now, then, Stope."

"Ah. Twelve hours ahead of time. Good. Shows excellent judgment. I'm ready to complete the deal if you are," the fat man's slitlike lips were scissors chopping off the words.

"There'll be no deal. Not on your snapshots, anyhow."

"Wha-what?"

"They're worthless for blackmail purposes. They aren't exclusive," Jim announced.

"Crazy talk! Sure they're exclusive. Got my first tip twelve days ago. Overheard two men in saloon. Said they were signing up, shipping out. Gave me a hunch. I had Higgie and Rhymer apply at foundation office. Accepted. They went with first bus-load. Dumped in Arizona. Other men broke. Not Higgie and Rhymer. Hired a rancher to drive them to closest town. Airport. Took plane back to New York. No other reporters and photographers on job. Course our pix are exclusive."

"Temporarily," the millionaire criminologist agreed. "But not for long. Even if I paid you blackmail to suppress your findings, the news is bound to break in a day or so; maybe sooner. The minute the first stranded workers reach civilization they'll talk—and the story will become public."

Stope seemed to deflate. "True. But—"

"So why should I pay you for a silence that can't possibly last more than a few more hours? You were hoping to stampede me for a quick settlement. I don't stampede worth a tinker's dam."

Higgie Smith moved forward, flanked by Koenig and Lana McBride. "What is this, an act?" he demanded suspiciously.

"No act," the fat publisher looked sheepish. "Tried to pull a fast one. Anthony too smart."

The blonde girl made a bitter mouth. "Maybe you're both too smart. Maybe you're still pulling a fast one—on us. Perhaps Mr. Anthony has already bought you off, and this little scene is to make us think the scheme failed. Listen, Gabe. If you've already collected and think you can squeeze us out of the gravy—"

"Don't try it," Higgie Smith growled. "For a chisel like that I'd put a bullet through your fat gut."

Stope seemed genuinely scared.

"No payoff. Word of honor. I wouldn't hold out on you." He turned to Anthony. "Tell them," he pleaded.

"It's true," Jim said quietly. "I haven't given you any money. But I might pay a reasonable figure for those records of the phony foundation."

Higgie Smith, Rhymer Koenig, and Lana McBride looked bewildered; apparently they didn't know what Anthony was talking about. But Stope's expression was crafty rather than surprised. "Files missing, eh?" Then he shook his head. "Sorry."

"Meaning you haven't got them?"

"Right."

"You don't know what happened to Miss Carradyne?"

"Who's she? Oh, the foundation secretary. No. Can't tell you a thing. Wish I could."

The millionaire detective touched Gentry's arm. "Come along, Tom. We're wasting time here." And they left the apartment, followed by the sounds of bitter argument as the conspirators hurled recriminations at each other for the shakedown fortune which had slipped through their fingers.

DOWNSTAIRS, JIM DREW his aviator friend into the shadows of an areaway. "You realize what I've done?" he asked the flyer.

"Sure. You caused a falling out among thieves."

"More than that, I've let them know I'll pay cash for stolen property. Stope may have been lying. He may have those files. If so, he'll probably do what his pals accused him of doing: pull a double cross, try to sell the files to me and keep all the money for himself."

Tom blinked. "Gosh, pappy, then that gang of vultures would really blow their tops!"

"Exactly. And in the process, one of them might accidentally let something slip."

"Such as—?"

"The possibility of them being in the pay of the Axis to foster industrial disunity in this country. With the blackmail game as a sort of sideline."

"So now what happens?" Gentry asked.

The wealthy criminologist smiled bleakly. "I have a hunch Mr. L. Gabriel Stope will be going home shortly. I want you to trail him. If he digs up those files, get them. Even if you have to do it with brass knuckles."

"That would be a pleasure."

"Then we'll drop a hint that he sold the stuff to us for pay. His friends will do the rest when they hear that."

Tom chuckled with anticipation. "But what about you, Jim?"

"I'm starting out to hunt for Dorothy Dawson Carradyne," the sun-bronzed investigator responded. "I intend to find her if I have to turn New York upside down. Should that be necessary, we have just the organization to do it!" And he pivoted, made off into the night.

TOM GENTRY KNEW what his friend meant by organization. In every strata of Manhattan society, from newsboys and lowly char-women up through the middle classes of white collar workers and even reaching as far as bankers, sportsmen, and capitalists, you could find secret membership in the legendary Anthony legion—a fabulous regiment of the adventurous whose allegiance and devotion could always be counted upon in time of stress. Into the ordinary every-day humdrum of their lives, Jim Anthony had carried the occasional thrill of battle against lawlessness; they were his undercover shock-troops, a heterogeneous army of modern Vigilantes banded together to fight crime.

And on those infrequent occasions when Jim called them into action, hell always spilled over!

Gentry grinned to himself as he lurked, alone, across the street from the entrance of Lana McBride's apartment house. He knew matters would soon be coming to a head, and he took grim delight in having a hand in the game. The action couldn't start too soon to suit him!

Presently he tensed as he saw two figures emerging from the building, one tall and thin, the other chubby. The genial aviator recognized them as Rhymer Koenig and Higgins Smith; and for an instant he was tempted to loiter along behind them; find out where they went, what they did.

Then he remembered his instructions. He was posted here to flush out bigger game, so he remained reluctantly in hiding and allowed the ill-assorted pair to pursue their course unmolested. He wished, though, that he might have been twins for the next couple of hours....

"Oh-oh!" he whispered to himself. *"Stope!"*

It was true. The fat man had appeared and was now furtively moving toward the far corner with haste in his waddling walk and a leather brief case in his hand. The brief case seemed heavy, bulging.

To Tom Gentry, that leather bag was deeply significant. Maybe Stope had the foundation records in it. Maybe they'd been in Lana McBride's flat all the time, unknown to Rhymer Koenig and Higgie Smith. Possibly Stope and the McBride blonde were working together, planning a freeze-out which would leave Smith and Koenig minus their share of the proceeds.

"We'll soon see!" Tom told himself. And he began shadowing the fat publisher.

This was not exactly easy, for L. Gabriel Stope seemed worried by some inner fear of a tail. He kept glancing back over his shoulder, forcing Gentry time after time to duck into some darkened doorway. Presently, though, Tom's corpulent quarry scuttled through the entrance of another shoddy apartment house a few blocks distant; and here the chase ended.

UP A FLIGHT of stairs the fat man laboriously climbed, unaware of the silent, freckle-faced figure which followed. Then, in the second floor hallway, Stope produced a key, unlocked a door, and entered a flat.

Gentry caught just a fleeting glimpse of the interior before the door was closed. It was one of those old fashioned apartments where the rooms were laid out in a long line, like heads on a string. Access to them was gained by means of an inside hall that ran the length of the layout, the way a narrow passage runs along a Pullman compartment car.

Waiting until he could no longer hear the fat man's footfalls, Gentry tiptoed to the door and tried the knob. It refused him; the latch was snapped. He scowled, swore. What, he asked himself, would Jim Anthony do in a case like this?

He'd use his prized steels, of course.

But Tom had no steels. All he had was a pocket knife with a screwdriver blade. Well, it was worth a try—provided nobody came along and caught him! He set to work, unscrewing the face-plate under the knob.

Eventually it came loose and he made some tentative stabs at the lock proper. He was astounded when this actually brought results. "I burgled it!" he gasped.

And he slipped over the threshold.

Dead ahead, light gleamed pallidly. He made for the illumination's source, making no sound; and then, cautiously, he peered into what proved to be a kitchen.

L. Gabriel Stope stood over a white enameled table, fumbling at the catches of the brief case. There was a childlike expression of contentment on his fat features, an avaricious gleam in his eyes, a snake like up-curl to the corners of his slitted lips. Now he reached into the bag, fondly.

Watching, Tom Gentry gathered himself to spring. The instant he saw those foundation records he would be ready to pounce and grab; to smack the publisher senseless if he made so much as one protesting yelp.

Stope's two hands came out of the brief case, bearing a cold roast chicken!

STUNNED DISAPPOINTMENT SLUGGED through Gentry's heart as he realized he'd been on a false trail. Correspondence, hell! This fat slob had merely brought home the main course of the feast which had been broken up at Lana McBride's place. And now he was carving the golden brown fowl with a kitchen knife, slicing off a juicy slab of the breast, conveying the succulent white meat to his traplike mouth.

Tom's own mouth watered. He suddenly recalled that his last meal had been dinner at the Waldorf-Anthony; a dinner interrupted by the murder of that Uvaldi fellow. Hunger began to clamor in the aviator's belly as he saw Stope munching a vast morsel of chicken and licking the grease off his fingers.

Gloating, smacking sounds came from the fat man's lips. For a single raging second, Gentry considered catapulting into the kitchen to snatch at least a drumstick for himself. And then, suddenly, a shot sounded.

The barking report blammed from the kitchen's open window, a few inches over the sill. There was a swift blurt of orange flame streaking across the room with L. Gabriel Stope as its target. The pudgy publisher screamed, dropped the chicken, grabbed at his left shoulder. Spinning, he collapsed into a chair—which went to pieces under his weight, dumped him floundering to the floor.

Tom Gentry said: "Cripes!" and instinctively launched himself into view; made a flying leap over Stope's sprawled form. Stope saw him and screeched again, wildly. "Murderer!" he yowled. "You shot me—!"

Paying no heed to the accusation, Tom gained the windowsill. There was a fire escape landing just outside, with the rusty rungs of an iron ladder leading downward. Somebody was on that ladder, descending with jerky speed.

The happy-go-lucky aviator didn't even hesitate. He clambered out, started down. His soles smacked the alley pavement just as a thin, slight figure raced away.

"No you don't!" Tom roared. He sprinted with all his might; overhauled the fleeing man at the mouth of the alley and nailed him. "Got you!"

His victim squirmed to face him. *"Monsieur* Gentry—!" he exclaimed.

He was Dr. Francois Montclair.

CHAPTER IX

PENTHOUSE PARTY

STANDING IN THE FOYER of his rooftop penthouse, Jim Anthony faced two visitors. For the millionaire criminologist, trouble seemed to be coming in carload lots tonight. He'd been home less than an hour, just long enough to get his famous organization moving and to make some startling discoveries; and now he had a new worry to contend with.

Higgie Smith and Rhymer Koenig.

He scowled at them. "I've already told you, gentlemen, that I'm not interested in buying your blackmail pictures."

"We didn't come to sell them to you, sir," Smith answered, a vindictive glitter in blue eyes which were no longer naive. "Although blackmail's what I want to talk about."

"Yes?"

The chubby reporter nodded. "Gabe Stope tried to put the bite on you. How much will you pay us to testify against him? You can send him up for attempted extortion; get even for all the grief he's caused you. All Rhymer and I want is some cash—and a promise of immunity."

Abruptly, Anthony had a feeling that he would like to fumigate the room when he got rid of these two lice. But his bronzed countenance was expressionless as he said: "Sending your employer to jail doesn't interest me. I might pay you for certain information, though."

"Name it then, and if we can, sir, we will try to give the answer," Rhymer Koenig looked pleased with his impromptu doggerel. "Gabe is dirty, Gabe is deep; we hate his guts, the moon-faced creep!"

Jim was not amused. "I want to know who's behind Stope. Has he any foreign connections?"

"Foreign connections—?" Higgins Smith stiffened. "Hell, no. I never heard of such a thing."

"He gets no funds from overseas?"

"Funds! He never has two dimes to rub together. Not for salaries, anyhow. He always manages to buy himself steaks; stuff his bloated paunch. But as for any big dough—nix!"

"You're sure of that?"

Higgie was about to embroider his negative theme, but there came a sudden interruption from the penthouse elevator. The cage opened and two newcomers surged into the foyer: Lieutenant Trotter and L. Gabriel Stope himself, with his shoulder bandaged and his arm in a sling.

Trotter had a satisfied smirk on his face. "Where's Gentry?" he demanded.

"Not here," Anthony's sixth sense warned him that more troubles were about to pile up on those he already had. "Why? What's wrong?"

"Oh, nothing," the homicide official sneered elaborately in Jim's teeth. "Nothing at all. Not a thing." Then he roared: "Except I want him on a charge of attempted murder!"

"*What?*"

The fat magazine publisher chimed in venomously. "You heard right, Mr. Anthony. Your freckled friend tried to kill me."

WHILE THIS STARTLING announcement was being made, the private lift had silently descended in its shaft, drawn downward by someone pressing the button in the hotel's main lobby. Equally unnoticed, the noiseless car now came back up again to penthouse level and its sliding door whispered open.

From the elevator's streamlined interior stepped Tom Gentry and the haggard little French refugee, Francois Montclair. Tom called:

"Hey, Jim! I've been zig-zagging all over town, ducking the cop—co—ka-humph! Oh-oh! Wrong floor. Excuse it, please." As he caught sight of Trotter and Stope, the genial aviator attempted to reverse himself and pull Montclair back into the cage with him.

He was too late. The headquarters detective emitted a snarl of triumph and nabbed him. "No you don't! So you've been ducking the cops all over town, hanh? Well, you picked the wrong spot to duck this time. You're under arrest."

"Who, me?"

"Yes, you."

"What for? What's the beef?"

Trotter feigned a weary sigh. "What's the beef, he asks me! You see this man here, don't you?"

"Man?" Tom looked at Stope. "Is it a man? I thought it was a lump of blubber. Yeah, I see him."

"And you see the bandage on his shoulder."

"Sure."

"Well, that's where your bullet plugged him. The slug you aimed at his heart. Stick out your hands for the cuffs."

Gentry summoned a look of injured indignation and glared at the fat publisher. "Did you go to the law and accuse me of winging you, for cripes' sake?"

"I didn't have to," Stope said. "Law came to me. Neighbors heard the shot, phoned headquarters. Police asked questions. I told them what happened." He didn't seem happy about it, though. His manner indicated he'd have preferred to let the whole thing drop if it hadn't been for Trotter.

Jim Anthony stepped to the fore. "What about it, Tom?" he asked quietly. "Did you shoot him?"

"Gosh, no, pappy!" Then the aviator glowered at Stope. "I want you to answer something, Fatso."

"Go ahead."

"Which way were you facing when you stopped the pill?"

"Toward kitchen window. Eating chicken."

"And which way did the slug go in your shoulder?"

"From—from the front."

"Where was I when you first saw me?" Gentry probed.

"Kitchen door. Behind. But—but—"

TOM SPREAD HIS hands at Trotter, palms upward. "See? This ape's trying to frame me. What really happened, I saw him get blasted from the window. I leaped for the sill and chased the gunsel down the fire ladder." He summoned a noble expression. "My duty as a citizen, you know."

Trotter was growing more crimson by the instant. "Stow it! Don't preach! What became of the guy with the gun?"

"He got away clean," Gentry lied unblushingly, not risking a glance at Francois Montclair.

The homicide lieutenant swung on Stope and exploded like a cannon cracker. "Why did you try to pin it on this lug? What's the idea?"

"I—I really thought he—" the fat publisher choked out the truth for once in his life, but couldn't make it sound convincing.

Jim Anthony made a suggestion. "Perhaps it was another little blackmail idea."

"Blackmail?" Stope paled. For the first time he seemed to notice the presence of Higgie Smith and Rhymer Koenig; then it dawned on him that they'd sold him out. "You two!" he extended a fat, accusing finger. "Now I get it! *It was one of you that shot me!* You'd made threats—"

Even Anthony had to admit, in secret, that Stope was clever as hell. With an eel's slippery skill he had adroitly eluded a pitfall; and by this new accusation he had managed to put his two staff members in an awkward spot. Any testimony they might offer against him from now on would be vitiated, disbelieved, thrown out of court. A case of the pot calling the kettle black.

Lieutenant Trotter buried his face in his hands and moaned disconsolately. "Ye gods and little gremlins, what've I done to deserve this? Every time I make an arrest it blows up in my teeth like a loaded cigar! Will everybody kindly get out of my road while I go quietly nuts?" And he stumbled over to the elevator like a man in a horrid nightmare.

Anthony called after him. "Take these vermin with you and turn them loose." He indicated Stope, Koenig and Higgie Smith. "They make the place smell bad."

THE ATMOSPHERE SEEMED a trifle clearer when Trotter and the *Focus Magazine* trio had departed; but there was still a suspicion of tension. Especially when the millionaire criminologist stared speculatively at his freckled friend.

"You lied, Tom."

"Yeah, pappy, I sure did."

"You lied about not catching the gunsel."

"That's right."

"Who was he?"

Gentry jerked a thumb. "Frenchie, here."

"Dr. Montclair? Good God!"

"I fronted for him," Tom said. "After the way he explained things, I couldn't do anything else."

Francois Montclair looked haggard, rueful and grateful all at once. "It is of the truth, *Monsieur* Anthony," he confessed. "I shot that *canaille* of a Stope. I tried to kill him. My aim, she was miserable. I point at the heart, I hit the shoulder. I win no medals for marksmanship, *hein?*"

"But why, in heaven's name?" Jim demanded. "Why should you attempt a thing like that?"

"It is simple, *Monsieur* Anthony. Me, I am a refugee. Driven from my homeland by pigs who would have executed me if they had caught me. I come to America. I am penniless. You take me into your industrial empire, your confidence."

The millionaire made a disparaging gesture. "I need men of your ability. It was no favor. It was business."

"Oui. Yet the fact remains. You give me a new chance, a new hope, a new life. Then this so-accursed Stope appears. He makes the trouble for you, my benefactor. He is no better than a Nazi rat. So, *Pouf!* I shoot him." The little Frenchman shrugged as if his act had been the most natural thing in the world.

Anthony began pacing the thick rug. His face was set in a grim mold; lines of worry appeared around the corners of his mouth.

"What's the matter, pappy?" Tom Gentry asked. "After all, I got Frenchie clear. Nobody suspects him. And Stope's in no position to bellyache."

"I'm not thinking about that."

"Then what *are* you thinking about?"

"Two things I discovered after I posted you to trail Stope," the wealthy criminologist answered heavily. "I returned here to the hotel; started my organization moving. Then, by accident, I found something in this very penthouse."

"What was it, Jim?"

"A dictaphone. It had been planted here to enable somebody to eavesdrop on my private conversations."

The aviator stiffened. "Gosh! Where'd it lead to?"

"An unused trunk room on Five. I traced it there. And then I found Dorothy Dawson Carradyne."

Tom's eyes bulged. "Did you make her talk?"

"She'll never talk again," Anthony said bitterly. "That was why I was upset when Trotter came in a while ago. You see, I've made no report on it as yet; but Dorothy Carradyne was dead when I found her. She'd been dead for quite some time."

CHAPTER X

FOCUS ON SABOTAGE

BARELY A FEW BRIEF hours before dawn, Jim Anthony finally finished summing up his interpretation of all the ugly events that had happened. Pacing the floor, burning numberless cigarettes, stopping occasionally for a drink, he had steadily given voice to his theories and his convictions.

"I'm positive it's the work of Axis agents," he concluded. "Not just one, but many—with a single clever, crafty, cunning brain leading them. This whole plan springs from Berlin."

"Yeah, Jim?"

The hawk-like criminologist seemed not to hear Gentry's murmur. "A scheme to disrupt the harmony that exists between labor and the Anthony industries. A plot to make all workers reluctant in the future to move from one city to another for war positions. Not to mention the temporary loss of manpower through bickering and strikes because busloads of men were stranded. Even after I get that mess straightened out, the bad taste will linger."

"But look, pappy—"

"I might not have had the slightest inkling of trouble until it was too late—if it hadn't been for that poor Uvaldi fellow. I know now that he got off a bus somewhere in Pennsylvania; came back here to kill me because he thought I was responsible. Someone killed him first, though; someone on the other side of the restaurant, who escaped in the darkness. That murder was for the purpose of keeping me in ignorance of conditions until the storm broke."

"What about Stope's blackmail stunt?"

"A side issue. We're dealing with a master mind, man or woman, who has money, nerve, daring—and plenty of underlings for the actual dirty work. Think of the ramifications. This Foundation for the Relocation of War Manpower, for instance. Offices in New York, Philadelphia, Baltimore. The bus charters. The gunsel bus-drivers. The bank accounts. The phony letterheads with forged signatures. Masked killers and snatch artists in hijacked cabs. The thing's so big it staggers you."

"Listen, Jim. This Carradyne dame—"

"Poisoned. Potassium cyanide. Instant death."

"Could she have been the brains? And killed herself when she saw you were closing in?"

"I DON'T KNOW," Anthony said. "She may have been a suicide, or she could have been murdered; brought here to the hotel under duress and forcibly given the fatal dose because she knew or suspected too much. Suppose she saw the face of the man who slugged you unconscious in the foundation office? That alone would have been her death warrant, even if she'd been innocent otherwise; a mere dupe of the sabotage mob. Her corpse may have been left in the trunk room by the dictagraph receiver just to make it appear that she was implicated. I won't be sure until after the banks open in the morning."

Tom stared. "Banks? What have they got to do with it?"

"Everything, I hope. The answer to the riddle—or at least a means whereby I can repair the damage that's been done."

"How come?"

"Well, you perhaps recall something she said when we interviewed her a few hours ago. She mentioned duplicate records in her safety deposit box."

"Yeah, she did speak of that."

"And do you remember where she placed the key to the filing cabinet which she locked in front of our eyes?"

Gentry sighed with reminiscent regret. "Inside her jacket."

"Right. So when I examined her corpse in the trunk room not long ago, I found another key in the same pocket. A bank key to a safety deposit box at the Commerce First National."

"Jeepers! You think the duplicates will be there?"

"I'm hoping so," Anthony's dark eyes were shrouded. "But in the meantime, I want you to help me bait a trap."

The aviator leaped to attention at the prospect of activity. "Sure, Jim. What's your plan?"

"You're to go to that blonde girl, Lana McBride—"

Tom choked a protest. "Aw, no, pappy! Not her! You ain't going to tell me *she's* mixed up with Axis agents! She's a little crooked, maybe, but not that crooked!"

"There you go again, letting a pretty face distort your common sense," the millionaire criminologist reproved him. "After all, the McBride girl is Gabriel Stope's secretary; which could be a blind for her other connections. Aside from that, whatever she learns will inevitably get back to Stope—and to his slimy underlings. Rhymer Koenig and Higgins Smith."

Gentry digested this. "By gosh, I wouldn't put anything past that pair of weasels! Even Rhymer's name, Koenig—that's a German monicker, ain't it?"

"Correct. And the character of a poverty stricken photographer would make an excellent disguise for the head of a ring of enemy agents who wished to stay under cover. Which is why I ask you to go to see Lana McBride."

"What am I to tell her that might get back to Koenig or the others?"

"The facts about Dorothy Dawson Carradyne's safety deposit box. Its possible contents. And a tip that I intend to go to the Merchants' Fourth Trust to inspect that box as soon as the bank opens its doors in the morning," Jim said.

"Hey, wait," the aviator checked up. "What's this about the Merchants' Fourth Trust? I thought you told me it was the Commerce First National?"

ANTHONY SMILED BLEAKLY. "I did. That's the trap part. If my suspicions are correct, the saboteur gang will do one of two things. First, they may try to make a getaway out of town when they learn I'm about to get the dope. If they do, they'll find themselves picked up. I'll have every road, tunnel, bridge, and depot under police surveillance."

"Suppose they sit tight, though?"

"In that case they'll probably make a concerted move on the Merchants' Fourth Trust to intercept me and take those records away from me in a daylight hijack."

Tom looked bewildered. "But you won't *be* at the Merchants' Fourth Trust! The box ain't there!"

"Exactly. Therefore, instead of hijacking me, the mob will run into the arms of the waiting cops. Meantime, you and I will go quietly to the Commerce First National where the box is actually located. Nobody will molest us, because we've thrown the saboteurs off the scent and into a trap several blocks distant. We kill two birds with one stone."

Gentry grinned suddenly. "I get it! We'll be picking up the evidence at the Commerce First National while the cops are picking up the Axis gang at the Merchants' Fourth Trust!" He hastened to the elevator. "I'm on my way to see Blondie!"

"Good," the millionaire detective approved. With sudden concern he turned to Francois Montclair. "Forgive me for talking so long. It's nearly dawn and you're utterly worn out; you've had a hard night. I suggest that you get some rest if you want to be in on the finish a few hours from now."

"Merci, Monsieur," the haggard little refugee thanked him. "As you say, the night has been of the difficult."

A FITFUL NAP didn't seem to have helped Montclair very much when payoff time rolled around. For that matter, Tom Gentry, too, looked drawn and worn in the morning sunlight. But Jim Anthony, who'd had no sleep at all, appeared as fresh and keenly attuned as a well trained athlete newly awakened from a full night's repose. His hawk-like eyes were sharp, his clean-shaven face glowing with bronze health, his stride vigorous as he and his weary companions made for the stately structure on Fifth Avenue which housed the Commerce First National Bank.

The massive doors were just opening for the start of the days' business transactions when the millionaire criminologist arrived there with Tom and Montclair. Three armored money-trucks bearing uniformed guards were in the act of parking before the big building, and Avenue traffic flowed smoothly in its accustomed morning grooves: delivery vans, private cars, the usual flood of cabs painted every color of the rainbow. Streams of pedestrians moved along the sidewalks: New York's motley assortment of workers en route to their jobs.

Anthony halted briefly. "Tom, I'm posting you here to wait. Not that it's necessary, but just as a safeguard. Come along, Dr. Montclair. We'll get that box."

Grumbling, Gentry took up his post at the entrance. Traffic, both vehicular and pedestrian, seemed to be thickening. Abruptly the freckled aviator stiffened as he noticed a fat figure crossing Fifth and heading in the direction of Lexington. It was L. Gabriel Stope—and that other bank, the Merchants' Fourth Trust, was located on Lexington Avenue! The bank where a trap had been baited and prepared!

Was the fat publisher approaching this trap, or was his appearance merely a coincidence? If coincidence was the explanation, *then why was he being followed at a discreet distance by Lana McBride, Rhymer Koenig, and Higgie Smith?*

TOM THOUGHT ABOUT the pre-dawn visit he had made to the McBride girl's apartment just a few hours ago. He had worked that pretty cleverly, he told himself. He'd pretended to be slightly drunk and very much infatuated. He had made a couple of tipsy passes at the golden-haired Lana, which she had repulsed—but not too indignantly. In her manner there had been more than a hint that she might be receptive to his attentions at some other time.

Then, before she persuaded him to leave, he had managed to impart certain false information to her, the way a drunken man might make loose conversation. And now she was headed for Lexington Avenue with Koenig and Smith, trailing Gabriel Stope in the direction of the Merchants' Fourth Trust.

It was entirely possible, of course, that they weren't intending to go anywhere near that bank trap. Maybe they had some other, more innocent destination; errands to perform. They vanished from Tom's view in a surge of traffic that seemed to grow more abnormally heavy every instant.

And then hell broke open.

The deadly action commenced at the exact instant of Jim Anthony's emerging from the depths of the Commerce First National. The millionaire criminologist had a flat green metal box tucked under his arm and Francois Montclair trotting along beside him. Jim saw Gentry standing guard; nodded to him. He tapped the box he was carrying, as if to indicate that everything had gone off without a hitch.

But Anthony's casual manner was a mask covering his actual tautness, his alert realization of danger. Deep within the wealthy detective's subconsciousness his weird sixth sense shrilled a warning. He froze.

Those three armored money trucks were still parked in a row at the curb; and now, viciously, suddenly, their doors flashed open. Uniformed guards erupted to the sidewalk, brandishing automatics and tommy-guns. They weren't guards, though. They were thugs in disguise. Nazi agents.

They closed in on Anthony.

The thing caught Tom Gentry flatfooted. All he could do was goggle at the scene and yell frantically: "Jim—look out! It's a heist!"

And then a seeming miracle took place.

ALONG FIFTH AVENUE in both directions, vehicular traffic came to an astounding halt. The broad street was suddenly blocked by a jam of motorcars packed in and wedged from one curb to the other. There were sleek limousines and battered jalopies; delivery trucks and garbage wagons; taxicabs, private coupés, sedans that ranged in size from midget Austins to swanky Cadillacs and Packards. A hellish din arose as each and every machine's horn started bleeping and yowling and braying.

Simultaneously, blurts of charging humanity began appearing from the vehicles. And on the sidewalks, that abnormally thick flow of pedestrians pressed inward, converging upon the uniformed thugs who had leaped out of the armored trucks.

"Gosh!" Tom Gentry gasped. "It's the Organization—Jim's Vigilantes!"

He was right. Scrubwomen and bankers, newsboys and dignified stock-brokers, janitors and society dowagers and stenographers and debutantes, soldiers and sailors and marines on furlough—the crush comprised a thrilling cross-section of America; the embattled citizenry of the United States waging war upon their homeland's enemies!

Guns barked. Fists thudded home. Tommy-guns were tom from the hands of the sabotage mob and used as clubs, with Jim Anthony himself in the thick of the fray, dealing out grim punishment with his battering knuckles.

Panic-stricken, the fake uniformed guards broke in terror and tried to regain the safety of their three armored trucks. It was a useless maneuver, a fruitless retreat. Even had they reached their sanctuary, they could not have driven a single yard—because Fifth Avenue was plugged by halted cars as effectually as if a solid wall had been built from curb to curb. Horrified, the saboteurs threw down their weapons and raised their pleading hands. From bashed and bleeding mouths came the concerted whine of cornered rats: *"Kamerad! Kamerad!* We surrender!"

Then, and only then, did Jim Anthony draw his own automatic from its shoulder holster. He pivoted, took aim at a furtively scurrying figure which was trying to burrow through the jammed throngs.

He fired just once. He sent a bullet through the escaping man's left leg; brought him down.

"Got you, Francois Montclair," he said quietly.

IN LIEUTENANT TROTTER'S office at police headquarters, Jim faced the crippled Nazi who had posed as a Free French refugee. "Toward the last, I knew you were the one I wanted; the brains behind this whole rotten plot."

Montclair squirmed, cursed him gutturally in German.

"You see," the wealthy criminologist went on, "I realized it had to be someone fairly close to me; someone with access to my signature, my business methods, my industries. And you were the only newcomer in my confidence. So my suspicions were justifiable under the circumstances."

Again the Nazi saboteur cursed him.

Jim ignored the oaths. "But I couldn't be certain until you made one false move; overplayed your hand. That was when you attempted to murder Gabriel Stope. The fat man was innocent of anything except blackmail; but because of his extortion scheme, he almost spoiled your own game. That is, he told me enough to make me realize I was up against an Axis plot. Therefore you tried to kill him—and sealed your own doom."

"*Schwein!* American dog! You trapped me! It was illegal! It was not according to the rules—!"

"You're a fine one to talk about rules," Anthony's smile was thin, mirthless. "As far as I'm concerned, I'll exterminate vermin with any means at hand. Sure I trapped you. In your hearing, I pretended to be baiting a snare for the *Focus Magazine* people. Actually the bait was for you—and you swallowed it, hook, line, and sinker. You thought I would be unprotected when I went after the safety deposit box at the Commerce First National. I intended for you to think that."

"It was unfair!"

Anthony said: "That's according to how you look at it. The main point is, I wanted to capture you; but I was equally anxious to nab your mob of henchmen. The bus drivers. The kidnap thugs. The man in my hotel restaurant who killed Nick Uvaldi. I wanted all of you to pay for Uvaldi's death, and the murder of innocent Dorothy Dawson Carradyne, and the stranding of the duped workers who were dumped on the desert. I knew you'd have your whole stinking mob on hand to hijack me when I came from the bank; so I arranged a plan to nail them. The plan worked—and now I'm turning the whole lot of you over to the F.B.I. in Washington."

"*Nein*—they'll hang us—!"

"I sincerely hope so," Jim Anthony said. Then he turned his back on the cringing Nazi and strode from the room.

LIEUTENANT TROTTER VISITED the Anthony penthouse the next evening; faced Jim and Gentry. "Did you get your own affairs straightened out?"

The millionaire nodded quietly—"Every last worker was located, given money and a job. As you know, the newspapers have headlined the story; revealed it as a Hitler plot. Consequently there's no disunity between labor and capital. Our plants are producing faster than ever."

"You know, of course," Trotter said, "I could pinch you for causing a traffic jam and riot on Fifth Avenue.

"Do you intend to?"

"Hell no. In fact, I'll drink with you if you'll invite me."

Tom Gentry reached for a bottle. "Three snorts coming right up, pappy," he chortled happily.

DEATH FOR A
FLYING DUTCHMAN

FROM THAT CATHEDRAL IN THE DESERT, DEATH AND
JIM ANTHONY RODE THE SAME PLANE. AND THOUSANDS
OF FEET HIGH THEY PLAYED OUT THEIR GRIM DRAMA—
WITH THOUSANDS OF LIVES AT STAKE.

MURDER WAS STALKING CLOSER to Tom Gentry with every passing tick of the clock, although he was unaware of it. In fact, the aviator was aware this evening only of a sulky feeling of dissatisfaction with his surroundings and his solitude. Tom, to put it briefly, was fed up with Hollywood and the whole movie industry. Even his apartment gave him the horrors, in spite of the fact that a nicer one couldn't have been found anywhere. What good was a layout like this, he asked himself, if there was nobody to share it with him?

Fervently he wished himself back in New York, taking his ease in Jim Anthony's spacious penthouse atop the Waldorf-Anthony Hotel; but wishing got him nowhere. For lack of anything better to do, he poured himself a stiff drink of Scotch and carried it to the mantelpiece mirror in the living room; raised the glass in a sour toast to his own freckled reflection.

"To you, Bright-Eyes," he made a bitter mouth. "The world's prize dope."

IN THIS HE was just a bit unfair to himself. True, he'd had nothing but trouble since coming to the west coast two weeks ago; but he couldn't have foreseen that, any more than he could know right now that a murder was about to take place at his threshold. Morosely he sipped his Scotch, thinking back over the circumstances which had brought him to California.

At first, the chance to become technical director on the new war-aviation epic being filmed by Stupendous Studios had seemed like a heaven-sent opportunity to escape the raw rigors of early spring-time in Manhattan—not to mention the girls he might meet in the picture colony. Moreover, the government was vastly interested in war

**Even above the roar of the plane's
motor that crash could be heard.**

movies; and Gentry's assignment had been practically a command
from Washington.

He'd soon learned, though, that there was a great deal more to
picture-making than the mere supervision of flying sequences called
for by the script of this "Burma Bombardier" production. He had
slammed his head squarely into studio politics from the very start;
and then, to make it worse, had come his unpleasant encounters with
Dorpf Van Dykmann.

Thinking about Van Dykmann brought a scowl to Tom's usually
serene countenance. The fellow was a big, handsome Dutchman; an
assistant director on the "Burma Bombardier" picture. He was also
a former Royal Netherlands Indies air force combat pilot. In which
capacity he'd battled the invading Japanese over Java and been shot
down, seriously wounded. And he seemed to think this experience
entitled him to the position of technical advisor, a job which had gone
to Gentry instead.

Tom could understand the big Dutchman's professional jealousy;
nor did he blame Van Dykmann for it. After all, the man was probably better qualified than Tom for the berth. But just or unjust, the

plum had dropped unsolicited in Tom's lap; and orders were orders no matter whose toes got stepped on.

By the same token, Gentry had done his best to stay on friendly terms with the hulking Hollander. He might have succeeded, too, if a girl hadn't complicated the set-up.

"You and your janes!" he addressed his mirrored reflection. "Why can't you learn to let the skirts alone and stick to business?"

Then he took back the remark. Martha Tildon wasn't an ordinary cutie. She was something extra special in the way of lovely brunette sweetness; a dazzling screen star who was even more alluring in private life. Playing the feminine lead in "Burma Bombardier," she had inevitably crossed Tom's impressionable path, with the inevitable result that he fell for her and began dating her.

And then he found out he had again stepped on the toes of Dorpf Van Dykmann, who considered Martha Tildon his personal property. In consequence, the Dutchman's professional jealousy took an angrier turn, as resentfully sullen as a smouldering volcano that might erupt at any moment.

In fact, it looked as if this blow-off was due tonight. Only ten minutes ago the handsome Hollander had phoned Tom, his tone thick with suppressed excitement. "Gentry?"

"Yeah."

"This is Van Dykmann. You vwill blease stay in your apartment until I arrife."

"Hunh? You mean you want to see me? You're coming here?"

"That is gorrect. I vwill be there bresently." Then the connection was broken.

TOM GENTRY THOUGHT he understood the purpose of this promised visit. Most likely the Dutch aviator wanted a showdown, maybe with bare knuckles. And while Tom was not in the habit of ducking fights, he hated to tangle with a wounded war veteran; a man not yet fully recovered from the effects of Jap machine gun bullets. "Gosh," he mourned, "I might make a mistake and hit him so hard I'd kill him!"

There was a prophetic quality about the thought, at least as far as Van Dykmann's death was concerned. Fortunately, however, Gentry didn't guess this. He drained the last of his Scotch; began pacing nervously back and forth. And then the door buzzer sounded.

Tom responded reluctantly; opened up to behold the Hollander facing him. "Come in, pal."

Van Dykmann's hair was yellow, wavy; his features bore deep seams bespeaking haggard worry. "So," he muttered. "I find you joost in time—"

Then, chopping across his words with whiplash sharpness, a gunshot blasted from somewhere farther down the corridor. And as the report slammed echoes from the walls, Dorpf Van Dykmann's big frame stiffened convulsively. He seemed to be drawing himself up to full height, as if coming to military attention the way a soldier prepares to salute.

In fact, his right hand came up a little toward the side of his head. The gesture was never completed, though. Instead, he toppled forward into Gentry's startled arms.

"Westminster... Abbey... I saw... Huttson... bomb..." he gasped. The meaningless phrase was the last he ever uttered. Abruptly a shudder coursed through him; then he grew limp, a dead weight in Tom Gentry's grasp.

And as Tom stared, he noticed a widening splotch of crimson staining the back of the flying Dutchman's coat where the bullet had entered. It must have been a dum-dum slug, from the size of the wound; a soft-nosed slug with its blunt point nicked to make it mushroom at the instant of impact against human flesh. It had torn a gaping hole all the way to Van Dykmann's heart, bringing instant death.

Gentry tried to shift the body, to get past it, to catapult into the hall and come to grips with the unseen gunsel. But the murdered man was heavy, limber, as difficult to hold as a sack of loose grain—and just as difficult to toss aside in the narrow confines of the doorway.

Racing footfalls pelted down the corridor staircase, receding, growing fainter each instant. In a neighboring apartment, somebody screamed. Around a bend in the hallway you could hear a door being opened.

Frantically Tom dragged his burden inside; kicked his own door shut. He dumped the Dutchman to the floor; took another hasty glance at the gaping bullet wound and realized he had a corpse for company. Dorpf Van Dykmann had escaped the Japanese, only to meet his end in Hollywood. A murderer's dum-dum had accomplished what the Japs had failed to do in the fighting over Java.

Again Gentry started for the hall; but as he reached for the doorknob his common sense told him it was too late. There would be no use trying to catch the killer now, he realized. Whoever had fired that shot would be well out of the building by this time, making a fast getaway. Meanwhile, another scream sounded nearby and you could hear people clumping into the corridor; tenants of adjacent apartments drawn by the gun's report.

Which meant that the cops, too, would soon be swarming into the place. Somebody would summon them; somebody always did. And when they found a dead man in Tom's living room—

"Boy, oh, boy!" the genial aviator repeated to himself, his freckles standing out like new copper pennies against the sudden pallor of his good-humored face. Then he leaped to his phone, lifted the receiver.

The lobby switchboard girl said: "Order, please?"

"Get me Jim Anthony in New York, sister."

"His number, sir?"

"At the Waldorf-Anthony Hotel. Person to person—and make it snappy. This is urgent!"

CHAPTER II

ENTER JIM ANTHONY

SINCE AIRLINE TRANSPORTATION IN war-time America was congested, overburdened and overworked, Jim Anthony flew his own personally designed passenger plane from New York to Los Angeles immediately after receiving Tom Gentry's frantic long distance message. And he wasted no time getting started.

Thanks to his semi-official connections with certain governmental law enforcement agencies in Washington, Jim had no trouble in obtaining permission for the transcontinental trip; but his was one of the first privately owned planes to come with official sanction into the airport since the Fourth Interceptor Command grounded all ships except those of the army, navy, and the established airlines.

As a result, he attracted considerable attention as his big, sleek monoplane swooped down out of the sky to a perfect landing. A few reporters, loitering around the airport, snapped suddenly alert, sensing headline news when they saw Jim's tall, impressive figure emerge from the streamlined ship.

"Who's that?" one green cub asked his companions.

An older news-hawk answered succinctly. "Jim Anthony, no less. One of the richest men in the country. Gold mines, oil wells, a string of hotels, a newspaper chain, war industries, and Heaven knows what else. Inherited his holdings from his father, a wild Irish soldier of fortune and capitalist. Then tripled the estate's value by plain good management."

"Looks like an Indian," the cub remarked.

"Sure. His mother was a Comanche princess. That's where he gets the bronze complexion and piercing eyes and hawk profile. A handsome guy, but dangerous if you're on the wrong side of the law."

"Sure," the younger reporter nodded. "I remember now. He's an amateur criminologist, isn't he?"

"Amateur, nuts! For my dough, he's smarter than any professional cop that ever wore a badge. Modern scientific methods are his hobby; but he can use strongarm stuff if he has to. Yep, he's Jim Anthony, the millionaire detective. Wonder why he flew out here to the coast?"

A third newspaperman chimed in. "I wouldn't be surprised if it's about that guy Gentry, the one that got arrested last night on a murder beef. They're pals, I understand. Let's go ask him for an interview."

They didn't get the chance, though, because the subject of their discussion had already crossed the field's paved apron and slipped through the employees' gate. Here Anthony was greeted by a tubby little man who stood waiting beside a very large and very glittering vee-sixteen limousine.

THE TUBBY LITTLE man was Lew Dandridge, production head of Stupendous Studios, the company which was filming "Burma Bombardier." A relieved exclamation bubbled on his fat lips as he pumped the millionaire criminologist's hand.

"Jim! Am I glad to see you, I'm asking! Troubles we got like I wouldn't wish on my worst enemy, God forbid; but we maybe are okay now, with you on the job. I hope."

Anthony smiled gravely. This was not the first time he'd met Dandridge in difficulties; more than once his banks had helped pull Stupendous out of temporary financial straits. Hence he was well acquainted with the studio and its tubby, talkative production chief; and he had a great deal of respect for the fat man's abilities. Lew Dandridge might resemble a naive billikin, but in his hairless head reposed a brain as shrewd as a steel trap, as keen as a scalpel.

"Thanks for meeting me, Lew. You'll take me to see Gentry right away?"

"Sure thing. Hop in. I'm driving myself these days; chauffeurs you positively can't get, you should believe me. Two I'm losing to the army,

In the chair he had so recently
occupied the script girl was dead.

one to the marines, so I hire a girl. So she joins the navy. The Waves,
y'understand." Expertly the little executive tooled his gaudy machine
across San Fernando Valley at a careful thirty-five miles an hour.

Anthony noticed that the car bore an "A" ration sticker on its windshield, and he was intrigued to think Dandridge was very likely spending his entire week's quota of gasoline on this trip to and from the

airport. He smiled briefly; then his features became an impassibe bronze mask.

"Tell me about the killing, Lew."

"Better I'm telling you about the Dutchman. A nice character, y'understand, but moody. Martha made me hire him."

"Martha?"

"Martha Tildon. My star. She's knowing this Dorpf Van Dykmann in Europe before the war. Met him on a vacation trip. So he shows up in Hollywood and Martha says to me, Lew, she's saying, you got to hire him as a personal favor."

"Hire him in what capacity?"

"Assistant director. In Holland he's a director and producer. Comes the war, that lousy Hitler invades the Low Countries. Van Dykmann gets away to the Indies. He's joining the Dutch Air Force and flying against the dirty Japs, which the yellow lice are ganging up on him in a dog-fight, y'understand, and shooting him out of the sky."

Jim nodded. "Then he came to Hollywood to recuperate from his war wounds and you gave him a job. Right?"

"Yes. But is he satisfied? No. He wants to be technical advisor on the flying sequences. This I am not doing, on account Washington sends us Tom Gentry. So the Dutchman is sore. So Gentry is making eyes at Martha Tildon—which after all he is only human and Martha is a lovely dish. So Van Dykmann was jealous. So now he's dead."

"Have you any idea who murdered him?"

The tubby man shrugged. "Ideas you're asking. What ideas are there? The cops say Gentry did it and tossed his gun out the window. They're finding it in the alley with his prints on it. Who am I to argue?"

A THOUGHTFUL FROWN crossed Anthony's face. Over the long distance phone, Tom hadn't told him about the gun and the prints—probably because the discovery hadn't yet been made at the time of the transcontinental call. Now that Jim did know it, the knowledge disturbed him.

From his Comanche princess mother he had inherited a weird sixth sense which always warned him when danger lurked ahead; a curious, premonitory intuition that had never failed him. Now it began to stir within his subconscious mind like a faint whisper, telling him he was moving toward a peril of far greater magnitude than he had suspected. Uncannily it came to him that this was no mere commonplace murder, no ordinary crime of sudden passion. There were unplumbed depths before him, murky and deadly as quicksand in a swamp....

He stared at the surrounding scenery of the valley. "Wait a minute, Lew. You're not headed downtown. This isn't the way to the Los Angeles courthouse and jail."

"And who's wanting to go to jail?"

"I do. To see Tom."

"So you'll be seeing him. He's at the studio."

The millionaire criminologist failed to conceal his astonishment. "The studio? Then he isn't in custody?"

"Sure he is. Two deputies are practically living in his vest pockets, y'understand. They're following him around like a shadow on the wall."

Anthony's lips quirked upward at the corners. "I see. You've been pulling strings at city hall."

"Strings?" Dandridge chuckled innocently, but there was more than a hint of shrewdness behind that innocence. "So we've got to have technical advice. So Gentry is technical advisor. So we can't shoot a picture in a cell, I'm asking you?"

Jim, although a New Yorker born, knew his Hollywood as well as the next man. This wouldn't be the first time a prisoner had been released by city and county authorities so that a movie could be finished. Such prisoners were returned to jail after nightfall, of course; but during the day they had comparative freedom of movement—with two or more plainclothes detectives constantly on hand to prevent any attempted getaway. There was nothing illegal about the situation; just a convenience and a courtesy to the motion picture industry, depending on the size and importance of the studio involved.

And Stupendous was an important studio. You couldn't mistake that fact when you saw its big white buildings sprawling over a twenty acre tract in the middle of San Fernando Valley, glistening richly in the warm noontime sunshine. Lew Dandridge flourished his limousine through the wrought iron gates; parked before the two-story main executive building.

"So," he announced. And he led Anthony upstairs to his own private office, where Tom Gentry stood waiting between two quiet headquarters men.

THE GENIAL AVIATOR'S freckled face seemed drawn, as if he'd passed a sleepless night; but his voice sounded jaunty enough as he sprang forward. "Hi, pappy. Welcome to wonderland." A wry grin twisted his mouth. "Wonderland, because you wonder how soon you can get away from it."

Anthony grasped his hand. "Hello, Tom. Can we talk somewhere alone?"

"Don't mind my two stooges," Tom grinned crookedly at his plain-clothes guards. "They're decent guys, but soft touches. I've already taken them for sixty-three cents, matching pennies."

One of the deputies said: "Give us time. We'll get it back. Okay, sonnyboy, you can go over in a corner and have a chat with your friend. We won't eavesdrop."

Anthony and Gentry moved toward a modernistic corner window, opposite a laboratory building across the studio street and well out of earshot. Then the aviator dropped his easy-going manner. "I'm in a spot, pappy. I've been framed to the eyebrows."

"Tell me exactly what happened."

Gentry sketched the essential details, finishing with: "So after I got through talking to you in New York I called the cops. They finally found a roscoe in the alley, and blamed if it didn't have my dabs on it."

"Your gun?" Jim's dark eyes glittered.

Tom shook his head. "Belonged to the prop department. I was using it yesterday to show Lew Dandridge a trick draw out on location; left it on a table in Martha Tildon's dressing trailer."

"Dandridge remembers this?"

"He remembers the trick draw, yeah. He says he didn't notice where I put the rod afterward."

"What about Miss Tildon?"

"She claims she never saw it. So does her maid. Anybody could have stepped into the trailer and picked it up, of course. The prints were blurred, as if somebody might have held it with his handkerchief or something."

The millionaire criminologist drew a deep breath. "Sounds like a frame, all right. A clever one. Who hated Van Dykmann to the point of killing him?"

"I wish I knew!"

"Well, then, who hated you to the point of framing you?"

"I don't know that, either."

Anthony said thoughtfully: "Give me a brief line on this picture you're making."

"It's about a lost American bomber squadron quartered in the Burma jungle, making a last ditch fight. The big punch scene is when they drop eggs on a Jap airplane assembly plant in Rangoon. Martha Tildon plays a Red Cross nurse. Her pal Betty Gault is an entertainer who's knocked around the Orient; hard-boiled, suspected of being an enemy agent. But in the payoff, when the squadron is shot to pieces and there isn't a full crew, Betty flies along in the last remaining ship; handles the bomb-sight and blasts the Jap assembly plant just before the plane crashes."

"Tell me about this Betty Gault."

"Swell kid. You'll like her. Tall, red-haired, came up the hard way—hoofer, tent shows, cheap stock companies in the sticks. Not as young as she used to was; thirty, maybe. But she's got a heart of solid gold; and she looks after Martha like a hen with one chick."

"How did she get along with Van Dykmann?"

"Didn't have much use for him," Tom admitted. "She figured he wasn't on the up-and-up as far as Martha Tildon was concerned. A wolf, if you catch my drift."

"Would she be capable of murdering him to protect Miss Tildon?"

Gentry looked shocked. "Betty? Nix, Jim. She ain't the killer type."

THERE'S NO SUCH thing as a killer type," Anthony said. "We can skip that part for a moment, though. Let's consider another angle: Martha Tildon herself. Do you think she'd shoot a man because his jealous infatuation annoyed her?"

"No, pappy, I don't."

"Okay. To get back to the movie. Has it been running smoothly or otherwise?"

"Smooth enough, considering the technical problems," Tom answered. "I mean, everybody got along with everybody else in the unit—all but the trouble between Van Dykmann and me. Which was something I couldn't help. The guy just didn't like the color of my teeth, I guess."

"He was friendly with everyone else?"

"Yeah."

"What are these technical problems you mentioned?"

"Well, all private flying is curtailed out here. It takes a special dispensation from the brass hats whenever we make an air scene; the army's using every plane they can lay hands on. After all, they need

"What's a little perjury to save a friend?" she asked.

them. I see where a bomber was lost last week on its test flight; they think it crashed somewhere in the mountains back of San Bernardino."

Anthony nodded. "I read about it; a Lockheed A-29. No trace of wreck or crew. What has that to do with the matter?"

"Nothing, only I wish we had the plane for this picture. Imagine making a bomber story without bombers! That's what I mean by technical problems."

"How do you manage?"

"Well, we've got some plywood mock-ups; phony ships that we line up on the ground to look like the real article. Then there are three kites that will actually fly; obsolete cabin jobs the prop department rebuilt and dressed up so they'll pass for twin-motored bombing planes in the air. Underpowered, though; pasted together with spit and baling wire. If we didn't have a mighty good bunch of stunt pilots, those crates would never rise two feet off the tarmac."

"Who are the pilots?"

"Bush flyers mostly," Gentry's eyes became animated, almost enthusiastic. "Too old for military service; and besides, Uncle Sam doesn't want guys that fly by the seat of their pants. They ain't scientific, but if you glued wings on a coffin any single one of those boys could hop from here to Tokyo."

"No suspects among them?"

"Nary a one. You'll find out when you meet them—*Hey! What the—?*"

Tom's sudden yelp was cut short as Anthony brought up a fist like a striking cobra and clipped the genial aviator full on the jaw. The explosive blow flattened Gentry like a chopped tree; then the wealthy criminologist stooped to make certain his freckled friend was genuinely unconscious.

Simultaneously the two plainclothes guards came surging across the room. "What cooks here, chum?"

Anthony's expression was enigmatic. "When a prisoner talks about escaping, it's time to put him where he won't get a chance. Better return Gentry to a cell and keep him there."

"You mean he was going to lam? Okay, we'll run him downtown. Thanks for the tip."

Tubby little Lew Dandridge emitted plaintive sounds. "Is this a business! So now what am I doing for a technical advisor?"

Jim Anthony's tone was wooden. "I'll take the job, Lew," he said stolidly.

CHAPTER III

LOCATION OF DEATH

THE LOCATION WHICH STUPENDOUS Studios had chosen for shooting the exterior flying sequences of *Burma Bombardier* was at the head of San Fernando Valley, near Saugus. Here the property department had fabricated a semblance of jungle, with a clearing that served as a makeshift airfield. Grips and prop men were wetting down this field to lay the dust when Anthony arrived on the scene with Lew Dandridge.

First to approach the glittering vee-sixteen limousine was a compact, grizzled man in flying togs. There were patches of grey at his temples, weather-beaten wrinkles deeply lining his face, a decided limp to his stride; but he carried himself with a truculent air of assurance, forceful rather than cocky, that gave him an almost youthful appearance.

The millionaire criminologist recognized him as an old aviation acquaintance, a man who'd flown planes all over the world—in South America, Africa, the bush country of northern Canada and Alaska. "Coke Robertson!" he exclaimed.

"Well, Jim, for Pete's sake!" Robertson extended a hard hand. "What are you doing here?"

"Technical director. And you?"

"I'm your number one boy, in that case," the older man's eyes wrinkled at the corners. "Flight leader of the Wingless Wonders. Come on over and meet the others."

He led Anthony across the field to where two more men in helmets, riding breeches and leather jackets idled in the sunshine. "Boys, this is Jim Anthony—and if you've never heard of him you must be deaf, dumb, and blind. He flies like an angel, fights like a devil, plays detective for a pastime and has more dough than a dozen adding machines could count."

ACKNOWLEDGING THE INTRODUCTION, Jim, without seeming to, covertly studied the two flyers who worked under Coke Robertson's orders. The first, Curly Carrol, was tall and painfully thin; a man who had apparently come through a recent siege of sickness, although his handclasp was firm enough.

"A pleasure, Mr. Anthony, suh," his voice had the hint of a Texas drawl.

Steve Sawyer, the other stunt pilot, was Carrol's exact opposite: a square shouldered, powerful fellow who wore his sandy hair cropped close to his skull like a German army officer, and whose left cheek bore what might have been a knife scar or maybe the mark of an old saber cut. Anthony was reminded of the duels fought by Prussian students for the sake of such scars, it being the German idea that a sword slash was a badge of courage and a mark of honor.

Sawyer didn't speak with an accent, though; and to some extent this destroyed the Prussian-officer illusion. "Glad to meet you, Jim," he said heartily, despite a certain shiftiness of eye. "Heard a lot about you, of course."

Anthony's response was equally cordial—and the cordiality was just as false as Sawyer's. Or at least the millionaire criminologist felt a note of insincerity in the other man's tone. A thing like that couldn't be a positive conviction, naturally; not on snap judgment, anyhow. All the same Jim felt his eerie intuitions stirring; experienced a sixth-sense that he had just met a dangerous man.

For that matter, all three of these stunt pilots might well be classed as dangerous; even killers. It developed that the tall, painfully thin Curly Carrol had been with the Flying Tigers in China until a month or so ago; and the scar-faced Steve Sawyer was a veteran of the Spanish civil war. Coke Robertson himself, the oldest of the trio, was flight leader by virtue of his greater experience in aerial combat; he'd flown for the Allies back in 1917.

Yes, each man had known what it was to deal death to an enemy. But would any one of them, Anthony asked himself, be capable of murdering Dorpf Van Dykmann by shooting him in the back? That was a question you couldn't answer offhand. It would require observation, study, an evaluation of character traits. In turn, this was going to take time.

And time was something Jim couldn't waste; for although he'd been in Hollywood only a couple of hours, he was certain *there had already been an attempt on his own life and Tom Gentry's!*

His stoic face betrayed no hint of his thoughts, however, as he and Coke Robertson strolled off across the field again, amiably chatting.

Dead ahead, four sinister-looking twin motored bomber planes squatted in the mud. "Real?" Anthony asked.

"Gosh, no," the grizzled flight leader growled. "Mock-ups of plywood. The only way you could get 'em off the ground is with a hydraulic jack. The ones we fly are almost as bad," he added sourly. "Like going up in a paper kite."

He seemed on the verge of saying more, then suddenly snapped his lips shut in a compressed line; stared toward the far side of the clearing. Anthony, following the direction of his gaze, saw a girl coming toward them; a tall, red-haired girl in jodhpurs and a white silk shirt.

"You, Robertson," she called.

The stunt flyer drew up; waited for her. "Yeah?"

"You've been pestering Martha again," the red-haired girl's voice held suppressed anger as she faced the compact man. "After I warned you to lay off."

He sneered faintly. "I should pay attention to your chatter? Get wise to yourself."

"I'm wise enough already, Coke. Martha doesn't want any part of you, understand? She's told you and I've told you. Now I'm telling you again."

"Maybe I don't hear you, girlie."

"You'd better hear me. Unless you'd sooner have me on your neck."

Robertson's smile was sardonic. "People have tried getting on my neck before, babe. They always get bucked off."

"Including the cops, smart guy?"

The flight leader's face darkened abruptly. "What about the cops? If you've got anything to say, spit it out." He clenched his fists and a sudden ugly light flared in his eyes.

JIM ANTHONY, LISTENING and watching and knowing Robertson's temper, held himself ready to go into action in case the angered flyer lost control and struck at the girl. For her part, she was apparently without the slightest vestige of fear.

"All right, I'll spit it out," she said. "You're making a play for Martha. So were two other men, Dorpf Van Dykmann and Tom Gentry."

"So what?"

"So Van Dykmann's dead and Gentry stands accused of killing him. Which puts them both out of the way; gives you what you may think is a clear track. Convenient, eh?"

Robertson's neck swelled, reddened. "Are you accusing me of a kill and a frame, girlie?"

"If the shoe fits, wear it," she retorted.

For an instant the man's nostrils pinched in as he sucked a labored breath into his lungs. Then, furiously, he spun around on his heel; stalked off across the field, ignoring the puddles of mud as if anger had made him too blind to see them.

"Lousy crumb!" the red-haired girl remarked. When she turned to the millionaire criminologist, though, her whole manner altered and softened. "You're Jim Anthony, aren't you?"

He nodded, noting the forthright quality of her clear green eyes, and he liked what he saw. "Yes, I'm Anthony. And you must be Betty Gault."

"Right," she thrust out her brown little hand, man fashion. "I suppose Tom Gentry described me to you, eh? That's how you recognized me."

"He did a good job of describing," Jim smiled.

"He would, the clown. I wish you'd come over to the trailer and assure Martha they aren't going to dump him in the gas chamber. Or are they?" she added swiftly.

The wealthy detective's smile vanished. "Not if I can help it. Yes, I'll go to the trailer with you." Secretly he was glad for this chance to meet Martha Tildon, who seemed to be the motivating influence behind a lot of animosities in this motion picture unit.

THE DRESSING TRAILER was expensive, built in the best Hollywood tradition; and the Tildon girl adorned its interior like an exquisite cameo against soft velvet. Even in the starched white plainness of the nurse's costume she wore for the forthcoming movie scene, she was astonishingly beautiful; dangerously so. And she turned the full power of her dainty charms on Jim Anthony the instant red-haired Betty Gault introduced him.

"I'm so happy you've come to help Tom," her voice had a husky, purring quality. When you came near her, you couldn't help feeling this sensuous aura which seemed to surround her like an invisible cloak. She added in little more than a whisper: "Tom's so sweet... and I know he k-killed Dorpf Van Dykmann just for poor little me...."

Jim's eyes slitted imperceptibly as he realized that this Tilden girl wasn't as guileless as she looked. She was putting on an act for him, and he wondered why.

He pushed them both flat, just as the airplane's guns opened up.

It was Betty Gault who furnished what might have been the answer. "Oh, for heaven's sake cut it out, Martha," she exclaimed with an air of annoyed impatience. "I've told you a hundred times Gentry isn't a killer. He could have broken that Dutchman in half with one hand if he'd wanted to. He's not the kind to shoot a man in the back."

"But his fingerprints…"

"Sure, his fingerprints. He explained about that. And you weren't even smart enough to back him up when he told how he left the prop gun here in the trailer."

Martha's eyes grew ingenuously large. "How could I back him up when I hadn't seen the pistol here?"

"You could have lied, then."

"That would be perjury, though."

The red-haired Gault girl made an indelicate sound with her lips. "What's a little perjury to save a friend? Sometimes, darling, I don't know why I bother with you. When you put on this dumb-Dora act, I could break your neck, so help me!"

"Oh, really, now—"

"Quit it will you? Mr. Anthony has been around. He isn't an exhibi-tor from Paducah you have to impress. Be natural."

For an instant Jim thought the brunette star was about to burst into tears. Then, to his amazement, she grinned engagingly. "Am I as corny as that, Betty?"

"Off the cob. And another thing. You've pulled the innocent baby stuff on Coke Robertson until he's walking around on his heels. That guy's dynamite, honey. You can push him just so far; then something blows up and somebody gets hurt. I'd sure hate to see you with a hole in your back like Dorpf Van Dykmann."

MARTHA TILDON TURNED to Anthony. "I'm sorry I gave you the ingenue routine, Jim. It's the ham in me, I guess. Forget it—and forget what I said about Tom Gentry killing that squarehead for my sake. He didn't do it for anybody's sake. I mean he didn't do it, period."

"Have you any idea who did? Or who might have?"

She looked thoughtful; seemed on the verge of making a reply. But just then there came a repeated call from outside the trailer: "Places, please! Places, please! Everybody on the set in two minutes."

This temporarily ended the discussion. The millionaire criminologist bowed out, leaving the two girls to repair their make-up and get ready for the scene about to be shot—a scene wherein Jap infantrymen stormed the airdrome from the surrounding jungle, only to be beaten off by machine gun fire from the grounded bomber planes.

Anthony watched from a position near the mobile camera crane at the edge of the clearing. Here, somewhat to his amusement, he found a canvas chair unfolded and waiting for him with his name already lettered on its back in quick-drying paint.

Tubby little Lew Dandridge pointed to it. "Yours personally, Jim. I had it fixed up for you, y'understand, on account nobody is important in pictures without he's having his name on a chair. Sit down."

Anthony complied, masking a smile. Presently, though, he discovered that his seat had belonged to a script clerk girl who was now compelled to stand; and he insisted on relinquishing it to her as soon as the action started. The chair was rightfully hers and he made her take it.

The action itself was tense, melodramatic. Martha Tildon and Betty Gault were picking their way across the muddy field when the Jap attack broke open. Then the leading man dashed at them, hurled them flat for safety, and continued across to the grounded planes with some of his buddies. And as the two girls crouched in a puddle of mire, the airplane guns opened up on the yellow enemy.

Everything went like clockwork. The lights were right, the cameras whirred and machine guns started stuttering their blank cartridges with an infernal clatter, like a dozen riveting machines hammering on hot steel. And then, for no apparent reason, Lew Dandridge shrieked: "*Cut!*" at the top of his lungs.

The cry was taken up, repeated by scores of underlings. Sudden silence descended; and in this silence Dandridge pointed a shaking finger. "My God—look—!"

Anthony felt the short hairs prickling at the nape of his neck. In the chair he himself had recently occupied, that script clerk girl was now curiously slumped.

She was quite dead. A bullet had torn through her skull.

CHAPTER IV

THIRD ATTACK

❝I'M SCARED," MARTHA TILDON shivered. She didn't seem to be acting, now. Her eyes were big and very dark against the pallor of her complexion. "It's all so—so hideous! First Van Dykmann, and then that script girl—!" Her hand trembled as it toyed with a dessert spoon.

She and Betty Gault were Jim Anthony's supper guests in one of the swankier restaurants on the Sunset Strip. Hours had passed since the murder of the script clerk on location; hours in which the millionaire criminologist had fruitlessly investigated trail after false trail. In spite of all his efforts, he'd got exactly nowhere—except to reach the unmistakable conclusion that he himself had been the intended victim.

At first Lew Dandridge had propounded the theory that a real slug had accidentally got into one of the machine gun belts; that the whole thing had been an unfortunate mischance. Anthony exploded this assumption, though, by pointing out that the death bullet had entered the back of the girl's skull and come out through her forehead. "And the machine guns were in front of her, not behind her," he had driven his point home.

Then he had back-tracked to the property jungle on a direct line with the flight of the murder missile; and here he'd found a rifle wired to the trunk of an imitation tree, its sights accurately trained toward the folding chair bearing his newly lettered name. Another wire attached to the weapon's trigger ran on through the jungle, ending in a concealed spot where anybody in the unit might have yanked it to discharge the gun.

The cleverness of this contrivance was two-fold. First, the unknown killer had left no damning fingerprints on the trigger; second, you couldn't prove anything by making the whole troupe submit to a paraffin test, because the shot had been fired by remote control and nobody's hand would reveal tell-tale evidence of having discharged a firearm.

BRIEFLY, THE THING could have been done by any of the extras who played Japanese attackers; or by someone else sneaking unobserved into the jungle just long enough to trip the wire. Even the brunette

Tildon girl and her red-haired friend, Betty Gault, were not entirely absolved of suspicion; for the wire was long enough to have reached that spot on the muddy airfield where they had both sprawled during the making of the scene. In the ensuing excitement, either one of them could have unostentatiously moved that wire back to the jungle's edge where Jim subsequently found it.

One fact was grimly clear. The rifle had been lined up with Jim's chair on the assumption that he would be sitting there; a natural assumption, since his name was painted on the chair back. To that extent, then, the clerk's death was an accident; Anthony, by relinquishing his seat to her, had unwittingly saved his own life at the cost of hers.

But murder was murder, whether the victim was a millionaire or an obscure studio employee. And Jim knew, now, that he was up against a brainy, crafty, and ruthless killer who wanted him out of the road; who feared discovery and was taking every possible step to prevent it.

He also realized that the person who'd rigged the remote control rifle must be the same one who had slain Dorpf Van Dykmann. There could be no other plausible explanation for what had happened on the location set—*or could there be?*

Logic said no; but Jim's uncanny sixth sense argued to the contrary. For some inexplicable reason he had a feeling that he was moving toward the middle of a dark morass, a deep and sinister swamp of plot and counterplot which went far beyond the mere murder of a flying Dutchman and a script clerk. There was a pattern here; a pattern that seemed formless at the moment, although in time it would take ugly shape.

Time! Always that element intruded itself, prodding the millionaire criminologist to a grim urgency. This was why he'd persuaded the two actresses to have supper with him, so that he could ply them with questions and perhaps find a single strand of information which would lead him to the puzzle's heart. Up to now, though, he hadn't learned much.

Betty Gault leaned toward him confidentially, her arms resting on the table. "If you ask me, Jim, there's your prime suspect. Coke Robertson." And she cast a veiled glance across the café.

The compact, grizzled stunt pilot sat in a corner booth with two companions: his flying associates on the "Burma Bombardier" picture, Curly Carrol and the scar-faced Steve Sawyer. Robertson was staring straight at the Anthony table, his eyes moodily riveted on Martha

Tildon with an expression that was half admiring, half sullen. He seemed more than a little drunk, too.

Martha dropped the spoon she'd been toying with, and it made a small silvery clatter. "But Betty, why w-would you say a thing like that?"

"I've already explained my notions. Coke is head over heels in love with you. He may have figured to get rid of two rivals at once by knocking off Van Dykmann and framing Tom Gentry for the kill."

"Even so, wh-why would he try to shoot Mr. Anthony?"

"When the world's greatest crime investigator shows up on a case, the guilty guy would try to remove him if he could. Our location set was a natural, with all those machine guns dubbing the noise of a rifle. Maybe Robertson planned to hide that rifle afterward but never got the chance. Maybe it didn't matter, since his prints weren't on it."

The dainty brunette star was stubborn. "I don't believe it. Coke may be as dangerous as you claim; but if he wanted to kill anybody it would be in a fair fight, not by a shot in the back. Why, I'd almost as soon suspect Lew Dandridge!"

"And what's wrong with Dandridge as a suspect?" Betty countered. "You're not forgetting how you became a star in the first place, I hope."

"Betty—!" the younger girl blushed painfully.

"I'm sorry, darling. I didn't mean to let any skeletons out of their closets. And I don't blame you for anything. If a producer offered to put *my* name in light, I'd probably be as human as the next—"

"But that… that was a long time ago. Lew and I are merely good friends, now."

"Sure, because you're established at the box office; a valuable piece of movie property. Lew don't dare ask favors as long as that holds true. All the same, do you think he likes the idea of other men reaching for what he once thought was his and lost?"

BREAKING IN ON this embarrassing revelation, a voice sounded from the aisle behind the table. "My name I'm hearing, is it? So I hope it's nothing bad."

The newcomer was Dandridge himself, tubby but immaculate in an expensively tailored tuxedo, his moon face bland, his eyes as naive as a baby's. But you could never tell about the Stupendous executive; you never knew what he was really thinking. Jim Anthony wondered how much of the conversation he'd overheard.

"We were discussing the murders," Jim said.

Dandridge made a sour mouth. "So is murder a nice subject at mealtime, I'm asking? It gives you an appetite? Better I'm breaking up the party and taking Martha home so we talk over the scenario of tomorrow's scenes. You know the old saying, no matter if anything happens, the show should got to go on."

The speech was delivered with an apologetic smile, but there was a hint of peremptory command in it; a command which brooked no disobedience. The producer wanted Martha Tildon to leave with him; and for all her palpable reluctance, the brunette star made ready to go.

Betty Gault also stood up. "Me too," she announced casually. "There's a spot in the script I want to ask about." Her off-hand manner didn't fool Anthony, though. He sensed her intention to stick close to Martha, just in case of need; and he couldn't help marking this Hollywood habit of saying one thing while meaning something else. Dandridge had it, Betty had it, nearly everybody in the picture industry seemed to have it.

Or anyhow everybody in the picture industry who might remotely be connected with the two murders....

AFTER DANDRIDGE AND the girls had left the restaurant, Jim settled his check and strolled across to Coke Robertson's booth; sat in without an invitation. "I've ordered drinks," he remarked pleasantly.

Robertson's weathered face deepened its wrinkles. "Dandridge beat your time, eh?" his tone could have been either jocular or sarcastic, which ever way you wanted to take it.

The millionaire criminologist chose not to be offended. "It looks that way. Well, I'd learned all I could."

"About the murders, suh?" Curly Carrol's Texas drawl betrayed immediate interest and his painfully thin body came erect.

Anthony nodded. "No use kidding you fellows. That's why I'm in town, yes. But not getting very far."

"Maybe you'd care to ask us some questions," Robertson had a drunken man's knack of knifing straight to the point. "Which is all right with me."

Jim thanked him. "Principally I'd like information on Dorpf Van Dykmann. Did you know him very well, Coke?"

"Not well enough to shoot him in the back."

"I didn't accuse you," Anthony reminded him evenly.

"No, but that Gault girl did."

"Forget her. She's not entirely in the clear, herself. What can you tell me about the Dutchman?"

"Nothing much. Never met him until we started working on the picture. To me he was just another guy."

Jim turned to Carrol. "And you, Curly? Did you ever encounter him when he was with the Netherlands Indies Air Force and you were with the Flying Tigers?"

The thin young man shook his head. "Sorry, suh. Java and China are pretty far apart, you know."

"Which makes it my turn," Steve Sawyer's saber scar twisted as he smiled. "I'll save you the trouble of asking. Yes, I knew Van Dykmann before Hollywood."

"Where?"

"Brazil. I was co-piloting for Lufthansa."

"That was a German line, wasn't it?"

The scar writhed again. "Yep," Sawyer agreed. "Had some Yankee flyers, though. Including me," he seemed to stress his Americanism.

"What was Van Dykmann doing down there?"

"Producing a movie for his Dutch outfit. Getting background shots and so forth. Chartered a plane. I flew it. He didn't like my style."

"And—?"

"We had words. He turned in a report to my boss. I was fired. Does that make me a murder suspect?"

The millionaire detective finished his drink. "No more than all the rest of you," he answered frankly. "I may as well lay my cards on the table. If I can, I intend to find the killer—for just one reason. To free Tom Gentry. Which reminds me, I want to go down to the jail and see Tom if you boys will excuse me." He stood up, moved out of the booth.

Curly Carrol stood up, too. "Got a car, suh? I'd be glad to run you downtown."

"Why, much obliged. Yes, I'll appreciate a lift."

So Anthony and the tall, thin Flying Tiger left the restaurant together; piled into Curly's battered little coupé. And then, five minutes later, death loomed out of the night to strike at them—and miss by inches.

CHAPTER V

DEAD MAN'S MESSAGE

MAYBE IT WAS ACCIDENTAL; or it could have been a deliberate murder attempt. Coming in Sunset, with that broad highway's usual glitter conspicuously missing because of dimout regulations affecting neon signs and street lights, Carrol's little machine was suddenly crowded curbward by a passing limousine that flashed by at maniac speed.

The limousine's headlamps were doused and it was running by its parking lights alone. Careening, weaving from side to side like an erratic black meteor, it overhauled the coupé and then recklessly swerved sidewise at the instant the two cars were abreast. Fender kissed against fender, lightly and without damage; there was a faint tunk as metal met metal.

Curly Carrol let out a startled yell as this happened. The limousine rocketed past, vanished. But Carrol, as he wrenched at his steering wheel, lost control of the coupé. It went angling toward an ornamental street lamp standard, heading straight for a crash that would spell destruction.

With a fighter pilot's trained reflexes the thin Texan unlatched his door. "Bail out!" he shouted frantically, preparing to hurl himself from the machine. "Save yourself! I can't hold her!"

For all Curly's speed of movement, Jim Anthony was faster. Superlatively timing himself to the split second, the millionaire criminologst reached across to seize and twist the wheel. Awkward though his posture was, his magnificent strength exerted inexorable pressure on the steering mechanism. With one hand he corrected the coupé's veering course, and with the other he grabbed at his companion; prevented him from leaping to what might have been death or serious injury.

There was a single breathless instant in which the battered coupé teetered, threatened to turn turtle. Then Jim yanked again at the wheel, compensating for the slaunchwise directional skid of screaming rear tires. Creaking, groaning, the little car righted itself not two feet from the curb and the ornamental street light pole.

"The gas!" Anthony growled. "Give it the gun, Curly. Get going, man. Follow that limousine. Take over!"

Carrol snapped out of his temporary panic, gripped the wheel and mashed his throttle to the floor-board. Like a clattering comet the coupé surged ahead with all the power its motor could muster. But that power was insufficient; even at top speed the pursuit was futile. This became obvious before three blocks had been traveled, when you could no longer see even so much as the red spark of the larger car's tail lamp.

"May as well slow down, Curly."

The thin pilot nodded, obeyed. "Yeah! Maybe I'd do better in a P-40. It's a cinch I don't handle a jalopy worth a curse." Then he grinned shyly at Anthony. "That was quick thinking, suh. You saved us from a smash, sure as shooting."

"Probably. A miss is as good as a mile, though. We didn't smash, which is the main thing."

"The main thing is that limousine. If I could get my hands on the drunken heel who was driving it—"

Jim's dark brows drew together. "Did you happen to see the driver?"

"No, suh."

"Or recognize the car itself?"

"No. What do you mean, recognize it?"

"I was wondering if it could have been the vee-sixteen Lew Dandridge uses."

"Dandridge, suh? But why should he—?"

"I wouldn't know. I'm just guessing, groping in the dark. If you don't feel like going on downtown I can get out and call for a cab."

"Oh, no, suh, my nerves aren't that shot." And Carrol resumed the interrupted jailward journey.

AT HOMICIDE HEADQUARTERS, Anthony conferred with Captain Floyd Spellman and his immediate subordinate, Lieutenant Donaldson. The two police officials looked worried, particularly when Jim spoke of his recent near-accident.

"You think it could have been somebody trying to get you?" Spellman asked heavily.

"I don't know. There's a possibility it was just a drunken driver; a coincidence. One thing's certain, however. It wasn't Tom Gentry. He's in a cell. And it wasn't Gentry who rigged that murder rifle on location. Which ought to clear him in your minds, as far as the Van Dykmann murder is concerned."

Donaldson stared. "Then you believe all this other stuff is hooked in with the Dutchman's death?"

"I'm pretty sure of it."

"Where's the proof?"

"I have none. Call it a hunch. Meantime, will you give me permission to see Gentry? There are some things I want to ask him."

Spellman scribbled on an official form; passed it over. An elevator whisked Anthony upward to the jail floor atop the imposingly tall white building; and presently the millionaire criminologist was inside his freckled friend's cell.

There was a purple bruise on Gentry's jaw and definite hostility in his greeting, a hostility that seemed more puzzled than embittered. "Well, Jim?"

Anthony thrust out his hand. "Come on, hot shot. Relax. I know what you're probably thinking. I slugged you when you weren't looking. I lied to those plainclothes dicks, told them you were planning to escape. It's my fault you were brought back behind bars. Would you like to know why?"

"It would make me feel better if you explained it, Jim."

"All right. Remember when we were talking by that corner window in Dandridge's studio office? Well, I saw a glitter opposite us in the lab building. *The glitter of a gun being aimed straight at you.*"

Tom's eyes widened. "Well, jeepers creepers, pappy, why didn't you say so? You mean you bopped me down to save me from a bullet?"

"A possible bullet," Jim grunted. "I couldn't be sure, but I had a feeling that was the score. Somebody was gunning either for you or for me; and I didn't have time to warn you. So I did the next best thing; knocked you stiff and leaned over to make certain you were safe. By leaning down, I also got myself out from the possible line of fire."

"Then you sent me back to the pokey because you loved me, is that it?" the genial aviator inquired wryly.

"To keep you from harm's way, yes."

For a moment all the picture's action centered in that one emotional passage.

"And what about yourself? You ain't hiding in a cell as far as I can see. If there's danger, what's the idea hogging it all? I want my share, pappy."

"You'll probably get it before we're finished. Temporarily you're more valuable to me right here where nobody can attempt to murder you the way they did me this afternoon." And Anthony gave a brief outline of the day's happenings.

Gentry clenched his fists when he heard about the rifle with the remote control. "The dirty lice!" he breathed. "Who could have done a trick like that?"

"I don't know, yet. But it explains what I meant by saying you're more valuable to me here in a cell, safe. Somehow I have a feeling you're the key to the case."

"In what way?"

"Between yourself and Van Dykmann rests the puzzle's answer, Tom. Somewhere in your contacts and associations with the Dutchman we'll find the missing pieces. Now, think hard. Are you positive he was coming to your apartment last night merely to have it out with you about Martha Tildon?"

Tom looked startled. "Sure. Why else?"

"That's what I'm trying to find out. Understand, I'm not dismissing the jealousy motivation in this thing. It keeps constantly cropping up, too often to be ignored; and always with the Tildon girl as its focus. Van Dykmann loved her and died. You were interested in her and got framed. Coke Robertson is infatuated with her and could be the killer. Lew Dandridge was once in love with her and perhaps he still is. He had my name lettered on what became a death chair; and it might have been his limousine which came near crashing into me tonight."

"And then there's Betty Gault," Tom mused.

"Exactly. With her instinct for protecting Martha regardless of consequences. In itself, a possible form of jealousy; the deeply psychological sort. And yet we can't ignore the chance that a different motivation may exist; something apart from Martha Tildon and entirely unrelated to the jealous factor."

"Such as what, Jim?"

"If I knew, I'd be better equipped to open a new line of investigation. Let's get back to Van Dykmann. Try to remember little details; incidents that have happened since you came to Hollywood."

GENTRY FROWNED. "I'VE told you most of it, pappy. He seemed to think I'd cheated him out of the technical advisor's job, for one thing. And he bucked me at every turn. Argued with me over flying maneuvers, objected to the fake bombing of the war plant, claimed it was too risky—"

"You mean the climax of the story where a Japanese airplane assembly line in Rangoon is supposed to be destroyed?"

Someone had tightened that noose around her neck until her neck snapped.

"Yeah. We've got permission to stage a mock attack on a genuine factory in Burbank. We won't drop any eggs, of course; just go through the motions with our phony bombing ships while a camera plane catches the action. The cutting room dubs in newsreel shots of a real war bombing; also a miniature factory set exploding. Finally we have a full sized set on a sound stage with actors and extras racing out of the wreckage."

"He didn't like the sequence over a real airplane plant. He thought we shouldn't do it, permission or no permission. Thought we might have an accident."

The millionaire criminologist revealed no expression on his sunbronzed features. "All right. Now try to remember everything possible concerning his death. His phone call, for instance, before he visited you."

"There wasn't much to it. He just told me to stay in my wigwam until he arrived. He had a funny, thick accent that always made him sound curt and arrogant."

"And when he showed up?"

"I opened the door and he said something about finding me just in time, whatever that meant. Then the gun went off and he flopped in my arms."

"He said nothing else?"

"Nothing that made sense. Let's see, I'll try to give it to you exactly the way I heard it: *'Westminster... Abbey... I saw... Huttson bomb...'* " Gentry did his best to imitate the murdered Dutchman's accent.

"That was all?"

"Yeah. Then he kicked the bucket. In fact, he was dead when he said it. Just a corpse raving."

Jim Anthony's dark, hawk-like eyes glowed weirdly. "I think you're wrong, Tom. If we can translate them, those words may be the mystery's solution."

CHAPTER VI

A MAN NAMED HUTTSON

NOT UNTIL LATE THE next afternoon did the wealthy investigator arrive on the location set of *Burma Bombardier* out in Saugus. Meantime, ever since his interview with Tom Gentry in the jail cell, he had been grimly busy. All night, and far into the morning, he'd been despatching cablegrams and radio messages; impatiently awaiting the answers. He'd had trans-Atlantic telephone conversations with various men in London and other part of the British Isles; men who served as reporters and war correspondents for the Anthony newspaper chain.

The results had been uniformly unsatisfactory; a series of blind alleys and disappointments. And now, as he drove a rented car onto the motion picture's jungle set, his mood was bleakly morose. He had only an indifferent nod for Coke Robertson when that grizzled stunt pilot tossed a quizzical greeting at him; a brief smile for Curly Carrol, whose coupé had come so close to a smash-up last night. The third member of the stunt-flying trio, scar-faced Steve Sawyer, was nowhere in view—and neither was Lew Dandridge, although the tubby little producer certainly had every reason to be on the job during the filming of today's important exterior shots.

The cameras, in fact, were rolling when Jim parked his hired coupé. Martha Tildon, looking like a dainty brunette angel, was doing a close-up love scene with the picture's leading man near a property bomber plane, and all activity seemed to be centered on this emotional passage.

Anthony wandered over to Martha's dressing trailer; discovered Betty Gault lolling inside, nervously puffing a cigarette. A smile of welcome, almost of relief, crossed her pert features as she saw the tall, sun-bronzed criminologist.

"Come in, Jim. Talk to me."

"Thanks, I'd like to." He entered the trailer and chose a seat across from her. "Feel like answering some questions, Betty?" he said quietly.

"Sure. Start the cross-examination and see if you can break me down, make me confess."

He ignored this flippancy because it was obviously forced; an attempt on the part of the red-haired girl to appear unworried. She was worried, though; it showed through her carefree manner despite her efforts at concealment. Anthony wondered why she should be secretly uneasy.

"I've been in contact with England," he mentioned.

"Really? What about?"

"A name which Dorpf Van Dykmann spoke before he died; a name he connected with the bombing of Westminster Abbey."

Betty shook her head. "I don't get it."

"Neither do I, yet. We know, of course, that Westminster Abbey was struck by bombs more than once during the Nazi raids on London year before last."

"Sure."

"And Dorpf Van Dykmann was in London at the time of the worst raids. I checked up on him, traced his movements. He escaped from Holland to England; later made his way to the South Seas and flew with the Dutch forces over Java and Sumatra."

"Well?"

JIM SHRUGGED. "THAT'S all. Van Dykmann lived through the London aerial blitz. With his last breath he mentioned a name in connection with those air raids. I've been trying to find out what he meant; what the hook-up could have been."

"Learn anything?"

"No. At first I thought he might have been alluding to some Nazi aviator who was perhaps shot down, captured; a prisoner of war. I operated on the assumption that this prisoner might have escaped from Britain, later, and somehow managed to come to the United States."

"I see," the red-haired girl's tone sharpened. "You figured maybe Van Dykmann spotted the escaped Nazi flyer here in Hollywood and was going to put the finger on him as an enemy alien. In which case the Nazi would be nabbed, thrown into a concentration camp."

"That's right. It would certainly be a motive for the Nazi to murder the man who'd recognized him."

"Swell theory," Betty said.

Jim made a bitter grimace. "Not swell enough. My English representatives shot it full of holes."

"How?"

"No German aviator has escaped from Britain since the blitz. Plenty were captured; but they're all accounted for. None missing. Particularly none with a name resembling the one Van Dykmann mentioned as he died. Which puts me just where I was when I started: up against a blank wall. Unless there's a man answering to that name somewhere here on this movie unit."

"And what is the name the Dutchman spoke?"

"Huttson," the millionaire criminologist responded. And then he watched the girl's reactions.

Save for a slight flickering of the eyelids, she seemed undisturbed. "Huttson? Never heard of him. Not with Stupendous, at least." Then she leaned forward. "Want to know something?"

"Yes, of course."

"I like you, Anthony," she said surprisingly. "I didn't expect to. Ordinarily I don't like rich guys. They divide into two classes; the Johns that hang around stage doors and the biggies that know all the answers— the ones who think they're giving a cutie a break when they condescend to talk to her. You're different. You're regular."

"Thanks, Betty. You're pretty regular yourself."

"SKIP THE FLOWERS," she sounded sour. "I haven't got my hand out for a handout. You and I live in different worlds. I'm just a hardboiled Gertie, see? But I've got a head, too. Sometimes I can actually think with it." She stared at him, hard. "How many times have they tried to kill you since you showed up in Hollywood?"

Her shrewd question startled him. "Several," he admitted.

"So okay. If I were you, Jimmy, my boy, I'd get out of town. But quick."

"That's what someone wants me to do. It's also what I don't intend to do. Aside from the fact that I wouldn't leave Gentry in a jackpot, I don't like the idea of being chased back to New York by a murderer."

"Would you rather be dead?"

He frowned. "That sounds almost like a threat."

"Oh. So now you suspect I'm the big bad wolf behind all the funny stuff. All right, pal; have it your way. But if you want it straight, I'm worried about your safety."

Her words jolted him. "Why should you be?"

She didn't evade his probing eyes. "Because you're the first guy that's interested me in a long time. Dopey, isn't it? Screwy! Take it or leave it."

"I'm inclined to take it," his voice softened oddly.

"Much obliged. Then take some advice, too. There's something going on around these diggings that I don't savvy, pardner. Maybe it's just a case of Coke Robertson or Lew Dandridge trying to muscle in on Martha's affections and driving off possible rivals. Maybe there's another man gone on her; somebody we don't suspect. Or maybe we got gremlins in the troupe. Gremlins that know how to shoot bullets. Me, I've got a hunch there's something cooking by gas on the front burner and the pot's about to boil over."

"What is it you think's cooking, Betty?"

She shook her head. "Even if I knew, I'm not sure I'd spill to you. You'd go tearing in to fix things and maybe get hurt. I'd feel pretty bad at your funeral, Anthony. I'm afraid I… might even c-cry a little."

He stared at her for a silent moment, realizing how very attractive she was when you saw her apart from Martha Tildon. The brunette star's beauty was of a daintier, softer sort; a subtle, more feminine type. But this Gault girl was every bit as alluring in her own forthright way. Her clear green eyes challenged you, and her symmetrical figure was superlatively contoured when you got around to noticing it....

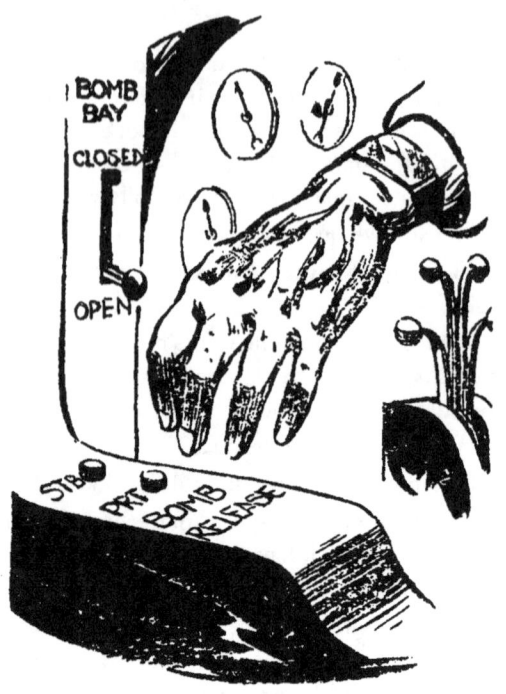

On sudden impulse, Jim went to her and lifted her; kissed her gravely on the mouth. "Thanks for the nicest compliment I've ever had, Betty," he said gently.

She nestled briefly against him, before she freed herself.

"Darn you for doing that. Now it'll haunt me the longest day I live. I'll remember it, and d-dream about it, and w-wish... oh, darn you!" She turned, raced out of the trailer and pelted across the muddy airfield as Coke Robertson had crossed it the day before. Only in Robertson's case, anger had blinded him; but the tears in Betty Gault's eyes were not anger.

ANTHONY WOULD HAVE followed her, except that he encountered Martha Tildon just then. Martha had finished her close-up love sequence with the production's leading man, the final scene of the afternoon's shooting schedule. Seeing Jim, she stopped him for a minute; exchanged a few words with him at the doorway of the portable dressing trailer. The delay was momentary, but meanwhile the Gault girl managed to disappear.

Lew Dandridge was standing by the camera set-up as Anthony approached a little later. The tubby, talkative producer was chatting with his group of stunt pilots—Coke Robertson, Curly Carrol, and the man with the scar-marked cheek, Steve Sawyer, who'd come on the set by this time.

The cicatrice on Sawyer's face writhed as he flashed a grin at the sun-bronzed millionaire. "Lipstick, no less. Is that part of the detective routine, Jim?"

Anthony used a handkerchief on his mouth; wiped away the red unguent which had been left there by Betty Gault's lips. "The Hollywood influence," he said lightly. "Twenty-four hours in this atmosphere and you're a wolf." Then, casually, to nobody in particular: "Which way did Betty go?"

"Home, I'm supposing," Lew Dandridge furnished the answer. "I saw her thumb a ride with Sammy as he's driving away. These days you double up on transportation, y'understand, on account it's not everybody has got a *B* or *C* ticket book for gasoline. So Sammy is giving her a lift to town."

"Sammy?" the wealthy criminologist lifted an eyebrow. "Sammy who?"

Dandridge looked astounded. "Our chief prop man, of course. I thought everybody is knowing Sammy Huttson."

CHAPTER VII

THE LONG SLEEP

LATE THAT SAME NIGHT Captain Spellman, down at headquarters, finally agreed to release Tom Gentry in Anthony's custody. The police official surrendered only after long argument; reluctantly signed the order that made Jim personally responsible for the genial aviator's guarantee not to leave Los Angeles.

Thus freed, Gentry drew a deep sigh of contentment as he settled himself in his wealthy friend's rented car. "Gosh, pappy, I thought you'd forgotten me. Or did you figure I was having a good time in my cell?"

"I pulled strings as soon as I had time to get around to it, Tom. There were other things that needed doing first."

"Such as what?"

"Such as spending the whole evening investigating a certain studio property man without his knowledge. Digging into his background, his history, his character. It was a job I might have handled sooner if you had a grain of sense."

An injured expression crossed Gentry's freckled countenance. "Is that a nice way to talk? Now what have I done wrong?"

"You failed to use your head. Remember what you told me Van Dykmann said as he died?"

"Sure. Westminster… Abbey… I saw… Huttson… bomb…"

"And the name Huttson meant absolutely nothing to you?"

"Not a thing, pappy. Not a blamed thing."

"That's fine," Jim growled. "That's simply swell. Especially when you've been rubbing elbows with a man named Huttson for the past two weeks."

The good-natured aviator stiffened indignantly. "Who, me?"

"Yes. I'm talking about the chief of the Stupendous property department. Sammy Huttson."

"Cripes!" Tom gasped. "Is that Sammy's last name? Well, I'll be a monkey's uncle! I never knew that, Jim. Honest, I didn't. Everybody on the lot calls the guy Sammy, so I called him Sammy too. That's how they do things in pictures. A prop man is just Bill or Joe or something. He don't rate a Mister, and he don't rate a chair with his name on it. How was I to guess he might be the one Van Dykmann was talking about?"

Anthony parked in front of the apartment building which was Gentry's temporary home; the building in which the flying Dutchman had been murdered on the theshold of Tom's flat, night before last. Jim had taken up quarters here since his own arrival; had been occupying his genial companion's rooms while the latter languished in jail. Now, as they entered the lobby, the millionaire scowled.

"No, Tom, I suppose you couldn't have guessed what Van Dykmann meant if you didn't know the prop man's last name."

"And I *still* don't know what he meant," Gentry insisted bitterly. "So he mentioned Huttson. So why?"

Anthony's scowl darkened. "That's the mystery, blast it. I've checked this Huttson fellow's record with a microscope—and I can't find a single connection linking him with the Dutchman. As for possible hatred between them, there wasn't any. They had no mutual contacts outside of the studio. They scarcely knew each other except in their professional capacities."

"What about the Westminster Abbey angle?"

"It refuses to mesh with Huttson. He was born and raised in Los Angeles. He's never been to London; never been out of California, in fact. So he couldn't have had anything to do with Van Dykmann in Europe—or here, either. And yet Betty Gault lied to me about him."

TOM'S EYES WIDENED. "She did? How?"

"I asked her if she knew anybody named Huttson. She said no. Five minutes later she drove away from location in Huttson's car. Thumbed a ride with him."

"Well, look, pappy. Maybe Betty's like me. Maybe she knows the guy only as Sammy. Maybe she wasn't hep to his other monicker. In that case she could have been leveling."

"It's possible, but not probable. Betty has been with Stupendous Studios a long time; long enough to be friendly with practically everyone on the payroll. There's some excuse for you, a newcomer; but she's an old timer. And her eyelids flickered when I mentioned Huttson's name. Immediately after that, she went directly to him and left the set with him."

"That looks funny," Gentry admitted. "But on the other hand, you say there ain't anything suspicious on Sammy's record. Why should Betty try to front for an innocent guy?"

The hawk-eyed criminologist didn't answer, because he'd spotted a call slip in his mail box behind the lobby desk. He made for the desk, asked the clerk for the slip; saw that it bore a telephone number and a notation requesting him to call this number after eleven o'clock tonight.

Upstairs in the apartment, it was barely five minutes after eleven as Jim complied with the request. He dialed, and presently a feminine voice answered; a voice quavery with excitement—or possibly terror.

"Hello?"

"This is Anthony. You left a message—"

"Yes, Jim. This is Betty Gault." Frantic urgency made her tone sound almost strident. "Listen. Can you come see me right away? I've got something to tell you; something I don't dare say over the phone. I th-think I'm being watched; the w-wire may be tapped. Please hurry..." Then the connection was broken, as if a knife had cut it.

Anthony hung up; pivoted. "Trouble, Tom. Let's go."

"Where?" Gentry made for the door at his friend's heels.

"Betty's apartment. She's learned something."

"About the kills?" Tom demanded tautly as they descended in the automatic elevator and sped toward the street.

The criminologist slid under the wheel of his U-drive coupé. Before he kicked the starter, though, he unshipped his shoulder holstered automatic and examined it; made sure it was in working order, with a full clip and a cartridge jacked into the firing chamber. "She didn't say," he finally answered the genial aviator's question. "But we'll soon see."

And he sent the car whooshing forward.

GENTRY TOOK THE lead when they reached Betty's address. He had called on the red-haired girl before, and he knew the way. The building was a two-story affair built of stucco in the shape of a U, with its open end facing the street. An inner patio or courtyard was surrounded by apartments; those on the first floor opened directly upon the tiled court, while the second floor flats were reached by means of an outdoor staircase leading up to a railed balcony. This balcony served as a sort of exterior corridor—an open-air hallway running past all the front doors on the upper story.

Betty Gault's number was 14-B. Tom pointed it out. "Shall I knock?"

"Yes."

But there was no response to the impact of Gentry's knuckles on the panel; and Anthony frowned in the shadows, experiencing a sudden ugly premonition. The girl should be expecting him, he told himself. She ought to be waiting near the door, ready to let him in.

"Try the knob, Tom."

"I am. It's locked."

Jim shouldered his freckled friend aside; and then, from a secret pocket of his coat, he withdrew his prized steels—those curious instruments of his own design, with which he could force the cleverest lock ever invented. He applied one of the queerly shaped blades to this latch, and his sensitive fingers expertly manipulated the tumblers.

The mechanism clicked faintly, metallically. The bolt slid from its keeper. The door swung open.

Tense with expectancy, the sun-bronzed millionaire drifted across the threshold as silently as one of his Comanche warrior ancestors stalking game in a dark forest. The living room before him was unlighted, its gloom relieved by a faint reflection filtering from another room to the rear where a shaded lamp seemed to be glowing. The door of this rear room was slightly ajar and Jim stalked toward it with Gentry following.

They gained the source of the light; saw that it was a boudoir. And then, as they entered, Tom whispered: "My God—look, Jim! It's—"

Anthony had already seen, and a futile riptide of rage welled into his heart. He knew, now, why Betty Gault hadn't responded to the knocks on her front door. She lay crumpled across the day-bed, pathetically motionless, her wavy red hair tousled. Someone had noosed a length of clothesline around her lovely throat; tightened the noose like a Cuban garrote. Her neck was broken.

In the millionaire criminologist's ears, her voice seemed to echo softly; to repeat what she'd said in the trailer dressing room that afternoon when he'd kissed her. "I'll remember it, and d-dream about the longest day I live...."

Well, her dreams would be uninterrupted from now on, if there was such a thing as dreaming in the long sleep of death.

CHAPTER VIII

WESTMINSTER ABBEY

AS A LONE-WOLF BATTLER against crime and the lawless forces of the nation's underworld, Jim Anthony had encountered murder in many forms; had looked upon many victims of homicide whose passing had brought him deep personal regret. A detective, even an amateur criminologist, learns to compensate for such things; to steel himself against emotion.

But he felt a poignant bitterness about the death of Betty Gault; a sense of loss that brought a curious tightness into his throat, a savage heaviness to his heart. And then came welcome rage, battering through him like a hot tide of lava and burning away all sorrow, so that nothing was left but the leaping flame of a desire for vengeance.

He reached for the telephone, snatched it from its cradle. As he dialed, Tom Gentry said: "The cops, Jim?"

"No. Time enough for them, later. Police ask questions, and questions mean delay. This is something I intend to finish personally. Tonight, if possible."

"Who you calling?"

"Lew Dandridge, for two reasons. First, to see if he's home. This kill is recent; within the past ten minutes. Maybe if we'd driven here a little faster, it wouldn't have happened."

"But we didn't. And it happened."

"And it'll be paid for," Anthony said grimly. "If I have to follow the murderer all the way to hell." Then, into the phone: "Mr. Dandridge's residence? Is Lew there? Just coming in, you say? Thanks. Put him on, please."

In a moment, the tubby producer's voice came over the line. "So who is calling?"

"Anthony."

"Hello, Jim. Funny thing, I am just thinking about you as I came home from some gin rummy with a bunch of friends which we all get together once a week at Mike Lyman's café, y'understand. Lew, I'm saying to myself, you better contact Jim Anthony about this bomber flight we got scheduled for early tomorrow morning, which Jim is technical advisor and better he's giving it some attention instead of fooling around with murders—"

Anthony interrupted this flow of apparently guileless prattle. "That's what I wanted to check on," he lied. "The bombing flight. I'd like to be sure about the condition of the plywood mock-up ships as well as the ones that really fly. Can you give me your chief prop man's address?"

"Sammy? Sure. Only what is so important about props? Should be you're looking up this Coke Robertson fellow, which I'm just seeing him a while ago at Hollywood and Vine, drunker than two billygoats y'understand. So in the morning he maybe has a hangover, he can't pilot a plane, so where are we then?"

"I'll attend to Coke. Just give me Sammy Huttson's address and leave everything to me."

DANDRIDGE GREW SILENT, apparently while consulting a pocket memo book. Then he supplied the requested information, for which Anthony thanked him and rang off.

The instant he hung up, the phone bell tinkled shrilly. Jim lifted the instrument again; placed it to his ear but didn't say anything into the transmitter.

At once he heard: "Betty? Martha calling. Listen. I wanted to ask you—"

"Sorry. You have the wrong number." He disconnected, while a scowl crossed his sun-bronzed features. Was it mere coincidence that had caused the brunette Tildon actress to ring at this particular time, or could she be aware of what had happened? Could she be checking up to see if the murder had yet been discovered? And where was she calling from?

There was no way of telling, now. Moreover, there were other matters that needed more immediate investigation. The millionaire criminologist turned. "Come along, Tom."

Gentry looked bewildered. "What gives with this Huttson, pappy? How come you asked Dandridge for his address?"

"Because we're going to see Huttson right now."

"But why?"

As they left the murdered girl's apartment and carefully shut the door after them, Jim explained tersely. "Betty Gault had some message for me; something she was afraid to say over the phone. She died before I reached her. And I think she was killed so she couldn't tell me what was on her mind."

"Well—?"

They piled into the rented car at the curb. "So now we back-track, Tom. We try to find out what she discovered this afternoon or tonight; the important information she wanted to give me. The thing that caused her death."

"But where does Huttson come into it?"

"Betty thumbed a lift in his car when she left the location set. That was the last I saw of her—until just now. Huttson may know something about her subsequent movements, between the time he drove her from the set until she left word for me to call her at her apartment. It's a slim hope, but our only one."

Gentry lighted two cigarettes, passed one of them to his millionaire friend at the wheel. "Poor kid. She was a nice guy, that redhead. I'd like to get my hands on whoever—Hey! What about Lew Dandridge? He was home, wasn't he? Sure, you talked to him. That lets him out, hunh?"

"He was just getting in as I phoned. Which cancels his alibi. He claims he saw Coke Robertson downtown, drunk; another possible red herring. Robertson could have been pretending drunkenness to attract attention to himself and establish the fact that he was at Hollywood and Vine at that specific time."

Tom's mouth twisted. "In other words, we ain't sure of anything about anybody."

"Not at the moment. But the pattern's getting clearer." Then Anthony parked before a house of the Swiss chalet type, an architectural trend of a previous decade to be found in abundance in that area bounded by Arlington, Crenshaw, Washington, and Venice. "This is where Huttson lives," he added soberly. "Come on—and be prepared for trouble."

THEY HAD NO trouble with Sammy Huttson, though. The prop man took a long time answering the doorbell; and when he did appear, he made an incongruously comic figure in the old fashioned striped flannel nightgown that swathed his undersized form. Yawning, rubbing his sleepy eyes, he blinked at his visitors, looking for all the world like a wrinkled little gnome.

"Mr. Gentry!" he exclaimed. "And—and Mr. Anthony, isn't it? We haven't met, but—"

The wealthy criminologist nodded. "May we come in? I've got some questions to ask you."

"Sure. Here's the living room. Sit down. You want to know about the sunrise flight, I suppose. Everything's set. I'll be on location by dawn; have the planes warmed up."

"Very good. But it's Betty Gault I happen to be interested in. You drove her back to town this afternoon—or rather, yesterday afternoon, since it's past midnight now. A new day."

Huttson lost his drowsy attitude and became more alert. "Yes, I gave her a lift. Why?"

"I want to know what she said to you. Everything."

"Well, now, that's funny. She certainly acted sort of screwy. She asked me—" Suddenly his wizened face went blank. "I guess I don't remember just what she *did* ask me."

Anthony restrained his own abrupt tautness. "Meaning you refuse to remember?"

"I wouldn't say that, exactly." There was a mulishly stubborn quality to the reply.

Tom Gentry stepped forward. "Shall I bop this shrimp, pappy? I can make him talk."

"No, that won't be necessary." Jim stared at the prop man a long moment. "Look, Huttson. Perhaps Betty swore you to silence; made you promise not to say anything about her conversation with you."

"That's right. Perhaps she did."

"Then you can forget your promise. Nothing you may say will affect Betty Gault now. She's beyond danger. And it's important that you tell me what I want to know."

There was a grim sincerity in Anthony's voice that seemed to impress the studio property chief. "We-e-ell," he hesitated. Then he said: "All right. I'll take your word for it, sir."

"Thank you. Now start with when she thumbed a ride with you. Try to give me the entire talk."

"I'll do my best. She began by asking me how much I knew about that Dutchman who was murdered, Dorpf Van Dykmann; whether I'd ever met him before, and if I'd had any connection with him over in Europe. I told her no, which was the truth."

"Okay. Go on."

"Then she asked me what I knew about the bombing of Westminster Abbey in London. I told her all I knew was what I read in the papers and seen in the newsreels. She said had I ever been to London myself? and I said no, I've never traveled outside of California."

Anthony nodded without expression. Undoubtedly these questions asked by Betty Gault had all been based upon what Jim himself had told her, there in Martha Tildon's dressing trailer. "Continue," he said.

"Well, sir, she kept coming back to this Westminster Abbey business. Was I sure I'd never been there? So finally I said to her the only Westminster Abbey I ever saw was the one out on the ranch."

"What ranch?" the wealthy criminologist's eyes took on a sudden weird glow, as if fires had been ignited behind them. "Speak up, man!"

HUTTSON LOOKED AMAZED. "What ranch, sir? Why, the Stupendous ranch. Away out San Fernando on the way to Ventura. Where we used to make all our exteriors in the old silent days. Cowboy westerns, costume period stuff, and so forth. Why, we've got whole cities set up out there. Frontier towns and medieval castles, African villages and heathen temples and New York streets and Heaven knows what."

"In use?"

"No, sir. All going to rack and ruin since gas rationing and the government ceiling on the cost of constructing any single set. Abandoned, you might say. A shame, too. Nowadays we do all our location shooting closer to town or else on the sound stages in the home lot."

"And Westminster Abbey?"

"One of the old sets on the ranch. Just about the biggest we ever built. Bigger than an airplane hangar. A complete reproduction of the real cathedral in London. It was used in our million dollar silent picture, the Ghost of Westminster. You remember it, with Ron Blaney starring."

Anthony's voice was tense. "Did Dorpf Van Dykmann ever go out there to the ranch?"

"Come to think of it, yes."

"When?"

"Betty asked me that, too. Sure, he went there the afternoon of the night he was killed."

"What for?"

"He was looking for some aviation props we didn't have here in town, I think. Anyhow, as soon as I told Betty she said she'd like to borrow my car for a little trip, and I loaned it to her because she promised to return it by dawn—"

"That's enough, Sammy. Forget we've talked to you. Go back to bed and get some sleep. I'll see you in the morning for that sunrise bombing flight; and you'd better arrange to pick up a ride with someone else, because Betty won't be bringing your car back to you."

CHAPTER IX

DAWN FLIGHT

FROM HIS SEAT BESIDE Anthony in the U-drive coupé, Tom Gentry lifted his hands in a bewildered gesture. "I don't get it, pappy. I don't get any part of it. Where are we headed now?"

"To the Stupendous ranch and Westminster Abbey—and the payoff," Anthony aimed toward Ventura Boulevard through the darkness of early morning. "I think we've got the final piece of the puzzle, now."

"How have we?" Tom demanded plaintively.

"The pattern has taken shape. Dorpf Van Dykmann went to the Westminster Abbey set. Subsequently he was killed. Betty Gault borrowed a car and went to that same set, I'm pretty sure. Then she, too, was murdered. Coincidence? I don't think so."

"But—"

"There's still another deadly parallel. Betty saw something in the cathedral set and wanted to tell me about it. Death stopped her. All right. Van Dykmann had seen the same thing, and he tried to pass the information to you."

"Why me?"

"Because you'd been sent here by Washington, which made you a sort of unofficial government agent. And the Dutchman died before he could talk, just like Betty; although he did manage to gasp a message which you failed to understand."

"Yes, the two murders are alike," Tom admitted. "I see what you mean by pattern. But this message—"

Anthony's voice grew brittle. "Think back. Remember how we discussed a certain missing bomber plane that vanished last week in the mountains back of San Bernardino on its test flight? It was supposed to have crashed, but there's been no trace found of wreckage or crew."

"Sure, I remember. It was a Lockheed A-29."

"That's the American designation for that particular type of attack bomber. Do you happen to know what it's called in Europe? In Britain, especially?"

Gentry said: "Yeah, certainly. Lockheed Hudson."

"And what were Van Dykmann's dying words?"

"I've told you a dozen times. *'Westminster... Abbey... I saw... Huttson... bomb...'* Then he ran out of breath. Permanently."

"And that's the answer," Anthony growled. "Van Dykmann was a European; a Hollander who'd lived in England. To him, a Lockheed A-29 was a Lockheed Hudson. Only he couldn't say Hudson as clearly as you can. He spoke with a thick accent. Now do you understand?"

"Huttson—Hudson—cripes! You mean—"

"I mean he was trying to tell you *he'd seen the missing Hudson bomber in the Westminster Abbey set.*"

THE THEORY STUNNED Gentry into momentary silence. "Good Lord, Jim!" the freckled aviator finally found his voice. "How could that be?"

"It's quite simple. Assume the vanished plane wasn't wrecked back of San Bernardino. Assume some member of the test crew was an enemy agent who forced the pilot to land in the desert, unseen. Assume the loyal crew members were then murdered, buried. Suppose more enemy agents were waiting at the prearranged landing place; expert mechanics."

"With trucks?"

"Exactly. Suppose they then took the Hudson apart, brought it back here piecemeal. That would account for the searching parties not finding wreckage or crew. Now assume the stolen bomber was to be re-assembled; put into flying condition again. You'd need a big building for that purpose. A concealed building which nobody would be likely to visit. Can you think of such a place?"

Gentry whistled. "An abandoned cathedral set on an unused movie ranch! But why, pappy? For what reason?"

"This Burma Bombardier picture you're working on," Jim said. "You've got official sanction to stage a mock bombing attack on a real airplane plant in Burbank. You're using property planes—underpowered ships reconstructed to resemble bombers, but incapable of carrying genuine bomb loads. Suppose an actual A-29 joined that flight at the last minute and dropped explosive eggs on the factory?"

"Gosh! Production of aircraft would be wrecked, hundreds of war-industry workers killed—"

"And morale seriously impaired," Anthony added. "Think of the uproar when people learned the government had okayed the flight. The whole country would suffer."

Tom started squirming. "Hell and damnation, Jim, you should have called the F.B.I.!"

"There wasn't time. It'll be nearly dawn when we get out to the ranch."

"But you could have told Dandridge when you were talking with him on the phone, there in Betty's apartment. He could have passed the word along—"

The millionaire shook his head. "I didn't know the set-up at that time. It was Sammy Huttson who supplied the information we needed, remember? And I'm not sure I trust him any more than I'd trust Dandridge himself. After all, this whole thing's hooked in with Dandridge's studio."

"In a way, yeah."

"IN EVERY WAY. The stolen bomber is on the Stupendous ranch. A scene from a Stupendous picture will mask the attack. Someone on a Stupendous location set rigged a remote control rifle to murder me for fear I'd learn the truth. A Stupendous script girl was killed in my stead. Betty Gault, a Stupendous actress, attempted to save me from subsequent danger by conducting her own independent investigation—and died."

"Always it's the studio," Tom admitted.

"Always. And I wouldn't be surprised if a stupendous stunt pilot plans to fly that Lockheed."

"Gosh! That narrows it down to just three guys!"

"Yes, and I've checked on all three. There's Coke Robertson, a Canadian by birth, with a killer reputation; a man who'd do almost anything if you paid him enough money. There's Curly Carrol, a New Yorker who went to Texas to sign up with a group of recruits for the Flying Tigers in China."

"And Steve Sawyer," Gentry put in. "There's something about him I don't like. Maybe the scar on his map—"

"Which might be a Prussian saber-duel slash. He wears his hair clipped German fashion and once was employed by a Nazi airline in South America. And—isn't that the Stupendous ranch dead ahead of us?" Jim broke off abruptly.

Tom peered through the highway's blackness. "I can't see it from here, pappy."

"There's a sign over the gate. Yes, this is it." Anthony's keen vision had spotted their destination; and now he swung the rented car hard to the right, where rolling fields sloped forbiddingly toward a range of foothills, acre after acre enclosed by barbed wire fence. From the public road you couldn't see any of the motion picture buildings even in daylight, let alone this pre-dawn darkness.

The gate was chained, padlocked; but Anthony's steels made short work of that. Then he doused his coupé's lights and drove forward along the winding private roadway, making every crooked turn with unerring accuracy—thanks to the use of a Hindu visual trick he'd learned years before from a yogi in India. By conscious effort he dilated the pupils of his eyes to abnormal size, thus seeing clearly in a blackness which would have left an ordinary man completely blind.

And now, around the escarpment of a foothill, the twisting trail leveled off in a hidden valley where loomed the jagged outlines of buildings that took fantastic shape in the gloom, like the unreal trappings of another world—a crazily jumbled world of French castles and Tibetan temples and Algerian railroad stations whose trains ran nowhere.

It was a nightmare scene of unreality; of utter, lifeless silence. And towering far above its serrated skyline appeared the counterfeit spires of Westminster Abbey, as if some malignantly jocular djinn had transported a slice of London here to this unearthly region of incongruities.

"Could you have been wrong?" Gentry whispered. "Seems like nobody's been here for three hundred years!"

"Sh! Follow me and keep quiet." They stole forward on foot, with Tom striving to match the noiseless movements of his wealthy friend. To him it seemed almost as if Jim had cast aside all vestiges of his Irish blood and had reverted completely to his Indian heritage—a hunter with the profile of an eagle cast in dark bronze.

THEY GAINED THE cathedral set, where Anthony's visual acuity discerned a small door. He pushed it open, grasping Tom's arm with the other hand. "You see?" he whispered.

There were hooded lights within the vast falsework structure; hissing Coleman lanterns shrouded to cast their brilliance downward. The incandescent white rays of these gasoline pressure lamps washed against the surrounding shadows to make a mottled pattern of light and gloom under the high, vaulted ceiling criss-crossed by wooden scaffoldings. And on the farther side of the vast interior a bomber squatted like an angry, camouflaged hornet.

"By the Lord Harry, Jim!" the genial Gentry gasped. "You were right. That's an A-29 Lockheed Hudson!" Then he pointed. "A load of eggs, too!"

He was not mistaken. Big, ugly looking cigar-shaped aerial missiles were being wheeled to the ship, loaded into its open bomb bay by scurrying men in flying jackets and leather helmets and aviation goggles that disguised them until they seemed like creatures from Mars.

Tom would have charged at them right then and there, recklessly and oblivious to danger; but Anthony seized him and held him back. "Easy, you idiot! There's six of them."

"That's only three to one, pappy. Let's go!"

"No. Too much depends on this. We mustn't fail. We daren't fail. Too many lives hinge on our next move; the lives of hundreds of aircraft workers. We can't take unnecessary chances now, Tom. Not until we've spiked this bombing flight, anyhow. Come on; circle this way. Flank attack." And the millionaire detective crouched low; crept forward around piles of discarded props and accumulated furniture, the remains of long forgotten silent pictures.

He wished desperately that he had something with which to strike directly at the plane, cripple it. That Lockheed was the focal point, the crux of the Nazi plot. Outside, a widening grey streak of dawn was staining the eastern horizon; turning slowly to pale blue tinged with faded green. Day was not far off; and at sunrise the fake bomber flight would take to the sky from the Stupendous jungle location back near

Saugus. Those mocked-up ships would ride the wings of the morning, heading for a sprawling aircraft plant in Burbank. And presently they would be joined by another bomber—a real one. The Lockheed which rested before him here in the cathedral set.

Nobody would think much about the Lockheed. It would excite no curiosity, for its markings were correct in every detail. It would seem to be merely an American plane up for a test flight, winging over to watch the fun. And then, suddenly, its bomb bay doors would open downward from the belly, loosing a rain of explosive death and destruction....

THAT MUSTN'T HAPPEN, Anthony told himself as he unshipped his automatic. He couldn't let it happen. He and Gentry had to get close enough to take those men by surprise; cover them and disarm them and capture them before they suspected the presence of intruders.

He moved nearer, with Tom at his elbow. Then, abruptly, the set was filled with unexpected sound. First came the high, grinding caterwaul of inertia starters; then a series of barking reports from full-throated exhaust pipes as the twin motors coughed on rich-mixtured fuel. Propeller blades flashed as they spun jerkily in the lantern light, then whirred with a swishing hiss of disturbed air. The engines settled down to a sharp, staccato drone, rhythmic with the muffled thunder of power straining at the throttle's leash.

The unforeseen noise startled Tom Gentry. He took a lurching step, his eyes on the plane and the goggled man who emerged from it after having started the motors warming up. Tom's shoulder caught against a piece of scenery precariously balanced. It toppled; fell with a ripping crash easily audible above the thrum of revving engines.

Anthony rasped a fervent oath. The last projectile had been loaded on the ship and its bomb bay had been closed. Now six pairs of goggled eyes turned toward the back-drop flat which Tom Gentry had accidentally dislodged. And at sight of the millionaire criminologist and his freckled friend, six hands flashed to holstered automatics.

"At them, Tom! Get in close so they won't dare shoot for fear of hitting each other!" Anthony shouted. Then he sailed straight at the cluster of enemy agents with his own gun clubbed, swinging like a bludgeon.

A helmeted figure lunged to meet him; tried to nail him with a flying tackle. Jim clipped the man full in the mouth with a pistol blow; pulped his lips to a gory smear and splintered his teeth and fractured his jaw. The fellow moaned, sagged, fell on his face like a hewn log.

There came a joyful bellow from behind Anthony. That was his genial companion surging into the fray. Two more Nazis closed in on Jim, one from each side.

"Coming, pappy!" Tom boomed. He took Anthony's nearest assailant with a kick in the stomach. The man folded forward, and Gentry gleefully maced him across the nape of the neck with a thudding bash that would have bent an iron rod. "Two down, four to go!"

OF THOSE REMAINING four, three had now hung themselves on the sun-bronzed detective's stalwart frame. They clung to him like savage leeches, battering him with fists and guns and heavy boots. A pistol barrel smashed at Jim's skull and he jerked his head aside barely in time to avoid it. The blow grazed his ear; struck his shoulder with numbing force.

Meanwhile the fourth goggled saboteur had detached himself from the others and was running toward the A-29. Anthony realized what this meant. At the far end of the Westminster Abbey set, huge doors were now open; had been flung wide some time during the mêlée. Beyond lay a long, sloping grassy runway; a clearing easily long enough for a plane to use in taking off. Murky dawn lighted this runway....

The fourth Nazi was climbing into the stolen Lockheed, now. It's engines were revved up, ready for action. A single pilot could lift the ship skyward: could handle the controls alone, leaving his henchmen to keep Anthony and Gentry engaged. And that same lone pilot could operate the bomb releases when it was time to drop his lethal cargo of explosives.

Tom Gentry slugged one of Anthony's three attackers; knocked him unconscious. Then Jim himself, with a superb surge of muscular coordination, used his almost superhuman strength to get free of the remaining pair. He sent them staggering; seized one around the waist, lifted him high, hurled him at the other. Both men went down in a tangle of flopping legs and arms.

"*Take them, Tom!*" He roared the command at the top of his lungs; and then he whirled, launched his finely trained athlete's body toward the Lockheed into which that final Nazi had scuttled. His quarry had crawled into the plane with such haste that he'd not even troubled to slam its door shut behind him—which would make no difference, ordinarily. The slipstream's backwash would take care of that detail.

But this was not an ordinary takeoff. True, the twin engines were yammering more loudly now, and the propeller blades blurring in silvery circles as they gained speed. As the ship started to move, though, Anthony literally hurled himself through the air; covered the intervening distance and caught the edge of the door an instant before it closed.

A mighty hurricane whipped at him from the starboard propeller, with fury enough to have dislodged a lesser man. The wealthy criminologist merely bent his head to the windstream that struck him like a giant's invisible fist. Inch by gasping inch he edged himself upward and into the Lockheed as it gathered forward momentum. The plane was outdoors, now; rocking along the grassy runway, lifting its tail, roaring defiance to the morning. Its heavy wheels spumed the earth, raised, bounced, raised again—and stayed that way.

Then, at the very instant the bomber took flight, Jim Anthony hauled himself inside.

But as he eluded the certain death that would have claimed him if he'd fallen to the ground at take-off speed, disaster ironically descended on him. The plane's door slammed shut under the pressure of the slipstream—and it struck his elbow a terrific blow. His automatic flew from paralyzed fingers; sailed through the closing crack, leaving him helpless and unarmed.

Up forward in the pilot's compartment, a head twisted around to stare back; a helmeted, goggled head you couldn't possibly recognize. You could recognize the Luger automatic which also came thrusting from that front compartment, though. Its muzzle drew a bead on the millionaire detective. And the man holding the gun said: "All right, Mr. Anthony. Come up here with me."

Jim made a bitter mouth. "Just as you say. *You're calling the tune, Curly Carrol.*"

CHAPTER X

SABOTAGE SALVAGE

HUNDREDS OF FEET ABOVE San Fernando Valley the Lockheed A-29 attack bomber cruised lazily but relentlessly in the direction of Burbank, home of vast aircraft factories jammed with war workers. Each passing instant brought destruction a little closer to those plants; and Jim Anthony sat in the co-pilot's seat of the deadly plane, temporarily incapable of averting the disaster a ruthless Nazi mind had schemed.

The tall, rangy man alongside him had long ago put the ship over on its automatic gyroscope controls. This robot mechanism did the flying, while the human pilot gave full attention to the task of keeping Jim covered with his Luger.

"So you knew me all the time," he grinned sardonically.

"I knew you were an imposter, yes. But I didn't realize why. A couple of hours ago I found out. Then it was too late to make a more successful effort to stop you."

"And how did you guess?"

Anthony shrugged. "Evidence. Piecing things together."

"I mean how did you guess I was the man?"

"That wasn't guesswork," the criminologist answered levelly. "When I learned the whole thing was a clever sabotage bombing plot, I knew the guilty person would be an aviator. A flyer connected with the Burma Bombardier unit. That narrowed it down to three suspects."

"Well?"

"I had already made a routine check on the stunt pilots of the picture company. Coke Robertson and Steve Sawyer had pasts and records that weren't too wholesome; but at least they were the men they claimed to be. You were not."

"Tell me how you reached this conclusion, my friend."

"Your Texas accent gave you away," Anthony said.

The man twitched as if something sharp had prodded him in a sensitive spot—his pride, probably. "Ridiculous! My southwestern drawl was perfect!"

"I agree. But Curly Carrol, the *genuine* Curly Carrol, was a native New Yorker. My findings showed that he had gone to Texas in search of employment. He stayed in Dallas just three weeks—and then joined a group of Flying Tiger recruits bound for China. No man could lose his New Yorkese and pick up a Texas drawl in three short weeks."

"Verdammte!" the thin pilot growled gutturally.

ANTHONY'S DARK EYES were smouldering slits. "So I knew you couldn't be the New York Curly Carrol. I think he must have been shot down by the Japs; either killed or captured. I think you, a Nazi agent, stole his identification papers."

"You are clever, my friend."

"Thanks. Clever enough to spot the weak place in your impersonation. You saw by Carrol's enlistment papers that he'd joined up in Dallas; therefore you assumed him to be a Texan and faked your accent accordingly. It was a bad mistake. It indicated that you weren't what you pretended to be. I asked myself why. And a while ago, when the rest of the puzzle clicked into place, I had my answer. You were the leader of the sabotage crew who'd stolen this Lockheed. You killed Van Dykmann and Betty Gault because they discovered the plane. You tried to kill me: once from the window of a studio building opposite Dandridge's office, then on the jungle set with a rifle, and again when you pretended to lose control of your car on Sunset Boulevard."

"That one was neat, eh?"

"You seemed to think so. A drunken driver in a limousine afforded you the spur-of-the-moment idea. You would have jumped out, bruised yourself a bit; but I'd have died when the coupé hit the lamp standard."

"Very clever indeed," the Hitler agent repeated. "And yet I think you are a fool after all, like any other stupid American swine. You tackled me single-handed in the cathedral instead of bringing a regiment of F.B.I. cowards."

"I didn't have time to call them."

"*Pfui!* You could have informed on me when you first learned that I was not Carrol. What you need is a lesson in German efficiency." The man's tone was taunting, mocking.

"When I first learned that you were not Carrol, I didn't know what your game was," Jim pointed out quietly. "I couldn't prove you were anything but a masquerader, which isn't a capital crime. After I did find out the truth, it was too late to do anything except move in with Gentry; try to nail you. Not you alone, but your whole filthy gang as well."

The Nazi's lips twisted cruelly. "In this, you may have succeeded. When I last saw them, my men seemed fairly well subdued. It is unimportant. If they hang, they die for the Fatherland and the Fuehrer. So will you, Mr. Anthony, in a way. You realize you are finished, *nicht wahr?*"

"I suppose so."

"You will be with me when I release my bombs," the impostor touched the trigger buttons beside his seat. "After the explosion we will climb high. I will knock you senseless and put on this parachute," he indicated a pack hanging on the partition behind him. "I shall jump to safety. The plane's gyro control will fly it toward the mountains, where it will eventually crash. I think there will be not much left of you for a funeral, my American friend."

ANTHONY DIDN'T ANSWER. His sharp eyes had picked up three other ships in the air: two patched, reconstructed, obsolescent transports rigged to resemble bombers, and above them a small camera plane. All were winging toward a distant blur of camouflaged buildings in the Burbank-Glendale area; and now the movie flight was joined by this Lockheed in which he himself rode toward destiny.

He thought bitterly of the ground defenses; the ack-ack guns that would remain silent until too late—silent because they'd been told to expect a motion picture sham attack. Until genuine bombs fell, nobody would realize the truth; that this was another instance of Nazi trickery and deceit.

The man at Jim's side was typical of that treacherous ideology; a Hun officer who'd spent years in the United States, picking up American mannerisms to perfect himself for just this sort of back-stabbing. Thanks to his traitor's training, hundreds or perhaps thousands of workers would lose their lives; tools and property and machines desperately needed by American fighting men would be destroyed.

The millionaire's fists clenched until the knuckles showed white. He must prevent the bombing, even at the cost of his own life. But how?

If he struck too soon, the Nazi would merely shoot him and go on with the scheme. It would be better to wait until the last moment, he decided. Then, just as his enemy reached for the bomb release triggers, it would be time to act. This, of course, would be in that split instant when the plane was almost directly above the aircraft plant.

One single second would do the trick. One second of delay, and the ship would be past its target. By then, Jim Anthony might be dead with a Luger slug through his heart. But the Nazi would be forced to bank and turn at a distance; make another bombing run at the factory. And the Lockheed's actions would arouse the suspicions of the ground defense soldiers below, resulting in a barrage of anti-aircraft fire....

It was the most difficult waiting Anthony had ever endured. His enemy deliberately allowed the movie planes to pass him. The speed of the A-29 was far greater than theirs, but he loafed back until the buildings underneath were clear and distinct in the sunrise despite their camouflage.

The Nazi didn't have a bomb-sight; didn't need one. At this low level, coming in slow, it would be like shooting fish in a barrel. The thin man's left hand moved like a darting rapier toward the release buttons.

That was the moment Jim had waited for. His captor's attention was diverted for the fraction of an instant. "Now!" the millionaire criminologist thundered.

And he dived at the German's throat.

Up came the Luger automatic, belching a dark-blurt of flame. Anthony felt the stinging, numbing impact of a bullet through the fleshy part of his left thigh. It almost kicked his leg out from under him, but not quite. He regained his balance; swung a desperate fist at his adversary's gun hand.

THE WEAPON SAILED from the cursing Nazi's grasp; flew from the control compartment back into the main cabin. Yowling, its owner deserted his post and dived after it. Jim plunged at his heels, while the Lockheed flew onward as steady as a rock with the robot gyroscope in command.

"*Verdammte—!*" the German agent babbled in the fuselage as he groped for his lost gun amid a maze of cables and a clutter of rigging controls which stretched on either side of the cabin's narrow catwalk floor.

Then he located the Luger and tugged at it. It seemed to be stuck; jammed under a thick wire that ran rearward toward the tail gunner's blister. There was no occupant in this post, of course; which was a good thing. For just then the wealthy, sun-bronzed detective pumped into his enemy with bruising, smashing concussion.

The Nazi skidded toward the plane's tail; and an apparent miracle followed. By yanking at his jammed automatic, the fellow had tripped a trapdoor release cable which was hooked with the rear gunner's platform. This was a floor section that swung down into the belly blister; but there was no gun station there in the present instance. A scream shrilled on the killer's lips as he plunged through the opening.

Then he vanished earthward, minus the parachute he'd never had time to put on. His maniac shrieks diminished in the lower distance; died completely. Anthony didn't watch for the moment when hurtling human flesh struck unyielding ground....

Instead, he pressed a palm to his wounded thigh; stanched the flow of blood and made wearily for the pilot's compartment. He threw the controls over to manual operation, banked the Lockheed in a graceful turn and headed toward the Stupendous location set out in Saugus.

TOM GENTRY WAS waiting for him at the jungle landing field. Their rented coupé stood nearby, with four trussed and unconscious Nazi murder-mechanics draped over fenders and hood. Tom had left the fifth saboteur out in the Westminster Abbey set. As he said later, what was the use of lugging in a corpse?

Right now, though, the genial Gentry rushed toward the Lockheed as his millionaire friend emerged. "Pappy! You made it!"

"Yes, Tom, I guess I did."

"Gosh! I've had the yeeping meemies ever since I phoned the Fourth Interceptor Command and told them the score. There'll be a sky full of P-38 pursuits hunting this crate in another minute, ready to knock it down… I had to tell them, Jim. Even if you'd got knocked down too. It was your life or… or the lives of hundreds of war workers…."

Anthony smiled bleakly. "That's okay. You faced a tough decision and you did the only thing you should do. But I didn't get knocked down, after all. I'm safe. The aircraft plant is safe. Even this stolen Hudson is safe; and God knows the army needs every one it can get."

"What about the guy that was flying it, pappy?"

"He'll never fly again, except perhaps in hell."

The freckled aviator whistled softly. "That way, hunh? Hey, you're bleeding! You've been hit!"

"A scratch, is all."

Just then Lew Dandridge came toward them with the lovely Martha Tildon in tow. "Jim, my boy, could you be giving me maybe a few minutes of your time to discuss a technical problem which is—"

"Stow it, bub," Tom Gentry growled. "Pappy's going to the hospital and then home to New York. Me, too."

The Tildon girl's eyes widened. "Oh, but Tom, darling, we need you."

"Yeah, just like I need two noses. Nuts to Hollywood, babe. Jim and I are headed home."

And for once in his life, Jim Anthony was content to abide by Gentry's decision. He was weary of the picture business; he wanted to go away. Far away. Perhaps, back in Manhattan, he'd manage partial forgetfulness. Maybe he wouldn't be quite so haunted by the memory of a red-haired, forthright girl named Betty Gault whose lips, in one brief kiss, had left a mark upon his heart that would never be fully erased.

HOMICIDE
HEIRESS

IT'S AN UNUSUAL CIRCUMSTANCE FOR JIM ANTHONY TO FIND
HIMSELF PENNILESS! AND IT'S EVEN MORE WEIRD WHEN
HE FINDS HIMSELF TO HAVE AN UNKNOWN BROTHER WHO
CLAIMS TO BE ENTITLED TO HALF HIS INHERITANCE! BUT
THE STRANGEST THING OF ALL IS THE BROTHER'S WIFE!

INTENSE DARKNESS HUNG LIKE a shroud over a certain side street in midtown Manhattan. The usual nightly wartime dimout was only partially responsible for this blackness, however; because in addition, the short block's sole street lamp had been surreptitiously extinguished by a furtive man who had scaled the pole and unscrewed the electric bulb.

Now, gun in hand, the man crouched with a companion in the resulting gloom. There was little traffic in the neighborhood, and none at all where the two stealthy figures lurked by the mouth of a narrow alley. Watchfully they waited, the safety mechanisms unlatched on their automatics and the surrounding shadows cutting them off from the outside world like a solid wall.

Presently the second man shivered nervously. "This setup is too screwy to suit me," he complained. "What if a cop saw you puttin' out that light?"

"Oh, I'd make out like I was drunk an' laugh it off."

"Yeah, but you're packin' a roscoe. You wouldn't laugh that off if a bull found it on you. A Sullivan Law rap ain't no joke in New York."

"Quit jitterin'," the first thug lipped sourly. "We're okay so far, ain't we?"

"Sure, only I wish—"

"So shut up. It's quarter to eight now. This Anthony monkey is supposed to be at the apartment by eight sharp, and we got to be all set for him when he shows up."

The nervous one breathed unsteadily. "All set!" he said in a querulous voice. "All set to make a pair of clay pigeons of ourselves!"

"I never seen no clay pigeons wearin' armor plate," the bolder gunsel chortled.

His accomplice shivered again. "So okay, we both got bulletproof vests on. But suppose they ain't all they're cracked up to be?"

"The vests is guaranteed. If anything goes haywire, we'll ask for a refund."

"Go ahead and make with the jokes," the nervous thug sulked. "But maybe you won't think it's so funny if Anthony hits us in the arms or gams, or maybe in the head, even."

"For Pete's sake lay off that kinda talk! You're givin' me the creeps. After all, we got to take some chance or we wouldn't earn our dough."

The troubled gunman sniffed. "Dough ain't everything. Me, I wouldn't mind if we was just hired to croak the bozo. But what gets me down is this idea of goin' up against him with blanks in our rods when he'll have real bullets. I don't savvy the play."

"We ain't supposed to savvy it, chump. We just do what we're told, which is make sure Anthony triggers at least one pill at us. The rest don't matter, see? Now pipe down."

AT THAT VERY moment, Jim Anthony, the subject of the conversation, was hanging up his phone in the luxuriously furnished living room of his penthouse apartment atop the Waldorf-Anthony Hotel. In white tie and tails he was a striking figure of a man, tall, muscular, superlatively athletic,

"Drop that gun! I mean it!" she blazed.

his every movement betraying the poise of health and the keen coordination of strength trained to a razor edge.

In sharp contrast to the starched whiteness of his shirt, his chiseled features were deeply sun-bronzed and his hair the black of jet. These things, coupled with the penetrating steadiness of his dark eyes and the hawk-like quality of his nose, gave him a marked resemblance to the legendary Indian warriors of the great western plains—a resemblance which was only natural, since his mother had been a full-blooded Comanche princess, bequeathing him his coppery complexion, his aquiline profile, and his amazing reserves of stamina and endurance.

Far different was the heritage which had been left to him by his Irish soldier-of-fortune father—a heritage of humor and of brilliant intellect, together with one of America's mightiest financial empires.

For at the time of his death the elder Anthony had been a captain of industry whose very name was a byword for untold wealth.

It was typical of Jim Anthony, though, that he'd never been content to accept these legacies as they were, but insisted upon improving them. Just as he had added to his physical inheritance by constant, rigorous exercise, so had he trained his fine mind by diligent study in dozens of universities all over the world, until there was no branch of science or art in which he did not excel.

Thus equipped, he had amassed new millions to add to the original fortune piled up by his father. The Anthony holdings now extended into every walk of American life: a nation-wide newspaper chain, oil fields and refineries, mines of every description, ship yards, factories, war industry plants and a string of hotels including New York's famed Waldorf-Anthony, where he maintained his penthouse residence.

Oddly enough, however, it was not as an industrialist and financier that Jim had gained his greatest reputation. Scientific criminology was his hobby—or rather, it had begun as a hobby, only to become a career. As an amateur detective, the mere mention of his name was enough to strike terror into the underworld; for, whenever Anthony started on the trail of a wrongdoer, he never stopped until he had brought his quarry to justice.

Perhaps his Indian strain was responsible for this manhunting instinct; a throw-back to some remote Comanche ancestor who had tracked down tribal enemies through the primitive wilderness of a bygone century. Whatever the reason, the millionaire investigator was far better known for the mysterious crimes he'd solved than for his wealth or his countless philanthropies and charities.

Tonight, replacing the telephone in its cradle, he picked up his overcoat and top hat and moved lithely toward his private automatic elevator which opened into the foyer of the apartment. Halfway across the thick Bokhara rug he stopped and began carefully searching his pockets and his wallet, a frown of annoyance darkening his suntanned countenance. Then he laughed, mirthfully and a little wryly, as he contemplated an absurd truth.

He would have to borrow taxi fare from his long-time friend and constant companion, Tom Gentry, the freckled, happy-go-lucky aviator. For Jim Anthony, one of the nation's richest men, found himself absolutely and utterly broke!

CHAPTER II

ATTACK

TOM GENTRY HOVE INTO view just in time to see the ludicrous expression of dismay on his friend's face. "Hi, pappy," he grinned, rather enjoying Jim's discomfiture because it was so ridiculous. "Busted again?"

"Afraid so, Tom," the wealthy criminologist admitted. "I guess I'll have to put the bite on you for a few markers, as they'd say in gangster pictures."

Even to Gentry, who knew the whole story, it seemed the pinnacle of impossibility for a multi-millionaire to be penniless. Of course the condition was only temporary; at least some of Anthony's fortune would soon be again available to him. But at the moment his entire estate was frozen in probate court as a result of unexpected litigation; he had been removed from control; his income was tied up; and he was actually being charged rent on the penthouse—which he owned!

"I've got fifty bucks," Tom produced five tens. "D'you think that will see you through?"

"Definitely. And much obliged."

The freckled aviator made a disparaging gesture. "The pleasure's all mine. I never thought I'd live to see the day, though, when I'd be doling out dough to one of the country's richest citizens."

Anthony smiled whimsically. The legal blow had fallen just two weeks ago, when the courts had been petitioned to reopen the matter of his inheritance under the terms of his father's will; *and that petition had been filed by a man claiming to be Jim's own half-brother!*

Steve Anthony was what this claimant called himself. Older than Jim by eight or ten years, he contended that he'd been born in Dublin. "My mother died when I was a baby," he stated to the court. "Then my father left Ireland and became a soldier of fortune, winding up in America where he took out naturalization papers and remarried—this second wife being a Comanche princess. Their son was Jim Anthony, who got every dollar the old man left; but as my father's first born child, I'm entitled to a full half of that estate."

On the surface, Steve's claim seemed plausible enough; particularly since he maintained that he'd been brought up by distant relatives and never learned of his real parentage until recently. "So of course, as soon as I found it out, I came to get what rightfully belongs to me," he concluded.

Whereupon the probate authorities had frozen the entire Anthony empire pending investigation and decision!

THE THING WAS awkward for Jim, although as yet he had not officially disputed the claim. To the hot-headed Gentry he pointed out, reasonably, that he knew little of his father's past before his arrival in the United States. The elder Anthony might well have had a previous wife—and a son about whom Jim knew nothing.

Right now, however, the happy-go-lucky aviator was in a truculent mood. "You're being jobbed," he insisted stubbornly as he handed the fifty dollars to his wealthy friend. Then he added in sudden concern: "Where you headed?"

"Over to Steve's apartment for a conference. His wife just phoned me."

Gentry's scowl was positively ferocious. "Why can't they come here instead of ordering you around? It burns me down, the airs they put on. Especially this Steve. Whether he's a brother of yours or not, I still say he's nothing but a chiseler. Shanty Irish."

"Maybe," the wealthy criminologist chuckled indulgently. "If he is my brother, though, I want him to have his share. It wouldn't exactly leave me a pauper." Then he grew serious. "And if he *isn't* my brother, we'll soon know."

"Yeah? How?"

"I've got the Organization working on it." Jim was referring to that strange, ill-assorted legion upon whom he sometimes called for assistance in times of stress. Drawn from all walks of life, the Anthony Organization numbered in its roster such varied people as bankers and scrubwomen, socialites and newsboys, street-sweepers and statesmen. Nor was this loyal army confined to New York alone. Its secret membership extended to every corner of the globe, bonded together by ties of friendship for a millionaire who devoted his life to a never-ending battle against crime in all its phases.

Tom Gentry felt a little better, hearing this. "Here's hoping they prove the guy is a crook!" he growled.

With an enigmatic smile, Jim turned toward the elevator. "I think we'll have the dope on him in a day or so, one way or the other." And he entered the cage, pressed the *Down* button; drifted from view.

GENTRY WAITED, UNTIL the indicator revealed the lobby; then he thumbed the control that brought it back up to penthouse level. Soberly he lowered himself to the seventh floor, emerged and accosted a passing maid in the corridor.

"Would you know if Mr. Griffith is in, sister?"

"Yes, sir, I'm sure he is."

Whistling thoughtfully, Tom strode to the door of Room 719 and tapped. A youthful voice told him to come in.

The man whose voice sounded so youthful proved surprisingly ancient in appearance. Evan Griffith was one of those rare old men who seem never to lose their sprightliness with the passing of the years. He must have been close to seventy; his thinning hair was white and his features wrinkled like faded parchment. His keen blue eyes, though, were as bright as polished amethysts, and his smile matched the boyish quality of his tone.

Carefully he unscrewed
the light bulb.

"Hello, son," he said around a cocked cigar whose fragrance mellowed the room. "Take a load off your feet."

"The load I'm toting is on my chest," Gentry told the dapper little oldster.

Evan Griffith blew a smoke ring. "Money trouble?"

"Yep. I just loaned Jim my last fifty bucks—and you'll be wanting the weekly penthouse rent day after tomorrow. What happens if we can't pay up?"

Like a spry gnome the ancient one leaped to his feet; began pacing the carpet "Look," he said. "Jim's father retained me as his chief attorney a good many years ago. I was one of his best friends; as close to him as you are to Jim. So close that he named me in his will as administrator of the estate."

"I know that, sir."

"You also know I retired from the law business, later—and lost my blooming shirt in the crash of Twenty-Nine. But Jim Anthony didn't let me down. He gave me a home, placed this hotel suite at my disposal, rent free. He even put me on a so-called salary as his legal advisor emeritus, you might say. Actually it was a sort of pension."

Gentry nodded.

"So okay," the old man puffed vigorously on his cigar until its lighted end glowed cherry red. "Along comes this self-styled half-brother of Jim's to lay claim to fifty per cent of the Anthony holdings. The whole shooting match is reopened in probate court. Under the law, as the estate's original administrator, I'm called back into harness, placed in charge to conserve the assets pending a decision. I'm supposed to be utterly impartial in the matter, granting no favors to one side or the other."

"Which is why you're charging rent on the penthouse—among other things," Tom put in.

"Precisely. In appearance, I've got to lean over backward, to prove my impartiality and disinterest. But actually, you know where my sympathies lie. I'd be a fine specimen of ingrate not to appreciate everything Jim's done for me in these past dozen years."

Gentry grinned at the ancient attorney's vehemence. There was something warming about the guy, a human quality that transcended age.

"All right," Griffith's brisk strides took him over to an old fashioned roll-top desk. He opened this and extracted a metal cash box. "Just between ourselves, I refuse to be a doddering old louse—or any other kind of louse. I'm not built that way. Jim Anthony's father was my pal. Jim himself is tops."

"You're telling me!"

"So I don't intend to let this screwball litigation embarrass him," the wrinkled lawyer snapped up the lid of his cash box, extracted a sheaf of currency. "I've saved a little scratch out of what Jim has given me. It's not much; just a couple of thousand bucks. But I'm turning it over to you for his use. With it, you can pay that silly hotel bill I'm forced to collect. You can keep him in Scotch and soda."

"That's mighty decent—"

Griffith waved a hand, cut off Tom's exclamation. "Skip that stuff, son. All I ask you to remember is that this is strictly a personal deal between ourselves. I don't want Jim thinking he's indebted to me. And I don't want the probate court to know about it or I might be accused of bias and get tossed out of the administrator's post. That mustn't happen, see? As long as I hold the job I can protect Jim's interests from inside."

"What about Steve's interests?"

Griffith's parchment wrinkles deepened in an impish grin. "I'll consider Steve's interests after Jim is taken care of."

"You don't think he's what he claims to be?"

"I think he's as phoney as a celluloid nickel. Now take this dough and stop worrying and get out of here. I'm an old man and I need my beauty sleep."

DOWNSTAIRS, JIM ANTHONY had chosen a cab from the rack at the hotel entrance, had given the hacker Steve's address, and relaxed against the tonneau's hard leather cushions. Now, as the vehicle rolled forward, he considered the possible reasons for the conference to which he'd been invited a few moments ago.

Twice the claimant and his wife had offered to settle out of court for a sum substantially less than fifty per cent of the entire estate; and twice Anthony had refused flatly to make such a deal. Not that he begrudged Steve a full share, provided he was entitled to it; blood relationship was something not to be ignored, and it would be rather pleasant, Jim thought, to have a brother as a partner in the management of the Anthony industrial system. But if the fellow turned out to be an imposter—well, that would be another matter.

He was still pondering the many facts of this problem as the cab turned into an unusually dark side street and drew up before a second-grade apartment structure; but when he started to alight, his mind snapped back to awareness of his surroundings. It was a sharp awareness, whetted by an instinctive premonition that peril impended.

That was another heritage which Jim's Comanche mother had bequeathed him: a curiously uncanny sort of sixth sense that never failed to ring a warning tocsin deep within his subconsciousness when jeopardy threatened. Times without number, this weird sense of danger had saved him from injury or even death—had enabled him to make the right move at the right instant. And the eerie feeling seized him now.

Automatically he pivoted on the pavement, utilizing a Hindu trick he had learned years ago from a *fakir* in Calcutta; the deliberate trick of dilating the pupils of his eyes by a conscious effort of will. Through this abnormal control of the optical muscles and nerve centers he had the ability to see in darkness as well as an ordinary man might see in broad daylight.

TWO SHADOWY, LOITERING figures were sulking forward from a black alley's maw, their movements furtive, right hands concealed in overcoat pockets, their hat brims pulled low over their faces. Anthony's cabby had left his position under the steering wheel and was waiting to be paid. Either he didn't notice the two men who were closing in, or, if he noticed them, he gave them no attention.

Not until the closest figure had whipped out a gun and fired, did the hacker realize the situation. Then he uttered a startled yelp and dived for the safety of his taxi. "Look out, mister—it's a holdup!"

To Anthony, that pistol shot spelled something grimmer than armed robbery. During his long years of battling crime, he had acquired countless underworld enemies; crooks who bore him murder-grudges and lived for the day when they might slake their thirst for vengeance by killing him.

With the speed of a leopard he hurled himself behind the uncertain shelter of the cab's open door, crouching close to it as he whipped out his own flat, shoulder-holstered automatic. In a single blur of motion he lined the weapon at his nearest assailant; squeezed the trigger. The gun belched a spear of yellowish flame, a blurt of thunderous sound.

An audible gasp came from the lips of Anthony's target. You could see the fellow twitch and stagger as if under the impact of an invisible fist-blow. Then he spun around, regained his balance, raced after his furtive accomplice who had already scuttled into the alley and vanished.

The millionaire criminologist scowled in puzzlement. His shot had been hasty, but he knew his expert marksmanship couldn't have missed at this short range. Moreover, his attacker had shown definite signs of being hit. And yet the man had remained on his feet; was catapulting away as if uninjured.

It didn't make sense. Jim's .28 slug should have done more damage than that, he told himself. True, its caliber wasn't heavy; for he carried only the smaller sized weapon when wearing evening attire. A .32 or

.38 would make too perceptible a bulge in an armpit rig. Even so, at close quarters his shot should have knocked that gunsel down.

He drew another bead on the fleeing thug, but it was too late. Not bothering to investigate the alley, Jim, with a shrug, returned to his cab; and then, as he crossed the sidewalk, his abnormally keen vision spotted something on the concrete. He stooped, picked it up, examined it curiously.

It was a .28 slug, flattened shapeless as if by impacting on a solid object—such as a bulletproof vest.

CHAPTER III

DEATH TAKES THE HEIR

ANTHONY'S HACKER WAS TREMBLING, white-faced when Jim returned to him. "Have they g-gone, chief? Have they gone?"

The sun-bronzed criminologist made a bitter mouth. "Yes, I'm sorry to say they got away."

"*Sorry* they g-got away? Man alive, the way they were gunning for you I should think you'd be glad!" The cabby removed his cap and mopped a pate as bald as a bowling ball. "You want me to call the law, chief?"

Anthony's smile was bleak. "That won't be necessary. Buck up. There's nothing to be scared of, now."

"Maybe not, only I ain't used to stuff like that. Ain't used to driving a hack at night, for that matter. It's my boy's, only he joined the Navy last month and I'm pinch-hitting for the duration."

Jim paid the fare; added a two dollar tip. "Luck to you, old timer. And to your boy. I envy him." Which was sincere, for Washington had decided that the millionaire's services were more necessary on the home front than in the armed forces. As a scientist, inventor, industrialist, and crime-investigator, he'd been ordered to remain in civilian life—a command he had obeyed without protest, even though it displeased him.

Now, watching the cab trundle off in the darkness, he frowned thoughtfully. He himself had better be moving, he knew. Those two gunshots might attract somebody who would ask questions he didn't care to answer at the moment, largely because he had no answer at hand. It was almost incredible that two such unbelievably timid killers had tried to ambush him.

In any case, he was already five minutes late for his conference. He went into the apartment building, ascended a staircase to the third floor, and knocked on the door of Steve Anthony's flat.

It was Steve's wife who opened up. "Hello, Jim. Come in. And we do appreciate the visit," she purred.

There was no other word as precisely descriptive for Nadia Anthony's throaty voice; it was low-pitched, vibrant, so sleekly feline you could almost stroke its fur. And the woman herself was somehow catlike. Her hair was a tawny silken mane, long-bobbed and curled inward where it cascaded around her shoulders; her eyes, green and lambent as a cat's, had an almost imperceptible slant. Sharp, white little teeth gleamed behind the scarlet of her smile, and a matching scarlet was lacquered on her long, pointed fingernails. Like a cat's claws dipped in blood, Anthony thought.

He sensed the innate danger of her, even while he admired her feminine perfection. Her evening gown was of some shimmery emerald stuff that clung to every nuance of her figure; she was tall, slender, hazardously provocative—and she knew it. She made capital of it. The fragrance of her expensive perfume seemed deliberately indiscreet, and so did that adhering green gown with its daring decolletage.

She stood aside for Jim to enter; but whether by accident or design, she contrived that his shoulder lightly touched against her as he passed. He chose to regard this as accidental. "Clumsy of me, Nadia. Sorry."

Funny laughter purred in her flawless throat. "Don't apologize." Then she faced him in the gaudily decorated living room, her beauty framed by a dark tapestry on the wall behind her. "That was a challenge, Jim, in case I didn't make it clear."

"Challenge?" he pretended not to understand.

AGAIN SHE LAUGHED, less theatrically this time. "All right, my handsome brother-in-law, so you don't want to play. You're a nice guy, even so." She poured drinks, handed him one. "Here's to the polite brush-off you just gave me. I guess I deserved it."

He raised his glass. "To a very fascinating woman."

She sipped the Scotch. "Funny thing. The more I see of you, the more I feel like some sort of burglar for going after your money."

He permitted a smile to quirk the corners of his lips, although he had a secret conviction that there was something spurious about this

The man twitched and staggered, but kept on running.

whole scene. Nadia seemed to be sparring for time, trying to delay his conference with her husband. He thought about the two thugs who had attacked him on the street a few moments ago; wondered if that, too, had been a delaying action.

If so, why?

These thoughts were not reflected on his impassive countenance, however. "Why should you feel like a burglar, my dear?" he fenced with the green-eyed woman.

"Well, I—"

"After all, if Steve is entitled to half my estate, I want him to have it. Incidentally, where is Steve? You said on the phone he had something important to show me."

She looked faintly uncomfortable. "That's right."

"Such as what?"

"Letters, proving his claim."

Aside from a slight glitter in his hawk-like eyes, the wealthy criminologist displayed no emotion. "Why don't you tell him I'm here to see these letters?"

"He—he'll bring them in presently. Or photographic copies, anyhow. That's what he's doing now. Developing the prints in his darkroom." This had the sound of a lie, made up on the spur of the moment; but before Anthony could pounce on it, there came a sudden interruption. Somebody opened the front door and surged into the room as abruptly as if he had been projected by giant rubber bands.

Swift reflexes swung Jim around to confront the newcomer, a jockey-sized man in fantastically loud clothes—a fellow whose sallow face was painfully thin, the thinness emphasized by deep smallpox scars. Pock-Face had been whistling, shrilly and merrily, when he first appeared; but at sight of Anthony his good humor vanished as if it had been erased by a damp sponge. He halted, giving the impression that it was necessary for him to dig his heels in the rug to check his progress.

"Oho!" he rasped. "So 'tis you, is it? And phwhat are ye doing here?"

Nadia Anthony stepped forward. "Now, Terence!"

"Lave me alone," he said rudely, his Irish brogue harsh, unpleasant "I'll not have this stuffed shirt bothering Steve. When we get done with him, we'll have all the stuffing and the shirt, too."

JIM SENSED ANGER welling in the green-eyed woman, but when she spoke, her voice was level enough. "You listen to me, Terry Shayne. You may be Steve's friend, but I'm his wife. And there are times when I know more than you do about Steve's private affairs."

"Ye don't say, now!"

"Yes, I do say. It so happens that Steve invited Jim to come here for a conference, and I'll thank you not to interfere. Do me a favor. Get out and stay out. The next time you show up as drunk as you are now, I'll have Steve handle you."

The little man glared at her with all the rancor of a bantam fighting cock; then, presently, he twisted his head on its scrawny neck and surveyed Anthony with faded eyes that seemed incapable of blinking. There was something malignant in that steady, unhurried stare, as if he wanted to fix each feature of the criminologist's face in his memory. A growl sounded in his throat.

Then, without a word, he turned and went to the door; opened it and stalked out, stiff-legged.

Nadia Anthony sighed. "I don't know why I tolerate that man, Jim. But he and Steve were raised together in Dublin; and later, when Steve first came to New York, Terence befriended him. I suppose I should overlook his bad manners for that reason, but he's pretty difficult."

The millionaire nodded politely. In secret, though, he wondered if the interruption had been prearranged—another excuse for delay. With each passing moment he was beginning to feel a sharper urge to see his supposed half-brother; an urge which was possibly heightened by all these transparent devices to prevent that meeting. His weird instincts were stirring again, warning him of peril, making him restless.

"Will you call Steve now, my dear?" he suggested. "Otherwise I think I must be leaving."

BEFORE NADIA COULD reply, the grim comedy was once again prolonged; this time by the entrance of a girl from one of the rear rooms. "I give up," she announced flatly as she appeared. "He's too fried for me to get anywhere with him—"

"*Betty!*" That was the green-eyed woman's voice, not purring or throaty now, but taut and crackling like the stroke of a whiplash.

The girl drew up short. She was small, dainty as an exquisite doll in a pert sport skirt and brushed-wool sweater that added warmth to her diminutive curves. Her raven hair framed a face of gamine piquancy, like a doll's face if the doll were made of smooth ivory.

She widened her big brown eyes; assumed an artfully babyish manner. "Oooh-h-h-h-h, I'm sorry. Little Betty didn't know you had company, darling! "

Nadia smiled, but there was anger behind it. "That's all right, lamb. You're not intruding." Then she turned to Jim. "This is my cousin, Betty Burke. You haven't met her before."

"Not formally," the wealthy criminologist acknowledged. "But we sat at adjoining tables night before last in Spike Telliero's club."

He wondered why this casual remark should produce such startling effect on the two women. The diminutive brunette Burke girl flushed; Nadia seemed stunned. "Spike Telliero?"

"Yes. He's a cabaret proprietor in the Fifties. Runs a quiet little gambling establishment in connection."

"I know, I know." Nadia turned on her cousin. "You were with Spike after I warned you to keep away from him!"

"But da-a-arling, I *like* him."

Anthony wearied of this by play; dropped his suave manner. "I came here to see Steve. For some reason you've been stalling, lying."

"Lying, Jim?" the green-eyed woman purred.

"Yes," he said bluntly. "You claimed he was in a darkroom to make photographic copies of some letters. But your cousin let it slip just now that he's drunk."

Nadia made a wry mouth. "Okay. So there isn't any darkroom."

"Or letters," Jim added.

"That's right I merely asked you to come up so we could try to persuade you into making a settlement out of court. And then I stalled, as you call it, because meanwhile Steve came home in no shape to talk sensibly. I hated to see your own brother in that disgusting condition. If I've wasted your time, I apologize; and if you feel like talking to a drunk, go ahead. You'll find him in the bedroom at the rear of the hall."

Anthony studied her, tried to analyze how much sincerity lay behind her confession. The story sounded far more plausible than any previous statement she'd made; and yet, deep within his subconscious mind, that eerie sixth sense kept telling him a trap was being baited to ensnare him.

He made his decision. Since this premonition had warned him, he could guard himself against danger. "Thanks, Nadia," he said. "I'll look in on Steve. Maybe I can help him."

He pivoted; strode into the rear hall.

THE MAN WHO claimed to be Jim Anthony's half-brother stood groggily in the middle of the dimly lighted room. He was big, broad shouldered, with the dark hair and irregular features of the Irish; and even Jim had to admit that there was a possible resemblance between Steve and himself. Right now, though, there was a lackluster quality to the older man's eyes; a looseness of mouth that bespoke insobriety.

"Well, well," he hiccupped. "Wha'sh you doing here, pal?"

"You wanted to talk to me."

"Who, me? You're sh-screwy."

Jim surveyed him narrowly; and at that instant a voice called: *"Hey, Steve!"*

For a second, the millionaire thought someone must have followed him into the room. The door behind him was ajar, and he turned to look. Nobody was there.

Simultaneously, Steve had swung around to face the room's only window. He stood there, irresolutely; and then gunfire blasted into the narrow confines of the place, the explosion beating like thunderous surf against Jim's ears.

With an instinctive movement the criminologist whipped his own automatic from its rig; lunged forward. Steve uttered an unintelligible, gurgling cry and toppled like an empty sack across Jim's path, impeding him for an instant. Anthony swore under his breath, and went leaping toward the window.

He was just in time to see a dark figure on the coping of a building's roof next door; a two-story structure across a narrow areaway. There was a plank stretched between the coping and the sill of this window at which Jim stood; and even as he reached it, the shadowy figure opposite shoved the board from its anchorage into the alley below.

Then, as the sun-bronzed millionaire took aim, that shadow-shape dropped behind the roof coping; vanished.

Anthony whirled to run through the apartment and downstairs with the idea of cutting off the murderer as he emerged to the street. But the gunsel, after firing one deadly shot, had tossed his weapon into the murder room; and as Jim wheeled around, he stepped on it.

His ankle turned and he went down heavily. Before he could regain his footing, Nadia flurried through the doorway. She saw Steve sprawled on the floor, a bullet through his head; saw the death gun, a .38 with smoke still trickling wispily from its ugly snout. She stared at Anthony.

"He—Steve's—oh, he's d-dead!"

"Yes, Nadia. Better phone the police."

She dived for the .38 and grabbed it before he could guess her intention. "You killed him!"

"Don't be ridiculous. Put that down. You'll spoil any fingerprints it may have."

"*Your* fingerprints!" she blazed. "Drop that other gun you've got in your hand. Fast. I mean it."

He obeyed. "You're making a mistake, Nadia." But even as he spoke the words, his jeopardy suddenly dawned on him and he realized the full significance of the trap into which he had tumbled.

CHAPTER IV

RELUCTANT ARREST

DETECTIVE LIEUTENANT TROTTER WAS accustomed to murder. As a member of New York's homicide bureau he had witnessed more than his share of death by violence; but never before had he been in a quandary like his present one.

For years, he and Jim Anthony had been antagonists. Because their training and points of view were so entirely at variance, they had clashed on more than one occasion; yet each had a vast respect for the other. For that reason the police official found it awkward to take the millionaire criminologist into custody on a murder charge.

"But I've got to," he growled at Jim. "It's my job!"

Anthony's eyes were steady. "I didn't kill Steve."

"Blast it, man, you *must* have!" Trotter exploded, his voice loud here in this room where death had struck. "You had the perfect motive. He was after your dough—"

"I didn't kill him."

"Then who did?"

"I've already told you. Somebody at the window. Someone who escaped on a plank to the roof next door."

"There wasn't any plank. We searched the alley from one end to the other."

"Then somebody removed it."

"Sorry, Jim. That's as thin as the fingerprint angle. There weren't any dabs on the gat except Nadia Anthony's, and we know *she* didn't kill her husband. So you must have wiped your prints off the rod before she grabbed it."

"Wrong. My prints were never on it," Anthony cast a glance across the room, where the green-eyed woman sat silently with the brunette Betty Burke.

Trotter shook his head. "Why be stubborn? We made a paraffin test of your hand. It showed positive. That proves you discharged a firearm."

"Yes. I fired my own .28 downstairs, earlier. I've explained about that. I've shown you the slug, flattened shapeless; and I demonstrated there's a cartridge missing from my gun's clip. Isn't that enough?"

"Nope. It stinks."

"So does this frame I'm in," Anthony retorted. "I'm convinced those two thugs attacked me in order to draw my fire. Bullet proof vests saved them from injury—and the trick left me with a hand that would show positive in the paraffin test."

"Meaning the murder was premeditated?"

"It would seem so. And I was intended to be the fall guy. I hadn't been alone with Steve thirty seconds when it happened. A thing like that couldn't be mere coincidence, particularly when every sort of stratagem and subterfuge was employed to keep me away from Steve until the proper moment."

On the far side of the room the slain man's green-eyed widow said distinctly: "You heel."

"Am I a heel for telling the truth, Nadia?"

"You're a heel for trying to save yourself by smearing me," she raged. "You know why I kept you away from Steve."

"I know what you said, yes."

"What I said was true. I didn't want you to see him when he was drunk. If you hint that I knew he was to be killed at a certain time, you lie."

Jim smiled thinly. "I hinted nothing. I stated facts. Can I help it if you draw conclusions?"

"This isn't getting us anywhere," Trotter broke in. He looked at Anthony. "Unless you can prove your story about those two thugs jumping you downstairs, there's not much I can do but book you on suspicion of murder."

"You were going to, anyway."

"Okay," the homicide official said. "You asked for it. Let's go."

Leaving the apartment through the usual cordon of policemen, reporters and photographers grouped in the hall, Jim noticed an undersized, pock-faced man glaring at him balefully by the staircase. It was that truculent little Irish bantam rooster, Terence Shayne, who had been Steve Anthony's friend.

"So ye killed me pal," his brogue was harsh, taut. "I'll be sending ye to hell for that." Incongruously, two tears formed in his faded eyes; ran down his pock-pitted cheeks. And somehow the tears mirrored more menace than the verbal threat; for a weeping man is a dangerous man.

IT WAS CLOSE to eleven that night before Tom Gentry finally showed up at Center Street, accompanied by the ancient attorney, Evan Griffith. They were conducted to Lieutenant Trotter's shabby office, where Jim Anthony presently appeared. Trotter politely withdrew, leaving Jim alone with his visitors.

"Gosh, pappy!" the freckled aviator exploded. "Why didn't you phone me sooner?"

"I couldn't. They wouldn't let me until a little while ago. Then Trotter had a change of heart; reduced my booking from the suspicion-of-murder charge to material witness. As soon as that happened, I was allowed to call you."

Gentry's good natured face was wrathful. "Of all the dopey setups, this takes the fur-lined spittoon! Ain't Trotter got a lick of sense? The idea of accusing you—!"

"The frame was clever, Tom," the millionaire criminologist pointed out. Then he told about the fake holdup; how he had fired a shot at his attackers, and how this had later caused his palm to show positive on the paraffin test.

Like a wrinkled but sprightly gnome, the dapper Griffith paced the office. "Hell's bells, son, why didn't you tell Trotter to hunt your taxi driver? If the cabby witnessed the assault, he can testify to that effect; which would explain away the paraffin evidence."

"Quite so," Anthony agreed. "That hacker is an important cog in my plans. But I didn't want to mention him in front of Steve's widow."

"Why not?"

"I have a feeling Nadia is connected with the frame-up—and if she knew about the cabby, she might take steps to keep him from helping me."

"By bribery, you mean?"

"Or worse," Jim said grimly.

The old lawyer cocked his cigar at a combative angle. "So all right. I'm going out to find a judge who'll issue a writ. Within the hour you'll be out of here hunting your hacker or you can kick my pants!"

"Wait," Anthony halted him. "In the first place, I can't let you act as my attorney."

"What's the matter? You think I'm too old?"

"Not at all. But remember, you're the administrator of the estate. And Steve's death won't stop the litigation. As his widow, Nadia now becomes the heiress—a sort of homicide heiress—if she can prove her husband was really my half-brother."

"By Godfrey, that's right!"

Jim went on: "An administrator must be impartial. How would it look if you took on the extra job of defending me in a criminal action?"

"It'd look lousy," Griffith agreed. "The probate court might appoint another administrator to replace me."

"Exactly. And that mustn't happen. In your present spot, you can protect my financial interest. You must concentrate on that. I'll get another lawyer for this murder mess."

The oldster's wrinkled face twisted in a grimace. "You're absolutely on the beam, son. I was haywire. I guess I'm losing my grip or I'd have realized the situation. You know, I think I'll start cultivating this Nadia dame."

Tom Gentry thought this was a swell idea. "She won't suspect you're working for Jim. She'll just try to influence you her way in money matters—and she might let some information drop about the murder!"

Anthony nodded. "Very good. As for you, Tom, you've got to locate that cabby. Work on it yourself; have the Organization help you. All I can tell you about him is that he's around sixty; bald; has a son who enlisted in the Navy last month. The cab belongs to the son and the old man's driving it while the boy is in the service."

"Got it, pappy. I'll dig the guy up if I have to use a shovel." Then Tom and Evan Griffith left.

A moment later, though, Gentry came into the office. "I had something for you, Jim. Didn't want to slip it to you while Griff was around."

"Such as what?" the millionaire asked.

Tom produced a wad of greenbacks; some of the money he had borrowed from the ancient attorney. "Dough. A couple hundred for incidental expenses. Maybe you can buy yourself a few dozen policemen." Whereupon the aviator grinningly departed again.

AS GENTRY STRODE down the police station's musty corridor, a door opened ahead of him and four persons emerged. One was Lieutenant Trotter, looking sour. He had two women with him: a diminutive brunette girl and a taller, tawny blonde with green eyes whom Tom immediately recognized as Nadia Anthony.

But it was the fourth member of the group who drew Gentry's startled attention. The man was chunky, impeccably clad in an expensive tuxedo that seemed out of place on his lumpy frame. His face was swarthy, his black eyes malicious, and under a spiked wisp of mustache his lips seemed curved in a perpetual sneer.

Anybody who had lived in New York for any length of time was bound to recognize this swarthy man as Spike Telliero, cabaret proprietor and gambler. He'd operated a speakeasy during prohibition, then turned it into one of Manhattan's leading night spots after repeal. But he was more widely known for his gambling than as the owner of a night club, for it was reputed that he would bet on anything if the odds were right.

At the moment, Telliero and Lieutenant Trotter were having heated words. "Listen, copper," Spike was saying. "Whether you like it or not, I'm declaring myself in, see?"

Whoever had maced him had dragged him to the
oven and turned on all the burners.

"That's funny. That's very funny indeed. Declaring yourself in on a murder case. What's your angle?"

Telliero slipped an arm around the waist of the doll-like brunette. "Betty Burke, here. She's my angle. I sort of go for her. Which means I'm looking out for her cousin, too—Nadia Anthony. Any time you put the pressure on these ladies, you're putting it on me. And I'm not a guy that likes to be pushed around by flatfeet."

"You may get pushed around more than you bargained for if you horn in the next time I call witnesses down here for questioning," Trotter retorted darkly. "Now scram, all of you."

Tom Gentry, not wishing to be caught in the role of an eavesdropper, turned along the corridor when he saw Telliero and the two women coming in his direction. But the swarthy gambler spotted him near the exit; called to him.

"Hey, you!"

Gentry halted. "Well?"

Hands in dinner-jacket pockets, Telliero approached him. "I wonder if you heard what I just told Trotter."

"Yes, I heard."

"Okay, sucker, that goes for you, too. Your rich pal is in a jackpot—and he tried to pull his sister-in-law, here, into the beef. You can tell him for me I won't stand still for that kind of stuff."

"Why not tell him yourself?" Tom's ire was rising.

"You can handle it, my big-eared friend. Anthony bumped his brother and he'll go over the road for it. He could have twice as much dough as he's got, and I still wouldn't let him smear these wrens."

Gentry's temper erupted. "How would you like to take a flying jump at the moon, monkey? You may have all the thugs in New York tied up with you, but if you fool around with me or Jim Anthony, you're liable to get your elbow in a sling. And don't be calling Jim a murderer, understand? You might have to eat your words when I locate his hacker—"

"Yeah? What hacker? What about him?"

The infuriated aviator realized he had been goaded into saying something he should have kept to himself. "Aw, skip it," he rasped.

But as he strode from headquarters, he felt the gambler's speculative gaze following him; and he had a notion that Nadia Anthony and her dainty brunette cousin were also staring after him in sudden interest.

IT WAS MIDNIGHT when the smoothly functioning "Organization" finally gave Gentry the information he was seeking. There was an independent cab driver named Pop Bartlett living in Brooklyn who answered the description furnished by the millionaire criminologist: bald, elderly, operating a taxi owned by his son who'd enlisted in the Navy. Along with this Bartlett's address, though, Tom was told something else that gave him an unpleasant sensation in the pit of the belly.

Somebody else, it seemed, had been conducting a quiet quest for that same hacker during the past hour; someone who was thus far unidentified.

The news was ominous. Could Spike Telliero, for some sinister reason, be this mysterious person hunting the cabby? Had Tom, by his indiscreet remark, put the gambler on the trail? "Gosh!" the freckled aviator whispered to himself, frantically. And he hailed a cab, had himself ferried post-haste to Brooklyn.

The trip seemed endless; but at long last the frantic flyer reached his destination—a four story walkup whose hall ways had a thick, rancid odor of stale cooking and imperfect ventilation. Ascending the creaky, dimly lighted stairs, Tom came to the flat he wanted. He knocked.

There was no answer.

He tried to tell himself his sudden panic was foolish. Maybe Pop Bartlett was still cruising the streets in search of a stray fare; maybe he wasn't one of those who quit at midnight and came home. Maybe—

Tom rapped again, then tried the knob. It turned easily, and the unlatched door swung inward; whereupon a noxious, invisible wave of gas enveloped Gentry, stinging his eyes and his nostrils, choking his throat.

He gasped, staggered backward, coughed the fumes from his lungs; filled his chest with the comparatively fresher air of the hall. Then, holding his breath, he plunged into the hacker's frowsy quarters.

A dim bulb burned in the kitchen, and you could hear a steady hissing sound from the dilapidated stove. Every petcock was turned open, both top burners and oven; the gas was escaping with deadly pressure. Tom leaped to the stove, closed its valves, lurched to a window, and flung it open. He took a deep gulp of the night air, then turned toward a slumped form sprawled on the worn linoleum.

The man was elderly, his bald head marred by a bruise as if he'd been slugged unconscious by a blackjack. Whoever had maced him had then dragged him near the open oven of the stove, turned on all the burners without lighting them.

Death had come quietly to Pop Bartlett, taxi-driver. He had never regained his senses after being struck down. And he would never furnish the testimony that might clear Jim Anthony.

CHAPTER V

DANGEROUS FREEDOM

LIEUTENANT TROTTER FAVORED TOM Gentry with a bleak, forbidding glare. "Okay, wise guy," he straightened up from an examination of the cabby's corpse. "What were you doing here?"

Gentry, who had immediately summoned the homicide official as soon as he discovered the murder, explained that the dead man had been Anthony's driver at the time of the holdup; had witnessed the criminologist firing at his assailants. "So I went hunting for him, knowing his testimony would help Jim. But when I got here—well, you see what I found."

"Are you trying to tell me this kill is connected with the murder of Steve Anthony?" Trotter made a disbelieving noise with his lips.

"I am," Tom snapped. "And this is one job you can't pin on Jim's coattails. He was in the jug when it happened."

Trotter looked grim. "That's where you're wrong, sonny-boy. Thirty minutes after you were at headquarters I turned Anthony loose on his own recognizance." Then he added: "So he *could* have bumped this guy, as far as alibi is concerned."

"Why would he do that?" Gentry yelped. "Blast it, I tell you Pop Bartlett could have testified for Jim. Nobody goes around killing witnesses who can get them out from under a homicide rap!"

"Not ordinarily," the police official agreed. "But this isn't an ordinary case. We're dealing with one of the richest men in the world; a man whose fortune has been threatened by an unexpected claimant. Money's one of the strongest murder motives known; and here the money runs up in the billions. How do I know what goes on in Jim Anthony's mind in a case like that? He might do anything, with so much at stake."

Tom's temper flared. "Yeah—and the claimant might do anything, too."

"The claimant happens to be dead," Trotter reminded him.

"You numbskull, he left a widow, didn't he? She's the one who inherits, now—if that claim holds water. Why don't you investigate Nadia? If you weren't such a lame-brain, you'd see the setup. Who else would benefit by killing Steve and framing Jim for it, I ask you?"

Nettled, Trotter thrust his chin forward. "That'll do out of you, pal. So I'm a lame-brain. So I dare you to say it again. By the Lord Harry, I'll heave your pants in the gow so fast it'll make you dizzy. Go on, beat it. Get out of here while you're still in one piece."

Gentry departed gladly. He felt that if he had to look at the lieutenant another instant he'd blow his top. And he was still in a bitter mood, thirty minutes later, when he stormed from the elevator into the Waldorf-Anthony penthouse.

HIS MILLIONAIRE FRIEND was already there, waiting for him, a sheaf of cablegrams and radio messages in his hand. "What's the matter, Tom? Who's been stepping on your toes?"

"Trotter, the halfwit."

"Indeed? Why?"

"Because I found your cabby—and he'd been croaked. Trotter seems to think you might have had a hand in it."

Anthony's hawk-like eyes narrowed to glittering slits. "The devil you say!"

"Yeah. And it's probably my fault the hacker was knocked off. I opened my big yapper once too often." Then Gentry explained how he had encountered Nadia Anthony, Betty Burke, and Spike Telliero at headquarters; how he had incautiously dropped a hint that he was about to search for the cabby. "So then I found out somebody else was

At that instant came the shot through the open door.

hunting that driver—and by the time I got to his tenement he was a goner."

"Telliero, eh?" the wealth criminologist muttered. "Strange how the puzzle is beginning to click into place."

Tom blinked. "Meaning what?"

"I've been doing some prowling since Trotter released me," Anthony said. "And I've learned several things. To begin with, Telliero has gone overboard for Nadia's cousin, the Burke girl."

"So I noticed."

"It also seems that the pock-marked Irishman, Terence Shayne, is in love with her."

"No kidding!"

"And finally," Jim said, "Steve himself, in spite of being a married man, was making a play for Betty. I'm told that he squired her to a lot of night clubs this past month; that he paid her an undue amount of attention."

"What are you driving at, pappy?"

The sun-bronzed millionaire frowned. "Consider the jealousy angle. Telliero might have resented my alleged half-brother's interest in the girl. Terence Shayne could've been equally jealous. And Nadia might well have resented her husband's attentions to her cute little cousin."

"Cripes! Then any one of those three people could have had a reason for killing Steve!"

"Yes."

"And by framing you for it, the guilty party figured to be in the clear—you being a natural fall guy because it would look as if your motive was to remove a man who'll put the finger on you for half your dough."

"That's the possibility, Tom."

The aviator digested all this for a long moment. Then he sputtered: "But hey, wait. If it was a jealous croaking, where does the estate come in? I figured this whole thing was hooked up with Steve's claim; like for instance his wife laying back until that suit was all entered, then knocking him off so she would fall into the gravy."

"There's been a certain development which more or less washes out that theory," Anthony said. Before he could elaborate on the statement, though, his ear caught a faint hum from the private elevator and he half turned toward its door, frowning. Usually no visitors were permitted to come up without first being announced from the lobby downstairs, but evidently in this case the desk clerk had been by-passed.

With a swift movement the millionaire criminologist unfastened his coat; stuffed into an inside pocket the sheaf of radio messages and cablegrams which he had been carrying in his hand. Then the elevator's pneumatic door whispered open and an undersized package of human dynamite erupted out of the cage.

The dynamite was Terence Shayne, his pale eyes baleful, the pock-scarred skin stretched taut over the bony structure of his thin face. He had a gun in his fist, its muzzle trained on Jim Anthony.

"This is it, ye scum," he said harshly.

Across the room, Gentry stood in frozen fascination, too far away from the man to jump him. Anthony, however, seemed as relaxed and calm as if there had been no peril present.

"This is what?" he inquired coolly.

The intruder's raw Irish brogue rasped like a bandsaw hitting a mahogany knot. "The end of ye, you rat. I'm going to put a slug through your black heart, the way ye did to poor Steve." And his trigger finger tightened, twitched in a preliminary to the thunder of gunfire that would follow.

Lieutenant Trotter, it appeared, had done the millionaire no favor by releasing him from custody.

CHAPTER VI

ALTERNATIVE DEAL

"**S**O YOU'RE TAKING THE law into your own hands," Anthony spoke almost lazily. He knew Shayne's nerves were on the ragged edge; realized that any unwarranted sharpness of his own voice might bring lethal flame from the fellow's weapon.

"That I am," the bantam Irishman's lips seemed to be stiff and dry, making it difficult for him to form words. " 'Tis the only kind of law to fix the likes of you."

"I didn't kill Steve, though."

"Ye lie!" Shayne moved slowly forward across the entrance foyer, which was separated from the larger room merely by an arch. "Ye murdered him in cold blood, so ye did. And yet you're free, sitting here in your elegant apartment, while he's on a marble slab."

"I didn't kill Steve," the criminologist repeated.

"Maybe ye convinced the law of that, but I know better. Or maybe ye bought off the cops instead of convincing them. Money can do lots for a man if he's got it. Well, I've got no money—but this gun in me fist makes us equal, Misther Anthony. And a bullet will make ye equal to Steve."

Gentry shifted his feet ever so slightly. "Look—"

"Don't try anything," Shayne snapped. "I've no quarrel with you, me bucko. Don't make me shoot you along with your murdering pal."

Jim's voice was unemotional. "He's right, Tom. Keep out of this. A homicide suspect is dangerous to fool with."

"What d'ye mean, homicide suspect?" the Irishman widened his faded eyes.

"I mean you," Anthony told him. "You're under as much suspicion as anybody in Steve's death."

"*Me?*"

"Exactly. Tell me something, Shayne. How do you feel regarding Nadia's cousin?"

" 'Tis Betty Burke you're talking about, I take it. I—well, I like her a lot, though she wouldn't wipe her pretty feet on the likes of me. 'Tis none of your business, anyhow."

"It's my business to know Steve was making a play for her," Jim said evenly.

"And what of that?"

"It might have aroused your jealousy."

"Ye—ye have the guts to accuse me of killing me best friend?"

"Somebody killed him and framed me for it. Think it over. It could have been you. It could have been that gambler, Telliero, who seems to have elected himself to the post of Miss Burke's guardian angel. Or it might have been Nadia Anthony herself when she saw her husband falling for another woman."

Shayne trembled visibly as sudden rage contorted his deeply pocked features. "Ye filthy-minded scum! Twisting like a snake to throw your guilt in three new directions! But ye'll not get away with it. Ye murdered Steve to keep him from getting his rightful share of your estate. Ye wanted it all for your greedy self, but ye'll not live to enjoy—"

"*Terry Shayne!*"

The peremptory call came from behind the pock-marked man, so unexpectedly that it halted him as if he had been lassoed. For a single instant he was off guard. He looked around.

That split second was all Jim Anthony needed. He launched himself at Shayne, knocked the gun from his grasp, sent it skittering across the room where Gentry grabbed it like a football player intercepting a forward pass. Then Anthony and the Irishman went down in a clawing tangle of arms and legs.

NADIA ANTHONY STOOD in the foyer. She had just emerged from the elevator, and it was her outcry which had distracted Shayne's attention. Now she stood stock-still, a hand pressed against her breast as if to silence her turbulent heart as she watched the battle taking place before her.

It wasn't much of a struggle, though. The millionaire criminologist eluded a knee that nearly caught him below the belt, neatly avoided probing fingers that tried to gouge out his eyes; then he pinioned his smaller adversary, using no more pressure than a father might apply to a recalcitrant child.

"Stop it," he said gravely to the squirming little man. "Be quiet. I don't want to hurt you."

From the foyer, Nadia said in a distinct voice: "Then you're a fool, Jim. You ought to break his neck."

All the fight seemed to leak out of Shayne as he heard this; or rather, his rage took a new direction. He ceased struggling against Anthony; cursed the green-eyed woman. "Curse ye for a traitor! So you'd turn on me when I'm trying to settle the scores with your husband's murderer!"

Her lips curled in contempt. "Who asked you to settle scores? Who asked you to interfere? From the look of things, you've interfered once too often. And met your match."

"Fine talk from the likes of ye, taking sides with the devil that killed Steve!" Then, slowly, a dazed expression crossed his face as he looked up at Jim. "Or was I wrong after all in thinking ye did it?"

Anthony released the little man; helped him to his feet. "If you realize your error, you may go."

"Ix-nay, pappy!" Tom Gentry protested swiftly. "The guy's too dangerous to turn loose. Where he belongs is in the bastille. Let me call the cops to come take him away."

"I don't think that will be necessary now. Will it, Shayne?" the criminologist asked softly.

Shayne was like a man coming out of some deep hypnotic rigor. "No, Mr. Anthony. 'Tis not you I'll be making trouble for, after tonight." His faded eyes were baleful, though, as he turned them on Nadia.

Then, silently, he made for the elevator.

A LONG MOMENT passed before Jim Anthony spoke to the widow in the emerald evening gown "I owe you a debt of gratitude. If you hadn't appeared when you did, Shayne might have shot me."

Her smile was spuriously compassionate and her voice throatily purring. "That's all right, Jim. But you can't entirely blame Terence. He idolized the ground Steve walked on. He was like a—a crazy man when he learned of the murder."

"I know."

"Even so, I thought I had him under control. Or at least when I sent him home with Spike I felt sure he wouldn't make any trouble."

"Telliero, eh?"

"Yes. Why look at me that way, Jim?"

"Because I'm interested in your connections with Telliero."

Her eyes were green pools of pseudo innocence. "Connections? Spike just happens to be an old acquaintance, is all."

"He also happens to be in love with your cousin."

"Well, yes, he *does* seem to be infatuated with Betty. I don't exactly approve, though. In fact, you heard me tell her so. That was in my apartment, remember? When you mentioned seeing them together. I sort of lost patience with her."

Anthony nodded. "I remember very well. It was just before I went in to Steve's room and saw him shot down." His tone deepened. "There's something I want to ask you, Nadia."

"Yes? Go ahead."

"To put it bluntly, did you know Steve had been paying attention to Betty?"

She seemed surprised. "Why—why, n-no!"

"Well, it's true. And knowing the sort of man Telliero is, I think he might have resented it."

"You m-mean—?" There was no question about her astonishment being real, now. "You mean Telliero might have had Steve m-murdered—?"

"I'm considering the possibility," the wealthy criminologist said. "If it were true, and Telliero had framed me to cover his own tracks, it would have been advantageous if he could have persuaded Shayne to shoot me."

"I understand. Being d-dead, you couldn't fight back."

"Right."

She drew a deep breath. "What you've just said makes it easier for me to explain a proposition I want to offer you, Jim."

"Ah. So that's why you're here. You have a proposition. In regard to money, perhaps? The claim on my estate?"

"Well, yes, in a way."

Anthony strode to his telephone. "Wait, before you make your offer." He called the downstairs desk, spoke inaudibly, obtained a hotel switchboard connection and spoke again. Presently, ringing off, he asked Gentry to pour four drinks.

"Why four, pappy? There's only three of us."

"You'll see," Jim said. And by the time the aviator had mixed soda with Scotch in four glasses, the elevator door opened in the foyer.

IT WAS EVAN Griffith who stepped from the cage.

The ancient, wrinkled attorney looked just as dapper in pajamas and flowered, brocaded dressing gown as he did in street attire. The ever-present cigar was cocked jauntily between his lips, its lighted end making glowing fire-patterns as he spoke.

"What cooks, Jim?" Then he saw Nadia. "Oho. Company."

Anthony waited until Tom had passed the glasses around. "Sorry to disturb you, Griff. But I think you should be on hand when the lady speaks her piece."

"Hah? What? What piece?"

"She'd like a settlement of her claims, I believe. Am I correct, Nadia?"

The green-eyed woman looked uneasy. "Yes and no. That is, I mean—"

"You mean as Steve's widow you're entitled to what his share would have been if he had lived," Jim supplied. Then he produced the sheaf of radio messages which Gentry had seen him studying a while ago. "So now I'll tell you what that share amounts to. *Precisely nothing.*"

If he had expected his bombshell to shatter her composure, he was disappointed. She merely smiled, impudently. "So you managed to find out, eh?"

"Yes, from my foreign organization; the Dublin branch. Steve Anthony was his real name, but he wasn't my half-brother. He wasn't related to me in any way."

"You're smart, Jim."

"Smart enough to realize your game. Legally you hadn't a leg to stand on, but you hoped to stampede me into making a deal out of court to release my estate from litigation. You kept asking a private settlement because you knew your claim wouldn't stand investigation."

Across the room, Tom Gentry coughed in his drink. "Well I'll be a monkey's uncle."

"Me too, son," Evan Griffith piped up. He pointed his cigar accusingly at Nadia. "Your husband was an impostor, hah? By Jove, that wins the marbles!"

The woman shrugged indolently, gracefully. "We were hoping it would win us more than marbles, but I'm afraid Jim, here, was a bit too clever for us. Not that it matters much now, with Steve dead. At least he can't be prosecuted for the trick."

Griffith's youthful eyes sparkled angrily. "No, but *you* can be, young lady. As a party to the attempted fraud—"

"Nuts to you, you old goat!" she flared back. "Try to prove I was a party to it, I dare you! I'll swear on a stack of cook books I thought Steve's claim was valid; that I was his innocent dupe. And I'll make it stick."

Tom Gentry whistled admiringly. "What a woman!"

She ignored this. To Anthony she purred: "Will you go down with me in the elevator, Jim? I have one more thing to say to you before goodbye."

"Yes, Nadia, of course." Politely he escorted her into the cage; sent it whispering downward. "What is it you have to tell me?"

She rested a hand on his arm. "Something I couldn't say in front of witnesses, for fear you'd nail me on a blackmail charge. Perhaps it is extortion, in a sense."

"Extortion? You have no claim on the estate."

"That's true. But I've got something almost as good. My price is five million dollars."

"For what?" he stared at her.

She met his stare with a triumphant smile. "Information, Jimmy, my boy."

"What kind?"

"The information I was about to give you when you interrupted me by phoning Griffith to join our little conference. I resented his intrusion; resented his attitude. So now I've decided to sell what I might have given free."

"Come to the point, Nadia."

"Okay. For five million dollars cash I'll produce evidence to clear you of all suspicion in Steve's murder," she said.

CHAPTER VII

FIND THE WOMAN!

AS THEY STEPPED INTO the famous lobby of the Waldorf-Anthony, Jim led his exquisitely gowned guest to a secluded divan. "Then you know who killed your husband?"

"No. I merely know you didn't kill him."

"How long have you had this knowledge?"

"I don't think that matters, Jim."

"It matters if you've withheld vital evidence from the police and saved it as a bargaining weapon to use on me."

She smiled wisely. "Let's not fence, James. You have no witnesses to prove I'm using it as a bargaining weapon. This is just between ourselves; and if worst comes to worst, I've left myself well protected."

"How?"

"I can always say the shock of Steve's death unnerved me. We had run up debts, anticipating a share of your fortune; but suddenly he's gone, leaving me to fight alone. If I withheld information from the police, it was because grief made me forget what Betty had told me."

Anthony pounced on this. "So Betty's the one who has the evidence!"

"Yes. But don't think you can force it out of her unless you pry me first. If I tell her to, she'll forget everything she saw."

"And what did she see?"

"Something that meshes with your theory about Spike Telliero having Steve murdered because of jealousy. Not that the job could be pinned on Spike, you understand. In fact, it can't be pinned on anybody; but especially it can't be pinned on you." She cast him an arch glance. "That's all you're interested in, I should think."

He neither denied nor confirmed it. "What did Betty see?" he repeated.

"A figure at Steve's window. A figure that fired the murder shot, tossed the gun into the room, and escaped by means of a plank across the areaway to the opposite roof. And she saw the plank being tossed down into the alley."

"In other words, she confirms my own statement."

Nadia nodded. "She can do more. She saw where the killer hid that board when he got downstairs. She was watching."

A thought leaped into Jim's mind. "The plank might have some fingerprints on it!"

"Maybe. At least Betty's story would put you in the clear. Is that worth money to you?"

He studied her. "Suppose I report this conversation to Trotter?"

"I'll deny it," she answered promptly. "And Betty will forget the whole thing."

A sardonic smile came to the millionaire criminologist's lips. "You're shrewd, Nadia. I'm afraid I'll have to deal with you on your own terms."

"Now you're talking sense."

HE OFFERED HER a cigarette, took one himself. "But if you ask my personal opinion, I'd say this extortion scheme was what you'd planned from the very start. You knew you could never get by with the fake half-brother stunt. That was just a prelude to the real play."

"Ah?" she purred.

"Yes. You picked up a man named Steve Anthony somewhere; married him and convinced him he would fall into a fortune if he'd do as he was told. He foolishly agreed, not knowing he was marked for murder. The idea all along was to kill him, frame me for it, and make me buy my way out of that frame!"

"You'd have a sweet time proving it, Jimmy."

"Yes, I know I would. First it would be necessary to uncover the person who's really behind the deal. The man you're working for. Frankly, I don't think you're the brains of the plot. There must be someone higher up."

"What gives you that impression?" she drawled.

"Observation backed by intuition. You mentioned running up a lot of debts. In other words, somebody advanced the front money for your activities, gambling on tremendous returns for his investment."

"Even if you were right, you'll never know who that man was," she said indifferently.

Anthony's white teeth flashed against the contrasting bronze of his chiseled features. "Spike Telliero likes to gamble for high stakes. Especially when he thinks he has a sure thing. Maybe he's the brain guy."

For the first time since the interview had begun, the woman lost some of her poise. "You can't—" she said swiftly, then bit back the words. She added in a calmer tone: "I wouldn't advise you to pursue that line of thought much farther, James. It mightn't be healthy."

After a minute the man passed him unchallenged, into the gambling rooms.

"How so?"

"We've got you under the gun. You're suspected of murder and we have a witness who can clear you. On the other hand, we might produce a witness to testify you into the hot seat."

"That's what will happen if I make trouble?"

"Yes; so don't make trouble. Pay off like a nice little boy and everything will be fine. You have until noon tomorrow. Take your choice: fork over five million or go to the chair." Lazily she rose, blew him a kiss, drifted across the lobby, and undulated from the hotel.

UPSTAIRS IN THE penthouse, Tom Gentry was just telling Evan Griffith his loan of two thousand dollars to Jim could now be repaid within a day or so, as soon as the probate litigation could be quashed and the Anthony assets unfrozen. As he made the remark, the millionaire criminologist himself strode from the elevator.

Tom leaped to his feet. "You got rid of her, pappy?"

"Not entirely." Anthony outlined the conversation he had had with Nadia.

Griffith looked suddenly very old; too old and too stunned to speak. Unlike the ancient lawyer, Gentry was voluble; a cascade of questions burst from him. "What are you going to do, Jim? What are your plans? How do you figure you can turn the tables on the dame?"

"I'm not sure I'll be able to."

"Hey, wait! You ain't going to take it lying down, are you?" Tom protested.

"It all depends. Betty Burke is the key to the case."

"Then let's find her! We'll make her tell the truth if I have to slap her bow-legged!" And for once in his life, the freckled aviator knew a consuming desire to use his fists on a woman if it were necessary. In fact, he was almost hoping that it would be necessary!

CHAPTER VIII

WAS IT SHAYNE?

"YOU'RE RIGHT," JIM TOLD Gentry. "We've got to talk to Betty Burke, but there's someone else that I'd like to talk with first."

The aviator looked at him questioningly. "Who's that Jim?"

"Terence Shayne."

Gentry looked startled. "Cripes, pappy, didn't you have enough of that crazy Irishman when he was up here? A little more and he'd have been the death of you."

"I know it," Anthony admitted, "but things have changed since then. Nadia as good as admitted to me that they never expected their claim against my estate to stand up. That being true, they could only hope to hurry me into an out of court settlement, or they have planned this murder frame from the first."

"They?" Tom Gentry cocked an eyebrow.

"Whoever planned this thing. I don't think that Nadia was the brains behind all this. Now do you see why I must talk with Shayne? Shayne was Steve Anthony's friend long before Steve married. Shayne will know how Steve met Nadia in the first place; who introduced them, and what Nadia's background was before her marriage."

"I get it," Gentry said. "You think that Shayne can tell you the name of the master-mind even though the fool may not realize what he knows, himself."

"Something like that," Anthony agreed.

"Wait," Gentry was getting excited. "What about this? Shayne could have been the master mind himself. He could have read about you in the newspapers, and knowing a guy named Anthony might have started him thinking."

"It's possible," Anthony admitted, his face set in a thoughtful frown. "At any rate, I want to talk with him before I contact Betty Burke."

"What's wrong with my contacting her?" Gentry tried not to sound too eager. "After all, she's a woman, and I understand women."

Anthony was tempted to remind his friend of the women whom the aviator had definitely failed to understand, but he forbore. It was a sore subject with Gentry, and he could see no real harm in Tom keeping track of the small brunette, while he tracked down the Irishman.

"Be careful," he warned. "Remember that she's Spike Telliero's girl, and that he'll be quick to take offense."

"Trust me," Gentry promised. "I've got it all figured out. That baby needs kid-glove handling, and I'm the little boy to give it to her." He grinned as they moved toward the elevator. "Half an hour with me, and she'll forget all about that gambler."

JIM ANTHONY REMEMBERED the words as his taxi carried him across town toward the apartment in which Shayne lived and the thought of Tom and what his friend might do filled him with uneasiness. He wished now that he had had Gentry accompany him, but he had thought that the belligerent little Irishman would be more easy to handle if he came alone.

The building resembled the one in which Nadia Anthony lived and was only two blocks distant. The basement was occupied by a small book shop, reached by a set of stairs to the right of the building's entrance.

He gave the shop but a passing glance as he went into the small foyer and found Terence Shayne's name on a small card above a mail box.

He climbed carpeted stairs, and rapped on the Irishman's door.

It opened almost at once and Anthony was surprised to see the little man was still fully dressed.

"I thought you'd be in bed by now?" Shayne had been gaping at his unexpected visitor. He closed his mouth slowly. Anthony realized that the man was still laboring under a tremendous strain.

"Can't sleep," his brogue was not as noticeable now as it had been. "Just sitting."

He did not ask Anthony to come in, nor did he show any curiosity about the visit.

Anthony followed him into the cheerless room. The windows were tight-shut, the air foul with tobacco smoke.

Shayne cleared a chair of its collected newspapers and motioned Anthony to sit down. For himself, he sank onto the edge of a sagging couch and clasped his bony hands over his knees.

"Ye wanted to see me?"

"I did," Anthony told him. "You were a friend of Steve's?"

"The best in the world," the man admitted. "We was boys together, me and Steve, and there was none like him."

"I'm sorry," Anthony said. "You may not believe that, Terence, but I am. I think that he was attacked by the same people that have been attacking me."

"You mean that woman?" Shayne looked up quickly, and two spots of high crimson color burned against the cheek-bones of his narrow face. "Never trusted her, I didn't. Warned Steve she would bring nothing but trouble, and after I found out he was your half-brother…"

"He wasn't my brother," Anthony corrected in a sober voice. "I've had the Dublin records checked. Steve Anthony was not born until a year and a half after my father left Ireland."

TERENCE SHAYNE CONSIDERED this information in silence, but he showed no surprise, and Anthony continued.

"Who was it that started this business about my estate? Where did Steve get the idea that he was my half-brother?"

"The woman, it was her idea." Shayne's voice deepened with anger as he talked. "Steve didn't know who his old man was. No more do I.

"I hate to see a little girl in a jam," he whispered in her ear.

But that woman, she kept saying how Anthony was no common name, and how 'twas an everlasting shame that he was no relation of yours."

He took a deep breath as if his anger choked him, and then went on. "Finally she asks him about himself, and has some lawyer look it up, and comes running one night, her eyes shining like stars, and it's excited she is. 'You're the heir,' she says, and she has it all wrote out on a paper, legal-like."

"Were they married then?"

The pock-marked man shook his head. "No, right afterward. I said to Steve, she's after your money, but he just laughed, and they didn't ask me to the wedding. I should have known she was phoney then, but

I didn't know it 'til tonight when she come to your place like no decent woman would, and Steve hardly cold.

"She killed him, Mister Anthony, sir. As sure as you're sitting in that chair, I know she killed him, but I don't know why."

"How'd they happen to meet?" Anthony asked.

" 'Twas in the book shop below stairs," the little Irishman told him. "A great reader was Steve, always his nose in a book, but when they married, she closed down the shop, and it hasn't been open since."

Anthony considered. "Were they friendly with any man?" he asked the Irishman, "anyone who might have been helping them with this case against me?"

The weazened face clouded with thought "No, I can't say… but hold, there was a man and, a curse upon me brain, for I can't call his name! But if I were to see it in print, I would know it at once."

"Not much chance of that," the wealthy criminologist told him.

"If we could but get into the book shop," the little man said. "There's a list of the customers, printed on cards, and this man was a customer, for I've seen him leaving with books under his arm. But I've no got the key, and the janitor is away for the night."

"We might be able to get in if you don't mind coming downstairs," Anthony told him, thinking of his trusty steels.

"And it's me that doesn't mind," Terence Shayne said. "Sure and I'd walk over the hot coals of hell without my shoes if it would bring that woman to justice."

He came off the couch, moving with more spirit than at any time since Anthony's arrival, and led the way to the door.

AROUND THEM THE deep silence of the night filled the dusty hall and despite the deadening carpet which blanketed the stair-treads, the stairs themselves creaked beneath their weight.

In the street, the stillness matched the quiet of the hall and Shayne unconsciously lowered his voice until it was the barest whisper. "Down here."

The four steps which led to the book shop entrance were in deep shadow, and Anthony was forced to resort to the Hindu trick of enlarging his pupils by a conscious effort of will.

The outlines of the door appeared before his enlarged eyes and he moved silently toward it, his steels already in his hand.

The door itself gave him little worry. Locksmith's ingenuity was not great enough to build a lock which these steels could not open.

His strong, supple fingers slid them into the lock, and with a touch as delicate as any watchmaker, he probed it, feeling out the tumblers.

There was a slight click as the bolt went over and Anthony eased the door open. A rush of stale air greeted him, showing that the shop had not been open for some time. He dropped the steels into their place and drew out a small flash-lamp of his own construction.

The lamp was for the benefit of the little Irishman who had followed him gingerly down the dark steps of the entry-way and who now stood just outside the open door, blinking in an effort to see through the gloom.

With the tiny beam from the flash as a guide, Terence Shayne advanced into the shop. There was an admiring note in his voice as he told Anthony.

"Slickest I ever saw a lock picked. I been hearing about you but I didn't believe what I heard."

Anthony was secretly amused by the little man's praise, but there was no time to waste. "Where are those files kept?" he asked.

"Top desk drawer, on the right," Shayne whispered hoarsely. "Drawer's cut out for a file. Slick arrangement."

Anthony moved around the desk. He did not mean to stay here while Shayne went through the file. There was too much chance of discovery by a late-returning tenant or a patrolling policeman. Far better to take the whole drawer up to the Irishman's apartment where they could go through it at their leisure.

He had pulled the drawer half way from the desk, holding the light in his left hand, when something made him turn. He did not think that it was a sound, which his sharp ears had caught. More likely it was his uncanny sixth sense, warning him of impending danger.

"Look out," the words were involuntary. At the same moment he clicked the switch, cutting off the flash, and leaving the shop in darkness.

But his action was too late. Through the open door of the shop came a lance of exploding flame, and mingled with the sound of the gun was a groan which Anthony knew must come from Terence Shayne.

HE DROPPED THE light and his hand moved like a streak to where his own gun nestled under his arm. The next instant it was in his hand and he was moving around the desk, guided by his unusual sight.

He gained the door and using the casing as a partial shield, he peered out into the night. He could see nothing, but his quick ear caught the almost imperceptible sound of an idling car motor.

Even as he heard it, it raced into quick life, and far down the street his eyes caught the flick of light as headlamps cut on.

Then the car pulled away with a jarring rush and an instant later disappeared around the next corner.

Jim Anthony turned back into the shop. He did not need the light to find Shayne's huddled body, nor to tell that the man was dead.

As he straightened, his face was a hard, bronzed mask, hidden by the sheltering darkness. For a moment he stood there, hesitating above the small body, then he moved quickly toward the desk, pulled out the drawer which held the file and glided swiftly toward the door.

Already there were sounds to show that the shot had aroused some of the sleepers in the neighborhood. Jim Anthony did not wish to be found here. Already he was under suspicion for the death of his 'brother,' and he could not afford to be found, alone, after midnight with the body of Steve Anthony's best friend, a man who had threatened to kill him earlier in the evening.

CHAPTER IX

MESSAGE FROM GENTRY

THE LOBBY OF THE Waldorf-Anthony Hotel was almost deserted when the tall, sun-bronzed millionaire pushed open the revolving door. Under his arm he still carried the desk drawer which he had taken from the book shop.

It was bulky and unwieldy, and several of the bell-hops came awake to stare at him in surprise.

The desk clerk made a quick sign with his hand indicating that be had a message for Anthony.

Jim crossed the lobby with long swinging strides. It was very late, but such was his amazing vitality that he seemed as fresh as if he had spent the night in bed.

"What is it, Charles?"

The clerk said respectfully, "It's Mr. Griffith, sir. He called the desk a half hour ago and wished to be informed as soon as you arrived."

"Very good," Anthony told him. "Will you ring Mr. Griffith's room and tell him that I'll be right up. And, by the way, put this box in the office somewhere, will you. See that nothing happens to it. It isn't exactly my property."

The file-drawer out of the way, Anthony turned quickly from the desk and using the public rather than the private elevator was lifted to the seventh floor. A moment later, Evan Griffith was admitting him.

"Glad you got here." The lawyer was fully dressed and his ever-present cigar was cocked at a rakish angle. "Gentry called me a while back. It seems that he went over to see that Burke girl and found that she wasn't home. He talked to Nadia Anthony and they both suspected that she might be at Telliero's place. Gentry's gone over there."

Anthony swore under his breath and the old lawyer nodded his understanding. "That's the way I felt, son. Tom's all right; a good boy with a heart the size of a basket, but he acts without thinking, and that Telliero is bad stuff to monkey with. If you hadn't showed up, I was heading over there myself."

Anthony shrugged. "Well, stop worrying, I'll go over and check up, just to see that Tom doesn't get himself into too much trouble."

"I'll come with you," the old man suggested. "That is, unless you mind."

"Why should I mind? But I hate to keep you out of bed."

Evan Griffith snorted. "Bed, bed is for youngsters and weaklings. That's the trouble with the world. People are getting soft. In my day we worked twelve hours and played the rest of the time." He turned and picked up a coat from the bed and struggled into it, scorning Anthony's offer to help.

"Hope Gentry's all right," he puffed as he settled his hat at a rakish angle on the side of his old head. "Never know what these hot-heads will do. Haven't got the sense of a billy goat, the lot of them." He turned and led the way to the door.

AT THE MOMENT Tom Gentry was far from all right. The freckled aviator had been in a number of difficult spots in his adventurous life, but none in which he had felt more helpless.

After leaving the big hotel, he had taken a cab directly to Nadia Anthony's apartment. He did not know where Betty Burke could be found but he was certain that Nadia would know and he meant to extract the information by hook or crook.

His reception at the apartment was of a much more friendly nature than he had expected for he found Steve Anthony's widow pacing the floor nervously and when he asked for the girl she seized his arm, standing so close to him that her perfume came up to make him a little dizzy.

"I've been worried about the little fool," her voice was low and throaty like the twanging string of a violin. "I told her not to go out tonight. I told her to keep away from that gambler."

"Oh, you mean Telliero?" Gentry managed to keep his mind on Betty despite this other woman's nearness. "That's bad business. He isn't the kind of person that little girls should play with."

"That's what I told her," Nadia Anthony insisted. "But she refuses to listen to me."

"Maybe she'll listen to me," Gentry suggested. "Mind if I use your phone?" He turned and walked past her toward the instrument, intending to call the hotel desk and leave a message for Anthony, but once he had his connection, he changed his mind and asked to be connected with Evan Griffith's room instead.

The lawyer sounded out of breath when he answered.

"Sorry to bother you," Tom explained, "but Jim Anthony will be coming back to the hotel in a few minutes, looking for me. Tell him that I came over to Nadia Anthony's, but that the Burke girl isn't here. She's down at Spike Telliero's and I'm going there to talk to her."

Evan Griffith's voice was still not clear. It was as if the old man was having difficulty in shaking off the bonds of sleep which drugged his mind. "Where is Jim? What's he doing?"

"He had an errand," Gentry said, not wishing to tell exactly what Jim's errand had been since Nadia Anthony was obviously listening to the conversation. "I expected to get back to the hotel before him, but I've been delayed, and if I go on to Telliero's, I don't know when I'll be back."

"I'll tell Jim, but be careful, boy. That's a bad place, a tough place. Maybe I'd better come down and go over there with you."

The idea that Evan Griffith should accompany him as a kind of a bodyguard, struck Gentry as funny, but he managed not to laugh as he said: "That won't be necessary. I'll make out okay, don't worry about me. Just tell Jim what I said." He hung up and turned around to find that Nadia Anthony had moved forward until she stood within three feet of him.

HER EYES WERE shadowed and dark, and there was a little line of tiredness around her mouth, but she managed to smile.

"You're nice, Tom Gentry, nice to help me."

It was on the tip of Tom's tongue to tell her that he most certainly was not doing this to help her.

She saw his expression and smiled her shrewd smile. "You think that you're smart, don't you, Tom? You and Jim Anthony are so wise that no mere woman can compete with you."

"What do you mean?"

"I know why you want to see Betty," she told him. "It's so obvious that I'd have to be an utter fool not to guess. But you're wasting your time. You couldn't make Betty talk if you were with her for hours. That's why I did not hesitate to tell you where she is. A man can go into Telliero's and perhaps get her to come home, where a woman couldn't, but it will do you no good, Gentry, no good at all."

"You want to bet on that?" The tone of her words roused Gentry's combative spirit. "Give me half an hour with that baby and she'll be telling, not only her own right name but yours also. You'd better ride along with me, lady. If you don't, I'll dig this alibi out of her before we're two blocks from Telliero's."

The smile stayed on Nadia's lips as if it were pinned in place, but her eyes had hardened. "No," she said. "You are very amusing, Mister Gentry, but I have no fear that you can persuade Betty to talk."

Her words were bold and self-confident, but her actions as soon as Gentry had left, did not bear them out, for she turned quickly to the phone, ordered a cab, and left the apartment.

CHAPTER X

THE CHIPS ARE DOWN

THERE WAS NOTHING OSTENTATIOUS about Spike Telliero's club in the Fifties. He had started with a speakeasy in the dead days of prohibition, and something of the character of the speakeasy lingered about the place.

The entrance was narrow, not well lighted, and gave no outward evidence of the size or the importance of the place. There was another reason why Spike did not attempt to draw public notice to his club. His clients were carefully chosen, and it was as hard to get a table reservation at Telliero's as it is to get a pass to the White House.

But there was a second Telliero's even more exclusive than the small supper room, and open to only a portion of the upstairs clientele. This was the gambling room, reached by a maze of passages which were well and carefully guarded.

Gentry looked around the upper floor without much expectation of finding the girl whom he was seeking. If she were here at all, she would, in all likelihood, be below stairs, either in the gambling rooms or in Telliero's private office.

Nor was he disappointed, for she was nowhere in sight. The supper room was almost deserted. Four men lingered at one of the rear tables, arguing among themselves while a sleepy waiter stood hopefully by.

In Gentry's pocket was a collection of cards, gathered through the years, which would admit the bearer to almost every spot in town. He sorted through the collection, found the right card, and presented it to a horse-faced man at the rear of the main foyer.

The man wore a tuxedo in the mistaken assumption that he looked like a waiter. He didn't. In fact he looked like nothing quite human, and Gentry, despite his easy-going, natural gaiety, which made him the friend of almost everyone he met, felt a chill as he met the reptilian eyes.

The man examined him with care, trying to assure himself that Gentry was sober, then, finally satisfied, he pulled a masking curtain aside and exposed a door which he opened.

Gentry stepped through. The door swung shut behind him and he found himself alone on a flight of wooden stairs which led downward to a cement passage way below.

He followed this passage to an iron door, set in a bare brick wall, wondering as he progressed whether this door would be fastened, and if so, how he should attract the attention of those on the other side.

But apparently they were notified from above, for as he reached it, the door swung inward to expose a second tuxedo-garbed man.

This guardian might have been the twin of the one whom Gentry had just seen above stairs, save that he had a face that was almost completely chinless.

But the chin failed to be reassuring, for his eyes and the loose slackness of his mouth gave his face a definitely sinister cast, and Gentry shivered as he passed him unchallenged and moved quickly to the door which led into the gambling rooms.

IT WAS LIKE stepping into another world. Rich drapes entirely hid the rough brick of the walls. Heavy, thick napped carpet deadened all sound, and fluorescent lights, concealed in the ceiling, flooded the whole place with their soft glow.

At the far end was a discreet bar while along one side were layouts for "Wheel of Fortune," "Chuck-a-luck," and "Twenty-One." There were three roulette wheels in the center of the floor and by far the largest portion of the crowd was grouped around them.

Gentry stood in the doorway, looking around. It was several minutes before he located the girl. She was so tiny that her black head did not show above the crowd.

She was at the last table, and she was so intent upon the spinning wheel that she was not conscious of Tom's approach until he had worked his way through the press to her side.

Before her was a large stack of colored markers, and her small fingers toyed with them nervously while she watched the little ivory ball as it danced about the wheel, rolling in the opposite direction to the spinning numbers.

It slowed finally, struck one of the metal tabs, bounced and settled into four.

"Black, low, and even." The houseman's voice was a drone. He reached out and cleared the board of all chips save those on four. There were two of Betty Burke's markers on the winning number and the man behind the wheel shoved the stacks of chips toward her.

"Having fun?" Gentry spoke, his lips almost touching the dark hair above her small ear.

She turned, startled. The gambling excitement had put two spots of high color into her dark cheeks and her eyes were sparkling. Some of the sparkle disappeared as she realized who he was.

Her eyes clouded, her lips set, and she turned away so that her shoulder was toward him.

Tom Gentry was far from daunted. Other women had tried to snub him in the past. "You'd better be nice," he warned, still speaking in an undertone, close to her ear. "I know a little girl that's headed right for trouble, and I don't like it. I hate to see a girl in a jam."

"Leave me alone." Annoyance made her tone louder than she had intended, and several players turned to look at them.

"See!" said Gentry, still whispering. "You're attracting attention. Now, we don't want that, do we? You wouldn't want all these fine people to know that you were mixed up in a murder case, would you? Better come over to the bar and let me buy a drink while we talk it over."

"We have nothing to talk about."

"I think we do," he told her. People were watching them now and the houseman behind the table moved his hand toward a concealed switch.

GENTRY DID NOT see the motion. He did not know that anything was the matter until several tuxedo garbed men had converged upon the table.

There was nothing ostentatious about their actions. It was easy to see that they were used to dealing with trouble, with a minimum of annoyance to the other guests.

Gentry was still arguing, when suddenly one of the guards shouldered in between him and the girl. Gentry twisted his head angrily.

"Say, look out where you're going."

"Take it easy, Jack." It was a second guard, on Gentry's other side. His hands locked on Tom's arm, just above the elbow. "No trouble now. You'll live longer that way."

Before the aviator could recover from his bewildered surprise, they had swung him neatly away from the table and were propelling him across the room toward a door at the far end of the bar.

He started to struggle but stopped it almost at once, for both men had peculiar locks upon his arms and they twisted simultaneously. Sharp pains shot up into Gentry's shoulders and he was forced forward as his arms were wrenched in their sockets.

He stopped struggling, but he was fuming anger when he was thrust through the door into the expensively furnished office beyond.

Spike Telliero was counting money. There was a great deal of it, and it was laid out on a long director's table in neat piles, ready to be banded in thousand dollar packages.

Gentry's captors relaxed their grip slightly and the freckled aviator freed himself with a quick jerk. A third man had brought in Betty and closed the door. Telliero paused in his counting and turned around.

His chunky figure stiffened as he recognized Gentry and the points of his spike-mustache seemed to stand out more sharply. "So," his

The gambler went over backwards
under Tom's punch.

voice had an oily softness which carried more threat than any curses. "It's you!"

"It's me." Gentry straightened his coat and took a step toward the swarthy gambler. "What's the idea of having your punks strong arm me? I come here, quietly minding my own business, and you set the wolf pack on my shoulders. Make them come on one at a time and I'll lick the bunch, you included."

Telliero's dark eyes ranged across the group and when he spoke there was a slight sneer in his tone. "It might interest you to know, Mister Gentry, that I was entirely unconscious of your presence until you came into this room. It seems that my wolf pack as you call them, acted on their own initiative. What about it, boys?"

"He was bothering the dame," one of the men said, harshly.

Telliero's eyes hardened until they resembled glittering black marbles as he looked, first toward Betty and then at the still angry Gentry.

"Perhaps," his voice was grating now, and the thin veneer of education which he reserved for patrons slipped away. "Perhaps you didn't hear what I said down at headquarters. I told that copper that this girl belonged to me, and that I wouldn't stand for anyone shoving her around. I meant it, see, and I meant it when I said that you and your stuff-shirted murdering friend had better watch out."

"Don't call him that," Gentry's anger was close to the boiling point.

"I'll call him anything I please," Telliero smirked with contempt. "To me he's a heel that goes around cheating women and murdering his relatives, the no-good…"

HE NEVER FINISHED the sentence for the freckled aviator had leaped forward. With his left hand, he caught the front of Telliero's soft-bosomed dinner shirt. His right, in the form of a hard knuckled fist shot out to crash against the gambler's jaw.

Telliero's head snapped back, and he would have fallen save for Gentry's clutching grip on his shirt. But Gentry was not ready for his victim to fall. He measured the man's jaw with precision and his second jarring blow was much harder than the first.

At the exact instant that his knuckles rapped against the swarthy jaw, he released his grip on the shirt front The gambler went over backwards, his chunky body making a little arc in the air, his shoulder blades striking the table, knocking it over onto its side and scattering the money broadcast, like a flood of floating green leaves.

But Tom Gentry had no time to observe the result of his handiwork for the three guards descended upon him from behind and it seemed to the battling Gentry that a thousand, buzzing, angry locusts were striking all at once.

Despite his efforts at defense, the very weight of their number carried him to the floor. A blackjack struck his shoulder a deadening blow, a second almost tore the ear from the side of his head, and his senses swam as a heavy toe caught him square on the point of the chin.

Tom Gentry loved a good fight, but this was no fight the way that it was being waged, and he had given up hope of ever leaving the office alive when another factor was projected into the battle.

The door from the gambling room burst open, and for an instant Jim Anthony was framed in its casing, looking like a tall, dark avenger out of the past.

MARKED MONEY

HIS HAWK-LIKE EYES TOOK in the confused scene at a glance and then, with a cry which might have done credit to a remote Indian ancestor he flung himself into the fray.

His powerful fingers locked in the collar of the top guard and with unbelievable strength, he jerked the man to his feet and hurled him across the room with such force that he struck the wall and fell sideways, the breath knocked out of him.

The second guard saw the motion from the corner of his eye and came up off the floor, cat-like to meet Jim's attack, his blackjack swinging in a wide arc.

Anthony took the force of the blow on his forearm and drove his free fist deep into the man's stomach. His assailant sat down, hard. The third man rolled across Gentry's prostrate body in an effort to escape, but Anthony caught the flying tail of his coat, jerked him to his feet and shook him until his teeth rattled.

He pulled the blackjack from the thug's wrist, got the gun from his pocket, and pushed him over against the desk. Then he bent above his battered friend. "Tom! Tom! Are you okay?"

Gentry managed to sit up dizzily and blink at his friend out of eyes which were swelling rapidly.

"Cripes, pappy, another couple of minutes and I'd have been bait for the undertaker. You certainly are Johnny on the spot." With Anthony's help, he managed to drag himself to his feet and began to feel his sides as if in search of broken ribs.

Finding that he was still in one piece, he looked around and was startled to see Nadia Anthony in the open doorway with Evan Griffith peering across her shoulder like an elderly, slightly startled eagle.

"Where'd she come from?"

"We found her waiting outside," Anthony explained. "I thought that the door keepers might know her so we brought her along. Lucky we did, otherwise we wouldn't have gotten in so fast."

Gentry grinned at the silent, unsmiling woman. "So, you weren't so sure of your little cousin as you made out. You had to tag along, just in case."

"Shut that door." It was Spike Telliero. He had struggled to his feet, and stood, swaying a little, one hand on the desk, the other fingering his swollen jaw. "Want all the customers in on this beef? Get out there, Louis, and tell the floor men to send them home. Tell them there's no trouble. Tell them anything."

The guard hurried to obey, and Nadia Anthony, trailed by Evan Griffith, came into the room. The door closed behind them. The man that Anthony had hit in the stomach was on his feet, helping his remaining partner to rise.

All the fight seemed to have gone out of both of them, but not out of Telliero. Despite his swollen jaw, the gambler was as belligerent as ever. "Pick up that money," he commanded. "Bring it here."

They got down on their knees, gathering up the bills in handfuls and he counted it as they brought it to him. When the last bill had been retrieved from beneath the edge of the fallen table, he looked up, his swarthy face twisted in anger.

"Come on, who's holding out? There's a thousand missing."

The two men looked at each other and then at their chief, shaking their heads.

He considered them for a moment of angry silence, then his attention shifted to the battered Gentry and one of his stubby fingers shot out accusingly.

"So you grabbed it."

Gentry, whose ruffled temper had not been entirely soothed, started forward, his fists clenched, but Anthony laid a restraining hand on his shoulder and pulled him back. "Wait, Tom, let me handle this."

"I'll handle it," Gentry muttered darkly. "I'll make that grease-ball eat that spiked mustache. Calling me a thief. Where does he get that stuff?"

ANTHONY PAID NO attention to his angry friend, but addressed the chunky gambler. "What makes you think that Gentry took your money?"

"He was on the floor, wasn't he," Telliero flared. "It's either him or one of the boys, and I'd sooner trust them than him."

Anthony's temper was close to the breaking point, but he managed to hold his voice level. "And just what do you intend to do about it?"

"If he's so all-fired innocent," Telliero sneered, "maybe he won't object to being searched."

"And just what would a search prove?" Anthony was still holding himself under careful reign. "Gentry might easily have a thousand dollars of his own money in his pocket. Money is money. You couldn't well tell the difference."

"That's what you think," the gambler was still sneering. "Every bill that goes through this joint has a tiny red dot placed in the last figure of the serial number. I like to know how much house dough is won across the tables each night, and how much new money comes in. That's one way to tell."

Anthony's bronzed face was thoughtful. "I see, and if the money in Gentry's pocket belonged to you, it would have a red dot?"

"Like this." The gambler picked up a bill from the desk and extended it toward Anthony, indicating a tiny dot that was barely distinguishable.

The criminologist looked at it for a moment, then stopped back. "All right, Tom, let them search you."

Gentry stared at him with unbelieving eyes. "Cripes, pappy, I tell you that I didn't pick up any money… you don't think…"

"Never mind," Anthony said, sharply. "Let them search you."

"Blamed if I will." Gentry was hurt by his friend's seeming lack of trust. He pulled his wallet from his pocket and tossed it on the desk. "Go ahead, grease-ball, look all you want to. My money's in there, all but a couple of bucks in my pants. Maybe you want to see them too."

Spike Telliero did not answer. Instead he caught up the wallet with eager fingers and pulled the thick sheaf of bills into sight.

He smoothed them out, bending forward so that he could see more clearly, then he looked up, his black eyes shining with malicious triumph. "So, Mister Jim Anthony, your friend is a thief. The dot is on these bills."

Once again Tom Gentry surged forward, his fists knotted, and this time it took all of Anthony's superb strength to hold him back.

"Wait, Tom."

"But he's lying. It isn't possible. I didn't—"

"Never mind," Anthony told him. "You'll understand in a minute." He turned to Telliero.

"You're quite a gambler, aren't you, Spike? You'll bet on anything, even on the chance that I might have a brother and that if I did, he would be entitled to half of my fortune."

The black eyes which had been malice-filled only a moment before viewed Anthony with growing suspicion. "What now?"

"You lose," Anthony told him. "It might have looked like a good gamble from your point of view, Spike, but in reality it wasn't. You see, my alleged half-brother was not born until a year and a half after my father left Ireland. They should have told you that, Spike. It wasn't fair. They should have told you from the first that the whole idea was nothing but a shakedown, that their idea was to get a quick settlement from me because of the nuisance of having my estate tied up."

Spike Telliero was still staring at him. "What's all this?" his voice was loaded with suspicion now.

"The truth," said Anthony, and he sounded weary. "They needed money for a front, Spike. That's where you came in. How much did you give them? How much were you expecting to get in return?"

IF ANTHONY EXPECTED a direct answer, he was disappointed because the gambler was no longer looking at him. Telliero's black eyes were turned toward the two women who stood silent, and white faced against the far wall.

"What's he saying?" the chunky man demanded harshly. "What's all this about Steve not being his brother?"

"I thought that they might have neglected to tell you." Anthony's voice had a maddening smoothness. "You see, Spike, they were afraid that if they told you the whole story, you wouldn't advance the money. They planned to get a quick settlement from me and then vanish. When that didn't turn out, they changed the plan. Steve wasn't of any more use to them, so they killed him. But they used the poor fool, even in death. They arranged his murder carefully. I was framed, and then, Nadia offered me a trade. For money, a lot of money, she offered to furnish me with an alibi.

"Ask them, Spike. Ask them if you were going to get part of that money, or if they were playing you for a sucker, too."

"I'm asking." Spike Telliero's hoarse words cut through the air like a knife. "What about it, Betty? Where did I come in?"

Betty Burke's baby face was very white, and her words had a little jumpy, nervous sound. "Why, Spike, darling, you know I wouldn't do anything to hurt you."

"The nuts you wouldn't, babe. I know a double cross when I see one. If you'd been on the level, you'd have told me the works. I'd have played with you until hell froze, but I'm not sitting around, letting a couple of smart dames slip me the double O. The chips are down, sweetheart, and I'm paying off in my own way."

"Wait," Anthony cut in sharply. "They helped plan it, yes, and they helped carry it out. But neither of them was the real man behind the play."

He glanced toward Evan Griffith and the lawyer's face looked older than Tom Gentry had ever seen it "Why'd you do it, Griff? Haven't I always played fair with you? Haven't I always given you everything you needed? Then why try to rob me and frame me for a murder *which you yourself committed?*"

The oldster looked startled. "Me, Jim? Have you lost your senses?"

"Almost," Anthony said. "I've known for hours that you were behind this thing. But I tried not to believe it. I tried desperately to prove myself wrong. Instead, I've merely piled up evidence against you. You're caught. Griff. These women will turn against you to save themselves. You haven't a chance."

"I tell you—"

"No, Griff, old friend. This marked money in Gentry's wallet: Tom didn't pick it up off the floor. It's part of the cash which you handed him to give me. A while ago I overheard Tom telling you we'd soon be able to repay your loan, so I know he got that cash from you. You, in turn, got it from Telliero. It's part of the funds he furnished to Nadia Anthony to carry on this scheme."

"That's no proof—"

"Not in itself. But there are other things. My taxi driver, for instance; the only witness who could, perhaps, have cleared me. He was murdered. Other people knew about him, vaguely. Telliero for one. But you were the only person who knew what he looked like, knew his son was in the Navy, and that the old man was driving the cab for the duration. *You were in Trotter's an office when I gave Tom Gentry that description.*"

"Smart, aren't you?" the lawyer was beginning to crack.

Anthony ignored the words. "I have a certain card in my pocket," he went on. "A card from the customer file of Nadia Anthony's circulating library. All through this case, you've pretended that you and Nadia were strangers, yet the card shows that you were a customer of her book shop for over two years. Terence Shayne led me to the file, hunting your name which he could not recall, but you must have feared him, for you trailed me there, and shot down the little Irishman. You covered it well, you must have rushed back to the hotel, since you were there when Gentry called."

The freckled aviator showed excitement "Say, he sounded out of breath when he answered. I thought he was just sleepy, but he must have been running."

"Another piece fitted into the puzzle," Anthony said. "The whole plot was hatched in that book shop, hatched because a man named Anthony had moved into the building, a man who did not know his father, a man who had but recently came from Ireland. You may deny it, but one of the women will crack. One of them will send you to the chair."

EVAN GRIFFITH MOVED with a speed surprising to one of his age, and the gun which appeared in his hand did not tremble as he covered the room.

"All of you stay where you are. Don't move. I'm not afraid of any of you. When you're old, you stop being afraid. But I'm not going to die in the chair, my smart young friend. I'll die where I choose.

"I've had fun with this, because I hated you. You never guessed that I did hate you, but I do. I hate you because I've had to take as your charity, that which should have been mine by right. I served your father for twenty years. I was his administrator, his executor, yet he left me nothing.

"And out of the millions which were yours solely by accident of birth, you doled me out pennies, me who had helped your father build his fortune."

Anthony's face seemed to be molded from burnished metal. He did not speak, and the old attorney went on, his words driven by the intensity of his hate.

"So my chance came. The man who bore your name showed up. I knew that the estate would be reopened when he filed his claim, and that I would be recalled to serve as administrator again. I would be in the saddle for a time. I could dole out the pennies, and watch you squirm.

"The money itself did not matter. I am too old to want much, but I used these fools and their greed as my tools." He indicated the staring women with a little wave of his hand.

"I've had my fun," he went on. "I hoped you would die in the chair. I planned it carefully. A man has to hate to crawl across a board and shoot down a drunken fool," his voice was rising, and rich, red color was driving the grey from his withered cheeks.

"But luck turned away from me and I'll have to do it myself. I'm going to kill you." The last words were almost a scream.

"No," said Anthony. He spoke without hurry, without raising his voice. "You lose again, Griff. You won't choose your means of death. You may not live to pull that trigger. It's apoplexy, Griff. You've been afraid of it for years. You won't pull that trigger because you can't. You can't, so don't try."

Evan Griffith was trying. It was as if a struggle were going on inside the man's scrawny body. And suddenly with a gasping cry which was not human, he collapsed, falling sideways. He lay quite still where he had dropped, his eyes closed, his breathing heavy, uneven, and high color pumping up into his face.

Anthony was beside him in an instant. The rest of the room's occupants seemed stunned, the women recovering first, leaping toward the door.

Spike Telliero grabbed them, and dragged them back. "No you don't. I'm not holding the sack for you dolls."

Gentry was at Anthony's side as the millionaire straightened. "What is it, pappy?"

"A stroke," Anthony told him.

"You certainly call them." Gentry sounded a little awed.

"Any competent doctor would have observed the same signs. I've been expecting it for some time. The excitement was too much. I doubt that he will recover. He may, in fact, not regain consciousness. Of course, my mentioning apoplexy probably did him no good. You've heard of the power of suggestion."

"I hope you never suggest that I have a tail," Gentry told him. "But pappy, how come you let him get the drop on us? Surely you knew he'd have a gun?"

"I didn't," Anthony turned. "I had him covered with my sleeve gun the whole time, but I didn't want to shoot the old boy if I could help it. I kept remembering that he had been my father's friend." His eyes shifted and hardened as he considered the two women that Telliero was still holding.

Gentry followed the look and asked in an undertone. "What happens to them?"

Anthony shrugged. "They'll probably take a plea. It seems that Telliero has stepped over onto our side. I don't believe he had anything to do with it save furnishing the front money.

"After all, Griff did the actual killing. It's strange what hate will make people do."

CURSE OF THE MASTERS

ONE AFTER ANOTHER, THE PURCHASERS OF RARE OLD
PAINTINGS ARE FOUND MURDERED, GARROTED. AND IN EACH
CASE THE CRIME HAS FOLLOWED AN APPRAISAL MADE BY
PROFESSOR WHELSTROM. IT'S HARD TO BELIEVE THAT THE
FAMOUS ART EXPERT OR HIS LOVELY DAUGHTER CAN BE
IMPLICATED, YET JIM ANTHONY FINDS IT EVEN HARDER TO
BELIEVE THERE ARE SUPERNATURAL FORCES AT WORK

THE ROOM WAS LONG and narrow, dark and richly furnished to match its fumed oak paneling which might have belonged in some mediaeval Gothic cloister instead of a private residence in midtown Manhattan. A small reading lamp glowed on the broad, polished surface of an ornately carved desk; but this lamp was far from sufficient to dispel the gloomy shadows of the vaulted chamber.

Much more effective illumination came from two diffusion-type reflector lights which were trained upon an oil painting at the opposite end of the room. In the direct glow of these mellow rays, the framed canvas took on a warmth you could almost feel. It was a large picture, rich with siennas and umbers, a painting to gladden the heart of almost any collector; yet the man who owned it was bitterly displeased.

He sat slumped in the desk chair, his expression angry, storms of wrath flickering in his deep-set eyes. A scowl furrowed his forehead as he contemplated the painting, and a muttered curse formed itself on his grim lips. "Damnable thieves!"

In that great, shadow-swathed room his whisper seemed to mock him with malignant little echoes; almost as if the picture itself had cast back a taunt in his teeth. Gradually his fury grew, until blue veins stood out on his temples like worms writhing under the skin. "Thieves!" he said again, louder now; and the sound of his own voice was weird against the gloom.

Twice his hand went out toward the telephone on the polished desk surface, and twice he pulled it back. The third time he picked up the instrument, cast a last glare at the framed picture, then dialed a number and waited impatiently.

When he had his connection, he spoke sharply into the transmitter. "Mr. Anthony, please. Yes, James Anthony." He drummed on the

193

The wire was fixed. The man was dead. Like wraiths, the killers fled.

desk with heavy, blunt fingers. Then, presently: "Anthony? This is J. Devereaux Bowden. You won't remember me."

The voice that drifted back over the wire was pleasantly resonant. "On the contrary, Mr. Bowden, I remember you quite well. I think we met at an exhibit of modern painting a year ago last December at the Metropolitan."

"Hm-m-mph! Didn't think, you'd recall a casual introduction as long ago as that. Well, no matter. Point is, I purchased a picture through the Monarch Gallery last week."

"And—?" the voice inquired politely.

"And I talked to Professor Whelstrom about it this afternoon. So now I want to see you. Right here. At once."

"Wouldn't tomorrow do? I'm engaged this evening."

The man at the desk snorted. "Engaged, hell! I'm busy, too. But not too busy to demand a showdown. There's something damned funny going on, Anthony. I don't like it."

"What do you mean by funny?"

"Monkey business, I mean! And I'll not say any more over the phone. If there's talking to be done, do it face to face; that's my motto. Your name heads the list of Monarch Gallery directors, doesn't it? Hm-m-mph! Then you're the one I want to see. I'll expect you in half an hour."

As if to brook no further argument, the angry man slammed up his receiver. Otherwise, though, he didn't move. Slumped once more in the desk chair, he glowered at the big painting on its distant easel with the expression of one whose best friend had double-crossed him.

Seated thus, buried in embittered reveries, he did not hear the click of the latch as the door behind him was thrust ominously open....

JIM ANTHONY, MILLIONAIRE industrialist and amateur student of criminology, put down his phone when he realized that the man at the other end of the connection had hung up. Across the huge living room of his penthouse apartment atop the world famous Waldorf-Anthony Hotel, Tom Gentry was mixing two tall glasses of Scotch and soda.

Adding a final splash to each glass, Gentry carried them forward and handed one to Anthony. As he performed this service, he noticed the puzzled look on Jim's dark, sun-bronzed face.

"What gives, pappy?" the freckled, genial aviator demanded. He was Jim Anthony's closest friend and constant companion, and he could sense the hawk-like millionaire's slightest change of mood. "Another jerk trying to sell you a guinea pig farm?"

Anthony took a long pull at his drink. "Something more serious than that, Tom. That was J. Devereaux Bowden on the line. At least that's what he claimed his name was; and judging from his tone, he considers himself an important personage. Important enough to order me around."

"Oh, yeah? And why should this J. Devereaux What's-His-Name be picking your head?"

"I don't know," Jim finished his Scotch and frowned thoughtfully. When he frowned, his resemblance to an Indian chieftain was striking. This was not particularly surprising, since his mother had been a full blooded princess of the Comanche tribe.

His father, on the other hand, had been a roystering Irish soldier of fortune turned capitalist; a man who, by skill and hard work and sheer financial wizardry, had piled up one of the world's greatest industrial empires. This vast wealth he had passed on to his only son—along with the shrewdness which had enabled him to accumulate it in the first place.

Young, tall, darkly handsome, and immoderately rich, Jim Anthony might have become a playboy to end all playboys; but he had too active a mind and too splendid a body to be satisfied with a polo-playing country club existence. Upon his graduation from top flight universities all over the globe, he had first turned his talents to the increasing of his financial inheritance—a job in which he was even more successful than his father; for within a few years he had become twice as wealthy as the elder Anthony had been. Factories, war industries, mines, oil-fields and refineries, a nation-wide string of metropolitan newspapers, a coast-to-coast chain of hotels: all these varied investments were included in Jim Anthony's holdings. And he operated them so skillfully that they seemed almost to run themselves, leaving him with time on his hands.

But the quest for money was not exciting enough to hold him; and this unspent time demanded new outlets for his boundless energy. The sciences and arts next took his attention, until he had achieved mastery of them in all their branches and thus reached a fresh impasse of boredom.

It was then that he had turned to the study of criminology as a hobby—and the hobby eventually became a career. Before long, Jim's fame as an amateur scientific detective became international; and the mere mention of his name was enough to strike terror into the hearts of lawbreakers. Into the battle against crime he brought superlative courage, keen wits, an amazing fund of knowledge, the physical perfection of a finely trained athlete, and a hunting instinct inherited from his Indian ancestors. Through his mother's Comanche strain he possessed still another heritage: a kind of mystic sixth sense, weird, uncanny, completely inexplicable, but never wrong.

It was this sixth sense that was working now, warning him of unseen dangers ahead; telling him that there was something more behind the recent telephone call than the grumblings of an angry man.

He looked soberly at Tom Gentry. "I think we had better pay Mr. J. Devereaux Bowden a visit."

"You mean right now?" Gentry uttered a shrill protest. "But we can't do that, pappy! Or have you forgotten those two gorgeous quails we've got a date with? I fixed everything for us to pick them up at the theater and—"

"Sorry, Tom. I have a feeling that this call may turn out to be much more important than your girls."

The freckled aviator displayed anguish. "That ain't possible. If you'd seen these chicks, you wouldn't say such a thing."

But as with most arguments between them, Gentry wound up on the loser's side. A few minutes later he was hunched in a corner of the millionaire's specially built convertible, wallowing in unhappy silence. Jim Anthony drove with the touch of a man who knows and loves his car, for he enjoyed nothing better than to ride through the night with the top down. This evening, though, the top was raised against a gathering mist which gave definite promise of heavy rain within the hour, just as Jim's uncanny sixth sense brought him a foreboding of peril ahead....

IN THAT NARROW, vaulted room of sentient shadows where an angry man had slammed up his telephone receiver, a rear door swung ominously open and two unseen figures entered soundlessly. Nor did the angry man realize he had visitors until he was startled by a mocking voice at his shoulder.

"So, Mr. Bowden, you are not satisfied with your bargain?"

The man in the chair twitched erect, turning to face the forbidding gloom from which the voice had come. He could see nothing, for the little light on the desk was directly in his eyes and the portion of the room occupied by the unknown speaker was cloaked in sinister darkness.

"Wh-who are you?"

"One who appreciates fine paintings," the voice held an evil undercurrent that was caught up by whispering echoes. "One who believes that such masterpieces should remain in Europe and not be exposed to the crudities of the new world. This picture you purchased was stolen, Mr. Bowden. Stolen from its rightful home. It must be returned."

The embittered man had by now recovered from the first shock of fear caused by the presence of his unseen visitor. He was a fighter by nature and by training, and he squared his shoulders; thrust out his heavy jaw.

"That's ridiculous," he barked, using the tone which had made him both hated and respected at a thousand directors' meetings during his business career. "No picture is stolen when it's smuggled out of occupied Europe to keep it from falling into the hands of Nazi thieves. Besides, in this case, that doesn't apply. If a man is gullible enough to be taken in by a bunch of crooks—well, I was a sucker and I'm going to do something about it."

"No, Mr. Bowden, you will do nothing about it. You will write no more complaining letters, and there will be no painting to substantiate your complaints."

"Ah. I get it. Steal the evidence, would you?" The man sprang from his chair, cursing. "Not unless it's over my dead body!" He was not as young as he once had been, but his powerful form still retained chunky strength, enhanced now by rage.

The sinister voice chuckled malignantly. "Over your dead body, eh? Well, you've asked for it. Take him, Spider."

That was all the warning the angry man ever had; for as he'd talked, the second intruder had slipped unnoticed to the rear of his chair, sheltered by the room's heavy shadows. Now this second interloper leaped to action. His body was curiously misshapen, his legs normal but his torso very short and his ape-like arms abnormally long.

With a deft flick that came of practice and training, he flipped a loop of thin, strong wire over his victim's head. Before the doomed man could realize what was happening, the wire loop tightened like a strangling garrote; cut sharply into flesh and sinew and gristle. Spasmodic agony jerked the dying man, caused his arms to flail blindly and his legs to kick at nothingness. Then he went limp in his chair; did not move again.

Two figures now glided out of the darkness, moving swiftly and without sound. Their work was quickly and effectively accomplished; then, moving like wraiths fleeing a troubled graveyard, they sped from the silent room. The door latch clicked; and now the vaulted chamber was left to its lonely occupant, with only a length of twisted wire about his gullet to bear evidence of death's grim handiwork.

THE RESIDENCE OF J. Devereaux Bowden was one of the old houses which jam each other along the crosstown streets in the middle sixties. This particular structure was narrow, three stories high, and its entrance door was reached by a flight of four brownstone steps. Jim Anthony climbed the stoop and pressed the bell button, with the unwilling Tom Gentry at his heels but still muttering to himself.

The butler who opened the door was very old. "Yes, sir?" he inquired.

Anthony extended his card. "I have an appointment with Mr. Bowden. He phoned me thirty minutes ago."

Astonishment widened the butler's rheumy eyes. "Strange, sir. Mr. Bowden said nothing to me about expecting you." He hesitated, peering at the millionaire's engraved calling card.

"Let's blow, pappy," Tom Gentry whispered impatiently. "If the guy's too dumb to tell the servants you're expected, he's a dope. And we've got no time to waste on dopes."

"Quiet," the millionaire locked his fingers around Gentry's arm and squeezed lightly. The freckled aviator was an athlete in his own right, a man whose muscles were corded and hard; but the steel bands which were his wealthy friend's fingers bit into the flesh until Tom winced.

"Who are you? What do you want
at this hour?" she asked.

Then Anthony said to the butler: "Please announce us to your master. From the way he spoke on the phone, I think he's anxious to see me."

The ancient servitor hesitated; but Jim's appearance was decidedly reassuring in top hat, white tie, and tails. "Very well, sir. Will you wait in the drawing room, sir?" And he creaked his rheumatic bones up the padded stairs.

An instant later he yelled.

It was almost as if Jim Anthony had been expecting that quavery outcry, for he was in lithe motion before its echoes had died. Like an arrow he ascended the staircase three steps at a time, with Gentry panting in his wake. They reached an open doorway on the second floor; burst into a long, vaulted room with a rush of speed that almost toppled the butler off his feet.

The servant had paused just inside the threshhold, frozen by horror. His lips moved, but no sound issued. All he could do was point a trembling finger at the desk beyond him.

The light on that desk made a little puddle of glow in the deep sea of surrounding shadows; and the glow bathed a man slumped awkwardly in the desk chair as if asleep. But the posture was an uncomfortable one; a position no sleeping man could maintain without soon awakening.

Anthony's subtle sixth sense buzzed within his subconscious mind. He thrust the unsteady butler at Gentry. "Take care of him, Tom." Then he glided forward, employing a visual trick he'd learned years ago from a Hindu yogi in Calcutta—the trick of dilating the pupils of his eyes by conscious effort, so that he could see almost as well in darkness as the ordinary man could see in daylight.

Now this ocular control enabled him to spot something which had not been noticed by Tom Gentry or the ancient servant: a thin loop of wire cruelly encircling the throat of the man in the chair. That wire was so deeply buried in folds of flesh as to be practically invisible; yet Anthony saw it and acted with chain-lightning speed. He gained the desk, propped the slumping figure upright; tried to loosen the wire garrote.

Simultaneously, Gentry found a wall switch and clicked it. A central chandelier blazed into brilliance, flooding the room with light. In this sudden radiance the millionaire criminologist finished his brief but all-encompassing examination of the inert form on the chair.

"What is it, pappy?" Tom demanded shakily.

Anthony's sun-bronzed face was an impassive mask. "This man has been murdered within the past few minutes," he answered tunelessly. "We must contact police headquarters."

CHAPTER II

PICTURE FRAME

AS SOON AS HE'D telephoned Centre Street and notified Lieutenant Trotter of the homicide bureau, Jim Anthony returned his attention to the butler. "You've been with Mr. Bowden a long time?" The old man nodded, his watery eyes vague—as if his ancient brain refused to grasp the significance of what had happened, "It... it's been twenty-five years come next August, sir. I can't believe he's dead. Who would wish to kill him?"

"Didn't he have enemies?" Anthony made his voice friendly.

"Enemies, sir? No, none. Not for the past ten years, anyhow."

"Why ten years?"

"He has been retired since then. Before that, he was chairman of the Bowden Dye and Chemical Corporation. Some of his business associates might have had disagreements with him in the old days, but those business associates have since passed away."

"He was well off financially?"

"Quite, sir. I might venture to call him wealthy."

"What about his heirs?"

"There are no relatives, sir. His wife died eight years ago. His money goes to various charities. I witnessed his will and he insisted that I read it. He bequeathed me an income of a hundred dollars a month during my own lifetime."

Gentry muttered an aside to the millionaire criminologist. "Hardly enough to commit murder for, pappy."

"Of course not. Be still, Tom." Anthony turned back to the butler. "Did anything out of the ordinary happen today?"

Unexpectedly the servant stiffened. "Yes, sir. Mr. Bowden was too angry to eat his dinner."

"Was that uncommon?"

"Oh, very, sir. Mr. Bowden used to have a terrible temper, if I may say so. His wife's death was due to a stroke resulting from one of their arguments. From then on, he set himself to control his rages. And he succeeded, sir. I never again saw him infuriated—until today."

"What aroused his anger in this case?"

The butler wagged his head. "I don't know, sir. It was after Professor Whelstrom came to look at the painting this afternoon. He left about five; and from then on, Mr. Bowden was in an ugly mood."

"He was sore at this Professor Who-zit?" the irrepressible Gentry asked.

"I think not, sir. They shook hands, and I heard Mr. Bowden thank him for coming. 'I'll take it up immediately,' Was what Mr. Bowden said. 'I'm glad you were honest with me about that damned picture.' Those were his exact words."

Anthony had been looking around the room, but now his glittering black eyes bored into the butler's. "What picture?"

"The one on the easel over there, sir," the servant pointed. Then he seemed completely bewildered. "Wh-why, where is it? *It's g-gone!*"

"There was a painting in that frame?"

"Y-yes, sir. A very valuable one. A Titian which had been in the Antwerp Museum and was smuggled out of Europe ahead of the Nazi invasion. It's—it's been stolen!"

"Was it here after Professor Whelstrom left?"

The butler nodded. "Of course, sir. I came up here less than an hour ago, thinking perhaps Mr. Bowden had changed his mind and would eat some dinner. He growled at me to get out. The painting was here then. The only lights in the room were that little desk lamp and two others arranged to reflect on the easel. Mr. Bowden was sitting here glaring at it."

Anthony moved swiftly to the empty gilt frame; inspected it. "It was a clever haul," he said.

"Yeah. They'd have to be clever to figure on lifting a Titian. That's an old master, ain't it? Plenty valuable?" Tom asked.

"I wasn't thinking of the picture's value," Anthony answered gravely. "What I meant was, whoever stole this picture knew something about art and the care of paintings. The ordinary thief would have cut the canvas from the frame."

"Well?"

"There was no cutting here. The frame was removed, then the tacks were pulled which held the canvas to the stretcher bars. There are the bars," he indicated the four wooden stretchers in a neat pile on the floor. "And the tacks," he added, pointing to the scattered brads.

Tom pursed his lips. "Experts, huh?"

"It would seem so. The thief, or thieves, came prepared. In all likelihood a tube was brought along, into which the canvas could be rolled for easy transportation from the house."

"Gosh! What about this professor guy? What's he a professor of? Art, maybe? A wise mug who'd know enough to—"

Instead of answering, Anthony went back to the butler and asked a question of his own. "This Whelstrom. There used to be an expert of that name at the Manhattan Museum. I haven't heard of him in several years and assumed him to be dead. Could he be the one who called today?"

"Take cover!" he warned. "We're
being used for clay pigeons."

"I really couldn't say, sir. I don't know anything about him. Mr. Bowden made the arrangements himself, by phone."

Gentry strode across the room, "A fine thing, wrapping a wire around a man's goozle and croaking him just to steal a painting. Why go to all that trouble? Why bother to knock him off when they could just as well have tied him up and let it go at that?"

"Perhaps he recognized the burglar or burglars," Anthony suggested.

Tom snapped his fingers. "That fits this Professor Whelstrom, doesn't it? I mean Whelstrom comes here to look at the picture. Later he sneaks back to swipe it—and Bowden tabs him. So bingo! Bowden gets the big chill. It's open and shut."

Before the millionaire criminologist could comment on this theory, a bell jangled through the lower floor of the old residence. "That should be the police, Tom. Go down and let them in. We'll see what Trotter thinks."

DETECTIVE LIEUTENANT TROTTER was a big man with a red face and a domineering voice; but the voice was no more domineering than the lieutenant himself. Long years of experience had made him an efficient police official—in his own way. His way was strictly that of the old-time cop, however; and his law was that of the night-stick. It was inevitable that his methods of conducting a murder investigation would clash with the more modern ideas of a scientific criminologist like Jim Anthony; and it was likewise inevitable that Anthony's international successes as an amateur detective would arouse a certain amount of resentment in Trotter.

In spite of this underlying antagonism, which was professional rather than personal, the two men bore a mutual respect for each other; a respect that Trotter usually kept well concealed beneath his blustery surface. He was concealing it now, as he listened to Anthony's summary of the things that had happened.

When the millionaire criminologist finished talking, Trotter turned to the butler and questioned him at length; but he got no more from the man than Anthony had already elicited.

"It's screwy!" the homicide official rasped. "Why should a smart crook put himself behind an eight ball by committing a murder he didn't have to pull?"

Hiding a faint smile, Anthony said: "There's a logical answer. If Bowden recognized the picture thief, murder would be the one way to keep him from identifying the thief later."

"Yeah, that's possible," Trotter admitted. "Still, it don't get us anywhere. The question is, who was the guy?"

"I don't know, as yet."

"As yet!" the lieutenant pounced on the words. "Meaning you figure to dip into the mess, eh?"

"Perhaps. After all, I have a personal interest in the matter—now."

"What do you mean, now? And what were you doing here in the first place? How come you're the one that discovered this kill?" Trotter swelled with sudden wrath.

Jim kept his voice impassive. "I received a phone call from Bowden this evening, demanding that I come here right away. I didn't like his tone; and I already had an engagement. But he was insistent; so I decided it might be wise to drop in."

"Wait a minute," the homicide detective narrowed his eyes. "I know you well enough to realize you don't rush to see people just because they get tough on the phone."

"True. But Bowden's toughness had something behind it; something that interested me."

"Oh, yeah? Such as what?"

"A mention of the Monarch Art Gallery," Jim said.

BY THIS TIME Trotter had turned over the four canvas stretchers to one of his fingerprint experts, who now approached and reported a complete absence of prints. The lieutenant brushed this information aside; stared at Anthony. "What about the Monarch Art Gallery?"

"Well, some time back I was contacted by a man named Leo Gerard. You may not be familiar with Gerard's history, but several years ago he was one of New York's leading art dealers."

"Okay. Go on."

Anthony continued unhurriedly. "Gerard told me that a number of priceless art pieces—statues, paintings, and so forth—had been saved from the Nazis in Holland, Belgium, and France. These art objects were smuggled to London by members of the underground movements in those countries, with the idea of shipping them to America for sale—the proceeds of such sales to be devoted to the fight against the Axis tyranny."

"That makes sense. What did this Gerard contact you for?"

"He wanted me, as well as two or three other men, to advance the funds for shipping costs and the renting of a gallery for display purposes. The corporation was to be a non-profit affair. Gerard donated his time and services, while we of the board of directors put up the financing. All money realized from sales to American art collectors would go directly into the war effort."

"You took a flyer at it, eh?"

The sun-bronzed millionaire nodded. "I'm chairman of the Monarch Gallery, yes."

"And this murdered man, this J. Devereaux Bowden; you say he mentioned the Monarch Gallery to you over the phone?"

"That's right. He said he had bought a picture there recently. He told me he had talked to a certain Professor Whelstrom about that painting. And he demanded to see me immediately for a showdown— whatever he meant by that. He grumbled something about monkey business going on, then he hung up on me."

Trotter lifted a lip. "A wild story if I ever heard one! A man calls you up about a picture, you rush over, find him bumped off and the picture missing. Do you expect me to believe that?"

"It's your privilege to doubt me. I've told you the truth; all of it. I can add nothing more at present."

"Yah. At present. There you go again, practically tossing a challenge in my face," Trotter snarled.

Jim saw no reason to deny this. "In a way, the matter is personal with me. First, because Bowden phoned me shortly before he was killed. And second, because of my association with the Monarch Gallery. If there's a connection between the gallery and Bowden's murder, I intend to find it."

"Suppose I tell you to keep out of police business?"

"I'm afraid I'd ignore the order, lieutenant."

"Suppose I decide to toss you in the cooler as a material witness?"

Anthony's eyes sharpened and so did his voice. "I don't think you'll do that. My attorneys would have me out again in less than an hour."

For a long instant they stared at each other, the burly headquarters detective and the tall, lithe, amateur investigator. It was Trotter whose glance was first to drop. "Okay," he growled in a tone that sounded almost defensive.

LATER, IN THE big convertible, Gentry chuckled as he and Jim headed across town. "You sure made that flat-foot haul in his horns, pappy. It did me good to see him put in his place."

"Don't fool yourself," Anthony tooled the sleek machine around a corner. "Nobody puts Trotter in his place. He's like a termite. Stop him one way and he bores in another direction."

"I'll say," Tom agreed heartily. "He's the biggest bore I've ever met. Hey, step on it. We can just make the theater if we hurry."

"No theater, Tom. We're going to visit the Monarch Gallery and try to find out what was troubling Mr. J. Devereaux Bowden before he died."

CHAPTER III

REFUGEE GALLERY

THE BUILDING WAS OLD, stately, imposing. Once it had housed a bank, which had failed during the depression. With all the tellers' cages removed and its high-ceilinged marble interior decorated by twin rows of lofty supporting columns, it now made the perfect setting for an exhibition of paintings and sculpture imported from Europe. Leo Gerard, manager of the enterprise, had displayed shrewd acumen in selecting this as headquarters for a permanent art gallery.

When Anthony parked before the massive structure, he observed lights still burning within the show-room, partially masked from the street by dimout drapes. Then, as he and his genial aviator friend emerged from the car, the first drops of rain came pelting down out of storm-pregnant clouds.

"Cripes!" Tom yelped. "Looks like a wet night ahead. I'm glad we don't have to go chasing all around the country in weather like this!"

"Don't be too sure. The evening's young yet," Anthony answered, shoving his weight against the entrance door and stepping into the main exhibit room.

From the high roof, artificial daylight sifted downward, bathing the interior with brilliance. A balcony once used by bank officials ranged around three sides of the rectangular place, supported by the marble columns; and under this balcony small show-rooms had been divided by means of temporary partitions in order to segregate the collected art treasures according to origin and nationality.

There were perhaps seven or eight connoisseurs and prospective customers in the place, viewing the various collections. "Business must be good," Gentry muttered. "Imagine keeping a joint like this open past nine at night!"

Jim Anthony said nothing, for he was gripped by a feeling of impending peril; a premonition of utter evil. There was something malign in this place, something threatening; his sixth sense warned him of it in terms so harsh that he almost felt the hairs prickling at the nape of his neck. He tried to shake off the sensation, but it persisted even when an obsequious little stout man came forward to greet him.

"Well, well, Mr. Anthony! This is a pleasure, sir, seeing you here!"

Jim accepted the man's handclasp, which was surprisingly firm in contrast to his mild bookkeeperish manner. His name was Harrison Hunt, and he had been Leo Gerard's personal secretary for a number of years—a sort of glorified stenographer in pants, Tom Gentry had once called him.

Not that Tom's jesting description was malicious. He merely based it on the fact that Hunt was the sort of person who could dress well, wear pince-nez glasses on a long black ribbon, and go around thumping on a bass drum, yet still attract absolutely no attention in a crowd. New York is full of his kind; he represented the submerged white collar class—the backbone of the nation but just as unobtrusive. Again quoting Gentry, the backbone carries the load but the face gets all the gravy; and Harrison Hunt's face was one you could look at a dozen times without remembering a single feature five minutes afterward.

Anthony smiled gravely. "I'd like to talk to Mr. Gerard if he's here."

"Oh, yes, sir, he's here. At the moment, though, he's engaged with a couple from Brookline, Massachusetts, who can't decide between a Van Gogh and an alleged Reynolds. He should be finished with them presently, I'm sure."

"I'll wait," the millionaire said. "How are things going?"

"Quite well," Hunt rubbed his hands in the manner of a certified public accountant who is pleasantly amazed to find his ledgers in perfect balance. "Better than we had any right to expect, considering our high prices. Oh, there comes Mr. Gerard's customers now. That means he's free."

Nodding thanks, Anthony steered Gentry to the balcony staircase and they ascended, knocked on a door, entered a small but tastefully furnished private office.

THE MAN WHO arose to greet them was tall, thin, pompous. His iron grey hair was chopped short in the fashion of a Prussian army officer; but this resemblance ceased with the haircut, for his upper lip was decorated by a flowing mustache merging at the corners of his thin mouth with an imperial which came down to a goatee's point under his prominent chin, giving him almost a Satanic look.

"My friend!" Leo Gerard exclaimed, coming forward to seize Anthony by both hands. "How glad I am to have you call on me! Come in, come in. We shall talk, and you will put the taste of those imbecile customers out of my mouth! The fools—what do they know about art? Undecided between a Reynolds and a Van Gogh. Bah! That is like trying to choose between mushrooms and limousines; there's no point of similarity! They buy pictures as one would buy chairs or tables, merely to cover a blank space on the wall. I wonder that some of the masters do not rise from the tomb to place a curse upon our heads for selling their work to idiots!"

To Tom Gentry there was something phony about the man; something hammily theatrical. Even his voice seemed studiously oratorical, like an

The strangler had already done his job, they saw.

old time elocution teacher—or a pompous politician making a stump speech for reelection. Even his talk about curses from the grave struck Tom as a lot of appleseeds.

But Jim Anthony took a different view. "A curse? Perhaps that's the answer. Perhaps the old masters really *have* put an evil destiny on their paintings."

The tall art dealer widened his eyes as if suspicious of being kidded. "Meaning what, sir?"

"A man named J. Devereaux Bowden has just died—violently," Anthony said. Then, tersely, he told Gerard what had happened. As he spoke, he watched the art dealer's reactions.

Gerard, surprisingly enough, displayed little emotion aside from nervously fingering his pointed beard. "Strange," he muttered. "Almost too strange for coincidence. Two other customers of Monarch Gallery have met the same fate in the past month."

"What?" Tom Gentry exclaimed.

The bearded man opened a desk drawer, removed two index cards and handed them to Anthony. Glancing at them, the millionaire saw that neither of the names meant anything to him; nor did the addresses, one in Philadelphia, the other in Baltimore.

"These two men were murdered?"

The art dealer inclined his head. "Yes, according to the news reports. Each had purchased a painting from us. And in both cases, those paintings were stolen."

TOM GENTRY WHISTLED inaudibly and felt a shiver coursing down his spine; but Anthony remained completely calm, his sun-bronzed features as expressionless as an Indian mask. His voice, too, was without inflection as he said: "Mr. Gerard, do you know a Professor Whelstrom?"

"Wh-why, yes."

"Is he that same Whelstrom who used to be curator of art for the Manhattan Museum?"

"The same." Some of the bearded man's composure returned. "Why do you ask?"

"He called on Bowden this afternoon, a few hours before the murder. Can you tell me anything about that visit?"

"A little. Whelstrom retired some years ago to his country place; but he lost his savings since then and has been supporting himself and his daughter by appraising private collections. I was instrumental in getting him several such assignments; in fact, I sent him to Bowden."

"Would you consider Whelstrom trustworthy?"

"Scrupulously so," the dealer flushed. "Otherwise I wouldn't have recommended him to our patrons."

"Did you recommend him to either of the customers who were killed? The ones in Baltimore and Philadelphia?"

Gerard started violently. "Why, I… my God, I never gave it a thought!" He thumbed hastily through a memo book. "Good heavens, I sent Whelstrom to both those poor devils! But surely you don't suspect—?"

"Cripes, it's past the suspicion stage!" Tom Gentry cut into the conversation. "If you ask me, buying a picture from this joint ain't the healthiest thing in the world. Three customers croaked, and you sicced this professor bozo onto each one of them."

"Incredible!" the gallery manager whispered. "It must be a coincidence. After all, I've sent Whelstrom to other clients who are still unharmed. He *can't* be involved in those robberies and murders!"

Gentry made a disparaging noise with his lips. "Maybe you got a better theory?"

"As a matter of fact, I have."

"A curse, for instance?" the freckled aviator was heavily sarcastic. "The curse of the old masters?"

Gerard reddened again. "No. Nothing as supernatural as that. I'd be more inclined to suspect Nazi agents. Remember, all these art treasures came from conquered lands now overrun by Hitler. I needn't remind you that the money from each sale goes to the war effort against the Axis."

"So what?" Tom demanded.

"So perhaps espionage agents are stealing the paintings for secret shipment back to Berlin, and murdering the purchasers in order to frighten future buyers away. Why, if these killings continue, it won't be long until we have to close our doors. No collector will buy from us for fear he would be signing his own death warrant!"

Anthony frowned. "It sounds plausible," he said. "And it will bear investigating. Are you willing to co-operate with me, Mr. Gerard?"

"In every way possible," the art dealer spread his hands. "I am at your command."

"Good. I want a dossier on every person who has bought paintings from the Monarch Gallery since it opened. And I want the address of Professor Whelstrom."

Gerard seemed painfully eager to comply. He pressed a button on his desk, and his rotund little secretary popped in. Curt orders sent Harrison Hunt scurrying, to return presently with a typed list. "A complete record, sir."

Thanking the obsequious secretary and shaking hands with Leo Gerard, the millionaire criminologist took his departure with the list in his pocket and Tom Gentry at his heels. Outdoors, the premonitory sprinkle of raindrops had by now turned to a deluge; the dimmed-out streets were canyons of darkness whipped by the storm's growing fury.

Snugly in the convertible, Tom shivered. "What a night! We're going home now, aren't we, I hope?"

His wealthy friend nodded, heading toward the Waldorf-Anthony. "Yes. But not to stay. I want to send a couple of wires; then we're going for a drive in the country."

"Country? In weather like this? Gosh, pappy, we ain't got web feet!"

"Web feet or no web feet," Anthony answered grimly, "I intend to have a talk with Professor Whelstrom!"

CHAPTER IV

SINISTER HOUSE

IT WAS MIDNIGHT WHEN the convertible's headlights broomed a tunnel of brilliance along the side road leading to the Whelstrom residence a few miles off the Hudson River highway. Jim Anthony had spent thirty minutes at his hotel, despatching telegrams to Baltimore and Philadelphia; then this trip up-country had consumed another hour and a half—all of it in a torrential downpour too heavy for the big car's windshield wipers to cope with. Now, as the hands of the clock on the instrument panel pointed to twelve sharp, the criminologist and his companion had finally gained their destination.

Rain-burdened banks of untrimmed lilacs bordered the driveway leading to the house, their dripping leaves making eerie whispers as the automobile brushed them. To Anthony's sixth sense it seemed almost as if the whispers were warning him to turn back; to run from this region of storm-swept darkness while there was still time. Jeopardy lay ahead like a silent, invisible presence; and even Tom Gentry seemed to feel an unseen menace.

"Br-r-r-r!" he shuddered. "I'm getting the drizzling creeps, pappy. This don't look like a place where anybody'd live—unless he was a werewolf or something. Are you sure that Gerard ginzo gave you the right directions?"

"I hope he did. At least we know the house must be occupied. It's been raining so hard you can't see any wheel tracks on the drive; but there are no weeds growing in it, which proves it's in use."

"We *would* pick tonight to come out here. Me, I'm ready to drift back to town any time you are."

Anthony didn't answer, for his attention was suddenly riveted upon the building which loomed abruptly before him; an old house almost entirely obscured by a grove of wind-lashed maples. As a residence it was enormous, following no particular architectural pattern, but rambling as if its several wings had been added indiscriminately from time to time at the whim of successive generations of owners.

Tom squinted through the storm. "Darker than the inside of a brunette blackbird!" he commented. "Either everybody's gone to bed or nobody's home."

But Anthony's sharper vision had detected a faint glow at an upper window; a weird flicker which vanished even as he saw it. He parked at the driveway's nearest point to the house and sat for a moment, silently studying it.

The original portion, evidently dating back to the days of New York State's first Dutch settlers, was a square box of field stone that looked more like a fort than a dwelling. To this had been added the later rambling wings, until there must have been more than twenty rooms upstairs and down. The exterior was in shabby repair.

Over the constant beat of rain drumming on the convertible's soft top, the wealthy investigator finally raised his voice. "I guess we may as well make a dash for it, Tom. Come on." He opened his door; loped forward with Gentry following.

That was when the gunshot sounded.

THE FLASH ITSELF was fortuitously covered by a simultaneous flicker of lightning and the report drowned by a volleying thunder-clap from low-hanging clouds. Anthony might not have realized a shot had been fired, except that Gentry grunted a sharp, sudden oath

He rolled back the boulder. They were deep in the maple grove.

and stumbled a little. Then the aviator recovered his stride; slapped at his left arm.

"What's the matter, Tom?"

"Damn bee stung me. What are bees doing out in the rain, though?" Gentry brought his hand away from the hurt place and tried to stare at his fingers in the darkness.

Jim Anthony's abnormally acute night-vision revealed a fact which Tom's own sight had not detected. The freckled flyer's fingers were streaked with red, which rapidly dissolved under the pelting rain. "Tom, you idiot, that was no bee! *It was a bullet!*" And the millionaire criminologist plunged at his friend, shoved him staggering in a zigzag course. "You've been shot!"

As Jim spoke, a second slug whined from nowhere; thwacked against the bole of a maple. Gentry yelped, ducked. "Take cover, pappy, we're being used for clay pigeons!"

Both men scuttled behind trees. Anthony's own shoulder-holstered automatic leaped into his fist as he peered through the storm, hoping for a third flame-flash at which he could fire. None came. He called: "Tom. Where are you? How badly were you hit?"

"Over here," Gentry's voice sounded disgusted. "Just a nick. I've been scratched worse by pins in a laundered shirt. But you ought to see the hole in my coat sleeve. It's a dilly."

"Get your gun out."

"What's in my fist ain't a stick of chewing gum," Tom clipped back grimly. "Let's get that dirty jerk, whoever he is. You take the right. I'll sneak around to the left. Okay?"

"Okay." Anthony was already on the move, as noiselessly as one of his Comanche ancestors stalking game in the wilderness. In spite of his silent skill, though, he spotted no sign of motion; nothing to shoot at.

Presently his preternatural vision discerned Gentry approaching. "Find anybody, Tom?"

"Nary a trace."

"Then we'll try the house." Together they climbed the sagging porch steps; and then, from within, there sounded a bellowing explosion like the blast of a cannon.

Gentry's drenched figure twitched. "What was that?"

"More gunfire. Sounded like an old fashioned Colt .45 using a black powder cartridge instead of modern smokeless cordite." The criminologist rushed at the door, pounded on it.

Hollow echoes reverberated inside. These were followed by hesitant footfalls; the sound of a bolt being slowly drawn. Then the heavy portal creaked open on complaining hinges; exposed a wide, cheerless hallway.

A woman stood at the threshold with a flickering candle in her left hand—and a smoking revolver in her right.

CANDLE GLOW PUT dull glints in the woman's coal black hair; reflected weirdly in her dark, large eyes. She was tall and thin, but by no means angular. Her complexion was clear, translucent, almost waxen in its lack of color—a pallor that matched the whiteness of her white satin hostess coat, relieved startlingly by the vivid crimson of her lips.

The heavy gun was steady in her grasp, and when she spoke it was in a deeply pitched voice of contralto timbre, vibrant and somehow weird because of its hollowness. "Who are you? What do you want at such an hour?" She raised the pistol slightly. "Let me warn you that my revolver is in perfect working order. I just tested it by firing into the hearth."

Anthony wondered about that. Maybe she was telling the truth in order to impress him that she was capable of defending herself; but on the other hand, it might be her way of explaining the fact that the weapon had been discharged—a cover-up to alibi her own firing of two slugs at the millionaire criminologist and his companion.

If she really was the one who had triggered those bushwhack bullets, though, she must have done it from a window of the house. Certainly she had not been outdoors, for her slippered feet were dry and there was no trace of rain upon her hair.

"You don't need that gun," Anthony said slowly. "We aren't your enemies."

"That remains to be seen." Then she repeated: "Who are you? What do you want?"

"I'm James Anthony, and I'm looking for Professor Whelstrom."

"My father is not at home."

Gentry fidgeted.

Anthony spoke again to the brunette girl. "So you're Whelstrom's daughter. Do you expect him soon?" He added: "I'm chairman of the board of directors for the Monarch Gallery, and Mr. Gerard, the gallery manager, sent me here."

"I've heard of you." For the barest instant there was a hint of expression in her eyes; then they regained their hostile blankness. "I'm not certain my father will come home tonight. He dislikes storms."

"Would you permit us to come in and wait a while—at least until we can dry our clothes a little and attend to my friend's wound?"

Kathi Whelstrom tensed. "Wound?"

"We were shot at as we approached your house."

She seemed suddenly to realize she still held her revolver on her visitors; and, choking back a tiny cry, she lowered the weapon. "Shot at! But—but then you may th-think I—oh-h-, no! Surely you won't suspect me of—?"

"May we come in?" Anthony reiterated his request.

"Of course. Please do." She backed into the hall, stood aside for Jim and Gentry to enter. They crossed the threshold and closed the door after them; followed the professor's daughter into a big, book-lined room whose floor was three steps below the level of the hallway.

HERE IN THIS sunken library the girl lighted two more candles in hurricane lamps. Shadows danced like ghosts across the rows of book-shelves. "The electricity is off. The storm, I suppose. And the phone isn't working. That's why I haven't heard from my father, I'm positive. He usually lets me know when he won't be home from the city. I get frightened when I'm alone here all night. The house is very old. Some claim it's haunted. At one time there was a stockade to keep out the Indians. Father bought the place when he retired from the museum. It had been in the same family for generations before that. But I'm boring you. You're wet. Let me light the fireplace. May I get you a little sherry? I'm afraid I have nothing else to offer. Oh, yes, and your friend's wound—"

The words had come from her lips in a steady torrent, a freshet of conversation that mirrored her inner tautness as she touched a match to kindling on the big hearth. Then she seemed to run out of breath, like a mechanical doll whose spring has unwound.

Tom Gentry made an embarrassed gesture. "Don't bother about me, sister. I ain't hurt." He rolled up his coat sleeve, displayed a shallow nick on his arm, not much more than a burn. It had already stopped bleeding.

"I'll bring some iodine with the sherry," the girl said. With a candle to guide her, she drifted from the room; her slippered feet made no sound as she moved, and her departure had a ghostlike quality which Gentry didn't like at all.

"Gosh, pappy," he whispered. "What kind of setup is this? That cupcake makes my blood run cold. Reminds me of vampire stories I used to read in the horror magazines."

"This is no vampire story, Tom. It's something a lot more genuine—and ugly. Sh-h-h, she's coming back."

Whelstrom's daughter reappeared with glasses, a decanter of sherry, a roll of sterilized bandage, and an iodine bottle. Deftly she dressed Tom's arm, then poured two generous drinks of wine for her callers.

Anthony sipped appreciatively. "Your father is an expert on sherry as well as art, apparently. I met him years ago, while he was still with the Manhattan Museum. I was surprised to discover that he's still active."

"Beggars can't be choosers," she made a bitter mouth. "He's active because we need the small fees he makes by appraising private collections. Otherwise we'd starve."

"Does he get many such assignments?"

"Recently, yes, thanks to your Mr. Gerard of the Monarch Gallery. Gerard gave him the job that took him to New York today. A couple of weeks ago it was Baltimore, and last week Philadelphia. He's too old to make so many trips, though. I wish it weren't so… so necessary."

"Did he tell you anything about the paintings he examined in those two cities?" Anthony probed casually.

"No, he never discusses his work with me. Years ago he tried to make me into an artist but I failed miserably. He swallowed his disappointment well enough; but he doesn't discuss pictures with me any more." She sighed. "In fact, these last few weeks he doesn't discuss anything. I think he's not well; or else there's something preying on his mind."

Gentry cast a significant glance at Anthony. "Yeah, I'll bet he's uneasy. So would I be, in his shoes."

"What do you mean by that?" she confronted the aviator. Then, receiving no reply, she turned to Anthony. "Why have you come to see my father? What do you want to talk to him about?"

"A couple of paintings he appraised."

Her dark eyes grew unreadable. "Are they so very important, to bring you out on a night like this?"

Before Jim could answer, there came a sudden brief yelp from Tom Gentry; a gasped outcry that stretched itself into a prolonged howl receding in the distance.

Anthony pivoted, stared. His freckled friend was nowhere in sight; had vanished like a rabbit in a magician's hat.

CHAPTER V

FIND THE EXPERT

BY THE RIGHT OF the big Dutch Colonial fireplace, where Gentry had been standing an instant ago, there was now a yawning and cavernous aperture instead of bookshelves. From this opening came a dank gush of fetid air, bearing on its breath a series of muffled thumps and fervent curses. Then the thumps ceased—but the curses continued.

Jim Anthony whipped out his automatic and plunged toward the black orifice. "What in hell's name is this?"

"It—it's another secret passage," Kathi Whelstrom tottered forward. "One I didn't know w-was there!"

"Secret passage?"

"The place is full of them. One leads to the ruins of an old block-house which used to be p-part of the stockade. Another is a tunnel to an abandoned well. Most of these early Dutch dwellings had them in c-case of Indian attack. But your f-friend—"

Anthony had already gained the forbidding aperture. From his pocket he now drew a miniature flashlight of his own invention and design, small as a fountain pen but almost as powerful as an automobile headlamp. He triggered its blue-white brilliance into the opening; perceived irregular stone steps leading steeply downward.

"Tom!" he thundered. "Answer me! Are you all right?"

Up rasped Gentry's response. "Wait until I count my arms and legs and teeth. Yeah; no pieces missing. Boy, did I bounce! I hit every step on the way down."

The wealthy detective descended; came presently to a subterranean passageway paved with flat stones. Here the glow of his torch revealed a very bedraggled, very shaken Tom Gentry who demanded to know what had happened. "One minute I'm standing by the hearth, leaning against the mantel. The next minute something opens up and swallows me like an oyster. Cripes, I should have worn a parachute!"

"Never mind that. Let's get out of here."

"What? And not explore the dungeons for skeletons and buried treasure and stuff?" Tom essayed a wry attempt at humor.

As it happened, though, his jest turned out to be well founded; for as Anthony nudged him firmly toward the stone steps, the flashlight's ray accidentally glared on something propped in one corner. "Pappy, look—a picture!"

Jim's hawk-like eyes narrowed to glittering slits. The framed painting was thick with dust that almost wholly obscured the portraiture proper—a likeness of a man stiffly posed, clad in the costume of the early Dutch settlers."

"Ain't that an old master?" Gentry whispered.

"It's old enough," the millionaire admitted. "Looks like a Dummer."

"Yeah, I'll say. Dumber than hell, from the expression on his kisser." Tom picked it up.

"I meant a Jeremiah Dummer. He was a Colonial portrait artist. Come on. Easy on these steps, boy. You're still shaky."

Gentry denied this. "I'm okay. At least I'm not too shaky to savvy the score. You take Professor Whelstrom, an art expert that goes broke. Being broke gives him funny ideas. So he goes around valuing private collections—and picking the pictures he wants. In other words, while he's exporting these paintings, he's also casing the houses. Afterward he sneaks back and gloms the things. Three times he gets caught and has to croak somebody."

"Possibly," Anthony said.

"Sure. And with these hidden passages in his house he could hide half the old masters in the United States. We just found one, didn't we? So he's got connections with collectors who wouldn't ask too many questions if they got a chance to buy some paintings cheap. Or for that matter, maybe he's acting as a Nazi agent; being paid by Hitler to pull these robberies."

"You subscribe to Leo Gerard's theory, then?"

Tom shrugged. "What's the difference? No matter what his motive is, Professor Whelstrom's the guilty guy. I'll bet he's right here in the joint now, laughing at us while his creepy daughter gives us a stall. Maybe it was him that fired those shots at us and nicked my arm— *Hey, what the—?*"

The sudden exclamation burst from Gentry's lips as he gained the top of the secret staircase. Then he pointed.

There was nothing but a blank wall dead ahead. The concealed entrance door had swung shut. They were locked in.

FAINTLY FROM THE library, Kathi Whelstrom's throaty voice sounded through thick masonry. "Mr. Anthony—the panel closed as I tried to see how the counterbalancing mechanism worked! Now I c-can't get it open again!"

Gentry made bitter noises. "She's a liar. I didn't trust her from the first. She wants to hold us here until her old man can scram!"

"Easy, Tom. Try to remember what spot you leaned against when the panel opened."

As if by magic the gun left her
hand and Anthony had it.

The aviator scowled in concentration. "The book-shelf. I had my hand on a hunk of scrollwork but I don't know if that had anything to do with it."

"Miss Whelstrom!" Anthony shouted. Then he repeated Tom's information to her. "Press against the bookcase and touch all the scrollwork you can find."

"I—I'm doing that. Nothing happens, though."

"She's stalling," Gentry growled. "One side, pappy. I'll kick the thing open."

"No. Sh-h-h. I have a better plan." Silently the criminologist pulled his friend back down the stone stairs. Then, guided by the bright electric torch, they scuttled along the subterranean tunnel. Gradually it slanted upward, until, a few hundred yards farther, it gave access to three rubble-littered flagstones set into raw earth, one above the other, like crude steps. Above these a large boulder loomed.

Anthony braced his shoulder to the granite barrier; shoved mightily. It budged, came dislodged, rolled outward. Gusts of rain slammed at his bronzed features. "The exit, Tom! Deep in the Maple grove. Come on, out with you!"

The two men emerged into the pelting storm, waited only long enough for Jim to replace the boulder. Then they catapulted toward the Whelstrom house with a brief pause at Anthony's convertible where they stowed the ancient portrait they'd found in the hidden passage. This done, they made for the dwelling's sagging porch; pounded on the heavy front door.

It opened. Kathi Whelstrom stared at them, her eyes shocked, her cheeks ashen. "You—how d-did you—?"

"We found a way out," Anthony dismissed the matter casually. "And now, since your father isn't here and apparently won't be coming home tonight, I think we'll leave for the city."

She shivered under the white satin hostess coat. "I—I was afraid you might be imprisoned in that horrible tunnel until—oh-h-h, I don't know what I *did* think! You might have suffocated, or—or—"

The millionaire studied her, wondering if her concern had been genuine or a clever bit of acting. One thing was certain: if she had deliberately closed that secret door, her father was no longer in the house. If he'd been there to begin with, he'd used this opportunity to get away. On the other hand, Kathi might be telling the truth....

"Is there any special place where the professor stays when he remains in town overnight, Miss Whelstrom?"

She nodded; mentioned without hesitation the name of a theatrical hotel off Times Square. "But—but must you leave now? In this storm? Can't y-you stay until—?"

"Sorry, my dear. We have work to do. Good night, and thanks for your hospitality." With which enigmatic remark, Anthony took Gentry by the arm and led him off the porch.

IN TURNING HIS convertible back toward the driveway, Jim contrived to sweep a path of light through the darkness with his headlamps; a swath which momentarily illumined the surrounding grounds as well as a barnlike building behind the residence proper. Later, en route to the main highway, his speculative thoughts were broken by a remark from Tom.

"You know what, pappy? I bet she heard her old man coming home, was why she locked us up. She wanted to give him a chance to slip indoors without us spotting him."

"I thought of that. So I covered the barn garage with a sweep of our headlights. The doors were open. No car inside. And Whelstrom wouldn't have arrived on foot; not all the way from the nearest rail-road station or bus stop. A man of his age wouldn't hike seven miles in this rain."

"Then he was already in the house and scrammed while we were in the tunnel. It was no accident that we got locked in. Did you ever see such a dame?"

"Rather attractive," Jim assented.

"Attractive?" the word was an explosion on Gentry's lips. "A ghoul like her that looks like she'd stepped out of a tomb?"

The criminologist chuckled. "It's a miracle, no less. At last you've met a girl without falling for her. Now I've seen everything!"

IT WAS NEARLY three in the morning when they parked the convert-ible and entered the shabby midtown hotel where Kathi Whelstrom said her father always stopped. A drowsy desk clerk saw them approaching. He reached for his register.

Anthony shook his head. "No, thanks. We're not looking for accom-modations. Have you a Professor Whelstrom staying here?"

"Well, he's registered. He isn't in, though."

"You're sure?"

"Positive. He checked in around five-thirty this evening, just after I came on duty. He went upstairs, then came back down again and made a call from the desk phone here. Got an appointment with somebody and went out. I haven't seen him since."

The millionaire fished a twenty dollar bill from his wallet. "Could you let me see his room, just to make positive?"

Twenty dollars was big money to the clerk. He grabbed at it with the alacrity of a trout striking bait. "Yes, *sir!*" Two minutes later he conducted Anthony and Gentry to a door on the second floor, opened it, made a light, stepped aside.

The room was commonplace, the carpet threadbare, the chair and bed and writing desk sturdy but inexpensive. The bed itself was unmussed, the covers not even turned down; and a battered Gladstone bag lay open on the counterpane, displaying well mended sox, shirt, underwear, and pajamas. All were neatly folded as if in readiness for use—but they had not been used.

Whelstrom's name was tooled into the leather bag; mute testimony that this indeed had been the chamber he'd intended to occupy. Yet he'd gone out—and had not returned to it.

"Blind trail, pappy," Tom Gentry whispered. "We've thrown snake-eyes again. Looks like the professor is just the little guy that wasn't there. Quicksilver Whelstrom, the man you can't put your thumb on!"

Anthony pulled another twenty from his billfold; turned to the clerk. "You say he made a phone call before he left?"

"Yes, sir." Avid eyes licked the money.

"I don't suppose you could remember anything about that call? An overheard remark, a chance name, anything?"

"Come to think of it, yes, sir. He dialed a number, then asked for somebody named Gerard. My own name sounds something like that. Sherrard. Naturally when I heard Professor Whelstrom speak it, I sort of listened a little."

"And?"

"He seemed almost angry. He mentioned this Gerard deliberately avoiding him the past couple of weeks when he'd tried to see him. Whatever the answer was, it seemed to soothe the professor. So then he said something about going right over for a talk."

"Going over where?"

"That I couldn't tell you, sir." The twenty changed hands. "Thank you, sir. Thank you very much indeed!"

OUTSIDE IN THE car, Tom Gentry lighted two cigarettes, passed one to Anthony. "Well, Jim, there it is. Whelstrom and Leo Gerard are in cahoots, by golly."

"How do you make that out?"

"Like adding two and two. The bearded guy manages the gallery. So he knows everything about when a painting is sold. He recommends Whelstrom to the buyer. Whelstrom cases the customer's house, pretending to be an expert appraiser. Boom! After a while they pull a heist—with homicide trimmings if necessary."

"But what about the phone call Whelstrom made from his hotel?" Anthony argued. "That indicated Gerard had been avoiding him."

Tom brushed this off with a wave of his cigarette. "An act, pappy. Just a cover-up in case anybody was listening in. One crook pretending to duck another one so they'd both look honest."

"Pretty thin," the criminologist commented. "I'm afraid it goes deeper than that."

"Nuts," Gentry sulked. "I'll bet you my flying license Mr. Leo Gerard could tell you right now where the professor is holed up." He flipped ashes. "Me, I don't like that bearded bozo's looks. He's a phony."

"He knows his art."

"Yeah, and so does Whelstrom. And you said it was an expert job of swiping that Titian out of its frame in the room where Bowden got bumped." The aviator spread his hands. "So Gerard and Whelstrom are experts. So I say they're both guilty."

Anthony lapsed into silence, which remained unbroken until he and Tom were back in their penthouse atop the Waldorf-Anthony. Here a sheaf of telegrams awaited the investigator; wires in response to those he had despatched to Baltimore and Philadelphia a few hours ago.

The replies came from confidential sources in those two cities; men who worked on his daily newspapers there, or in his industrial plants. He finished reading the messages; looked moodily at Gentry.

"We're getting closer to the curse on those old masters, Tom. The two previous robberies and murders seem to have been committed by the same person or persons who killed Bowden."

"How do you know?"

"The paintings were removed from their stretchers, just like Bowden's Titian. And the owners were garrotted by loops of thin wire."

CHAPTER VI

PICTURE OF DEATH

ONLY A FEW HOURS' sleep refreshed Tom Gentry immeasurably, although he might have rested longer except for a long distance telephone call which awakened him around ten in the morning. He was having a solitary breakfast in the penthouse when Jim Anthony stepped from the private elevator and joined him.

"Spare a cup of coffee, Tom?"

The aviator poured it. "Blamed if I see how you can look so chipper without any rest," he complained. "Here I had to hit the hay or drop in my tracks. But all you did was change clothes and go out again at three-thirty in the morning after driving around all night in the rain!"

"You rested well, I hope?" Jim's teeth flashed in a smile.

"Yeah. That's more than you can say. Where have you been, pappy?"

"Doing a bit of high class burglary."

"You—*hunh?*"

The millionaire nodded. "I decided to play your hunch."

"What hunch?"

"Concerning Leo Gerard being in criminal association with Professor Whelstrom. If that were true, I thought perhaps Whelstrom might be hiding in Gerard's house."

Tom choked on a crumb of toast. "You busted into the guy's wigwam?"

"Among other places, yes. I fine-combed it without waking a soul. And Whelstrom wasn't there."

"Gerard doesn't know you called on him?"

"No. He snored the whole time. So today, we'll pay him an official visit at the Monarch Gallery." Anthony blended a pony of brandy with his coffee and sipped with relish. "We'll talk to him this afternoon."

"Why not this morning? Why not right now?"

The criminologist leaned back. "At the moment Mr. Gerard has his hands pretty full. The police are grilling him."

"So that's one of the things you found out on your little expedition, eh?"

"Yes. Lieutenant Trotter finally got around to covering some of the ground you and I covered last night. I prefer not to interrupt a policeman at his work."

"Especially *that* policeman," Gentry said sagely. "He seems to be following a lot of your moves, pappy. He contacted Whelstrom's spooky daughter this morning."

Jim narrowed his eyes. "How do you know?"

"She phoned me long distance about an hour ago while you were still gone. Evidently her line has been fixed up since the storm. She said Trotter had called her, bright and early, to ask if her father was at home."

"Ah," Anthony murmured. "So the lieutenant is checking the Whelstrom angle."

"Looks that way. Anyhow, she told him no, her old gent wasn't on deck. But it worried her to think the cops were hunting for him. Right away she rang that hotel off Times Square; found out the professor was missing from his room."

"Then she phoned here?" Jim asked.

"That's right. She was in a tizzy. Demanded to know what we'd done with her father. And why were the bulls on daddy's tail?"

In response to Jim's deft fingers the vault swung open.

"What did you tell her, Tom?"

"Not a thing. I figure she was feeding me a lot of malarky. She knows where Whelstrom is, and she's just covering him up by pretending he's vanished."

Anthony finished his coffee royal. "Somehow I almost hope you're right, boy," he said in a grave voice. "But I'm afraid you're wrong." Then he pulled an envelope from his pocket, and from the envelope he spilled a few flakes of what resembled vari-colored paints. With these flakes there were some white strands of thread which might have been raveled from cloth. He placed the assortment on sheets of paper.

"What's that stuff?" the freckled aviator asked.

"Loot from two other burglaries I committed before dawn," an enigmatic expression was on Anthony's dark face. Then he strode into his private scientific laboratory; closed the door.

A LITTLE BEFORE two that afternoon, some judicious inquiries brought Jim Anthony the knowledge that the manager of the Monarch Gallery, Leo Gerard, had been released after a whole morning at headquarters. At two sharp, Anthony and Gentry parked in front of the gallery; entered the former bank building.

In the ante-room adjoining Gerard's personal office, Harrison Hunt sprang from his desk to greet them. The chubby little man had lost his bland-book-keeper manner of last night. In its stead was a nervousness that might have been ludicrous except for the fact that he was obviously in earnest. Having his employer and himself questioned by the homicide department was a new experience for him; one he didn't relish. He'd been polishing his pince-nez glasses, but now he allowed them to dangle from their broad black ribbon as he leaped to his feet.

"Good afternoon, Mr. Anthony. And Mr. Gentry. Thank g-goodness you've come! You have no idea what Mr. Gerard and I have endured in the past few hours. That Lieutenant Trotter person—" his voice broke.

The millionaire nodded. "Trotter can be hardboiled at times."

"Hardboiled is scarcely the word, sir."

Tom Gentry snorted. "You're lucky he didn't give you your lumps with a length of rubber hose, pal."

"Great heavens, does he do th-things like th-that?"

"So I've heard," Tom needled the man for the sheer joy of seeing him turn pale. Then Anthony put a stop to it by taking the aviator's arm and steering him toward the door of Leo Gerard's sanctum.

Gerard himself was pacing the rug as they entered. He pivoted, his ordinarily well-kept beard straggly. "Gentlemen! I wondered when I would see you!"

"I waited until I was sure Trotter was through with you," Anthony answered. "What line of questioning did he pursue?"

Gerard rumpled his bristly haircut. "Every line possible. He seems to have the idea there's a connection between Mr. Bowden's murder and the Monarch Gallery—all because the Titian which was stolen from Bowden's home had been purchased here."

"Did he mention Professor Whelstrom?"

"Yes. He claims Whelstrom has disappeared. And he acted as if I might know something about it. That's absurd! Why should I keep check of Whelstrom's movements?"

The criminologist dropped a casual bombshell. "I understand the professor phoned you here at the gallery yesterday evening around five-thirty from his hotel, then came over to see you. He hasn't been seen since."

"What? But—but he didn't visit me! I had no phone call from him!" The art dealer pressed the buzzer on his desk and Harrison Hunt popped into the room. "Was Professor Whelstrom here yesterday, Harry?"

"No, sir. Not to my knowledge."

"Did he phone me?"

"If he did, sir, I wasn't aware of it. Not while I was on duty. Of course I took my usual time off for supper."

LEO GERARD'S FACE went brick-red. "Are you hinting the professor came to see me when you were gone, Harry? Would you dare call me a liar?"

"Oh no, sir. I merely meant—"

"Get out!" the bearded man snapped. "Go back to your typewriter where you belong." He seemed furious to think his rotund secretary had refused to corroborate him, and Tom Gentry wondered if this could be the anger of a man gnawed by the pangs of guilt.

Anthony, however, displayed no outward indications of interest in Leo Gerard's burst of temper. Instead, the criminologist said: "I wonder if you'd mind conducting me on a little tour, Mr. Gerard? I'd like to inspect some of the paintings being offered on sale."

"Why, certainly. Come along." Gerard looked puzzled, though—because he knew the millionaire was already familiar with the gallery's art treasures. He appeared even more bewildered, downstairs, when Jim subjected several paintings to scrutiny under a pocket magnifying glass. "One would almost think you suspected these pictures of not being genuine, sir!"

"They're genuine enough," Anthony answered impassively. "I'm satisfied of that."

Tom Gentry pointed. "They must be, pappy, judging from the number of guards around the joint. I've spotted four or five guys in plainclothes already. If they ain't flatfeet, I'm crazy."

"Right, Tom, except that some are F.B.I agents. These paintings are old masters; priceless. Nearly all belong to governments-in-exile. If anything happened to them, it might mean international complications; so the Department of Justice helps guard them."

Just as Anthony finished speaking, Harrison Hunt came scurrying across the gallery with a burly uniformed policeman. "Mr. Gerard, sir," the chubby man panted, "this officer wants to see you. Lieutenant Trotter sent him."

The policeman confirmed this. "Yeah. If you're Gerard, you're to come with me." Then he eyed the criminologist. Recognition dawned. "Aren't you Jim Anthony?"

"I am."

"I heard Trotter put out a call for you, too. He sent over to your hotel for you. Maybe you'd better come along."

"Can you tell me what it's all about?"

The cop shrugged. "I'll leave that for Lieutenant Trotter if you don't mind." Then he led Leo Gerard, Harrison Hunt, Anthony, and Gentry out to a waiting police sedan; and presently they discovered themselves parked in front of an ornate apartment building on Riverside Drive. "End of line, folks," the officer announced. "Let's go in."

An elevator whisked them up to an expensive suite in one of the structure's spired towers. Here, at the main door of the costly apartment, Trotter was waiting.

Jaw thrust grimly forward, he beckoned with an arrogant hand. "Well, well," he commended the cop. "You got Anthony, too. That's fine. That makes the party complete. Step right inside, my friends. I want to show you something."

He conducted them through several rooms to a combined library and den. Here he halted, pointed.

A dead man lay sprawled on the Bokhara rug, his features hideously engorged, and a thin loop of wire noose-tight about his neck. Beyond, on an easel, there was a gilt picture frame.

It was empty.

CHAPTER VII

GUN GIRL

HARRISON HUNT'S COUNTENANCE TURNED a sickly grey as his popping eyes stared at the body. "Good heavens, th-that's Mr. Willis Ballard—the retired railroad magnate! The one who bought a Corot from us last month!"

"By God, you're right," Leo Gerard whispered harshly. He worried his goatee with trembling fingers. "Wh-what happened?"

Lieutenant Trotter stood with shoulders hunched. "He was murdered, that's what happened. Just a slight case of homicide, is all." The sarcasm was almost vicious.

"How long has he been dead?" Anthony asked quietly.

"Since from eight o'clock to ten last night is as near as my medical examiner can figure it. In other words, either just before or just after J. Devereaux Bowden was killed by the same kind of wire loop."

"Any other points of similarity?"

"The empty picture frame. The wooden stretchers on the floor. The tacks scattered where the painting was removed. Is that similar enough for you?"

Jim nodded. "The curse of the masters."

"Hunh? What was that you said?"

"Nothing. Skip it. By the way, when was the body found?"

"Within the past hour," Trotter growled. "Ballard lived alone except for a valet. It was the valet's night off last night and he didn't come back to the apartment until after lunch today. Soon as he saw his boss dead, he flashed headquarters."

"Any fingerprints? Clues?"

"Fingerprints, no. Clues, yeah. One clue." The lieutenant paused to make his next words more effective. "A guy visited J. Devereaux

Bowden. So last night both Bowden and Ballard were murdered. Now *I'll* ask a question—and I want a straight answer. *Where is Professor Whelstrom?*"

LEO GERARD EMITTED a strangled cry. "You mean Whelstrom called here at this apartment yesterday?"

"So the valet tells me," Trotter said grimly. "He stayed maybe thirty minutes, inspecting paintings. Then he left; and right away Ballard phoned the Monarch Gallery."

Harrison Hunt took a step forward. "Yes. I took his call."

All eyes turned to the chubby secretary. Trotter yowled: "Oh, you did, eh? And what did he want?"

"He asked for Mr. Gerard, who happened to be out to lunch. I inquired if he cared to leave a message."

"Well, did he leave one?"

The portly little man was politely dignified. "Had he left a message, sir, I would have given it to Mr. Gerard. No, there was no message; merely an inquiry as to whether or not we still were offering a certain Holbein for sale."

Tom Gentry, irrepressible even in a room where death had all too recently struck, burst out: "Holbein? Gosh, I didn't know an art gallery sold cows as well as pictures."

"Quiet, Tom," Anthony said. "Holbein was a famous painter in Europe. You're thinking of Holstein cattle."

"Oh. Excuse me, pappy."

Harrison Hunt looked more pained by the aviator's ignorance than by the interruption. "Anyhow, I told Mr. Ballard we still had the Holbein and he said he was considering buying it. He told me he would come in to take another look at it in a few days. That's all there was to the conversation."

"But it's not all there is to this murder case," Trotter bellowed furiously. He whirled on Jim Anthony. "You've been holding out on me!"

"In what way?" the criminologist raised an eyebrow.

"You were out to Whelstrom's house last night. You wired Baltimore and Philadelphia about two other kills that happened just the same way Ballard and Bowden were knocked off. Don't deny it. I've been checking on you."

The sun-bronzed millionaire's expression was wooden. "No denial, lieutenant. I told you in advance that I intended to investigate this mystery. I meant it."

"Yeah. And *I* meant it when I said for you to lay off. When I want a case all fouled up, I'll foul it up myself."

"You mean you don't want me around," Anthony smiled. He turned toward the door.

Trotter intercepted him. "Not so fast. First I want to know where to find Professor Whelstrom."

"Sorry. I'd tell you if I could."

"Meaning the great Jim Anthony didn't locate the guy? The super detective failed on a mission?" Trotter sneered.

Tom Gentry, truculent as a fighting cock, took up the cudgels in his friend's defense. "What's the matter with the police department, the missing persons bureau? Why don't you dumb flatfeet find Whelstrom if you want him so bad? What do you want Jim to do, hand you the professor on a platter while you sit with your finger on your nose?"

Then, while Trotter was still apoplectically inarticulate, Tom grabbed Anthony's arm. "Let's powder, pappy. Something stinks around here and it ain't the corpse. It's a guy with a lieutenant's badge."

They left; and Trotter didn't stop them.

BY THE TIME a taxi had carried Anthony and Gentry back to the Monarch Gallery where they'd left the convertible, it was late in the afternoon. It took another fifteen or twenty minutes to drive to the Waldorf-Anthony Hotel. Then they entered the famous hotel lobby; made for Jim's private automatic elevator which would lift them up to the penthouse.

A desk clerk came toward them as they were getting into the cage. "Beg pardon, Mr. Anthony. There's a lady upstairs, sir, waiting for you."

"A lady? Did she give her name?"

"No, sir. She said she had an appointment with you. Claimed you had told her to wait in the penthouse foyer. I permitted her to go up. Was that correct, sir?"

"Quite all right," Anthony assured him without change of expression. Then he closed the door of the elevator while Gentry thumbed the controls.

As the car silently ascended, Tom made injured gestures with his hands. "Shame on you, pappy. You've been holding out on me. Making dates with dames and not cutting me in on the secret!"

"Don't be absurd. I didn't make any dates."

"You mean you don't know who this chick is?"

"I haven't the slightest idea," Anthony answered. But when he stepped from the elevator at the penthouse level, he soon learned the identity of his visitor.

She was Kathi Whelstrom, and in her hand she held the same .45 Colt revolver she'd displayed the previous midnight in her up-country dwelling.

FOR AN INSTANT the criminologist didn't notice the gun, which was partially concealed by the purse in her other hand. Jim was too busy admiring her somber beauty; the eerie loveliness of her waxen face, the vivid scarlet of her lips, the glossy blackness of her hair enclosed in a white satin turban that seemed to complement her darkly glowing eyes.

Then, finally, he saw the weapon. "Well!" he remarked impassively and stopped in his tracks. With a swift look he commanded Gentry also to halt.

The girl's voice was frigid as a graveyard breeze. "What have you done to my father?"

"What have I done—?" Jim took a forward step.

"Stay where you are. No tricks. I was warned against them."

"And who warned you?" he asked.

"The police. Lieutenant Trotter said you were in this thing. Clear up to your neck, were the words he used. He told me if anything had happened to my father in connection with the Monarch Gallery, you would probably know more about it than anyone else."

Anthony was annoyed. "That sounds like Trotter."

"Are you hinting that the police would lie to me?" she demanded. "If so, save your breath. I know something's happened to dad. I've been to his hotel room. He wouldn't have gone away leaving his bag open unless he intended to return. Yet he didn't return."

The millionaire nodded. "I'm sure you're right, Miss Whelstrom. I have evidence to confirm it; something I found among his effects. Let me show you." He moved casually toward a desk beyond the girl, stepping sidewise as he passed her.

She turned, keeping him covered. Thanks to Anthony's stratagem, she now stood with her back to Tom Gentry. Before she could realize this, Anthony yelled: "Take her, Tom!"

Her head twisted around. For a second she stared toward Gentry—who was too startled to make any move in her direction. But while her attention was diverted, Jim plunged at her. As if by magic the gun was no longer in her fist. Anthony had it.

She rubbed her fingers. "A trick!" she stormed.

"Can you blame me? After all, when a lady pulls a pistol on me…" he shrugged.

"Then you didn't f-find anything in my father's hotel room! That was a lie!"

The criminologist admitted this. "Sorry. As a matter of fact, I wish I did have a clue that would lead me to him. There are a number of questions I'd like to ask him."

"Regarding the robberies and m-murders? Are you hinting dad had anything to d-do with… those c-crimes?"

"Frankly, I don't know."

Her dark eyes flamed. "I w-wish I'd shot you when you walked from that elevator; I—I suppose you'll keep me prisoner?"

"No. Not at all."

"If you let me leave, I warn you I'll go straight to the police," she said bitterly.

"With my blessing," Anthony smiled. "I'd rather see Trotter have you on his hands." Then he opened the elevator door for her; watched the cage carry her downward.

Tom Gentry mopped his forehead. "What a quail! I'm certain her children will all turn out to be werewolves." Then he sobered. "But don't fall for the act, Jim. She knows where her old man is. That was a buildup to divert suspicion from him."

Instead of answering, Anthony said: "Order dinner, Tom. And mix a drink for each of us. We'll need it before the night's over."

"Why? What gives?"

The criminologist pulled a typewritten paper from his pocket. It was the list he had obtained from the Monarch Gallery of all its customers and sales. "Remember I told you I did some high class burglarizing last night—or rather, early this morning while you were asleep?"

"Yeah. You brought back some flakes of paint and shreds of raveled cloth; took them in your lab."

"Right. They were samples from two paintings the Monarch Gallery sold. I broke into the owners' homes; took tiny scrapings and ravelings for spectroscopic, chemical, and microscope analysis."

"Well?"

"Well, tonight we go out for more samples," Anthony said.

CHAPTER VIII

BURGLAR'S JEOPARDY

BETWEEN SUPPERTIME AND MIDNIGHT, Jim Anthony was too busy for conversation. The freckled aviator kept well out of his friend's way; but he was puzzled by Jim's many activities. First there were numberless phone calls which Anthony made to a score of members of his "Organization"—that fabulous legion of stockbrokers and shoe shine boys, dowagers and scrub-women, debutantes and ribbon clerks. Jim's amateur operatives included every strata of society; people who owed allegiance to the criminologist in his never-ending fight against law-breakers. When he called on them, they dropped whatever they were doing and formed a sort of vigilante posse—for the sheer pleasure of adventure.

Tonight Anthony seemed anxious to have his strangely assorted legion locate a man named Lenzke in the art quarter of Greenwich Village. A copyist was what Jim called this Lenzke; although Tom Gentry hadn't the foggiest notion what it meant.

Then Anthony set himself to the task of fitting up a compact leather case with various instruments and chemicals.

He selected the contents with infinite patience, pausing every now and then to answer his phone when it rang. Each time this happened, he seemed to be getting a report from some Organization member; and with every new report, his sun-bronzed face took on a more puzzled scowl.

Finally, around midnight, the last call came in. Anthony listened gravely, then rang off and turned to Gentry. "Well, it appears that Lenzke has vanished from his haunts as utterly and completely as Professor Whelstrom disappeared."

"Meaning what, pappy?"

"Meaning it's time for us to get started."

THE HOUSE WAS a Long Island mansion, lightless and silent at this late hour. Anthony chose a side window; worked on the steel sash with certain secret instruments of his own invention. Within two minutes the window was open—and its burglar alarm did not even whisper.

Gentry shivered. "Pretty risky, pappy. This joint's as big as a young hotel. Won't there be guards?"

"If so, we eluded them."

"Who owns the layout?"

"A man named Robert Leslie. Made a fortune in Oklahoma oil, retired, and put some of the money into oil paintings. His private gallery is in the left wing. Come along. No noise."

Guided by Anthony's abnormally acute vision, they stole forward through a darkness so thick you could almost feel it. Presently they gained the mansion's private art museum: a long room cleverly arranged to display its treasure to the best advantage. Here Anthony made use of his specially designed flashlight, until its hooded beam came to rest on a framed painting which Jim's practiced eye recognized.

"That's it," he whispered.

"That's what, pappy?"

"The Velasquez which Robert Leslie bought last month from the Monarch Gallery." As he spoke, the criminologist carefully placed his powerful light on a small stand and adjusted its control so that it cast a diffused glow on the picture rather than a sharp, bright beam. In consequence; the balance of the long chamber remained cloaked in shadows. Tom watched his friend opening the fitted leather case. "What cooks?"

"I want to determine if this picture is real or fake."

"How can you tell?"

Jim's low-pitched voice droned almost inaudibly as he worked with the contents of the kit. "In a number of ways. Laboratory tests are best, of course. That's why I brought samples to my lab at the penthouse this morning. But now we must work faster; do the job right here. No time to spare."

"That still don't answer my question. How can you tell a fake from a genuine old master?"

"Well, there are a lot of good copyists in the world; men who make their living doing nothing else. It's perfectly legitimate; a number of small public galleries feature copies which at times reveal better work-manship than the originals."

"Copyists! That's what you called that Lenzke guy, ain't it? The one you had the Organization tracing tonight?"

"Yes. He seems to have vanished about six months ago; but he was one of the best in America. Never made a blunder unless it was intentional."

"What do you mean, blunder?"

Anthony took a powerful lens from his kit, quartered the Velasquez into inch squares; began examining each square minutely. "Amusing errors sometimes creep into the work of copyists. A little gallery in the Mohawk Valley had what was considered an excellent copy of a Rembrandt. The original was quite dark in tone and so was the copy made from it. Later the original was cleaned, restored by experts—and found to be one of the lightest examples of Rembrandt's work. The dark tone which the copyist so faithfully reproduced was nothing but accumulated dirt!"

"That's a hot one," Gentry chuckled. He watched his criminolo-gist friend, who had finished examining the painting and was now flaking off tiny particles of color from a corner of the canvas. "What's the caper, Jim?"

Anthony tested the fragments by dropping them into miniature glass tubes filled with chemicals. "A paint-solvent experiment," he timed the reaction with a stop-watch. "Oils take at least six months to season and dry thoroughly. As the years pass, the drying process naturally continues. There are a number of tricks for artificially aging pictures, but it's difficult to deceive the expert. This happens to be a test I developed myself. By the elapsed dissolving time I can tell whether those flakes are new or centuries old."

"Why are you putting more flakes in those other tubes?"

"For precipitation in granule form. A pigment-separation process. In the early days the old masters ground all their colors by hand. Natu-rally there were irregularities, since the grinding wasn't even. Modern pigments are machine-ground; the fragments are all exactly the same." Anthony filtered the color-precipitate and briefly examined it under a miniature but high-powered microscope. Then he turned back to the painting.

LIFTING IT CAREFULLY away from the wall, he used a surgeon's scalpel on the rough edge of the canvas under the frame. A few flakes

The slug was aimed at Anthony
but it struck the man he dangled
before him like a child.

resembling dried glue came away on the blade. These went into another glass tube.

"Now what, pappy?"

"A test for size."

"Quit ribbing me. For size you use a tape measure."

Anthony's white teeth flashed against his coppery complexion. "This is a different kind of size. Webster defines it as any glutinous material used for glazing the surface of paper, fiber or cloth—a stiffener. Most modern sizing is common glue and chalk. It prepares the canvas for painting."

"Oh."

"In the early days, each artist used a special size of his own personal formula. Some of the combinations were odd; flour, eggs, milk, all sorts of curious ingredients in varying quantities. Many of the old masters' formulas are known today—and chemical tests will sometimes show whether a painting is genuine or faked, merely by an analysis of the sizing. If it matches the formula which that particular old master is known to have used, it's a good sign. But if it's glue and chalk, you have a modern counterfeit."

"I'll be damned!" Gentry commented. "Hey, now what?"

Anthony was working a loose thread from the edge of the tautly stretched painting, raveling it cautiously. "Old canvas varied greatly in texture because it was hand-loomed. Modern cloth is machine made. Microscopic study reveals the difference. There are ways of artificially aging canvas; and of course it can still be hand-woven for fraudulent purposes."

"What about this Velasquez? Do you suspect it's a fake?"

"Yes."

"But hell's bells, you know the Monarch Gallery ain't selling anything but the real article!"

"Very true. Yet this is not a genuine Velasquez. We have the strange situation of a man buying a real old master but hanging a copy in his gallery—an excellent copy. Offhand, I think it's the work of Lenzke."

"The guy you were trying to find tonight?"

"Yes. I seemed to detect his craftsmanship in the fakes I inspected last night, too. That was why I wanted to have a talk with him."

"There were two other phonies from the Monarch Gallery?" Tom gasped. "Gosh, I don't get it!"

"Neither did I, at first. The pattern is becoming much plainer, though. A customer buys a genuine original; but a substitute, a copy, is what's delivered to him. The real old master never reaches his house. If the buyer discovers he's been victimized and makes a complaint, he is murdered to shut him up. And the evidence, the fake painting, is stolen in order to cover all traces of the crime."

Gentry made a strangling sound.

BY NOW, ANTHONY was packing his kit. "Can you see where Whelstrom enters the setup, Tom? He's the expert who appraised a lot of the Monarch Gallery pictures after they were sold and delivered. Every time he found a substitute he reported it to the duped owner. The owner then registered a complaint—and was murdered. That's your connection between the professor and the killings. It explains why four customers have died shortly after Whelstrom called on them. Whelstrom honestly told them they had been jobbed; that they hadn't received the original pictures they had paid for. Armed with this knowledge, they each demanded a showdown from the gallery. The showdown they got was a wire loop around the throat. Understand?"

The millionaire criminologist closed his kit at the same time he closed his theory. He had been so interested, both in his talk and in the packing of the apparatus case, that his sixth sense momentarily was lulled; failed to warn him of peril. But now, suddenly, he realized that his genial friend had not answered him; that the last sound Gentry had uttered was a curious sort of strangling noise....

Anthony whirled toward his companion, who had been standing in complete darkness just beyond the circle of glow cast by the hooded flashlight. A dull thumping sound drummed abruptly on the carpeted floor, coming from a source which ordinary eyes could not have seen because of the heavy shadows.

But Jim Anthony's eyes were not normal ones. By conscious effort he dilated the pupils; distended them wide. A harsh curse leaped to his lips as he beheld Gentry arched backward, flailing and struggling in the grasp of a blackclad, misshapen figure. Tom's head was drawn askew, and there was a loop of wire tightly around his neck, throttling his life out.

Jim plunged headlong at the grotesque strangler, whose ape-like arms and short torso gave him an appearance oddly resembling a black spider. Even as the criminologist moved, something flamed from the darkness at the other end of the room. There was a tiny puffing sound with the flash; the hot scorch of a silenced bullet barely creasing Anthony's ribs.

Subconsciously he realized there was a second killer here in the chamber; someone with a Maxim-equipped gun. But there was no time to think about that new danger, now. In another moment Tom Gentry would be past all help. The wire garrote was cutting into his gullet, starving his lungs of breath.

THE DRIVING FORCE of Anthony's wild charge bashed the spider-like strangler backward. Gentry sagged down as the noose loosened on his windpipe. He clawed at it, tore it away, gasped a sob of air into his panting chest "Pappy—!" his voice was a whispering croak.

The millionaire was too busy to answer. He grabbed for the black-clad murderer, got his hand around the fellow's throat, lifted him straight into the air the way a hangman's rope dangles an executed criminal on the gibbet. Then, at the same instant, another silenced shot spat from the far end of the long room.

The slug was aimed at Anthony; but it struck the man he dangled before him like a shield. The grotesque figure jerked, twitched convulsively and went limp. Death had bored a tunnel into his unprotected back.

Jim dropped the corpse, pivoted, catapulted toward the hidden gunman. But he tripped over Gentry's prone form and went sprawling. As he fell, his hand streaked inside his coat; came out with an automatic. He never had a chance to use it, though. Evidently his second enemy had gone suddenly yellow, for there was no sign of him anywhere; nothing but receding footfalls that faded and were lost.

The criminologist grabbed for his flashlight; surged upright and started in pursuit. Then a vagrant light-ray fell on Tom Gentry; revealed the aviator untwisting the last strand of wire from his neck. Tom meant more than all the fleeing criminals in the world. Anthony made his decision, abandoned the chase, and knelt by his friend.

"Are you all right, boy? Talk to me!"

"Yeah… I'll be… okay. Help me… stand up. Gosh, that guy certainly… had me wired… without sound! He sneaked up… behind me and the first… thing I knew… br-r-r!"

"Let's have a look at him," Jim growled. He played his light on the misshapen corpse; revealed a face he had never seen before and hoped never to see again. It was brutish, unshaven, the nose so flattened that the nostrils were mere holes slanting upward instead of down.

Gentry shuddered. "Boy, if I'd seen that nightmare before he jumped me, he wouldn't have had to use a noose. I'd have perished from fright. Let's get out of here!"

"Not yet. First I want to sneak upstairs and see the owner of this place. I'd like to talk to him; and we can't just go away and leave this body. Nor do I want to call the police myself.

I'd rather wait a little while before we start arguing with the law."

Tom wasn't sold on the idea, but he knew he couldn't change Anthony's mind. They located the main hall of the big dwelling, ascended the broad staircase, found the master bedroom. Double white doors facing the stairhead gave admittance to it. The two friends entered silently.

Dead ahead there was a huge four-poster bed. A reclining form lay motionless under the covers. Anthony leaned down. "Mr. Leslie. Wake up."

There was no response. There would never be a response. That misshapen strangler had already been here to twist a wire loop about the sleeper's throat. Another Monarch Gallery patron had been murdered.

CHAPTER IX

GALLERY OF DEATH

DEPARTING FROM THE MANSION as silently as they had come, Jim Anthony and his freckled companion crossed the grounds, scaled a surrounding wall and made for their convertible. Gentry's teeth chattered. "I thought I was a goner when the spider guy decorated me with a wire necktie, but to go upstairs and find Leslie bumped really gave me the horrors!"

"Sh-h-h," the criminologist warned. "There's a car parked near ours. Someone's in it; maybe the person who fired that silenced gun."

"Lying in ambush for us, eh? The dirty crumb!"

"Quiet! You duck around to the right. I'll circle the other way and we'll take him from two directions at once." With automatics drawn, Anthony and Tom separated; noiselessly executed this flanking maneuver.

With the suddenness of an explosion, Anthony's flashlight stabbed a beam into the eyes of the person sitting in that second car; while at the same instant, Gentry opened its door on the other side and thundered: "Freese, louse— Hey, pappy! For the love of Whozis, *it's Whelstrom's daughter!*"

"So I see. Well, Miss Whelstrom, have you anything to say?"

Her face was death-pale in the glow of Jim's torch. "Please—you're blinding me—" Then she regained a small measure of composure. "Yes, I have plenty to say. But not to you. To the police." Her weird contralto voice was vibrant with triumph.

"The police?"

She made a bitter mouth. "I've been following you ever since you left your hotel. I hoped you might lead me to my father. You didn't. But at least I've learned you're a housebreaker."

"Are you sure you aren't equally guilty?"

"What d-do you mean by that? Are you accusing me of entering that residence after you? Well, you're wrong! I merely sat here and waited for you to come out. Now I've got enough on you to put you in jail where you belong!"

Tom Gentry made displeased sounds. "By damn, I always thought I could never have enough dames around me; but you're one I'd be glad to trade in cheap for a new model. I bet when my hearse carries me to the graveyard, you'll be sitting by the driver. Think of it, Jim. Here's the gorgeous ghoul who did the silent triggering and had Spider-Man for a stooge!"

"What silent triggering?" the girl tensed.

ANTHONY STUDIED HER. "You deny knowing what just happened in the Leslie residence?"

"Yes. How can I know when I wasn't in there?"

"Then perhaps you won't object to being searched." He hauled her from the car. "Sorry if I seem unchivalrous."

Meanwhile, Gentry was exploring her coupé. Now he announced: "No silenced gat here, Jim. Nor in her handbag."

"Nothing on her person, either," Anthony said.

"Sure not. She ditched the roscoe. That's obvious."

Kathi Whelstrom squirmed in the criminologist's grasp. "What are you madmen talking about? Let me go! I haven't done anything except f-follow you and w-wait—"

"If that's true, let me ask you a question," Anthony's voice was grim. "While you were sitting here, did you see any one leave the house or the grounds?"

"No. But I heard a car speed away. It must have been on the other side of the estate, hidden by the wall. I couldn't see it. Why? Wh-what's happened? Has—has anything—?"

Gentry snorted. "She's lying, pappy."

"Maybe. Maybe not. But we daren't set her free right now and have her go to the police, spoil my plans."

"That's exactly what I intend to do," the girl said.

"Sorry to contradict you, Miss Whelstrom. I'm afraid you'll have to come along with me on a final burglary."

"I—I don't understand!"

"You will, when we break into the Monarch Gallery. I hope we will all understand a great many things then. Provided we aren't shot by some of the F.B.I. guards."

BACK IN TOWN, Anthony parked his convertible in a dark alley behind the former bank building which now housed a king's ransom in art treasures. There was a small rear door, seldom used except for emergencies; but tonight was an emergency as far as Jim was concerned. From a secret pocket of his coat he withdrew his prized steels, those same cleverly designed implements with which he had forced a window of that mansion on Long Island a while ago. Once more he manipulated them.

The door swung open.

Dim lights burned within the vaulted structure, revealing the small exhibit rooms, the marble columns, the surrounding mezzanine balcony. Footfalls trudged in the distance, echoing hollowly as guards paced their posts. Ahead lay the staircase leading to the offices above.

But Anthony turned in the opposite direction, beckoning Tom to follow with the girl. There was no need for the aviator to warn her not to make an outcry, for she seemed to realize the slightest sound might bring gunfire.

Jim had been in the building many times, and his photographic memory held a clear picture of where he wanted to go. He made unerringly to a door on the right, which led to a flight of steps plunging downward into a deep basement. This underground chamber was vast, musty, pitch dark. For the sake of his companions the millionaire clicked on his pocket torch. In its sudden beam, a great grey rat scurried for cover.

Gentry pointed. "Look over there, Jim!" his croaking whisper was harsh. "Am I screwy, or was that rat eating supper off a restaurant plate?"

Fantastic though this sounded, it was true. On opposite walls of the monolithic cellar there were two giant steel vault doors; huge, circular metal portals countersunk into the walls proper, closed now and securely fastened by means of triple-combination dials as big as automobile steering wheels. The vault on the left was where the former bank had once kept its currency and securities; the one on the right was even larger, indicating that once upon a time it had been the bank's safety deposit room for rental customers.

On the floor alongside this vast circular door there was a tray containing the remnants of a meal: dishes, knife, and fork, a cup showing the dregs of coffee. The scurrying rat had indeed been eating from the tray until Anthony's light scared it off.

TOM SHOOK HIS head dizzily. "Who would want supper served in a spooky joint like this?"

"A prisoner, perhaps," the criminologist answered.

"Prisoner? What prisoner? Where?"

"Maybe in the old safety deposit vault."

"Ix-nay, pappy. Nobody could be in there unless he was dead. He'd suffocate without air!"

"On the contrary, the vault is ventilated," Anthony said. "Remember, it was once used as a rental-storage room for the valuables of bank patrons. If someone wanted to keep a man captive, I can think of no better place. Even if a prisoner shouted, you'd never hear him through the thick steel door."

As he spoke, the millionaire made toward the vault; scrutinized its triple-dial locking mechanism. Fortunately there was no time lock in connection with this. While Gentry and the Whelstrom girl stared in amazement, Anthony's deft fingers went to work on the three dial wheels.

These were hubbed so snugly into the metal that not even a cigarette paper could have been inserted around the pivots. Yet one of Jim's steels was so delicate that he managed to slip it where he wanted it. Then he slowly turned the dial with one hand. With the other he clasped the steel implement, whose vibrations relayed the clicking of hidden giant tumblers. Thus he felt out the combination; and he repeated the same successful experiment on the remaining two locks. Abruptly the huge inner bolts were heard to slide, and the delicately balanced vault portal was ready to be pulled open by a mere touch.

"Gosh!" Gentry whispered. "If you weren't already wealthy, you soon could be! I bet you could peter the gold vaults down at Fort Knox!"

Jim didn't answer. Instead, he inched the tremendous circular door outward in its full arc. Light from the interior glowed on his hawk-like countenance; bright artificial daylight that illuminated the safety deposit room and its haggard tenant.

The man's hair was unkempt, shoulder-long; his beard matted and grey to match the unhealthy pallor of his emaciated cheeks. His frame was wasted, his eyes deeply sunken in hollow sockets. Nearby there was an easel bearing an unfinished painting, together with palette, brushes, tubes of oil paints. These were the only furnishings except for the crude cot on which the man sat despondently.

Nor could he have moved even if he had wanted to. His ankles were chained to a steel ring in the floor, and his wrists manacled in old fashioned slave irons!

Slowly he raised his glance. Then, in a voice dulled by disuse, he muttered: "You're not Spider."

"No," Anthony answered quietly. "I'm a friend who recognized your code messages. I've come to rescue you, Mr. Lenzke."

OUTSIDE THE VAULT, Tom Gentry gasped: "Gosh, Jim, is this Lenzke, the copyist guy you were hunting?"

The unkempt man responded: "Yes, I am Lenzke."

"But—but great guns and little gremlins, pappy, what's this about coded messages?"

Anthony's tone was grim. "Remember I told you Lenzke was such an expert copyist that he never made a blunder unless it was intentional? Well, on the various fakes I examined, I detected the unmistakable craftsmanship of Lenzke. But I also noticed errors; a hand in the wrong position, eyes of incorrect color, certain discrepancies of light and shadow."

"Those mistakes were deliberate," the shackled man said dully. "I hoped someone would see them, realize something was wrong and institute a search for me. Thank God it worked."

Anthony stooped, used his steels on the prisoner's leg-fetters. "How long have you been held here?"

"More than six months, as far as I can estimate."

"How were you kidnaped?"

"I was lured to a hotel by a letter from Leo Gerard, damn his soul. He promised me some work and I needed the money. But a masked man knocked me unconscious. I woke up in this vault. The masked man looked like a… a spider…"

Tom Gentry snapped his fingers. "See, Jim? That's the strangler ape he's talking about! The guy that got knocked off tonight!"

"Right, Tom."

"And Leo Gerard was his boss. As manager of Monarch Gallery, he sold genuine old masters but delivered fakes painted by Lenzke. It's open and shut!" Tom almost shouted.

The shackled copyist rattled his wrist-chains. "You must not think I painted those fakes voluntarily. I was starved into obedience. Unless I worked, I got no food." He hesitated. "Listen. I hear someone coming—"

The warning was too late to do any good. Even as Gentry, Anthony, and the Whelstrom girl spun around to stare across the cellar, two husky men raced down the steps and confronted them with submachine guns. "Okay, you people. Get your hands up."

CHATTER X

RIDDLE OF THE MASTERS

ONE OF THE ARMED men displayed the small gold badge of a Department of Justice operative. "We're F.B.I. guards. You're all under arrest—and maybe you'd like to tell us what goes on here?"

The millionaire criminologist's face revealed no expression. He kept his arms raised as he answered: "I'm Jim Anthony and these are my friends. You've interrupted me as I was near the solution of a series of murders."

"Jim Anthony, eh? That'll do to tell, brother. But I'm not listening. How did you get into this building?"

"I broke in."

"You admit it, do you? Fine. Burglary. Attempted theft. This will cost you some years, mister."

"Before you make the mistake of arresting me while a murderer runs loose, I suggest you summon Lieutenant Trotter of the homicide bureau," Jim said impassively. "He will identify all of us. And you had better tell him to round up the staff of the Monarch Gallery; bring them here. Everyone from Leo Gerard, the manager, on down the line." The second G-man looked hesitant.

"Maybe this man's telling the truth," he said to his companion. "It wouldn't hurt to play ball with him that far."

"Okay. Guard them while I go up and phone."

Anthony breathed a sigh of relief. The sinister story would soon be ended; and a guilty person would be made to pay in full for the crimes that had been committed....

IT WAS A motley gathering of people who clustered in the underground room an hour later. Trotter was accompanied by several of his underlings; Leo Gerard had brought his chubby secretary, Harrison Hunt, as well as minor employees of the gallery ranging from clerks to doormen.

A raging oath roared from the lips of the copyist, Lenzke, when he caught sight of Gerard. "You swine! *You're* the one whose letter lured me into a kidnaping! *You* had your spider-man imprison me in the vault, force me to paint fakes!" And he plunged at the gallery manager, brandishing his chained wrists.

Gerard squealed unhappily; ducked behind a G-man for protection. "You're c-crazy! I never wrote—" His goatee waggled when he choked out the frantic denial.

"Lay off!" Trotter roared, grabbing Lenzke and pinioning him helpless. "What cooks around here? You, Anthony! Can you explain this mess?"

The millionaire criminologist nodded. "Customers bought old masters, but copies were delivered; substitutes which Lenzke was forced to paint. Professor Whelstrom appraised some of them, found them to be counterfeit, and so notified the purchasers. Each patron then complained to the gallery—and was murdered to shut him up."

"Who pulled the kills?"

"A spider man. He's dead now. His boss accidentally shot him tonight with a silenced gun."

Trotter glowered. "And who is this secret boss?"

"Hell, that's easy," Tom Gentry grunted. "Leo Gerard."

Anthony shook his head. "Wrong, Tom. We're dealing with an unusually clever thief; someone who delivered fake paintings and kept the genuine originals."

"Sure. Gerard."

"No. There's one vital clue which clears Gerard. He's the man who recommended Professor Whelstrom to the gallery customers as an expert appraiser. If Gerard had been guilty, he wouldn't have dared send an expert to call on the buyers—because Whelstrom was bound to recognize the pictures as fakes and make a report to that effect. Gerard *must* be innocent. When he recommended Professor Whelstrom, he proved he didn't know any counterfeit paintings had been delivered."

Tom blinked. "I get it. Then Whelstrom himself must be your man."

"That's a lie!" the professor's daughter cried. "My father is an honest man!"

Anthony patted her on the shoulder. "Yes, Kathi, he was entirely honest."

"What do you mean, was? Do you think he—he's—?"

"Easy, my dear. Be brave. Your father was discovering too many of the fake paintings. As a result of his reports, too many customers complained and had to be killed. In brief, the professor had become a menace to our hidden criminal."

"So he was… m-murdered," she whispered.

"I'm afraid so. He phoned the gallery, tried to contact Leo Gerard. He thought Gerard was deliberately avoiding him."

The art dealer squalled: "I was not avoiding him! I never had any messages from him! I never had any complaints from our customers!"

"Quite so," Anthony agreed. "And there's the answer to the riddle. Only one person was in a position to intercept your phone calls and sidetrack them; to destroy any letters of complaint. Only one person could have seen those complaining letters and arranged to have the duped patrons murdered. Purchasers who didn't protest were allowed to live; the others died. Only one individual on the gallery's staff knew the inside workings of all Monarch transactions. *Harrison Hunt.*"

THE CHUBBY SECRETARY opened his mouth and laughed. "Are you kidding?"

"I'm accusing you of multiple murder; of retaining the genuine old masters for which you delivered substitutes," the criminologist stated flatly. "You planned to keep the genuine originals for future sale to buyers who wouldn't mind purchasing stolen art treasures."

Hunt laughed again, evilly. "Prove it."

"I believe I can. In fact, I think I can disclose where you have hidden the priceless paintings you stole."

"Really?"

"Yes. If you used the old safety deposit vault to keep your prisoner, Lenzke, hidden, then it's logical to assume that you used the other vault—the currency vault—in which to store the pictures." Anthony turned toward the opposite cellar wall, where there was a second huge circular door. "You're caught, Hunt. You may as well give us the combination."

The portly secretary's eyes glittered behind the pince-nez glasses. "I don't know the combination. Even if I knew it, I wouldn't tell you. Why should I incriminate myself?"

"Then I'll open the vault without it."

"You can't. Nobody can."

Tom Gentry's teeth flashed, although he wasn't smiling. "Oh, *brother*, how wrong you are! You should've been here a while back, when pappy petered the other one. Show him, Jim."

The criminologist nodded, fell to work. Three minutes later, the vault door swung outward on its hinges. A concert of gasps went up from the watchers when they saw what the crackproof aperture contained.

"The paintings!" Trotter bellowed.

Then Kathi Whelstrom shrilled: "Father—!" and leaped into the vault, went to her knees beside a huddled figure. "He—he's d-dead—strangled with a wire noose—!"

It was true. Professor Whelstrom's corpse lay beneath stacked canvasses, the genuine old masters which buyers had paid for but never received. The girl sobbed disconsolately.

Anthony stared at Harrison Hunt. "You lured him here when he tried to phone Gerard. You killed him, but had no place to hide his body except this temporary one."

"You haven't a shred of proof," the chubby man grinned.

Then the brunette girl straightened, raised her throaty voice. "Mr. Anthony—look! My father must have lived a little while after he was thrust in here! He scrawled a message on the f-floor in his own blood. It says: *Harrison Hunt killed me!*"

That was the final straw. It broke the secretary's nerve. He jumped backward, and there was suddenly a gun in his fist. "All right. So the old creep put the finger on me, after all. But you won't take me, wise guys. The first man who moves gets a slug in his belly."

As if to pile fantasy on fantasy, somebody screamed: "I'll take that risk!" and lunged at the chubby man. Hunt's gun barked; spat flame.

The bullet struck Lenzke full in the chest; but the copyist didn't even stagger. "You're responsible for the six months of hell I endured. Now it's my turn." Another bullet smashed him, but he kept moving forward. Then he raised his manacled fists—and the long length of chain connecting his old fashioned handcuffs formed a loop which settled around Hunt's thick neck.

Jim Anthony tried to spurt across the cellar. Gentry blocked him. "Let it ride, pappy. Remember, he tailed us to that mansion on Long Island and tried to croak us with silent slugs. I say let it ride."

"Out of my way, Tom! Don't be a fool! Let the law take its proper course!" the criminologist grated as he side-stepped his freckled friend. He was too late, though. The chain noose had already broken Harrison Hunt's neck in a manner weirdly similar to the wire-loop murders which were now atoned for. The rotund corpse sagged, fell inert. Then Lenzke, the self-appointed executioner, fell motionless across the body of the man he had just slain. The copyist's revenge was complete; but it had been at the price of his own life.

DAWN STREAKED THE eastern horizon and tinted the skyline of Manhattan with grey; brushed the windows of Jim Anthony's penthouse. Anthony, Gentry, and Kathi Whelstrom stepped from the private elevator into the foyer.

"You saved the day, Kathi," the criminologist said softly. "When you mentioned that accusation your father had written with his own blood as he died, you caused Hunt to make the move which ended his ugly career."

Her pale face was wan. "I lied. There was no message."

"Yes, I know," Anthony nodded. "The professor couldn't possibly have scrawled anything on the floor of the vault. Not when he'd been garrotted."

Gentry's eyes popped. "You mean it was a trick to make Harrison Hunt give himself away? Ain't that something!"

From a closet, Anthony withdrew a big square of painted canvas which he handed to the brunette girl. "And here, Kathi, is your inheritance—a genuine Jeremiah Dummler portrait that Tom and I found in the secret passage under your house. An excellent example of early American Colonial art; and, as such, worth a small fortune. It belongs to you, because it was part of the home your father bought; must have been hidden in the tunnel since the days of the first owner."

"You—you mean—?"

"At least you'll not have to worry about money," Jim smiled. "This Dummler is easily worth fifty thousand dollars; perhaps more. In fact, I'll buy it from you if you care to sell. You needn't decide now. I'll visit you and ask you for your answer some day soon."

Her dark eyes bespoke the gratitude she couldn't seem to put into words. And later, when she had left the penthouse, Gentry said: "You know something, pappy? That doll ain't such a bad dish, after all. Let me know when you're ready to call on her. I think I'd like to go along and see if she'll date."

"No, Tom. This was one girl you weren't interested in. Don't be changing your mind about her now—because if there are any dates to be had with Kathi Whelstrom, your Uncle Jim Anthony is going to get them."

PIPELINE TO MURDER

HE LIKED TO RIDE IN EXPENSIVE CARS, SO HE ALWAYS
DROVE AROUND IN A HEARSE. BUT WHERE HE THOUGHT
HE WAS SAFE BEHIND BULLET-PROOF GLASS, HE
DISCOVERED HE WAS PARTICULARLY OPEN TO ATTACK

STAR-STUDDED DARKNESS OF AN Oklahoma evening spread its shadows over Tulsa's municipal airport; shrouded the paved landing strip runways and the concrete apron in front of the modernistic passenger Station. Above the building, lights gleamed from the glassed-in cupola of the traffic control tower, over which a constantly revolving searchlight sent its sharp finger of brightness probing circularly through the night.

In the upper skies a thrumming drone could be heard, growing ever louder as an oncoming twin motored passenger plane approached the field, losing altitude. Now the sleek silver ship's wingtip riding lamps, one green, one red, could be discerned against the deep purple background, like twinkling meteors. Two powerful landing lights abruptly blazed out of the aircraft's streamlined nose, their beams converging on the ground below.

In response, the airport's own floodlamps snapped on like a glittering necklace encircling the rectangular clearing. Washed by this sudden radiance, the shadows fled from the field toward a thicker darkness beyond its borders. Overhead, the sharp bark of throttled engines blended with a banshee whistling of idling propellers.

At the same instant, a sinister black vehicle swung in from the highway; passed the administration building and halted without sound in the parking space reserved for cabs and private automobiles calling for arriving passengers. This long black conveyance was the only one meeting the descending ship; but it was neither a taxi nor a limousine.

It was something far more ominous—a specially built Cadillac hearse!

ABOVE THE LIGHTED field, the twin motored cabin plane swooped like a bird of prey, its landing gear lowering like talons. At the controls

sat a man whose smooth touch bespoke thousands of flying hours; a happy-go-lucky, genial young veteran of the days when you flew a wired-up Jenny by the seat of your pants and a hand compass. This was Tom Gentry, a grin on his freckled countenance as he banked the ship and put it into a long glide.

"Smack-dab on the beam, pappy," he chortled, pointing to the lights below.

In the co-pilot's seat, the owner of the plane nodded absently. Jim Anthony, multi-millionaire inventor, scientist, sportsman, and industrialist, was accustomed to perfect flying from his aviator friend. An expert airman himself, anything less than perfection on Tom's part would have disappointed him.

He spoke no praise, though, for his thoughts were on another matter. A frown marked his sun-bronzed face and there was a penetrating glitter visible in his dark, hawk-like eyes as he felt the craft drift to a deft three point landing.

Gentry gunned the starboard motor to turn the plane and taxi it toward the tarmac. "Hope Bill Long Thumb is here to meet us," he remarked. "My curiosity is all of a twitter about that letter he wrote you."

Jim Anthony, too, was curious. Intuition told him that Tulsa might hold a mystery to tax even his own abilities as an investigator. In his mind's eye he again scanned the message that had reached him this morning at his penthouse residence atop the famed Waldorf-Anthony Hotel in New York.

Anthony ducked and the man could not stop his headlong rush.

"Dear Jim:
Understand the Washington brass hats are sending you here to Tulsa

to check that new tangled pipeline being promoted by Franklin Foster. I realize the east needs more oil and transportation facilities are at a premium in these war times, but between you and me, I think Foster's scheme is phony.

As a petroleum engineer I can't see where any wooden pipeline can stand up, even if treated with Foster's alleged secret preservative. What does he know about preserving wood? He's a shyster corporation lawyer, not a chemist.

Besides, wooden pipe needs steel collar and sleeve connections to join the sections and seal them against leakage. How can he get a priority on the tons of metal required for a thousand mile experimental line? That's the joker in the deal.

As I view it, Foster is persuading suckers to invest in his screwball scheme when he knows he can't obtain steel priorities. He'll probably use that as an excuse for not going ahead with construction, meantime pocketing the money.

You can see I don't trust the little heel, especially since one of his backers is a crooked gambler named Martelli. Don't quote me, though. I've got enough trouble! In fact, as one redskin to another, I'm yelling for help in a personal matter.

My great grandfather went to the happy hunting grounds last month, leaving ten million smackers to my grand-dad and assorted relatives. I'll get a slice myself if I live; but two of my uncles were killed last week in supposed auto accidents. I inspected each car's steering gear later, and they'd been tampered with.

Maybe we other heirs are slated to be wiped out, too. I'm not a suspicious Injun, but something tells me all is not kosher in Oklahoma. Since you're my best friend as well as the world's greatest detective, I hope you'll find time while you're in Tulsa to put on your war paint and look into these deaths. I'll meet you at the airport.

Bill Long Thumb."

IN CALLING JIM Anthony the world's greatest detective, Long Thumb had not underestimated. For in all the history of crime and its punishment, no manhunter ever lived whose deeds could equal those of this tall, sun-bronzed criminologist now arriving in Tulsa.

From his swashbuckling father, an Irish-American soldier of fortune, and a renowned capitalist, Jim had inherited a mighty financial empire which included a nation wide chain of newspapers, a string of hotels, countless manufacturing enterprises and a vast array of mines and oil fields. Sage management had increased his holdings until he had become one of America's wealthiest men.

Restless, he had then cast about for a hobby; and his interest had turned to scientific criminology. Perhaps Jim's Indian strain was responsible for this hunter's instinct, for his mother had been a full blooded Comanche princess. And in time, the very name Jim Anthony was enough to strike terror to the heart of a nation's underworld.

Into his battle against crime, Jim brought superlative equipment. Rangy, handsome, his dark eyes and chiseled bronze features betraying his Comanche ancestry, he had a steely strength bulwarked by vast reserves of energy and vitality, the result of constant rigorous exercise. To this was added an intellect as swift as a rapier; an education obtained in major universities all over the world.

College was where he had first met Bill Long Thumb, a Cherokee tribesman specializing in oil research. A warm friendship had sprung up between them, although they'd traveled separate paths in the past few years. Anthony's tremendous industrial empire was currently engaged in all-out war production under Jim's personal supervision— a task requiring his undivided attention except when the government called upon his many expert knowledges, such as this present Oklahoma trip to investigate a pipeline project.

Long Thumb, however, had won a captain's commission in the army at the outbreak of the war; and he was in uniform now as he came forward to greet Anthony and Gentry at the airport exit. A heavy-set, muscular man, he smiled a warm welcome.

"Gosh, am I glad you're here!" he thrust out a hard, copper-colored hand. "My kid cousins have turned up for a division of the estate and I've been holding my breath every moment for fear something might happen to them."

Anthony's voice was gravely resonant. "Have there been any indications of trouble?"

"Plenty. My grand-dad has been shot at twice. Luckily, he had bullet proof glass in his chariot, so he wasn't hurt. Incidentally, he came along with me tonight to give you a lift."

"Decent of him," Jim said.

LONG THUMB CHUCKLED. "Maybe, and then again maybe not. The old boy is no dope. He realizes he's under the gun, along with the rest of the heirs to that ten million clams. He also knows about the letter I wrote you regarding my two uncles being knocked off. So if he's nice to you, it's because he hopes you'll work on the mystery."

"I will if I have time," Anthony said soberly. "But first I must check those wooden pipeline specifications."

The Cherokee captain lowered his tone. "Which reminds me, I wish you'd forget I called Franklin Foster a phony. Don't allow my opinion to influence you."

"Why? Have you changed your mind about him?"

"No. But he just told me you're the one who'll either grant or deny his priority application on steel fittings. It wouldn't be fair for me to prejudice you against him in advance. Maybe I was wrong; maybe his scheme is on the square. That's for you to decide."

Jim smiled. "I respect your judgment, Bill."

"Thanks. But after all, it's none of my business. *I* haven't got any dough invested in the thing."

"Do you know anyone who has?"

Long Thumb made a wry mouth. "Yes. My grandfather. He's completely sold on the idea. In fact, he brought Foster along with us to meet you. Sh-h-h. Here he comes now."

The man who trotted briskly around a corner of the administration building toward them was almost absurdly small by comparison with the pompous esteem in which he seemed to hold himself. As Tom Gentry remarked later, "If he was two inches shorter, the guy could double for a circus midget."

The description came very close to being accurate. Franklin Foster was small-boned, slim, wiry; and even the built-up heels of his shoes failed to bring his height to a full five feet. In his loud tweeds and jaunty fedora he somehow gave you the impression, at first glance, of a schoolboy dressed up in an effort to appear adult. He had an over-sized black cigar cocked incongruously in his tiny mouth as if to prove his manhood.

On closer inspection, though, this schoolboy impression vanished. His face was definitely that of a man in the middle thirties, perhaps close to the forty mark. Shrewd eyes, sharp as gimlets, peered unthinkingly from a surrounding network of wrinkles; and when he spoke, his voice was surprisingly robust.

His handclasp was firm, too. "Mr. Anthony? I'm Foster. Glad to meet you, sir. Welcome to Tulsa, the oil capital of the world. Fine city.

One of the best. A fitting headquarters for the development of my new pipeline idea. Destined to make history for the petroleum industry."

He also shook hands with Tom Gentry; but he seemed pointedly to ignore Bill Long Thumb, as if captains were beneath his dignity. For all the little fellow's lack of size he acted like a man who spoke only to brigadier generals—or multimillionaires like Jim Anthony.

"Shall we get going?" he boomed. "The Chief is waiting, you know. Waiting in his hearse. Ha-ha."

Gentry twitched visibly, then relaxed. "My ears must be slipping," he remarked. "I thought you said hearse."

BY THIS TIME they had rounded the corner of the airport's administration building. Long Thumb, chuckling, pointed to the black vehicle ahead. "Mr. Foster did say hearse."

"You mean you *ride* in it?"

"It's my grandfather's favorite mode of travel."

The freckled aviator balked in his tracks. "Look. A rib is a rib, but this definitely ain't funny."

"It isn't meant to be," Anthony interposed. "Try to see the Indian psychology, Tom. Chief Fire-Bird is wealthy. The oil lands controlled by his family cover a good part of the southwest, and that hearse is the fanciest car he could find."

"Does he collect coffins, too?"

"Be serious," Jim smiled. "Why should the dead ride in better cars than the living? To the Chief's unfettered point of view that doesn't make sense. So he buys a hearse."

Gentry shuddered. "I should have stayed in New York where Indians live in penthouses and own newspapers. This kills me."

"It might, if you make any remarks about the hearse where the Chief can hear you," Long Thumb said. "He might whip out a scalping knife and peel you like a banana." He winked at Anthony. "Am I right, Jim?"

The millionaire criminologist joined in the jest by nodding gravely. Tom caught the twinkle in his friend's eye, though, and realized he was being kidded. He grinned. "What else does the old guy do for a pastime besides whittling scalps?"

"He gambles," Long Thumb was serious now. "It's a mania with him. With my whole family, for that matter. Not even the shadow of murder can stop them. I'll lay you a bet they'll all wind up at Martelli's place before the night's over."

Then the little group reached the waiting hearse, and Chief Fire-Bird stepped forward to greet them.

IN APPEARANCE, THE elderly Indian might have walked straight out of a character drawing. His face, unmarked by age, was notable for its mahogany hue, its high cheekbones and piercing eyes and beak-like nose. Two long braids of black hair hung over his shoulders, and a derby hat perched squarely on the center of his head. He was almost as tall as Jim Anthony's own six-feet-plus; but it was his costume that caused Gentry to stare in open-mouthed bewilderment.

He wore the trousers to a tuxedo, the cuffs neatly folded and stuffed into expensive high-heeled cowboy boots. His white dress shirt had a starched, pleated front and a wing collar with black bow tie. Instead of a tuxedo jacket, however, he wore a quilted velvet lounging coat; and the whole ensemble was topped off by a gaudy Indian blanket draped shawl fashion across his shoulders, a touch which left Tom Gentry speechless.

"Fire-Bird salutes his red brother," the old man shook hands with Anthony. Then, to Tom, he added: "How!"

"How what?" the aviator demanded.

The chief laughed merrily. "Just plain 'how.' It's supposed to be the traditional Cherokee greeting. Don't you want me to remain in character? Never mind; skip it." He turned back to Jim. "I've reserved a suite for you at the Hotel Mayan, but first you must come out to my house for a talk."

A liveried chauffeur opened the rear door of the hearse. Its glass enclosed interior looked less somber with the dome light on. There were no metal rollers in the floor for coffins to rest upon; instead, it was richly carpeted and furnished with several upholstered easy chairs which could be arranged as you saw fit.

Anthony and Gentry entered first, followed by Franklin Foster, then Bill Long Thumb. Chief Fire-Bird was last, and he chose to sit Indian fashion, cross-legged on the floor, like a tailor. The chauffeur shut the door, moved smartly to the front compartment and slid under the wheel. Instants later the hearse was purring onto the highway, as smoothly as a whisper.

Gentry started off toward the right, where the skyline of the petroleum metropolis jabbed upward from higher ground like a bit of New York itself. Tall buildings rose spirelike against the horizon, monolithic monuments to the oil industry. Two of the tallest were especially spectacular because of theatrical lighting effects: the Philtower with its mighty revolving beacon and the National Bank of Tulsa with its ever changing floodlights which bathed the upper spire in all the colors of the rainbow, greens melting into reds and yellows and blues—a giant kaleidoscope against the night sky.

"I'd hate to use this chariot for a heavy date," Tom muttered, indicating the unobstructed view through the glass sides of the hearse. "Your personal life is certainly not your own in a traveling mortuary, is it? I feel like a goldfish in a bowl of water."

Anthony nudged him silent, for a sudden premonition had come to the

It was the old Indian's costume that caught Tom's attention.

millionaire detective. From his Comanche mother, Jim had inherited a weird, almost supernatural sixth sense which never failed to warn him when danger approached; and this sixth sense was stirring now, whispering of peril very close.

The hearse was whisking south on Sheridan toward the suburbs of the oil metropolis; just passing a shadow-draped golf course on the left. From the golf course driveway, headlights suddenly blazed as a car emerged. For an instant this glare bisected the hearse, throwing its passengers into sharp relief. Then they had passed and the car swung in behind them.

Jim's warning premonition grew in intensity. That other car increased its speed, sweeping up to the side of the hearse as if to pass. But it did not go by; and Anthony, turning to stare at the sedan, suddenly exploded into violent motion as he saw the muzzle of a revolver protruding from one of the machine's rear windows.

With a sweep of his hand, Jim slapped Gentry to the hearse's floor. "Duck, everybody!" he roared.

His voice was drowned in the sudden crash of gunfire and a shattering of glass. Three times the revolver belched thunderous flame. Then the sedan's engine whined eerily and the car itself shot ahead as if powered by a rocket motor.

Instead of pursuing, the hearse drew to a halt at the side of the highway. The liveried chauffeur hopped down, ran around to the rear door; opened it. "Did—did anybody—?"

Anthony switched on the dome light overhead and surveyed his fellow passengers. Tom Gentry was okay; so were Chief Fire-Bird and little Franklin Foster. But Bill Long Thumb was slumped in his seat, curiously motionless.

CHAPTER II

DEATH'S SHADOW

A **DOZEN QUESTIONS WHICH** Detective Lieutenant John Halmar asked at police headquarters a little later elicited no helpful information. Chief Fire-Bird's voice was emotionless as he answered the homicide officer's queries. All he could offer was the statement that the hearse had been equipped with bullet proof glass, and that he could not understand how the slug had penetrated to kill his grandson.

Finally the police detective turned to Jim Anthony. "I know you by reputation, sir. Can you throw any light on this murder? Have you any theories?"

"Vague ones," the millionaire criminologist said. He mentioned the letter Long Thumb had written to him. "On the surface it would seem to be a plot to kill off some of the heirs to a ten million dollar oil estate, so that the survivors might receive larger shares. Obviously the fewer heirs, the more each one will inherit."

"Hm-m-mm-m. That's reasonable. And we do know there've been previous attempts on Chief Fire-Bird's life."

Jim nodded. "Plus the deaths of Bill Long Thumb's two uncles in supposed auto accidents. Still, Bill could have been wrong in thinking those accidents were deliberate; and his own murder may have had a far different motive."

"That remains to be seen," Anthony said. "For instance, he had very little confidence in a certain pipeline promotion which Washington has asked me to investigate. Somebody may have been afraid Bill would influence me against the project."

On the other side of the homicide office, Franklin Foster's face went crimson and he leaped to his feet like an infuriated bantam rooster. "Are you accusing me of engineering Long Thumb's murder?"

"Not at all. You aren't the only one interested in the pipeline. You have associates."

"They aren't killers!" Foster snapped angrily. "And neither am I."

"Let us hope you're right," Jim said levelly.

Foster's rage died as quickly as it had flared. Suddenly he seemed to remember Anthony's official status as the government representative who could grant or reject his priority application. "Sorry I blew up," he apologized. "I'll admit Long Thumb and I didn't like each other much; but I certainly had no desire to see him dead."

AT THE DESK, Lieutenant Halmar waved a hand for silence. A bleak smile curved his lips. "Personally, I don't think the pipeline project has anything to do with it. The killer is one of the heirs to that estate—and I intend to make a list of them; bring them down here for questioning."

"If you do, it will cost you your badge," came the surprising statement from Chief Fire-Bird. The elderly Indian spoke coldly, without rancor, but his hooded eyes were hot. "I've got influence in this town, remember."

Halmar looked uncomfortable. "Yes, but—"

"If this is a family murder, we'll keep it in the family. I don't need the police to protect me or my relatives; or to find the one who has become a traitor to his blood. If there is a viper in the nest, I'll deal justice in my own way—without interference."

The homicide official made a reluctant gesture of dismissal. "Okay, if you feel that way about it." But Jim Anthony, watching the man, knew this was merely a stratagem to placate Fire-Bird. Threats or no threats, the police department would continue working on the case. White man's law was not to be denied.

FRANKLIN FOSTER, OBVIOUSLY shaken, summoned a taxi and left police headquarters by himself after promising to lay his entire pipeline specifications before Anthony the following day. Then Jim and Gentry accompanied Chief Fire-Bird around the corner of Fourth Street to Elgin, where the hearse was parked.

Gentry voiced a protest. "You still figure to ride in this thing after what happened?"

"There is nothing wrong with it except the shattered glass side," the elderly Indian answered. Then he laid a gentle hand on Tom's shoulder. "You think I'm cold blooded, don't you? But you're wrong. Merely because a Cherokee conceals his grief is no indication that he doesn't feel it. I assure you my grandson's death touches me deeply. I realize the shot may have been meant for me; that I may be next on the list. But I am not afraid to face whatever might come."

And then the sinister black vehicle resumed its journey that had been interrupted by murder.

Chief Fire-Bird's home was a square brick house of mansion-like proportions near White City subdivision. Its tailored trimness was surrounded by grounds comprising a full city block, the terraced lawns hedged in by wrought iron fence, the front yard sporting several examples of atrocious marble statuary and iron deer. As the hearse purred into the private driveway, another car passed in the opposite direction, going out. It was a sleek sedan, and Anthony caught a momentary glimpse of its driver—a dapper, swarthy man who looked as if he might be either Spanish or Italian.

Seated beside this Latin-looking individual was one of the most startlingly beautiful women Jim had ever seen. She seemed tall and

There, in the center of the
bed, was the tarantula.

poised, like a professional model, and her hair was as black as midnight
coiffed to her head like glossy patent leather. Her complexion was as
smooth as ivory, relieved only by the splash of carmine which was
her sensuous mouth. She wore a low-cut evening gown, and her bare
shoulders were creamy perfection, as if sculptured in snow.

Anthony had only a brief glance at her; then the sedan went by. A
minute later the hearse drew up before Fire-Bird's pretentious resi-

dence and the elderly Indian gestured his guests into the house, stopping only to give instructions to his chauffeur. "Have that side glass replaced, Martin; and this time make sure it's bullet proof. I'll want the car in an hour."

Then he conducted Jim and Gentry indoors, leaving his blanket in the hearse. In the reception hall he exchanged his quilted smoking jacket for a dinner coat, which was held for him by a respectful butler. Hatless now, he looked like a successful businessman dressed for some social occasion—all except the cowboy boots and the two braids of hair hanging down over his shoulders.

IN THE LIBRARY, two girls moved quickly to the old chief's side as he entered the room. Anthony's sweeping, carefully veiled scrutiny told him that the news of Bill Long Thumb's murder had already been reported here, for the girls were trembling and pale and visibly shocked.

"My granddaughters," Fire-Bird said. "Lady Barbara Kendrington and Miss Marie DuValle—Mr. Jim Anthony and Mr. Tom Gentry. Gentlemen, we three are all that remain of the family. I have no other immediate relatives."

Jim bowed courteously and gravely; but Gentry seemed too astonished to acknowledge the introduction. Subconsciously he had more or less expected Indian maids with beaded headbands, buckskin skirts, and fringed leather jackets. Instead, his astounded eyes beheld two perfectly groomed women who might have been models from the Powers agency.

Marie DuValle was red-haired and petite; a diminutive and vibrant girl whose emerald eyes matched the color of her clinging evening gown. Her cousin was taller, a statuesque blonde whose graceful movements betrayed regal breeding and a background of wealth, of assured social position.

These were the cousins Bill Long Thumb had mentioned at the airport, prior to his death; the ones who had turned up for their share of the estate. Gentry, studying them with bedazzled admiration, found himself wondering how either one could possibly be suspected of a plot to kill off their collateral heirs. It was unthinkable that such gorgeous creatures might be guilty of murder.

Jim Anthony, however, reserved judgment. More than once, in his career as an amateur criminologist, he had discovered that a pretty face can mask a killer's heart. Women even as young as Marie DuValle and

Barbara Kendrington were capable of dissimulation; and it was entirely possible that the grief which each girl revealed might be a sham.

Chief Fire-Bird spoke somberly. "You have heard about the attack, then? The death of your cousin?"

The statuesque blonde girl nodded. "We got the news from Martelli and his sister. They stopped by to tell us; to offer sympathy."

Anthony's card-index mind clicked to the name Martelli. Bill Long Thumb had mentioned the man in his letter; had called him a dishonest gambler, one of the backers of Franklin Foster's promotion scheme for a wooden pipeline.

Jim also recalled the sedan which had just left the grounds, driven by a Latin-looking man who'd had a very beautiful brunette woman beside him. The swarthy man must have been Martelli, he decided; and the sedan itself bore a curious resemblance to the machine from which death had struck at Long Thumb.

Meanwhile, Tom Gentry had recovered his unquenchable poise after the initial shock of being introduced to a pair of extremely pretty girls who looked nothing at all like Indian maids. He drew the diminutive, red-haired Marie DuValle off to one side. "Is Fire-Bird really your grandpa, baby?"

"But, yes," her accent was faintly Gallic. "Why do you ask?"

"Well, you don't look like a redskin, is all."

She smiled at his candor. "I am more French than Indian. My mother was the old chief's daughter, a halfbreed; my father was white, a French Canuck. *Voila,* that makes me—"

"A swell dish," the freckled aviator supplied gallantly. He indicated the stately blonde on the other side of the room. "How about your cousin? Where does she get that Lady So-and-So handle on her name?"

MARIE DuVALLE SMILED again, less genuinely this time. "Barbara's mother was another of Fire-Bird's daughters, married to an Englishman who came into a peerage. Oh yes, my darling cousin is quite entitled to be called Lady Barbara Kendrington. For all her haughty airs, though, she's as poor as I am; which is poorer than the proverbial church mouse. Never until the blitz has she been away from England."

"You don't like her much, do you?" Gentry asked shrewdly.

The girl's green eyes flashed a danger signal. "I like all my relatives, *Monsieur* Gentry—including my two uncles who died in automobile accidents and my cousin Bill Long Thumb who was killed this evening."

Tom realized he had accidentally probed a sensitive spot and he was on the verge of protesting that he had meant no insinuations; but across the room the voice of Chief Fire-Bird was a dignified thunder that compelled full attention.

"The whole thing is impossible!" the elderly Indian was saying to Jim Anthony. "Twice before, bullets have been fired at my car; and twice the glass protected me. Tonight it failed. I can scarcely credit it."

"The glass must have been changed," Jim said.

"Not without my chauffeur knowing. You were at headquarters when he was questioned. He knew nothing."

"How long has he been with you?"

"Almost twelve years. I trust him implicitly."

Lady Barbara broke in bitterly. "Maybe you do, grandfather; but I don't. In fact, I don't trust anyone after the things that have happened."

"Meaning you do not trust me, darling?" came a brittle drawl from Marie DuValle.

The taller blonde girl's smile was silk wrapped around poison. "Not even you, my sweet little cousin. Particularly when you are so romantically interested in that loathsome midget of a pipeline promoter, Franklin Foster."

"And what has he to do with it, *cherie?*"

"He needs money for his enterprise," Lady Barbara shrugged. "Perhaps you could supply it if you inherited a large enough portion of the estate."

Anger put a metallic glint into the brunette girl's emerald eyes. "And I suppose *you* are indifferent to money. You, with a run-down castle in England which would cost millions to repair and even more millions merely to drive out the rats that starve in the walls!"

Lady Barbara deliberately turned her back. "I think I shall go downtown. The atmosphere here is rather tawdry. Stifling would be a better word. An American might even say stinking." She walked from the room without glancing backward.

Marie DuValle cast a look of pure venom at her departing cousin.

"You see?" Chief Fire-Bird sounded tired. "It's a family affair, Mr. Anthony. A purely domestic quarrel. I have no right to ask an outsider to take an interest."

The millionaire criminologist disagreed. "Bill Long Thumb was my friend. I'm not exactly an outsider, sir. When an old classmate of mine is murdered—"

"His death will be avenged," the old man interrupted, "I'll see to that."

Anthony realized they weren't getting anywhere. "You're tired; you've had a shock. Tom and I will go on to the hotel and let you get some rest."

"We'll get no rest," the DuValle girl laughed harshly. "We never rest. We go where there are crowds, and we stay there—because we're afraid. Afraid to be alone!"

Even as she spoke, a weird screech knifed from somewhere in the upper reaches of the house; a muffled, spine-tingling outcry that made the short hairs stir at the nape of Tom Gentry's neck. "What the devil was that?" he burst out.

Fire-Bird shrugged. "My pet parrot," he answered. "He is hungry." And he left the room.

CHAPTER III

SPIDER THREAT

MARTIN LEE, THE CHAUFFEUR, was discreetly courteous. Despite Gentry's protests he had driven Tom and Anthony down-town to the Hotel Mayan; and now, at the corner of Fifth and Cheyenne where he had parked before the hotel entrance, he stood by the ominous black hearse as Jim questioned him.

"No, sir," he said in his careful voice. "I can't understand the glass breaking. After the last time the Chief was shot at, I put in a new panel myself."

"A one man job?" Anthony's eyes narrowed.

"Yes. There's a metal strip at the back; a locking arrangement. By removing it you can slide out the broken panel and put in a fresh one. I've done it twice, now. What with those other two attacks, the Chief bought several spare panes."

Anthony considered this, then tried a new tack. "We heard a peculiar sort of scream from the upper part of the house just as we were getting ready to leave. Would you know anything about it, Lee?"

"Green bird, sir," the chauffeur's tone was inscrutable. To Gentry, that seemed a queer way to speak about a parrot. "Will that be all, sir? I was told to return to the house at once."

Anthony dismissed the man. Then he and his freckled friend entered the expensively decorated Mayan lobby, where Gentry looked around with an air of pleased surprise. "Imagine anything as swell as this away out here in the wilds of Oklahoma! Gosh, pappy, it's almost as nice as the Waldorf-Anthony!"

"It should be," Jim smiled indulgently. "I own the majority stock in it."

"Yeah? Well, I wish you owned some stock in Fire-Bird's grand-daughters. Imagine that old buck having two angels in his tribe!— Oh-oh, here comes one of them now. Her Ladyship is with us, no less!"

Tom was right. Barbara Kendrington, looking like a lovely golden-haired goddess, came gracefully toward them across the lobby, oblivious to the stares of loiterers. An eager expression was in her limpid blue eyes, and there was a catch in her cool voice when she addressed the millionaire criminologist.

"Forgive me for waylaying you like this, Mr. Anthony. But I simply had to speak to you in private. That's why I came downtown ahead of you. Do you mind?"

"Not at all." At Jim's suggestion they went' to the hotel's Marine Room for cocktails. Over their drinks, the sun-bronzed investigator said: "What's troubling you?"

"These murders. There are certain things you should know. I tried to hint at them a while ago…"

"You mean Marie DuValle's romantic interest in Franklin Foster?"

THAT'S PART OF it," the girl nodded. "I mistrust that horrid little man. He tried to make overtures to me first; and when I ignored him, he turned his attentions to Marie. He's turned her head completely. But I know it's all false on his part. Money is his only interest. He's fanatically determined to obtain funds for his pipeline; and those who oppose him… die."

"Who opposed him, sweet stuff?" Gentry demanded.

"Bill Long Thumb, for one. And our two uncles who lost their lives in auto smash-ups. Chief Fire-Bird refuses to suspect Foster, though. How can the old man be so stubborn, so blind?"

The genial aviator sipped his drink. "Maybe he's smart. Maybe he figures his own neck will be safer if he stays on Foster's good side."

"That doesn't square with the facts," Anthony argued. "Remember, there have been two attempts on the Chief's life, despite his friendship with the promoter."

Lady Barbara shuddered. "Nobody's safe in that house! Friendships simply don't count. It's like being caged with wild beasts. That's not a figure of speech, either. It's actual fact."

"In what way?" Jim stared at her.

Like the rest of the family, she was a gambling fool.

"Green bird," she answered enigmatically.

"You mean the old boy's parrot?" Tom asked. "The one that screeches?"

The girl smiled mirthlessly. "If he told you it was a parrot, he lied. In fact, he lied when he said he and Marie and myself were the last surviving members of his family. There's a skeleton in the tribal closet; a living skeleton. Fire-Bird has one remaining son; the youngest—a man about forty. His name is Green Bird and they keep him locked up in a private suite under the eaves. He's a madman, a cunning, drunken throwback to primitive savagery."

"Well, I'll be damned!" Gentry gasped.

"Yes, it's a damnable business. Green Bird is not always crazy. Sometimes he's quite lucid. He realizes he is entitled to a full share of the estate, an equal division with the other heirs. If we all died, he'd get the entire fortune. Or so he thinks—not realizing he'd be declared mentally incompetent." She made a helpless gesture at Anthony. "You see how muddled it is? You see how much we need someone like you to p-protect us from this shadow of d-death?"

"I see many things," Jim Anthony answered.

LATER, IN THEIR seventh floor suite, Jim and his genial companion discussed what Lady Barbara Kendrington had said. "What's your opinion of that doll, pappy?" Tom asked.

"She's a very clever person. Perhaps too clever for her own good. Unpack your bags, junior. Get your tux. You and I are going slumming."

The aviator shook his head. "Nix. Not me. I've had enough of Tulsa for one night." He yawned. "Me, I'm hitting the feathers." And then, as he turned down the covers of his bed, he emitted a strangled yelp and jumped backward.

Anthony pivoted. "What the devil's wrong with you?"

Gentry's cheeks were so white that his freckles stood out in great golden blotches. Speechless, he pointed a shaking finger at the bed whose covers he had thrown back. There in the center of the lower white sheet, hairy and squat and venomous-looking, crouched a tarantula the size of a saucer.

The creature's malignant appearance was emphasized by its ugly blackness, which seemed all the blacker by contrast to the snowy sheet. It shifted its hairy legs slightly, but made no other movement. The happy-go-lucky aviator moaned softly, like a man afflicted with delirium tremens.

"It's alive!" he whispered.

Jim Anthony laughed briefly. "Of course it's alive."

"You think that's funny?" Tom sounded aggrieved. "I guess my sense of humor must be on a vacation."

"I wasn't laughing at the spider. I was laughing at our unknown friend who hopes to frighten us out of town."

Gentry blinked. "Come again, pappy. What do you mean, frighten us out of town? Are you trying to say this hairy monstrosity was planted?"

"I think so. After all, things like that aren't usually to be found in a hotel like the Mayan."

"Well, for Pete's sake! And to think I might have crawled under the covers with it! Br-r-r. What a way to die."

"You wouldn't necessarily die, Tom. You'd be sick, but the bite of that spider isn't usually fatal. In fact, it wouldn't be much more serious than the bite of a real tarantula."

"*Real* tarantula? This one's real enough for me."

"But he's not a true tarantula," Anthony crossed the room and opened the fitted black kit which he carried with him as a sort of portable scientific laboratory.

HE EXTRACTED A metal container, and poured one drop of colorless fluid into it. He then allowed most of the liquid's volatile fumes to dissipate, testing the rate of evaporation by close scrutiny. "Lycosa tarantula takes its name from the town of Taranto, in Apulia," he kept talking as he worked. "Whereas this specimen is much larger and belongs to the species Aviculariidae—the bird-eating spider."

"I'm one bird he ain't going to eat, pappy. I'm blowing town. Hey, what are you trying to do?"

"Capture him," Jim approached the bed with the metal receptacle in one hand and a coat hanger in the other. "Stop fretting. This won't take long."

Gentry's eyes bulged. "Now I've seen everything. A millionaire playing cowboy in a hotel bedroom, riding herd on a spider. You figure to brand him or just carve him into steaks?"

"Neither. I plan to conduct a little experiment. I don't believe this was an attempt to poison either of us, because as I've already told you, the bite wouldn't be fatal. Consider the creature's position in the bed."

"I already considered it. Right where I was about to sit."

"But near the pillows," Anthony corrected. "If the spider had been intended to bite you, though, it would undoubtedly have been planted farther down in the bed, where we would not have detected its presence until some harm had been done. Therefore the whole thing is either a threat or warning—and I intend to find the person who did it."

"How?"

"By seeing if anybody cares to claim this little fellow," Jim nudged the spider with the coat hanger. "Don't worry, there isn't any risk."

"Suppose he jumps at you?"

"He won't. The species can move quickly enough, but they can't see as well as you think. If handled gently, they can be prodded any way you want them to go."

"I want him to go away, pappy. Far, far away."

Smiling, Anthony used the coat hanger as a goad; steered his hairy, unwelcome visitor into the metal container. Then a curious thing happened. At contact with the faint fumes within the receptacle, the spider seemed to curl up and fall asleep.

"Anaesthetized," the criminologist said with satisfaction. "He'll wake up later."

Tom made a sour mouth. "But I won't be around to watch," he promised.

Clamping a perforated lid on the metal box, Anthony contradicted his genial friend. "Of course you will. Now get into your tux. We're still going slumming."

CHAPTER IV

MARTELLI AND CO.

THE ORNATE MIDNATION BUILDING at the corner of Fourth and Boston was one of Tulsa's earlier skyscrapers, partially dwarfed now by taller structures of more recent vintage. It was still imposing, however; and Tom Gentry was thoroughly impressed by the vaulted marble entrance lobby.

"Is this what you call slumming, Jim?"

"More or less," his wealthy friend thumbed an elevator bell. "You haven't seen anything yet."

"Why? What gives?"

"Gives a penthouse that puts my little shack atop the Waldorf-Anthony to shame. It used to be the home of the oil magnate who originally erected the building; a complete house constructed on the roof. Practically a mansion. The owner later transferred his activities to New York and died broke."

"Who lives here now?"

Anthony's voice was grim. "Martelli," he said, and gestured his friend into the elevator.

The car whisked them upward, and presently they stood in what had once been the reception hall of a magnificent residence, looking down into a sunken salon of ballroom dimensions. A quiet hum of voices arose, and you could hear the click of roulette wheels, the subdued clatter of dice bouncing on green baize, the flick of cards being dealt.

Gentry drew a sharp breath as he stared. The floor was richly carpeted, the windows were masked by expensive velvet drapes and the furnishings elaborately costly. Over the scene glowed indirect lighting from concealed fluorescent tubes set into the walls, a glamorous effulgence for men in evening attire and exquisitely gowned women. Here oil was still king, and despite a war of globe-quaking proportions, money was something to be recklessly tossed away.

"We've struck pay-dirt, pappy," the aviator muttered. "Ain't that my little Frenchie cutie over there, bucking the blackjack layout? Sure. That's Marie DuValle. And she's got Franklin Foster with her. Now, why should she fall for a midget?"

Even as Tom spoke, Foster glanced up and spotted the criminologist. He said something to the red-haired girl at his side, then trotted across the salon. "Mr. Anthony! Mr. Gentry! Why didn't you tell me you were coming here? We could have made a party."

Jim's voice was impassive. "I decided to drop in on the spur of the moment. Tom and I couldn't sleep, so—"

"I'll say we couldn't!" the freckled flyer cast a glance at the pocket in which Anthony was carrying a certain metal container. "Our suite had one too many tenants."

Jim warned his friend with a hooded glance. "Rather a busy place, this," he indicated his surroundings.

"Busy and strictly straight," Foster answered enthusiastically. "You'd be amazed at the play Martelli gets. It's a gold mine. I'm hoping to persuade him to invest in my pipeline, provided you grant my priority application on steel. Right, Marie?"

THE DuVALLE GIRL nodded indifferently. She was definitely not cordial; or perhaps she was merely anxious to return to her blackjack game. Anthony wondered if her silence was a pose: wondered if the sight of himself, alive and well, had disturbed her. Could she have known about the spider?

Meantime the little promoter kept chattering in his overly affable way. "Would you like to look around? Come along, I'll show you the whole layout. This is the main room. Over there beyond that door there are semi-private tables. Not actually private—but the ante is a bit high. You have to own plenty of oil wells to buck those games."

"Perhaps I can qualify," the millionaire detective's smile was disarming. "Let's peep in."

They moved to an inner room, Foster in the lead, Marie DuValle obviously annoyed at having to go along. And as they crossed the threshold of the smaller gaming chamber, Anthony beheld the regal blonde Lady Barbara Kendrington standing tautly at a roulette table, oblivious to the newcomers. Before her was a large stack of colored plastic counters, with which she constantly toyed as she kept her gaze glued on the whirling wheel with its dancing ivory ball.

In her eyes was the burning intensity of the true gambler—an expression which Jim had seen on other faces in gaming casinos all over the world. It brought a momentary frown to his own sun-bronzed countenance, for he knew that a person infected with gambling fever would beg, borrow, steal, or perhaps even murder in order to obtain funds with which to pursue the elusive goddess of chance.

He moved forward, watching her. She was playing a combination, resetting the numbers surrounding seventeen, shoving more and yet more of her dwindling stack of chips onto the layout. In two more spins she was wiped out. At once she demanded more markers from the croupier.

The house man hesitated, then despatched his assistant to an adjoining room. Instants later the assistant returned, accompanied by a sleek, swarthy man whose Latin-looking face Anthony immediately recognized. This was the fellow he had seen at the wheel of a sedan leaving the grounds of Chief Fire-Bird's house. This was the gambler, Martelli.

The roulette croupier darted a look at Martelli, who answered with an almost imperceptible nod. Then, obediently, the croupier pushed new chips at Lady Barbara and she resumed her wild plunging on the numbers around seventeen.

At the same instant, Franklin Foster beckoned Martelli over to meet Anthony and Gentry. The gambler suavely acknowledged the introductions. "Happy to have you with us, gentlemen. Would you care to try your luck?"

"Later, perhaps," Jim said. "I'm more interested in the fact that you extend credit to your patrons. Especially patrons who are anything but wealthy," he indicated the golden-haired girl.

The falling object was a huge pipe wrench, and Anthony ducked barely in time.

Martelli smiled with his lips, but not with his eyes. "Lady Barbara is to inherit a considerable fortune in the near future. I think I can afford the risk—within limits, of course."

"And those limits?"

The gambler shrugged. "Oh, a hundred thousand or so. Possibly more. She'll pay up when she gets her inheritance."

"If she lives," Anthony said softly.

Martelli seemed not to hear this; or, if he heard it, he ignored it. "Oklahoma is a dry state, but I think I might find a bottle of—shall we say soda water?—in my office if you would like to join me." His glance included Gentry, Foster, and Marie DuValle in the invitation.

"Thanks, I'd like nothing better," Anthony accepted, sensing that the offer had been made in a deliberate effort to steer him away from a touchy topic. "Shall we include Lady Barbara?"

Martelli couldn't well refuse, although you could tell he didn't appreciate the suggestion. At that same moment, Barbara Kendrington lost the last of her new chips and left the roulette table, spotted the gambler, came toward him.

"How about another five thousand, Martelli?"

"Come have a drink with us first," the swarthy man countered. "We're all going to my office."

She hesitated; seemed on the verge of refusing to drink with Marie DuValle and Franklin Foster. Then, measuring Anthony and Gentry, she appeared to decide that their presence made it all right. "Yes, I could use a spot of something."

THE GROUP DRIFTED along a corridor; passed an open doorway giving access to another private gambling room. Tom Gentry, casually looking in, emitted a surprised whistle when he saw Chief Fire-Bird standing before a faro bank which was being dealt for his solitary benefit. The elderly Indian was not alone at the table, though, for a woman stood beside him; a tall, spectacularly beautiful brunette woman.

"Look, pappy!" the aviator whispered to Anthony. "Cop a gander at what goes on!"

Jim had already noticed the scene and recognized the chief's stunning companion. She was the girl he had seen in that sedan with Martelli earlier in the evening. "Your sister?" he now asked the swarthy gambler.

Martelli nodded. "Yes, that's Lucille. She loves to look on when Fire-Bird plays. It fascinates her."

"Because he loses?"

"No. Because he always wins," Martelli made a wry mouth. "I certainly won't ever get rich from that particular member of the family. He's my special jinx."

Anthony, hearing this, watched the play more attentively, although he seemed to pay no attention. He saw the elderly Indian hesitate over a bet; saw Lucille Martelli make a tiny signal with her hand, unnoticed by the dealer. Fire-Bird changed his bet—and won.

Jim frowned. Something definitely didn't make sense. He wondered why Martelli's sister should back a patron's play. Normally you'd expect her to pull for her brother's establishment, and not against it. Yet obviously she had developed a system of signals which accounted for Fire-Bird's consistent winning.

There was a crazy pattern to this, the millionaire criminologist knew; but that pattern had not yet begun to take shape. It was still chaotic and formless, even to his own keenly perceptive mind; and the many tangled threads bothered him.

But there was one experiment which he wanted to try tonight; an experiment that might clear up at least part of the mystifying puzzle. Moving with deliberate intent, yet making it appear impromptu, Anthony strode into the private room and touched Fire-Bird's arm.

"We're all going to Martelli's office for a drink, sir. How about joining us?"

The old Indian turned, frowned, then looked quizzically at Lucille Martelli. "Shall we?"

"Yes, of course." Her voice was rich and throaty, and her eyes were calculating when she was presented to Anthony. Here, Jim decided, was a woman who would bear watching; a girl who knew exactly what she wanted and how to get it.

IT WAS QUITE a large cluster of persons who strolled into Martelli's office: Anthony, Gentry, Franklin Foster, Fire-Bird, Marie DuValle, Lady Barbara, Lucille Martelli, and the swarthy gambler himself. The room into which Martelli led them was not really an office, but a library of considerable size—the walls lined with well filled bookshelves, the lights discreetly shaded, the furnishings comfortable. Once it had been the private study of the oil magnate who had originally owned the building and the penthouse residence.

Martelli busied himself mixing drinks, apparently unmindful of the tension which was suddenly in the air like crackling electricity. Jim Anthony sensed this tautness, though, and turned it to his own advantage.

He smiled thinly at the English girl. "I congratulate you on your cleverness, Lady Barbara," he dropped a verbal bombshell.

Fire-Bird's golden-haired granddaughter stared. "Just how do you mean that?" her voice rose over the abrupt silence that settled upon the room.

"I refer to your highly original form of life insurance."

"Life insurance—?"

"Quite so," the sun-bronzed criminologist nodded. "Several of your relatives have been murdered. Perhaps you fear that you yourself may be next on the list. Therefore you pile up a staggering gambling debt to Mr. Martelli, a debt he can't hope to collect unless you remain alive to inherit your share of a certain oil estate. Obviously Martelli will do his best to protect your life until the debt is paid."

The girl's red lips parted. "That's rather shrewd of you, Mr. Anthony. As you say, it's a form of life insurance; expensive, but worth the cost."

"I wonder," Jim mused. "There are other angles, you know."

"Such as?"

"You might get in so deeply that your normal share of the estate would be insufficient to cover your losses. In that case it might become necessary to remove some of the other heirs so that you would inherit a larger amount."

She paled. "Are you accusing me of the murders?"

"Or me?" Martelli spoke harshly from across the room.

Anthony moved toward the gambler, producing a metal box out of his pocket en route. "I have accused nobody. In fact, while there might be several plausible suspects in this mass attempt on the lives of Chief Fire-Bird and his family, I find in each case a curious canceling-out of motive."

"Meaning what?" Fire-Bird himself asked the question.

"Well, take Lady Barbara," Jim said. "Fearing for her safety, she incurred a huge gambling debt as life insurance. If she were the killer, that would seem unnecessary."

"Thanks," the blonde girl's voice was icy.

"Then there's Martelli. Why should he murder any of the heirs when all of you constantly lose large sums at his tables? He gets your money without violence; therefore it would seem foolish for him to resort to such measures."

The gambler grinned sardonic appreciation of this logic.

Anthony continued: "Miss DuValle might possibly desire a larger share of the estate than she would ordinarily inherit, so that she could invest in Franklin Foster's pipeline; and the same possibility might be attributed to Foster himself. But Foster already seems to have sufficient backing for his project, with you, Chief, as one of the participants, and Martelli also behind the deal."

The DuValle girl laughed coldly. "You seem to have cleared all of us from suspicion, Mr. Anthony."

"Not quite. There is the Chief's mad son, Green Bird. There may be others I don't know about. Many questions remain unanswered—including this…" And the criminologist opened his small metal receptacle; dumped the spider on Martelli's desk.

He stepped back quickly, his narrowed eyes surveying the circle of faces around him, watching for some reflex expression of guilt. Instead, he saw only repugnance and horror; a reaction of stupefied astonishment, as if no person in the room had ever beheld the ugly tarantula before. Among the company, someone was a consummately clever actor or actress—or else the guilty one was not present.

For a full second, no one moved. Then Martelli, with a speed almost impossible for the eye to follow, thrust his right hand into an open drawer and hauled forth a snub-nosed .32 automatic. As Tom Gentry said later, it was the fastest draw he had ever witnessed, barring only Jim Anthony's own swiftness with a gun.

Martelli squeezed the trigger and the automatic spat orange flame, its explosive sound roaring like unleashed thunder. The spider on the desk seemed to disintegrate and vanish; and in its place a bullet hole appeared in the polished wood.

On Anthony's stoic countenance there was no expression of surprise at the gambler's unerring marksmanship. As for Martelli, he stared for an instant at the bullet hole; then his cold black eyes looked directly into Jim's.

"All right, pal," his voice had a ragged quality, as if he'd been running. "You've had your practical joke. Now it's my turn to tell you I didn't like it. You may be one of the richest and most powerful guys in the world, but I'm not impressed. Don't do anything like that again or I'll slap your ears down."

The man was white-faced, obviously building himself up to a towering rage that might result in a blind fury of further gunplay. Anthony realized this and tensed his muscles for action; but the need never came. At that moment a door banged inward and two men surged into the room. They were big, hard-looking, obviously on the alert for trouble—as fine a pair of bruisers as you would care to meet in some underworld slum.

"Hey, Spider, what cooks? We heard a shot—"

Martelli's anger vanished. He slipped his gun back in the desk drawer, and a suave, mechanical smile lifted the corners of his thin-lipped mouth. "Nothing, boys. I was just showing Mr. Anthony what we do to insects here in Tulsa. Get back to the salon and quiet the beef. Go on, scram."

The bouncers hesitated, then left. Jim Anthony, sensing the hostility around him, concluded that it was time he, too, took his departure. His experiment with the spider had apparently gained him little except the knowledge that Martelli was handy with a gun.

First promising Franklin Foster that he would accompany the promoter to the oil fields the next afternoon for an inspection of a short length of wooden pipeline that had been constructed for demonstration purposes, Jim took Gentry's arm. "We must be going, Tom. Good night, everybody."

Later, on the way back to the hotel, Gentry burst into excited chatter. "Gosh, pappy, did you hear what that big bruiser called Martelli? He called him Spider! Do you suppose it means anything? Could a spider be Martelli's trademark? Could he be the guy that left the tarantula in our suite?"

"Possibly. On the other hand, maybe he just didn't like the idea of someone else shoving his calling cards around; someone who was trying to put him under suspicion."

CHAPTER V

DERRICK OF DEATH

HALF AN HOUR'S DRIVE due east from Tulsa on State Highway 33 lay the experimental length of wooden pipeline. The oil field itself was an old one, rather small, near the grassy banks of the Verdigris River; and most of the wells had long since gone on the pump, since natural pressure was no longer sufficient to make a flow.

A few of the producing holes were newer, however, and their derricks still reared like wooden skeletons above them. From a dozen offsets, thick crude petroleum gurgled into branch pipes of small diameter. These, in turn, fed like the roots of a tree into a main pipeline leading to a large storage tank.

It was this main line, no more than half a mile long, which Franklin Foster had employed for his experimental wooden type of construction. The pool belonged, lock, stock and barrel, to Chief Fire-Bird, who had granted permission for the regular steel pipe to be bypassed in favor of the wooden pipeline.

Foster had laid his line in a shallow trench dug in the red clay, but he had not covered it with earth. Instead, he'd left the wooden pipe exposed for inspection purposes, to demonstrate the method of joining the sections with steel collars and inner sleeves—and to display the pipe's ability to stand up under pumping pressure. Since there was a slight upward grade to the storage tank, the crude oil had to be forced on its journey by a booster pump to overcome gravity.

It was midafternoon when the affable little promoter drove Jim Anthony and Tom Gentry onto the field and began explaining his methods. He seemed genuinely earnest; and Jim, as a government expert, made careful notes of all the details. Even Gentry displayed a certain reluctant interest, although the technology was utterly beyond him.

But the genial flyer was even more interested in another matter which had been bothering him all day. At his first opportunity he drew his wealthy criminologist friend aside.

"Hey, pappy!" he whispered guardedly. "Where were you this morning? I figured you'd need some extra sleep after the excitement at Martelli's last night. But when I woke up for breakfast, you were long gone; didn't come back to the hotel until time for Foster to pick us up and bring us out here."

ANTHONY STARED SPECULATIVELY across the heat-baked field as it shimmered in the sun; watched the red dust-devils whirling in an occasional gust of breeze. Here and there a few workers moved laggardly, inspecting pumps and clambering over derricks. "I was contacting the Tulsa branch of my Organization," he said.

His enigmatic words conveyed plenty of meaning to Gentry. A strange legion was the Anthony Organization; a nation-wide army of men and women drawn from all walks of life and every strata of society. It included bootblacks and bankers, merchants and chorus girls, newsboys and housewives and scrubwomen and sportsmen. No matter how large or how small the community, there was always a branch of this

**Out of control, the car plunged
over the embankment.**

fabulous legion whose membership had just one thing in common—a constant readiness to aid Jim Anthony in his never ending war upon crime. They represented a great cross-section of America, and they stood for the American way of life: the battle of right against wrong.

"You've started the machinery moving?" Tom asked.

"Yes. At least I've placed all suspects under surveillance," Anthony said. "I also had a long conference with Lieutenant Halmar down at homicide headquarters."

"What did you find out from him?"

"Not much. He's taking legal steps to put Chief Fire-Bird's crazy son under official restraint, send him to an asylum—just in case Green Bird is the one behind the murders. And speaking of legal matters, I learned something about Foster."

"What?"

"Our undersized friend is the attorney in charge of the oil estate inherited by the Fire-Bird family. Moreover, he seems to have some secret source of income beyond his law practise or his various promotion enterprises. Sh-h. He's calling me now."

True enough, the strutting little promoter stood at the base of a derrick, a cigar cocked in his mouth as he beckoned. "Here are some specifications and blueprints I'd like to show you, sir," he said as Jim approached.

A sheaf of papers fluttered in his hand, stirred by a vagrant wind that smelled of hot, dusty foliage; of green grass and trees by the cool riverbank and the sharper pungency of oil flowing from the earth's heart. Anthony bent over the blueprints; and then Tom Gentry, with a banshee yowl, hurled himself forward to impact bruisingly against the sun-bronzed criminologist.

"Jim! Watch out!"

Something flashed down out of the sky as Anthony staggered sidewise. The falling object was a huge pipe wrench that weighed easily fifteen pounds, maybe more. It struck the cement base of the derrick with clanging force; sent shattered pieces of concrete flying like sparks. And the spot where it landed was exactly where Jim had been standing an instant ago.

Gentry's plunging tackle had saved his friend's life. Now he pointed upward, his freckles prominent against the pallor of his cheeks. "On the top derrick platform, pappy! That guy up there—he dropped the wrench deliberately! He *aimed* it!"

AN EXPRESSION OF almost ludicrous concern spread across the countenance of Franklin Foster. "But—but th-that's impossible! Wh-who would do a thing like that? Accidents are always happening around oil derricks—"

Jim Anthony had not stopped to listen to this protest. He'd spotted the man on the rig's top platform, a bulky fellow in a pair of grease stained overalls. And now, moving with an amazing flash of speed, Jim started climbing.

Hand over hand he went surging up the side of the derrick, his superb muscles accomplishing the ascent with deceptive ease and breath-taking swiftness. Gaining the upper stage, he literally flung himself like a swinging pendulum up and over the edge; landed on his feet upon the platform, legs straddled and fists balled.

"Now, then," he said tunelessly.

The overall clad man backed away. "Lay offa me, mister. That wrench was a accident, see?"

"I think you're lying. Especially since I recognize you. It won't pay you to lie, my friend. I have ways of forcing the truth out of you; ways you might not enjoy."

"But I'm tellin' the truth," the fellow rasped. "Get outa my way. I'm goin' down and you ain't gonna stop me."

Jim's smile was bleak, mirthless menace. "That's where you're wrong. You don't go down until you tell me who hired you to drop that tool on me."

"Hired me? Nobody did." Abruptly the workman, like a cornered rat, charged at Jim, swinging terrifically. "You asked for it. Now take it!" And he aimed a savage roundhouse punch that would have knocked the millionaire criminologist off the platform had it landed.

It didn't land, though. Anthony stepped upside the blow, let it whistle harmlessly past his shoulder, and countered with a jolting, punishing uppercut that rocked the man back on his heels. He followed this with an explosive jab full to his bulkier adversary's mouth. The man spat blood and curses and the broken fragments of his wrecked front teeth.

"Will you talk?" Anthony grappled with him.

The thug's answer was shrill vituperation. "I'll kill you—I'll teach you to slug me—I'll throw you off—" Freeing himself, he lowered his head and rushed like an infuriated bull, trying to butt Jim to destruction.

Anthony dropped flat. The unexpected maneuver gave his enemy no target to smash against; and the man could not check his headlong rush in time to save himself. Screaming in a sudden frenzy of terror, the fellow tried to dig his heels into the planks of the platform; failed. Momentum carried him to the brink and over it. His flailing body arced into empty space and fell earthward, sickeningly....

DESCENDING TO THE derrick's base, Anthony faced a stunned Tom Gentry and a nauseated Franklin Foster, who seemed incapable of looking at the corpse.

Gentry was first to break the silence. He glared toward Foster. "Something tells me you ain't going to stay healthy very long, pal. What was the idea of luring Jim under this derrick so that guy could drop a spanner at him?"

"You—you don't th-think I had anything to do with it?" the man choked.

"I don't know. I'm asking you."

Foster appealed to Jim. "Don't let him say such th-things! I w-wouldn't have any reason to arrange a deathtrap for you, Mr. Anthony. You're the man I'm depending on for a steel priority! Why would I—?" his voice trailed off weakly.

Gentry made a disparaging noise. "Nuts! Maybe you don't want that priority. Maybe you're figuring to go south with the dough the suckers have invested in your crackpot pipeline. Maybe it'd spoil your plans if the government gave you a go-ahead signal on construction of the line."

Bewilderment spread across the promoter's features, as if he now realized how circumstances had placed him under suspicion. Once again he addressed a frantic appeal to the millionaire criminologist.

"Surely you don't believe any such fantastic theory! Aren't there others in Tulsa who'd be more logically interested in removing you from the scene? What about the person who has been killing off Chief Fire-Bird's family? Suppose the murderer is afraid of your detective abilities and is trying to eliminate you before you discover too much? After all, a lot of people were in Martelli's library last night when you and I made this date to come out here today. They all heard it. Any of them could have sent a man out ahead—"

Anthony nodded, his face expressionless, his eyes smouldering. "Very true. And there's one possibility you seem to have missed. Maybe the man intended to drop that wrench on you instead of me. Perhaps you were the intended victim."

"Heavens!" Foster squeaked. "I hadn't thought of that! But I have no enemies that I know of. I don't even recognize this dead man. Nobody could identify him now, the way his head was crushed by the fall."

"I recognized him before he went off the platform," Jim said grimly. "Do you remember the two bruisers who came rushing into Martelli's office after he shot that spider? Well, this was one of Martelli's men."

CHAPTER VI

MURDER HEARSE

CURIOUSLY THAT STATEMENT SEEMED to bludgeon Franklin Foster's senses like a blackjack blow. He reeled, swayed, recovered himself. "My God!" he gasped. "Martelli!" He turned, started to run.

Anthony caught him. "Where do you think you're going?"

"To the field office phone," the little man panted. "The county authorities must be notified."

"I'll attend to that," Jim said levelly. "For the time being, this man's death must appear to have been an accident to one of the regular derrick riggers. I don't want his identity disclosed to the police."

"Wh-why?"

"Because it might tip Martelli that we're wise to him. If I can keep him in the dark regarding the extent of my knowledge, I may find it easier to close the net around him. Now go ahead and phone your report of this 'accident'."

Foster licked his lips. "That's not the only phone call I'm going to make."

"Meaning what?"

"Meaning I'm scared. Maybe you were right last night when you hinted Martelli might be killing off the other heirs so Lady Barbara would inherit the whole fortune. At first I didn't quite believe it could be a mass family murder scheme; it seemed too fantastic. Bill Long Thumb was an outspoken man with plenty of enemies, any one of whom might have shot him. His uncles died in automobile smashups and I thought it was ridiculous to call those accidents murder. But now I'm convinced."

"Well?"

"Marie DuValle is the one I'm worried about now. Whether you believe it or not, I love her. I'm not interested in her inheritance. She means more to me than all the money and pipelines in the world. I'm going to get her out of town before something happens to her. I'm going to call her, tell her to meet me in West Tulsa. Then, I'm going to take her to Oklahoma City and keep her under cover."

By now a sparse group of oilfield workmen had raced to the derrick, drawn by the sight of the corpse. Jim Anthony left a foreman in charge of the body, with instructions to stand guard until the county police arrived. Then the criminologist and Tom Gentry accompanied Foster to the field office, half a mile distant, to make phone calls.

They contacted the law first; then Foster put through a connection to Marie DuValle at Chief Fire-Bird's residence in Tulsa. He spoke to her with desperate urgency; and when he rang off, he turned to Jim.

"I'll run you and Mr. Gentry back to town, drop you off at your hotel. After that you won't be seeing me for a while—not until the killer has been caught!"

IN FIRE-BIRD'S HOUSE, the diminutive DuValle girl trembled as she placed the phone in its cradle. An instant before she lowered the instrument, though, she thought she detected a metallic click on the line, as if one of the upstairs extensions had just been disconnected.

Already panic-stricken because of Franklin Foster's message, her fright now increased tenfold. Foster had told her he was at her grandfather's oil property on the Verdigris, and that it would take him an hour to drive back to town.

Perhaps the danger was already enfolding her, she thought frantically. Someone had apparently been listening in on her conversation from an upstairs extension—and yet she had been under the impression that she was alone in the house. Alone except for the servants—and a madman.

The thought of the Chief's crazy son, Green Bird, sent a shudder of fear through her very marrow. She had seen this insane uncle of hers only once; and that once had been enough. His glittering eyes and maniac, crazy smile had terrified her, and the memory still festered in her mind. Supposedly he was locked in his room on the top floor: but could he have escaped? Could he have been the one who'd tapped her phone call?

Blindly she went to the staircase, raced upward in search of her grandfather. Maybe he had come home from a trip downtown without her knowledge. She knocked on the closed door of his study, received no response and timidly tried the knob; found it unlatched. She entered.

THE LONG SHADOWS of late afternoon were already marching across the carpet, silent as the chamber itself. She stared all about; saw nobody. And she did not possess the courage to check on Green Bird's prison suite on the third floor.

Instead, she raced to her own room and began packing her luggage, first hastily, then with more care—for she had nearly an hour to kill before it would be time for her rendezvous with Franklin Foster. Dusk deepened as she worked, and with thickening darkness came a thickening of her fears. An idea struck her. Why should she waste time here in this somber mansion when she could wait in safety across the bridge in West Tulsa?

The thought seemed to lift a heavy pressure from her shoulders. Swiftly she finished cramming her belongings into her bags; went to the house phone and pressed the button marked Garage. A voice answered respectfully. "Yes?"

"Who is this?"

Stalled on the track, they waited while the car broke down.

"Martin Lee, ma'am. The chauffeur."

"Good! Bring the car around front. This is Miss DuValle. I want you to take me somewhere. At once."

"Yes, ma'am." And then, as the line went dead, a hideous blurt of laughter shrilled through the house from upstairs; maniac laughter, sinister and reasonless.

The red-haired girl stood frozen in her boudoir. For one horrifying instant she had thought that the sound had come from her own doorway, and that Green Bird was waiting there to seize her when she emerged.

She strained her ears for some sound from the corridor, but heard nothing; no breathing, no movement, no repetition of that cackling laugh. Strength flowed back into her terror-paralyzed body and she grasped her suitcase, moved to the door, cautiously thrust it open.

The hall was deserted.

Below, tires crunched on gravel. That would be the hearse as it pulled up before the residence. Marie DuValle went to a front window of the hallway overlooking the private drive. Directly beneath her, the liveried chauffeur was just opening the rear door of his somber black vehicle.

A bag in each hand, Chief Fire-Bird's red-haired granddaughter descended the staircase; walked out of the red brick house for the last time. Dusk's gloom had become almost complete darkness by now, and a shudder of repugnance rippled through the girl as she entered the hearse. Martin Lee must have already returned to the driver's compartment, she concluded; at least he wasn't on hand to close the door for her. She closed it herself, just as well satisfied. Now they could get started all the more quickly; and haste was what she wanted.

"To West Tulsa," she called through the sliding steel panel which separated her from the chauffeur up front. "Use the new bridge. And please hurry!"

THE HEARSE PURRED smoothly into motion, heading downtown toward Riverside Drive and then along the landscaped bank of the Arkansas, a broad stream now swollen and muddily red from recent rains in the distant watershed. Presently the girl tapped on the forward panel. "Faster, please!"

The partition slid open, and Marie's startled eyes beheld a face which was not Martin Lee's. She had a shadowy, fleeting glimpse of a figure slumped to the right of the driver; a lolling, inert figure in livery. That was the chauffeur; but he was not at the wheel.

The man who was driving the hearse had turned to peer back at his feminine passenger; and she, in turn, looked into his cunning, beady eyes. Recognition dawned on her, and with it a realization of her own peril; for the mad glitter in those eyes spelled her doom.

She screamed, and the sound filled the narrow confines of the hearse as the partitioning panel slid closed. For an instant she sat rooted in her chair, thralled by terror; then she leaped toward the rear door. The sinister vehicle was increasing its speed now, but that didn't matter to Marie DuValle. Her thoughts were centered upon only one thing. Escape. Reckless of risk, she meant to hurl herself to the roadway.

But the door refused to open when she wrenched at its inner handle. The latch was jammed—deliberately jammed, she sensed now as she clawed at it. Its catch must have been doctored in advance, before she'd entered the machine. When she shut herself in, she had sealed her own fate.

Another scream ripped from her agonized throat. She beat at the door with tiny fists, until the knuckles split and bled. It was useless. Suddenly she felt the hearse swerving into a turn, although the roadway at this point was straight.

Dimly through the vehicle's glass side she saw a figure as it leaped from the driver's compartment, abandoning the wheel, jumping to the soft foliage beside the highway. Then the hearse passed that sprawled form and plunged toward the embankment out of control.

Driverless, it lurched and swayed toward the brink of the Arkansas; teetered crazily there for an age-long instant. Then it toppled into the muddy river, end over end. There was a mighty, widening splash; then, upside down, the car sank in soft muck until only its wheels remained above the roiled water's muddy surface.

Marie DuValle's screams faded and were still.

CHAPTER VII

PHOTOSTAT CLUES

LESS THAN AN HOUR after Franklin Foster had dropped them at their hotel, Jim Anthony and Tom Gentry were again on the move. The wealthy criminologist had spent the intervening time in a series of telephone check-ups with various members of his Organization as well as a guarded conversation with Lieutenant Halmar of the homicide department; a talk in which he told the police official very little of what had actually happened at the oil field. Halmar, in turn, had nothing of interest to report.

Now, crossing the intersection of Third and Main, the genial Gentry looked dissatisfied. "I don't savvy your drift, Jim. That character who tried to bounce a wrench off your conk was one of Martelli's hoods. How come you ain't rushing over to ask the wop some knuckle questions?"

Anthony's smile was enigmatic in the reflection of red Neon lights from a store window. "One thing at a time. First I want a look at Franklin Foster's office."

"Foster? But that little squirt is out of the picture, now. He's just plain scared. You saw how he high-tailed it for West Tulsa as soon as he let us out of his car. He's got just one idea in mind—to get his girl friend out of town where she'll be safe."

Pushing along through the early night pedestrian traffic toward Boston and Third, the sun-bronzed millionaire nodded. "Precisely why I want to check on him. He seems overanxious to get away. Maybe he has Marie DuValle's safety in mind; maybe his own. But we do know he was unnaturally shocked when he learned it was one of Martelli's men who dropped that pipe wrench. Why does he fear Martelli, specifically? What is the source of his secret income? Why was the wrench dropped when both Foster and I were under the oil derrick?"

"Too many questions for me, pappy."

"And for me. Hence my desire to learn some of the answers." They entered the remodeled lobby of the three-story Grew Building, one of the city's older and less important downtown office structures which had recently been modernized. Here Franklin Foster maintained his business headquarters—the focal point of Anthony's current interest.

Using the stairway instead of revealing their presence by calling the elevator operator, Jim and Gentry ascended to Foster's second floor suite. In the dimly lighted second floor corridor, the criminologist posted Tom on sentry duty to warn him if anyone approached. Then, from a secret pocket of his coat, Anthony drew his prized steels—those uncanny instruments of his own design, with which he could force the cleverest lock ever devised.

A MOMENT'S MANIPULATION clicked the bolt of Franklin Foster's door. Jim called softly for his aviator friend to join him; and together they crossed the threshold into solid darkness, closing the door behind them.

"Need my flashlight, pappy?"

"Not yet. No use risking it until it's necessary." Years before, while in India, the millionaire had mastered a certain visual trick which had been taught to him by a Hindu yogi: the amazing trick of enlarging the pupils of his eyes by conscious muscular effort, so that he could see almost as well in darkness as an average man might see in full daylight.

Employing this system now, Anthony took Tom's arm and steered him through a reception room whose furnishings aroused no interest. Presently they came into Foster's private sanctum, where Jim made use of a hooded pocket torch.

In the dull glow you could discern an expensive desk, swivel chair, two guest chairs, costly rug, and a built-in bookcase full of law reports.

It was behind the book-cases
that he found the safe.

But the other walls were blank and there were no filing cabinets, no office safe where a man might store valuable papers or documents.

"Looks as if the little shrimp doesn't do much law business," Gentry whispered. "Or any other kind."

Jim shook his head. "Mustn't let an uncluttered desk deceive you. If there are records, they must be here somewhere."

"What makes you believe there might be?"

"Because I've observed Foster and analyzed him. He's a careful man, the kind that keeps full documentary files on everything with which he has any association. Those blueprints and specifications he showed me at the oil field were indications. I never saw anything more complete, down to the smallest detail."

While speaking, Anthony was opening and closing desk drawers; but when these revealed nothing of importance he turned his hawk-like eyes to a thoughtful scrutiny of the room itself. Presently his gaze halted on the built-in bookcase.

There was something about it that attracted his suspicion; a tiny, almost imperceptible fissure which seemed to separate a middle section from the lower and upper portions. This center sector seemed detached from its neighbors, as if resting unsupported. It consisted of three crammed shelves, and the books were certainly too weighty to stay there merely because the shelves were fastened to the rear wall. Something else gave strength and rigidity to the structure.

But what?

Jim took one of the thinnest of his steels and worked it into the fissure; ran it horizontally, then vertically along the sides. The left side was free, but the right side offered a hidden obstruction that felt, to Anthony's sensitive fingers on the steel instrument, like concealed hinges.

Again he probed, more carefully this time. Suddenly there was a faint metallic click—and the whole central bookcase section swung outward the way a door would swing. Set flush into the back wall was the circular metal face of a safe.

"I'll be jiggered!" Gentry whispered.

Tom's astonished admiration increased when he saw his friend take another steel instrument and work it behind the shiny combination knob. Now, holding this metal probe with one hand, Anthony began turning the dial with the other. His fingers twisted the knob with infinite slowness and vernier precision, while the steel instrument conveyed to his fingertips an almost imperceptible vibration as the tumblers fell. The job of noting these tumbler-position numbers required the keenest of vision, of hearing, of touch.

It seemed easy work for Jim Anthony, though. In less than five minutes he had worked out the lock's combination. Then, expertly, he opened the safe. It contained a large green strongbox, which he extracted and opened. From this he drew a series of fat manila envelopes, whose contents he spread on Franklin Foster's desk.

GENTRY PEERED OVER Jim's shoulder. The first envelope disgorged a number of vouchers, bank deposits, and a complete set of bookkeeping records in loose leaf form.

"What do you think of this, Tom?" the criminologist whispered grimly.

"Looks like a slice of big business. Somebody's been handling a lot of dough. But what were they selling?"

"Excitement, I think," Anthony said. "Pleasure. The pleasure of risk, of winning and losing large sums of money. In brief, I believe these are the records of a gambling house."

"Martelli's?"

"Yes. His initials are on the reports, and his endorsements on some of the canceled checks. But notice the division of profits. Martelli receives one fourth. The other three quarters go to someone whose initials are F.F."

"Franklin Foster!" Tom exclaimed. "He must be the guy who's backing that penthouse layout!"

"So it would appear. According to these figures, they began with a very small capital and the thing has grown to pretty big proportions; Foster the silent partner, Martelli the front."

Gentry whistled softly. "That explains why the little squirt got so scared when he found out it was one of Martelli's gunsels who dropped the pipe wrench. Maybe he thought Martelli was going to have him knocked off and get full control of the racket."

"Quite so."

"But wait," Tom said. "Foster hinted he was trying to sell Martelli on the idea of investing in his pipeline. How about that angle?"

Anthony smiled. "A cover-up. Martelli is little more than one of Foster's employees."

"Okay. Then why didn't Foster use his gambling profits to go ahead with the pipeline deal? Why was he scurrying around for outside capital from Chief Fire-Bird and other suckers? How can you explain that?"

"Easily enough. The gambling profits ran into thousands but a pipeline would need millions."

"Then you must figure the little bozo was sincere about his wooden pipe dream. He really wanted to build the line; and Bill Long Thumb was haywire when he called him a phony."

"It begins to look that way," Jim said. "Now let's see what else we have." He opened another envelope; frowned.

Gentry was impatient. "What is it, pappy?"

"A copy of a will filed for probate by Franklin Foster, lawyer. The will of Chief Fire-Bird's father—Bill Long Thumb's great grandfather."

"How does it read?"

"The estate is divided equally among all the heirs, with a provision that if any die before the date of final probate, the collateral heirs inherit the decedent's share."

"In other words, when the old redskin signed it, he cut in his whole family for a split, huh?"

"It would seem he signed their death warrants at the same time," Anthony answered grimly. "Wait; here's something else!" A hint of excitement tinctured his whisper.

"Something important?"

"Important enough to be the partial answer to our puzzle, I think," the millionaire criminologist responded. "It's the photo-static copy of an application for a marriage license issued for Chief Fire-Bird and—Lucille Martelli!"

"The gambler's sister! You mean she's married to the Chief? That gorgeous brunette dish?"

"I don't know. This is just the application. Hold everything while I do some checking." Jim reached for the phone on the desk, dialed it. Presently he spoke in a low tone and rang off.

Gentry fired two cigarettes, gave one to his sun-bronzed companion. "Who'd you call?"

"An Organization member who works in the county courthouse," the criminologist answered. "I've sent him to look something up. He'll report back."

THE NEXT THIRTY or forty minutes dragged interminably. Then there was the first suggestion of a jingle from the phone bell, and Anthony lifted the receiver swiftly to prevent a loud ring from attracting the attention of any possible passer-by in the outer corridor. "Yes?" A pause. "Good. Thanks." He disconnected thoughtfully.

Tom's eyes were expectant. "Well?"

"There is no record of Fire-Bird marrying Miss Martelli anywhere in Oklahoma. The license has not yet been used."

"Then why did they apply for it?" Anthony rapidly theorized. "I think the answer is in the date of the application, which is just one week prior to the filing of the will for probate. Here's the picture last month: Chief Fire-Bird's father is very rich, very old, dying. Presumably his fortune will go to Fire-Bird."

"Well?"

"Lucille Martelli determines to marry the Chief for the money she thinks he will inherit. That has happened more than once in the past, you know; young and pretty white women marrying elderly Indians for financial gain."

"Sure," Tom nodded.

Anthony continued: "Lucille makes a big play for Fire-Bird; even helps him win at gambling games. He falls for her. They apply for a marriage license. Then Great-Grandpa dies, his will is opened, and instead of Fire-Bird being sole heir, the estate is to be shared among a number of relatives."

"So Lucille backs out, eh?"

"Temporarily, yes."

Gentry pursed his lips. I get it. Martelli is promoting his sister's marriage to Chief Fire-Bird. When other heirs show up, Martelli decides to knock them off so Fire-Bird can inherit everything. The wedding is postponed until these murders are all finished. Some phony attacks are even made on the Chief himself, to throw suspicion on the various other heirs; to keep the poor old Cherokee from guessing the score. Fire-Bird thinks he's under the gun along with the rest of his family, when actually he's as safe as he'd be in church."

"You're pretty close to it, Tom," the criminologist said.

"Yeah. Then you showed up and took an interest. Martelli put a spider in your bed to scare you off. When you didn't scare, he sent one of his hoods to conk you with a wrench. Hell's hinges, pappy, it's high time we were going over to that dago's gambling joint. He needs to be taught a lesson!"

Anthony snapped off his flashlight. "Okay. What are we waiting for?"

CHAPTER VIII

GAMBLER'S GAMBIT

IT WAS STILL EARLY in the evening, and there was only a small crowd in Martelli's penthouse resort when Jim Anthony and Tom Gentry entered the reception hall. Not pausing in the outer salon, they directed their steps toward the swarthy gambler's office. Reaching the door of the converted library, they heard voices issuing from within the room. A woman was loudly demanding: "You can't cut me off this way, Spider. I want more credit."

"Sorry." That was Martelli, his suave tone as impersonal as a cube of ice. "I run this place for profit, Lady Barbara. You're into me deep enough, considering I'm not sure when I'll be paid—if ever."

"You know I'll square accounts with you as soon as I get my share of the estate."

"That's my point. I no longer consider you a good risk. I'm not certain you'll be alive to get your inheritance."

A hint of fear was discernible in Lady Barbara Kendrington's retort. "Are you threatening me, Martelli?"

"No. But since you admitted last night that you were buying life insurance by losing at my tables, I've decided not to sell you any more."

Without waiting to hear the blonde girl's answer, Jim Anthony shoved the door open and strode over the threshold with Gentry at his heels. Ignoring Lady Barbara, he faced Martelli.

The gambler arose from behind his desk. "I like people to knock before they intrude, mister."

"The time for politeness has passed," Jim said levelly. "I want to know about one of your gorillas; one of the pair who entered this room last night after you fired a shot at the spider. The one with the crooked nose."

Martelli exhibited a hint of surprise. "That would be Louie Sultzer. What about him?"

"Do you know where he is now?" Anthony countered.

"Why, no. He didn't show up for work this evening. Probably drunk somewhere, I suppose."

"Not drunk," the criminologist stated.

"Dead."

"Wh-wha-what—?"

"He fell from an oil derrick this afternoon while he was attempting to kill me. And I'm curious to know why he made that attempt. Perhaps you can enlighten me."

Martelli shoved his chair backward as if to give himself a greater clearance for sudden movement. Gentry, remembering the speed with which the gambler had pulled a gun from the desk the previous night, tensed himself to leap at the swarthy man if he so much as twitched a hand.

But Martelli remained motionless on his feet, staring at Anthony, his eyes betraying no desire for gunplay. "Are you trying to say I ordered Louie to rub you out?"

"I'm just asking. After all, he was your employee."

Martelli made a sour mouth. "I don't know anything about it, pal. I gave no such orders. I didn't even hire the guy to work here. My sister takes care of the personnel—"

HE WAS INTERRUPTED by someone who came crashing into the library, unannounced and wild-eyed with excitement. The newcomer was absurdly small, and he didn't even look dapper in his loud tweeds. He was the promoter and attorney, Franklin Foster; but something had stripped away his usual affable manner, leaving him breathless and white-faced.

"I can't find her!" he panted. "Is she here? Has anyone seen her?"

Anthony seized the little man's arm; shook him. "Get a grip on yourself. What are you talking about?"

"Marie DuValle. She didn't meet me in West Tulsa as we planned. I waited more than an hour, then went to the house. Nobody home but the servants and Green Bird. The hearse was gone. The chauffeur, too." Foster's lips twisted. "Where's Fire-Bird? Maybe he can tell me—"

"The Chief went to an Indian stomp dance this side of Sand Springs, just beyond Bruner Station on the interurban line," Martelli said. "My sister went with him. They left about half past four."

Foster wrenched himself from Anthony's grasp. "I'll find him and ask him." Then he blundered blindly from the room.

The millionaire criminologist picked up the phone from Martelli's desk. "You don't mind if I notify the police that Marie DuValle is missing?"

The gambler shrugged. "Why should I mind?"

Anthony had already started dialing. Presently he got his connection with headquarters; asked for Lieutenant Halmar of the homicide department. "Jim Anthony calling, lieutenant. I want to report a missing girl, Marie DuValle, one of the heirs to the Fire-Bird estate… What? You did? Where… oh, I see. Just a while ago, you say?… Thanks, lieutenant. I'll contact you later." Harshly etched lines deepened on Jim's sun-bronzed countenance as he replaced the receiver in its hook.

Tom Gentry blinked. "What's happened, pappy?"

"Miss DuValle is dead," the millionaire answered grimly. He studied the effect of his words on Martelli and Lady Barbara Kendrington.

Both seemed genuinely stunned. "How did it… wh-what killed Cousin Marie?" the English girl choked.

"The police just found Chief Fire-Bird's hearse upside down in the river, only its wheels showing. The girl was drowned. The chauffeur's neck was broken."

"An accident?" Martelli whispered.

"In appearance. Time may prove otherwise. I think we'd better have a showdown, my friend."

The gambler was as unmoving as the spider had been on the preceding night, crouching in Gentry's bed. "Meaning what, mister?"

"Meaning I took the liberty of opening Franklin Foster's private safe this evening. And I learned some curious secrets. For one thing, Foster is your silent partner in this gambling resort; the majority owner."

"So?" Still Martelli did not move.

"I also found a copy of the will left by Fire-Bird's father. Under its terms, the estate was to be split equally; but should any heirs die before a final settlement, their shares revert to the remaining members of the family."

"That's no secret," Martelli said raggedly.

"No, but the marriage license was."

"What marriage license?"

ANTHONY'S SMILE WAS sardonic. "The one which was issued to Chief Fire-Bird prior to his father's death, with your sister's name as party of the second part."

"That's a lie!" the gambler jerked taut.

"Check it yourself at the county courthouse. The license is made out to Fire-Bird and Lucille Martelli."

"Then it's not legal!" the swarthy man grated. "There isn't any Lucille Martelli. I have no sister."

Tom Gentry's eyes widened. "But—"

"She's my… my hostess here at the gambling club," Martelli made a visible effort to control himself. "I needed somebody to lend tone to the joint, so women would feel free to come in and buck my games. Lucille was an actress, stranded. Her real name doesn't matter. She was broke and I gave her a job. Why, the dirty, double-crossing witch! The two-timing tramp!"

The swarthy man's hand reached into a desk drawer; reappeared clenching the .32 automatic he had used on the spider the previous night. At sight of the gun, Tom Gentry started to dive at Martelli; but Anthony restrained him.

"Easy, Tom."

"Easy, hell! Look at him racing out of the joint. You going to let him get away like that?"

The millionaire criminologist kept his voice calm. "I think he won't go very far."

"Yeah? Where?"

"To that Indian stomp dance, probably—for a showdown with Lucille. From the beginning, I had a hunch she wasn't his sister. There was no family resemblance; and whenever he looked at her, the devotion in his eyes wasn't brotherly. He loved her, and she was giving him a raw deal."

The aviator blinked. "That's why you told him about the marriage license, hunh? You figured it might bring things to a head. You were up to your old tricks, setting one crook against another."

"Something of the sort," Jim admitted.

Then Gentry thought of something. "But hey, look. If Martelli wasn't hep to the wedding deal, it means he couldn't have been plotting those murders, either. He wouldn't have any reason for bumping off the heirs."

"Someone else had a reason, though," the hawk-eyed detective said grimly. "In fact, I'm beginning to see through many tangled motives. It even makes sense for Franklin Foster to have possessed a photostat copy of the Chief's marriage license."

"How so?"

Anthony smiled thoughtfully. "The Chief wanted his engagement and forthcoming marriage kept secret for a while. Foster learned about it, however, and procured a copy of the document. He probably used it as a lever to persuade Fire-Bird to back his pipeline scheme."

"Blackmail, eh?"

"Not quite that strong. Just a clinching sales argument used by a promoter who was frantically determined to obtain the necessary support for a pet project."

Tom puckered his mouth. "So now we know a lot of answers and what good does it do us? Everybody's gone to this stomp dance except us. Here we stand talking when we ought to be doing something. Or don't you care?"

"Yes, I care. In fact, we're going to the stomp dance too. I think you might enjoy watching it. It's a sort of Indian tribal picnic, you know; a ceremonial and feast. These days, most of them are held over near Pawhuska in the Osage country; but occasionally there's a smaller one in this vicinity. I guess it's time for us to start. Come along."

From across the room came a firm statement. "I'm going with you." This was Lady Barbara Kendrington talking.

She came gracefully forward now, cool, poised, completely in possession of her self-control except for the twitching of her long, tapered fingers—an unerring sign of nervousness and tension. "I don't understand everything that's happened; but I know I'm in danger and I'm not staying here alone."

Anthony offered his arm. "It might be wiser for you to be with us," he agreed.

DOWNSTAIRS IN FRONT of the building's lobby entrance, a ragged newsboy sidled furtively toward Jim Anthony and gave whispered evidence that the Organization was smoothly functioning. "Got a report for you, sir."

"Let's have it, sonny."

The lad spoke quickly out of the side of his mouth. "The Lucille jane and Chief Fire-Bird went out to the stomp dance. Martelli was to join them later. He just left, so I guess that's where he was headed."

"Very good. It checks with what I already know."

The boy looked disappointed. "Shucks, I thought I had news for you. Well, anyhow, this Lucille doll did something before she started. Something at the car-barn of the Sand Springs line."

"What was it?" Anthony's tone sharpened.

"She went to some mugg she knows; a motorman for the trolley outfit. He's to swipe an empty one-man car and run it down toward Sand Springs when there ain't no other scheduled trains usin' the tracks. I dunno what the idea is."

Anthony smiled. "Perhaps I do. Now listen. Here are your instructions." He whispered briefly.

"Gotcha," the newsboy grinned. "We'll be there."

Then the millionaire criminologist returned to Tom Gentry and Lady Barbara. A walk of two blocks took them to the taxi stand in front of the Hotel Tulsa. They piled into a cab and started on their journey toward jeopardy.

CHAPTER IX

DANCE OF DEATH

RUNNING PARALLEL TO THE highway were the tracks of the Tulsa-Sand Springs electric interurban line, running through suburban settlements, passing old Bruner Station with its Indian family burial ground in an open field under a lone pecan tree. Then the automobile road took a turn to the right, crossing the trolley tracks at grade and sweeping at an angle toward a deep dip, a sort of open storm drain for the overflow waters of a nearby creek.

Beyond lay Sand Springs Lake, a municipal park, and the little town of Sand Springs itself. Before you reached the outskirts, though, you went by a rolling strip of unimproved acreage which lay between the trees of the park and the waters of the creek. It was here that Tom Gentry caught his first glimpse of the Indian ceremonial stomp dance—a sight that would remain always in his memory.

Flaring torches and scattered campfires cast a weird crimson glow over the scene. Hundreds of tribesmen and their squaws had gathered for the festivities, and the men were shouting, dancing in huge circles to the throbbing beat of tom-tom drums. This off-beat rhythm was an ancient savage magic that seemed to get into your blood, set your heart to pounding in tune with the chanted war cries.

Nor was the throng entirely Indian; for there was a plentiful sprinkling of men and women whose lighter complexions betrayed white blood crossed with Cherokee. And there were dozens of all-white onlookers and tourists, drawn by the sight, attracted by the free barbecue which sent a redolent aroma of cooking meat into the air—succulent meat whose unmatched flavor could only be obtained by slow roasting over open fire-pits.

Thrum-tunka-*thrum,* the drums spoke ceaselessly; and the earth itself vibrated to the pounding of warrior feet as the dance went on. But Jim Anthony revealed little interest in the barbaric vestiges of an America that had vanished. Here before his eyes lay history; the nostalgic past of a proud race, the remnants of a people whose ranks were thinning, but whose hearts would remain forever unconquered until the end of time.

Half Comanche himself, the millionaire criminologist's blood raced in rhythm with the drums; but he forced his attention to the task at hand—the capturing of a murderer. And presently, as the taxi halted in the parking space at the edge of the clearing, he spotted the group he was looking for.

THEY STOOD BESIDE a green sedan, four of them, their faces eerily distinct in the firelight. There was Franklin Foster, looking small and shocked and angry. There was the beautiful brunette who called herself Lucille Martelli, coldly smiling. There was Spider Martelli himself with his hands raised, his features twisted with hatred under the menace of a Colt .44 in the sturdy right hand of Chief Fire-Bird.

The showdown had come at long last.

Anthony surged from his taxi. "Come along, Tom. Lady Barbara, you stay where you are." And he began running, with the genial aviator matching him stride for stride.

The blonde English girl refused to be left alone. Scrambling out of the cab, she pelted in pursuit. Her long, slender legs twinkled silkily as she ran; and her face was a pallid mask of apprehension.

Then Jim Anthony reached his goal. The suddenness of his unexpected arrival turned all eyes his way, and for an instant it seemed like a silent tableau patterned after some painted masterpiece. The sun-bronzed millionaire spoke, and his voice dispelled this illusion.

"You're aiming at the wrong person, Chief," he told the elderly Indian.

No emotion showed on Fire-Bird's coppery features, and his tone was dispassionate. "That's for me to decide. I know when I'm threatened. This paleface came at me with a gun," he indicated Martelli. He added contemptuously: "I took it away from him. He's lucky I didn't bend it around his neck."

Martelli's eyes glittered, but not from fright. Deadly anger was in his glare, and his words were thick with unsuppressed hate. "Yes, I came at you with a gun. I'm only sorry I picked you instead of Lucille. I should have plugged her first and taken my chances afterward."

"There have been enough killings, Spider," Anthony said. "I think the murder game is just about finished. The cards were stacked against you, but it's too late to change that now."

"It's never too late. My time will come."

Lucille laughed a brittle laugh. "Your time has come and gone, wop. You were a sucker from the start. You never threw anything but snake-eyes and you never will."

"Wait!" That was little Franklin Foster injecting his semi-hysteria into the conversation. "Whatever this is all about, I don't care. All I want is Marie DuValle. Somebody knows where she is. Somebody's got to know. For God's sake tell me and let me go to her!"

Anthony surveyed the undersized promoter, and there was just a hint of pity behind his accusing glance. "You'll find Miss DuValle in the morgue, my friend. And in a certain sense, you put her there."

"The m-morgue…? You mean… she's… d-dead?"

"Unfortunately, yes."

"My God!" the little man moaned. "Marie…" He looked suddenly old and broken, like a discarded toy doll fashioned in the semblance of a man. Then he squared his shoulders. "What do you mean by saying I put her in the morgue?"

"IT WAS YOUR telephone call that sent her to destruction. Had you not told her to meet you in West Tulsa it might not have happened— at least, not the way it did happen. She was marked for murder in any event; but you might have saved her if it hadn't been for your pipeline."

"I… I d-don't understand…"

"You wanted funds for your pipeline. You knew about the Chief applying for a marriage license; you obtained a photostat copy of the application and used it as a sort of club for the purpose of forcing the Chief to lend financial support to your enterprise. You realized he desired to keep his relations with Lucille a secret from Martelli, who loved her. They didn't want Martelli making trouble. And you employed that knowledge to gain your own ends."

"Wh-what's that got to do with it?" Foster quavered.

"If you had told me about the wedding plans, I might have uncovered the truth in time to save Miss Du Valle. But you chose to remain silent, and death struck again at the Fire-Bird family. Cold, calculating, premeditated death based upon one person's greed for a fortune."

Lucille undulated forward, her beautiful face vicious in the flickering firelight from the nearby stomp dance. "I don't like your insinuations, Mr. High-And-Mighty Anthony. If you're accusing me of those kills—"

"Why, no," Jim responded softly. He glanced away from her toward Lady Barbara Kendrington, then back again. "No, Lucille, I'm not accusing you of the kills. I'm only accusing you of being the motivating influence which caused them."

"Meaning?"

"Meaning you refused to marry the Chief until he became sole heir to his father's estate." Then Anthony whirled so swiftly that his movement was a mere blur. His hand lashed out, struck a nerve in the elderly Indian's gunwrist. The Colt .44 caromed through the air. "Catch it, Tom!" the criminologist called. And he fastened himself on his quarry. *"Fire-Bird, I'm handing you over to the police for multiple murder."*

CHIEF FIRE-BIRD MADE no attempt to struggle, for he seemed to realize it was useless to pit himself against Jim Anthony's strength. "You are a clever man, Mr. Anthony. I wonder if you're as clever as you think you are?" The millionaire detective chose to reply in the Cherokee tongue. "There is no cleverness in my heart, but only a heavy weight that I must unmask the evil deeds of a misguided tribal kinsman." Then he switched back to English. "You killed off the members of your own family, your own blood relatives, for their shares of the estate."

A gasp of astonishment came from Franklin Foster. "God! And I thought it was Martelli trying to marry his sister to the Chief and murdering the heirs so she would get the money!"

"She's no sister of mine," the gambler spat. "She's just a girl I picked up and fell for. I never got wise to what she was doing until Anthony opened my eyes."

Jim nodded. "I might have suspected you, Spider—except that the marriage license hadn't yet been used. If you had been behind the deal, your first move would have been to get Lucille safely installed as Fire-Bird's wife. Then you would have gone ahead with the murders, assured that the girl would eventually benefit. Since the marriage had not yet been consummated, I knew there must be another angle."

Lucille herself took a forward step; but Tom Gentry prodded her with Fire-Bird's .44 Colt. "Freeze, babe. This relic looks as if the Chief swiped it from Buffalo Bill, but I'm betting it can still shoot a terrific hole in a lady's brisket. You wouldn't want your tripes ventilated, would you?"

She subsided, her eyes cursing him silently.

Anthony again addressed himself to Fire-Bird. "Like many another Indian, you lost your sense of proportion because of a very beautiful white woman. She promised to become your wife. But when the will was opened, she learned that you would not inherit the entire estate. It was to be shared with your various nephews and grandchildren. She then refused to marry you unless you removed them; and you, blinded by your infatuation, agreed. That's the story the unused marriage license told me."

"It told you too much," the Chief said impassively.

"Yes. Too much about the automobile accidents which sent Bill Long Thumb's two uncles to their deaths. You sabotaged those steering gears. And you had bought extra glass panels for your hearse after some fake attacks had been made on you; attacks which you yourself arranged. Replacing the glass panels was a one-man job. You put a plain glass pane in the car instead of a bullet-proof window. And when one of your hired gunsels fired at the hearse last night, Bill Long Thumb died. Your own grandson! You even insured your own safety by squatting on the floor instead of sitting in a chair."

"Why take chances?" the Indian shrugged.

Anthony's hawk-like eyes were moody. "It was you who had a tarantula planted in my hotel room in an effort to scare me off when I indicated a desire to investigate Long Thumb's murder. It was you who sent a thug to drop a wrench on me at the oil field. You'd heard me promising Franklin Foster I would go with him to the pipeline, and you despatched this Louie Sultzer to liquidate me—Sultzer, one of Martelli's bouncers, but a man who had been originally hired by Lucille. And it was you who broke your chauffeur's neck, sent your hearse into the Arkansas River so that Marie DuValle would be drowned."

"Have you finished summing up my crimes?" Fire-Bird demanded quietly.

"I think so. I'm sorry it had to turn out this way. Lucille is really to blame more than yourself. She made you do these things. And she'll pay."

AMUSEMENT TINKLED IN the brunette woman's sudden laugh. "I won't pay, smart guy. I'll collect. I'm still going to marry the Chief, and he'll still get all the dough—all except his crazy son's share. And since Green Bird is mentally incompetent, we'll control his split, too. The rest of you are going to die. All of you. Right now. You've been covered ever since you started talking. Take care of them, Steve."

From the shadows behind the sedan a man appeared; a hulking bruiser with an automatic in each steady fist. He was the second bouncer from Martelli's gambling resort, and he drew a bead on Tom Gentry with one of his guns—Tom being the only armed person in the group.

"Drop it, pal."

Gentry might have detonated into reckless motion; might have risked a shot at the thug. Anthony stopped him with a glance, however, and Tom reluctantly let his .44 fall to the ground. He looked bewildered, for he had never before seen his millionaire friend surrender so easily.

Chief Fire-Bird stooped and retrieved his Colt. "This is working out better than I expected. You see, we had already arranged a certain plan to dispose of Martelli. We knew he was coming out here, to the stomp dance, and his feelings toward Lucille were rather a nuisance. Now he will be eliminated—and the rest of you with him. Ready, Lucille?"

"Ready," she opened the tonneau door of the green sedan.

Spider Martelli's face was set in harsh bravado, as if he understood that this was the end of the road. Little Franklin Foster trembled violently, while Lady Barbara Kendrington stood motionless and unconcerned, her stoic poise betraying the Cherokee heritage that flowed in her veins. Her superb bravery, her arctic calmness, made Tom Gentry bat his eyes. The blonde girl was the most gorgeous dish he'd ever encountered, he thought; but she must be less than human to reveal absolutely no trace of terror in the imminent face of death.

Franklin Foster's voice blurted desperately. "You can't kill us this way, Chief! Lucille, you can't shoot five people in cold blood!"

The brunette smiled readily. "We don't intend to. Into this sedan, everybody. And you, Steve, take the wheel," she addressed the gambling joint's bouncer. "Run the car up on the interurban tracks."

"Oh-oh!" Gentry growled. "You're going to stall us on that grade crossing!"

"You get smart, too," she laughed. "I've arranged for a special trolley to take care of the accident. Its motorman will jump off in time to save himself. See," she pointed to the deep dip in the highway through which overflowing creek water ran shallowly. "It's not uncommon for automobiles to splash water into their distributors as they go through that dip. Then they conk out as they drift up onto the tracks. Everyone will think that was what happened to you."

"I won't do it!" Foster quavered. "I won't get in the sedan! I refuse!"

"Suit yourself," Fire-Bird said. "We can always knock you on the head and put you in. That goes for the rest of you, too. Take your choice of being clubbed to death now, or dying when the trolley hits. And the first person who tries to get out of the machine—gets shot."

Martelli grinned. "Let's go. The cards are dealt and the hand didn't fall our way. We can't live forever. Who wants to?" Then he stared at Lucille. "So-long, sweetheart. I'll save a kiss for you in hell."

THE WHOLE THING was like a nightmare to Tom Gentry. Why didn't Anthony do something? The odds were only five to three: Jim, Tom, Martelli, Foster, and Lady Barbara against Fire-Bird, Lucille, and the gunsel. True, the Chief and the thug had pistols; but it would be better to go down fighting than to sit meekly in an automobile, awaiting certain destruction. Once they piled into that sedan they were done for. It didn't make sense.

Jim Anthony, though, seemed to think otherwise. He offered his arm to the English girl; assisted her into the tonneau and followed her. Gentry crawled in next, then Martelli and Foster, The thuggish bouncer slid under the wheel, rolled the car onto the grade crossing; stalled it there. His job finished, he leaped to safety; joined Fire-Bird and Lucille in the shadows beyond the railroad tracks.

Torchlight made little metallic glints on their guns, which were aimed at the sedan with silent menace. And now the rails began to hum and click, the sound growing louder with each passing instant as a trolley approached at high speed from the direction of Tulsa.

"Nuts to this!" Gentry snarled. He started to open the sedan door. "I'd rather be shot!"

"Sit still!" Anthony's voice was a low-pitched warning.

"Well, then, let me take the wheel and run this chariot off the tracks! Gosh, pappy, maybe we can get going fast enough so they can't catch us with bullets."

"There's no key in the ignition. The bruiser took it with him. Quiet."

Far down the humming trolley rails, the millionaire criminologist's keen eyes had already discerned a blue-white glare of brilliant light—the powerful electric headlamp of the oncoming interurban car, gleaming like a baleful Cyclops. Brighter grew this ominous radiance, and louder was the clicking of the steel rails singing their song of doom.

Now the electric car's headlight rays bathed the stalled sedan with eerie glow, revealing the strained faces of the occupants. Franklin Foster sat slumped, so exhausted by fear that he seemed no longer to care what happened. Lady Barbara held herself coolly erect at Anthony's side.

Martelli lighted a cigarette, outwardly unmoved by the swift approach of a death that looked impossible to stop. Gentry swore softly as the interurban car bore down. And he tensed himself for the inevitable, inexorable crash.

But there was no crash.

At the last split instant, brake-shoes screamed against steel wheels; poured out Niagaras of sparks. Bucking, rocking, shuddering, the trolley shrieked to a grinding halt—less than five feet from the stalled sedan.

And even before its forward motion was arrested, people began erupting from front and rear platforms like live lava out of a volcano. They came out of the doors and through the open windows—cowboys, oilfield riggers, scrubwomen, society dowagers, newsboys, policemen, even a few soldiers and sailors on furlough. Tom Gentry exploded like a firecracker.

"Jeepers jiminy—the Organization!"

His sun-bronzed criminologist friend was already in motion. Lunging from the automobile, Jim Anthony roared a command at his motley legion of followers. "There they are! Grab them!" he indicated Fire-Bird, Lucille, and the thug named Steve.

Chief Fire-Bird whirled, started to run. Anthony tackled him and brought him down. Lucille darted in another direction, straight toward the oncoming mob. The thug raised his two automatics and tried to shoot his way clear. One of the bullets smashed into the brunette woman's spine. She screamed once, horridly. Then she toppled.

Gentry nailed the gunsel with a rabbit punch that almost tore the fellow's head off.

It was the end of a long, ugly murder trail; and the one who seemed to have suffered most was Spider Martelli. The gambler was hunkering down, cradling Lucille in his lap. "Dead," he muttered brokenly. "The only woman I ever cared for...."

Anthony summoned his legion away and left Martelli alone with his grief.

IN THEIR HOTEL suite, later, Tom Gentry was packing his own luggage, and Jim Anthony's as well. Anthony, entering the room, stopped him.

"We aren't leaving Tulsa just yet, junior. I've still got that pipeline project to report on, remember?"

"Hunh?"

"Yes. I think Franklin Foster may put his promotion through, after all. When Fire-Bird is executed for murder, the entire estate will go to Green Bird and Lady Barbara. And since Green Bird is a mental case, Lady Barbara will be in full control. I believe she intends to invest in Foster's scheme—as a sort of solace to him because he lost the girl he loved, Barbara's cousin, Marie DuValle."